Praise for Jennie Marts

"Funny, complicated, and irresistible. Sometimes a cowboy isn't perfect but you got to love him anyway."
—Jodi Thomas, *New York Times* bestselling author, for *Caught Up in a Cowboy*

"Full of humor, heart, and hope, deliciously steamy but still sweet, with a secret at its heart."
—Joanne Kennedy, award-winning and bestselling author, for *Wish Upon a Cowboy*

"The perfect blend of humor, grit, and sexy cowboy spice. Delicious!"
—Kari Lynn Dell, award-winning and bestselling author for *Wish Upon a Cowboy*

"Readers will cherish the scorching sex, snappy dialogue, well-paced plot, and the appeal of the small Colorado town setting."
—*Publishers Weekly* for *You Had Me at Cowboy*

"Full of exquisite heat and passion…an enthralling combination of intense moments, playful banter, and great depth of emotion."
—*Harlequin Junkie* for *Caught Up in a Cowboy*

Also by Jennie Marts

Cowboys of Creedence
Caught Up in a Cowboy
You Had Me at Cowboy
It Started with a Cowboy
Wish Upon a Cowboy

a *Cowboy* STATE OF MIND

JENNIE MARTS

*This book is dedicated to Dr. William Bryant,
my father and my first hero.
Thanks for always believing in me, Dad.*

Published by Sourcebooks Casablanca, an imprint of Sourcebooks
P.O. Box 4410, Naperville, Illinois 60567-4410
(630) 961-3900
sourcebooks.com

Printed and bound in the United States of America.
OPM 10 9 8 7 6 5 4 3 2 1

CHAPTER 1

THE STILL-NAMELESS DOG JUMPED INTO THE CAB AS Zane Taylor opened the door of his pickup, and he absently patted its head and rubbed behind its ears. The dog leaned into him and got that blissed-out look on its face, and Zane's tension eased a little as it always did when he interacted with an animal. The late spring sun warmed Zane's back, and as soon as he turned his attention away from the dog, he felt the weight of the decision he bore on his shoulders. His former boss, Maggie, had been nagging him to come back to his old job on her Montana ranch. She'd taken in a herd of wild stallions, and she needed him. He'd gotten by so far with vague replies, but it was time to give her an answer. Time to get back on the road and out of Creedence. Except the reason he was so fired up to leave was also the reason he wasn't ready to walk away.

He shrugged the soreness from his shoulders. He'd had a good morning with Rebel, the headstrong black stallion he'd been working with for weeks now. Maybe the horse could feel the warmth in the air as well. Although it *was* Colorado, so they could still get a snowstorm or two before spring reluctantly slid into summer.

"Nice job today, horse whisperer," Logan Rivers, his current boss, and friend, hollered from the corral where he was putting another horse through the paces.

Zane waved a hand in his direction, ignoring the comment, as he turned the engine over and pulled the door shut. He wasn't fond of the nickname, even though Logan had been using it since they were in high school and working summers at Logan's family's ranch.

Zane could admit grudgingly that he did have a gift with horses, especially the dangerous or wild ones, somehow connecting with the animals better than he ever did with people.

The black-and-white border collie mix rested her head on Zane's leg, and he stroked her neck as he drove toward Creedence, where no one was a stranger and everyone knew not just *your* business, but your cousin's as well.

He lowered the windows and turned on the radio, contemplating the errands he needed to run after he grabbed a plate of biscuits and gravy at the diner. The thought made his mouth water. So did the thought of hopefully seeing a certain blond waitress who had been taking up way too many of his thoughts these last few months.

He slowed, his brow furrowing, as he recognized that same waitress's car sitting empty on the side of the road. The car was an old nondescript blue sedan, but there was no mistaking the colorful bumper stickers stuck to the trunk. A bright blue one read "What if the hokey-pokey really is what it's all about?" and the hot-pink one above the back taillight read "It was me. I let the dogs out."

His heart rate quickened as his gaze went from the

empty vehicle to a hundred yards up the road, where a woman walked along the side of the highway, her pony-tail bouncing with each step and a light-colored dog keeping pace at her heels. Which was pretty impressive, in and of itself, since the dog had only three legs.

But then, everything about Bryn Callahan was kind of bouncy, and she was just as impressive as her dog. The woman was always upbeat and positive. Even now, with her car sitting busted on the side of the road, her steps still seemed to spring, and the bright sunlight glinted off her blond hair.

He drove past the abandoned car and onto the dirt shoulder as he slowed to a stop beside her. "Need a ride?"

She turned, her expression wary, then her face broke into a grin, and it was like the sun shining through the clouds after a rainstorm.

"Hey, Zane," she said, the smile reaching all the way into her voice as she grasped the door handle. She looked steadily into his eyes, her gaze never wavering, never slid-ing sideways to stare at the three-inch, jagged scar start-ing at the corner of his eye and slicing down his cheek. Most people couldn't keep their eyes off it, but Bryn acted as if it wasn't there at all. "I sure do. I was supposed to start my shift at the diner ten minutes ago."

She opened the door, and the dog bounded in, hitting the floorboards, then springing onto the seat to wiggle and sniff noses with the border collie. They could have powered a wind farm, the way their tails were wagging and their little butts were shaking.

"Hey, Lucky." He leaned in as the dog leapt over the collie's back and into Zane's lap, where it proceeded to drench his face in fevered licks and puppy kisses. Lucky was like a hyper three-legged Tigger as he bounced from Zane's lap back to the collie, over to Bryn, and back to Zane.

"Lucky, get off him," Bryn scolded. She tried to push her way into the truck as she got her own slobbery reception from the collie.

Zane chuckled and grabbed her hand to help her into the cab. But his laugh stuck in his throat as heat shot down his spine and his mouth went dry. He swallowed and tried to focus on assisting her, instead of staring at the area of bare skin he glimpsed as the top of her dress buckled and gaped from her movement. It was just the side of her neck, but it was the exact spot he'd spent too much time thinking about kissing.

"Silly mutts." She laughed as she tossed her backpack on the floor and plopped into the seat. Her hand was soft, but her grip was solid, and for a moment, he wondered what would happen if he didn't let go. "Wow, what a greeting," she said, as she released his hand to buckle herself in.

Zane's eyes were drawn to her legs like bees to honey. The woman had great legs, already tan, and muscular and shapely from her work at the diner. Her white cross-trainers were scuffed with the red dirt from the road, and she had a smudge of dust across one ankle that Zane was severely tempted to reach down and brush away so he could let his fingers linger on her skin.

Bryn wore a pink waitress dress, the kind that zips up the front, with a white collar and a little breast pocket, and the fabric hugged her curvy figure in all the right spots. For just a moment, Zane imagined pulling down that zipper—with his teeth. His back started to sweat just thinking about it.

Simmer down, man. He took a deep breath, utilizing the stress-reducing exercise he'd learned in the military, and tried to think of something witty to say. He didn't usually let himself get carried away with those kinds of fantasies. But he didn't usually have Bryn in his truck, filling his cab with the sound of her easy laughter and the scent of her skin—traces of honeysuckle and vanilla and the smell of fresh sheets off the line on a warm summer day.

"That dog is serious about kissing. I haven't had that much action in months." He winked, then laughed with her, pulling his hand back to ruffle Lucky's ears as the dog settled into the seat next to the collie. He tried to play it off like a joke, to settle his pounding heart, when what he really wanted to do was pull her into his lap and kiss her face and throat the way Lucky had done to him. Well, not *exactly* the same way.

Bryn snorted and scratched the ears of the collie, who was softly whining as she pressed into Bryn's shoulder. "He's just happy to see you. It's been a while, ya know?"

"Yeah, I know." It had, in fact, been months since he'd seen her.

"Well, Lucky has noticed you haven't been around

much." She dropped her gaze and her voice as she focused on petting the dog. "We both have."

Both?

"Are you saying you missed me?"

"I didn't say *missed*. I said noticed."

His shoulders slumped. Of course she hadn't missed him.

She playfully nudged his elbow, and he felt the heat of her skin against his arm.

"Of course I missed you. You all but disappeared after the great Christmas pie bake-off in December."

He chuckled as he shook his head. "I still can't believe we made fifteen pies in four hours."

"I still can't believe you wore a frilly apron with a glittery cupcake on the front."

He raised an eyebrow. "What other kind of cupcake is there? And I liked that glittery color. I'm thinking of having it added to the paint job on my truck."

A laugh burst from her. "I dare you to."

He let his voice drop and offered her what he hoped was a flirtatious grin. "I do enjoy a good dare."

She chuckled, then lowered her gaze to the dog's shoulder, where she scratched its fur. "So, why *didn't* I hear from you? Was it something I said or did?"

Yeah, it was everything you did—everything that made me want and hope and wish for something more. "Nah. I was going to call you, but we got real busy at the ranch. Then I heard you started dating some rough-stock cowboy, and I didn't want to overstep."

"Is it overstepping to be my friend?"

He cocked his head, eyeing her. "Is that what you want me to be? Your friend?"

"Of course. I didn't give you my number for you to *not* call me."

Wrong question, dumbass. Should have asked her if *all* she wanted was to be his friend. He offered her a shrug. "I'm not much of a talker."

"That's perfect. Because I can talk up a blue streak, and I'm always on the lookout for a good listener."

He chuckled. "I can do that. I can probably even throw in an occasional grunt of agreement just so you know I'm paying attention."

She giggled softly, and the sound swirled in his chest, melting into him like molasses on a warm pancake. "That sounds great."

"I'm happy to lend an ear, but shouldn't your new boyfriend be the one listening?"

She huffed, then muttered, "Not hardly."

"Uh-oh. Trouble in paradise?" He hoped.

She shook her head. "No trouble. Not anymore. It's safe to say we broke up."

"Sorry to hear that." *Not really.*

"Don't be." Her expression hardened, but she didn't say anything more.

No problem. He didn't want to continue *any* conversation that had her shoulders slumping and pulled her lips into a tight frown. "What happened to your car?" Zane asked, drawing his gaze back to the road as he eased the truck onto the highway. Not that her broken-down car was a great topic, but at least it took the focus off her broken-down relationship.

"Who knows? This is the third time it's conked out since Christmas."

"Have you called someone about it?" *Like me.* Yeah right. Why would she call *him*? Hadn't they just established that he'd been avoiding her for the past several months?

"No. What good would it do to call someone when I don't have any money to pay them anyway? Last I checked, my bank account was holding steady at six dollars and eighty cents."

"I could take a look at it for you. And I wouldn't charge you more than a smile." Ugh. Did that really just come out of his mouth? It hadn't sounded half as dopey in his head.

"That would be very neighborly of you," she said, ignoring his dorky comment and flashing him a brilliant grin. "That's a price I can afford. But you don't have to. I know Logan's keeping you pretty busy out at Rivers Gulch."

Neighborly? He didn't want to seem neighborly. He'd been trying for flirty, but his efforts had apparently fallen flat. *Wait.* How did *she* know Logan had been keeping him busy at the ranch? Had she asked about him? "I've got time," he assured her. "I'll take a look at it when I'm done in town. See if I can spot the problem at least."

"That would be so great." She ruffled the neck of the

black-and-white dog, who had settled down next to her. She seemed to draw stray animals like a magnet. "You picked a name for your dog yet?"

"She's not my dog."

Bryn rolled her eyes and let out a small chuckle. "*You* might not think so, but *she* does. Every time I see your truck, she's ridin' shotgun. Why do you think she does that if she doesn't consider herself yours?"

He shrugged, his tone even and dry. "She must like my winning personality."

A laugh escaped Bryn's lips—a sound that filled the cab of the truck, and his heart, as if the door of a dark room had been cracked open to let in a shaft of light. "I'm sure that's it," Bryn said, still chuckling.

A grin tugged at the corners of his lips. This woman made him smile, even when she was giving him a hard time.

"How's your dad doing?" she asked.

The smile fell from his lips. "Stubborn as ever."

His dad's heart attack had brought him back to town earlier that winter, only long enough to get the old bastard back on his feet. But then Logan lost his hired hand and had offered Zane a job helping at the ranch and with the horses, and a couple of weeks had turned into a couple of months.

He and his dad had reached an uneasy truce. As long as Birch took his meds and stayed off the sauce, Zane agreed to remain in town. They mostly stayed out of each other's way, but occasionally found themselves watching a hockey game together, especially if the Colorado Summit were playing, and Creedence's hometown hero, Rockford James, was on the ice.

But lately Zane had felt the familiar itch—the need to move on when he'd stayed in one place too long and gotten too comfortable with having people around him. An itch that was made worse by the desire to see the blond waitress who was taking up space in his mind and under his skin. And that was an itch he had no business trying to scratch.

"He seems to be doing better lately," he told Bryn. "So I'll probably take off pretty soon. My old boss is harping on me to come back to Montana. She took in a new herd of wild stallions and needs someone to break them."

"Oh," Bryn said, the word a soft breath on her lips. "I didn't realize you were leaving. When are you going?"

He murmured something noncommittal about it not being today, then lifted his shoulders in a dismissive shrug as he pulled into the parking lot of the diner and parked in the shade of a giant elm tree.

"Then how about coming in and having some breakfast? On the house." She laid her hand on his arm and gave it a gentle squeeze. "It's the least I can do for giving me a ride into town."

He shook his head, only slightly, not wanting to move too much for fear of dislodging her hand. The weight of it settled something inside him. "You don't owe me a thing for the ride. I was happy to do it. But I will come in for a bite. I've been thinking about Gil's biscuits and gravy, and there's a pretty cute waitress I wouldn't mind getting a cup of coffee from."

She raised an eyebrow. "Oh yeah? You're gonna have to stand in line. That vixen, Vi, has a long line of suitors interested in her pouring them a cup of joe," she teased, letting go of his arm to gather her backpack and climb from the truck.

Viola Bell was as much a part of the diner as the black-and-white-checkered floor and the faded red vinyl seats of the booths lining the window. She was somewhere between forty-five and sixty-five—only her mama knew for sure, but Zane didn't think the waitress had changed a lick since his dad had started bringing him into the diner for breakfast when he was a kid. The woman had a sassy mouth, a saucy swing to her ample hips, and a mass of strawberry-red hair piled on her head that usually had at least two pens sticking out of its curly depths. She was tough but sweet, and had a string of truckers from California to Montana who planned stops in Creedence just for a plate of pie and a dish of Vi's sass.

Zane chuckled as he got out and followed Bryn toward the diner. She had a pretty saucy swing to her step as well, and his lips twitched in a grin as he enjoyed the view. Lucky bounced along next to her, his head upturned as if waiting for direction. Zane had rolled down the windows and left the collie in the truck. In this town, nobody locked their doors, and the dog hadn't jumped out of the truck yet, despite him giving her plenty of opportunities.

The air smelled of smoked meat mixed with the scent

of pine from the trees rising up the side of the mountain behind the diner. The Creedence Country Café sat on the edge of town. A cracked sidewalk ran alongside the road leading into the town square. Colorful purple and pink trumpet flowers spilled from the whiskey barrels in front of the door, the result of a recent renovation Creedence had undertaken in order to spruce up the town.

A dirty black pickup with out-of-state plates and a rusty horse trailer hooked to its bumper sat parked in front of the diner. The horse inside stamped and whinnied as Zane and Bryn approached the door. It butted its head against the side of the trailer and peered out at them with a frightened brown eye that was crusted and leaky with infected goop.

"Whoa there, it's all right," Zane assured it, his voice steady and calm as they drew closer.

"Oh no, do you see its eye?" Bryn asked. "Poor thing."

"No wonder it's infected. This trailer is disgusting," he said, peering in at the mess of manure and sparse bits of hay. It looked like the horse had been trampling in its own waste for days.

"It doesn't look like they've cleaned this trailer out ever." Bryn pulled her head back to avoid the foul smell. "And it's got to be baking hot in there." The horse's back was streaked with sweat and dust.

Bile rose in his throat, and Zane clamped his teeth together as his hands tightened into fists. He hated to see animals being abused. Especially when they didn't get the chance to turn old enough and strong enough to fight back. "I'd like to see the owner of this truck spend a day cooped up in there." Zane was tempted to loosen the latch as he walked by and let the horse free.

"I agree." Bryn lifted her hand toward the latch. "What if we just opened the back end of the trailer and the horse accidentally escaped?"

His lips curved in a wry grin. He liked the way this woman's brain worked. "I was thinking the same thing. But the horse is tied up, and even if we released the lead rope, where is it going to go?"

"I don't know. But I feel like we have to do something."

"Not our circus. Not our monkeys." Zane shook his head and stole a glance at the three-legged dog sitting devotedly at the waitress's feet. He put a hand on Bryn's back to guide her toward the diner entrance and softened his tone. "You can't save everybody, Bryn."

Her feet didn't move. She turned to stare at him, holding his gaze for just long enough to have sweat heating his back. "I'm still gonna try to save as many as I can."

Damn, but this woman had a habit of hitting him right in the heart. He gave a slight nod of his head, not trusting his voice to speak, as she tore her eyes from his and entered the restaurant.

"You're late," the fry cook yelled from the kitchen. Another staple of the café, Gil had been frying eggs and slinging hash at the roadside diner for as long as Zane could remember. He'd learned to cook in the Navy, and as gruff as Gil sounded, Zane knew the old sailor had a soft spot for Bryn. *Who didn't?*

"I know," Bryn answered, the dog trotting at her heels as she raced into the back. Lucky must have taken his customary spot in the back office because Bryn emerged from the kitchen alone a few seconds later, hastily tying a white apron around her waist. She reached for the coffee-pot as she apologized to Gil, Vi, and the few customers that filled the diner. "Sorry, y'all. My stupid car broke down."

"Again?" Ida Mae Phillips, an elderly woman, and a regular, who had taught Sunday school down at the Methodist church for over thirty years, asked from her customary table by the window. "You have got to do something about that dad-blamed vehicle."

"I know. I know." Bryn forced a smile at the two men sitting at the counter. The taller one wore a threadbare flannel shirt that was hard to tell if it was dirty or just faded. A chewed-up toothpick clung to his chapped lips. The other, a shorter guy whose body was muscled, yet his rounded belly gave away a habit of either too much beer or too many chicken wings, had on a T-shirt so wrinkled it looked like he'd slept in it. A green hat cov-ered his unwashed hair, a greasy stain soiling the bill. "It looks like you're all set for coffee, so what can I get you fellas to eat?"

Zane slid onto a stool at the counter, leaving an empty spot between him and the two guys drinking coffee. He didn't recognize either one, but that didn't surprise him. The diner was next to the highway, so in addition to the regular locals, plenty of truckers and road-trippers stopped in for "the county's best chicken-fried steak," as the sign above the diner boasted.

But these guys didn't fit one of those categories. They had a different air about them, with their grimy hair and dirty jeans, and the oily way one of them raked his eyes over Bryn's figure before giving her his breakfast order.

Zane was sure these were the guys driving the trailer, and just the sound of their voices nettled his nerves like rocks against a cheese grater.

Bryn kept her cool as she passed their order to Gil. She poured Zane a cup of coffee as she took his order next, then worked her way around the room, checking in with the other customers, exchanging comments about her car and the nice weather while she cleared plates and filled water glasses.

A freckle-faced boy of about five or six and his younger sister clambered onto the barstools next to Zane.

The curly-haired blond toddler looked up at him, her tiny pink lips pursed in a perfect bow as her brow furrowed. She pointed a small chubby finger at the scar on his cheek. "Ow-ie."

"It doesn't hurt anymore," he assured her in a soft voice accompanied by a quick wink, earning him an adorable giggle.

"Geez. What happened to your face, mister?" her brother asked, cringing as he drew his head back.

Zane lifted his shoulder in a slight shrug. "Got in a fight with a dragon."

The boy's eyes widened.

Zane's lips pulled into a smirk. "You should see the dragon's face."

"I'm sorry if they're bothering you," the kids' mother said as she started to sit on the stool next to the boy. She paused mid-squat, a wince crinkling her eyes, as she caught sight of his face. She straightened again as she wrapped a protective arm around the angelic toddler. "Come on, kids. I think we're going to sit in a booth today."

"But, Mom, you said we could sit at the counter," the boy whined.

"We will next time," she said, already lifting the toddler to her hip and pulling at the boy's hand. "I want to look out the window today."

Likely excuse. Zane ignored the hard ball of shame that tightened under his ribs as he turned away from the family and concentrated on his coffee. Wasn't the first time—and wouldn't be the last—that someone judged his character by the scar on his face and moved away from him.

"You shouldn't tease him like that," Bryn said.

His mouth pulled into a hard grimace. He hadn't heard her come back around the counter. Had she seen the whole embarrassing exchange? Not that he could do anything about it. He pointed to the marred tissue on his cheek. "I considered telling him I got this because I didn't listen to my parents. But I didn't want to scare him." *And because that answer was a little too close to the truth.* The ragged skin had been torn with the broken end of a beer bottle Birch had hit him with when Zane had finally chosen to *stop* listening to his dad and stand up to him instead.

"Yeah, imagining a fight with a dragon won't scare him at all. The kid's gonna think Creedence has a monster in its midst," she joked as she grabbed another order and hustled to deliver it.

It does. It's just in the form of a scar-faced man. Zane took another sip of coffee and turned his focus to watching Bryn work.

Her movements were quick and efficient, like every action she took had a purpose. He noted, and appreciated, the way her curvy hips swayed as she maneuvered between tables and around chairs. She wasn't tall exactly, probably only five seven or so—he knew this by how she had fit against his over-six-foot frame the one time he'd danced with her—but she carried herself that way: her spine straight, her shoulders pulled back. Maybe because of his time in the military, he admired a woman with good posture.

He found he admired a lot of things about Bryn Callahan: the way she put people at ease, her good heart. Just in the past few minutes, he'd seen her good-naturedly wipe up one child's spill and offer a high five and a sticker to another. She filled waters and stopped to give Ida Mae a hug before the former Sunday school teacher left the diner.

"How's our puzzle comin'?" Bryn asked, pausing on her way by to lean over the shoulder of old Doc Hunter.

The elderly widower held the newspaper up and pointed to a spot on the page. "What's a five-letter word for someone who likes to spend their time alone?"

"Happy," Zane muttered.

"I thought it was 'hermit' but it doesn't fit," Doc continued, either ignoring Zane, or more than likely not hearing him.

"Didn't we have this one last week?" Bryn asked, resting her hand on Doc's arm as she studied the puzzle. "What about 'loner'?"

"That fits," Doc said triumphantly, filling in the letters. "You've got such an eye for those letters. You're smart, just like my Madge was."

"You're the smart one. You always get the hard words. I just fill in the easy ones." She squeezed his shoulder, then checked to make sure his coffee was full before heading back toward the counter.

"You *are* smart," Zane told her as she refilled his cup.

"Smart aleck-y," she quipped with a grin as she grabbed a plate of pancakes and a bowl of oatmeal and headed back into the dining area.

He couldn't help but smile back. "That too."

She set the food in front of a man about her age wearing a set of mechanic's overalls.

He looked at the bowl of oatmeal, then back at Bryn. "What's this? I ordered hash browns."

"I know you did, Justin. But your wife called and said your cholesterol was up at your last checkup and to substitute oatmeal if you tried to order fried potatoes."

His shoulders slumped. "But I'm the one paying for the food."

She grinned. "Yeah, but I've known her longer."

His lips tugged up in a grin. "That old excuse. We were all three in the same third grade class."

"Yeah, but I met her first," Bryn teased. "Just eat the oatmeal."

"Fine," he grumbled as he picked up a spoon.

Zane had grown up in Creedence as well. He and Bryn had been a few years apart in school, but he hadn't paid much attention to her back then.

But she sure had his attention now. Watching her tuck a loose strand of hair behind her ear and listening to the sound of her laughter carrying through the diner had his gut doing the funny kind of flips he hadn't let himself feel in a long time.

And I have no business letting myself feel them now either, he thought as he dug into the warm plate of biscuits and gravy Bryn set in front of him. Not after what happened with Sarah. He'd loved her, but look how that turned out. Tragedy and pain. Even now, the sound of an ambulance siren still made his chest tighten and his stomach roil. He wasn't a bet any woman should take.

Bryn topped off the coffees of the two trailer guys as they ate, then leaned her hip against the counter. Her manner suggested cool nonchalance, but Zane knew different as he heard her ask casually, "Is that your horse out there?"

"Not ours," Flannel Shirt said, his tone boastful and derisive. "But she's in our trailer."

Bryn eyed them, the first hint of suspicion showing on her face. "Why do you have someone else's horse in your trailer? Who does she belong to?"

"No one. Not anymore."

Her brow furrowed in confusion. "I don't get it, but I noticed she didn't seem very happy."

"I'm sure she isn't," he answered, shrugging his shoulders. "But it doesn't matter. That nag is on her way to 'a farm in the country,' if you know what I mean." He used his fingers to make air quotes.

Bryn's eyes widened as a gasp escaped her lips. "You mean you're taking her to..." She obviously couldn't say the words, and her skin took on a greenish pallor.

Green Hat nodded, and his lips curved into a sly grin. "Yep. We're what you might call a 'waste disposal' company."

The color drained from Bryn's face. "You can't be serious."

"As a horse's heart attack." He talked around the bite of hash browns in his mouth as he elbowed the other man in the ribs and laughed at his own poor joke.

"But why?" she asked.

"Who knows? And who cares? Not our business to ask. We just collect the horse and the fee. Then it's our job to drop them off at the glue factory."

Just as "casual" as Bryn had been, Zane kept an eye on the conversation, and he swore he saw the light blink in Bryn's eyes as an idea occurred to her.

"Soooo if you've already collected the fee for her,

what happens if she never makes it to the…" She swallowed. "The final destination?"

Flannel Shirt shrugged again. "Nothing, I guess. Except they have one less horse to slaughter."

Bryn winced but wasn't swayed by their obvious attempt to rile her. "So what if you just let her go? Or what if I took her off your hands? I live on a farm, so from what you said earlier, you'd still be fulfilling your obligation."

Green Hat's eyes went dark and predatory. "Where is this farm? Maybe we could stop by and visit before we leave town."

A low growl formed in Zane's throat, and his knuckles went white around his fork as he considered jabbing the utensil into the dirt bag's eye.

Flannel Shirt put a hand on his partner's arm as he eyed Bryn, working the toothpick from one side of his mouth to the other. "I can see you really want this horse"—he eyed her name tag—"Bryn. So we might be able to arrange something. I'm Raleigh, and this here's my friend Gator. Why don't you tell us what you have in mind?"

"Not the same thing he does," she answered, flashing Gator a disdainful look. She forced her lips back into a smile as she regarded Raleigh. "How about I cover your breakfast *and* pack you a lunch for the road as well? I'll even throw in a couple of slices of pie."

He let out a scornful laugh. "How about you do all that *and* throw in a couple hundred bucks?"

Bryn's shoulders sank. "I don't have a couple hundred bucks." She pressed her lips together, then inhaled a deep breath before offering, "But I'd give you my car in exchange for letting me have the horse."

"The one you just told this whole place is broken down on the side of the road? No thanks."

"Yeah, what are we gonna do with a broken-down car?" Gator chimed in. As casual as she tried to act, they knew they had her. "Couple of guys like us, we work on a cash-only basis."

"I understand. I'm just a little low on cash right now." She glanced around the diner as if mentally counting up her morning tips. "And there's no way I can make that in tips today. But think about it: you giving me the horse only makes your job easier. That seems like a no-brainer for a couple of smart guys like you."

These two idiots are the "no-brainers." Zane held back a smirk as he reached for his wallet to pay his bill. He needed to get out of here before he did something foolish—like kick these guys out on their greasy butts and let the horse go. Or worse.

Raleigh tapped his finger on the counter, a thin line of grease visible under his nail. "No one's ever offered to buy our load before, but you have a point. If we don't have to drop off that horse, we can get home a day early. So maybe I'm feeling generous and willing to make a deal."

"I'm listening," Bryn said, crossing her arms protectively over her chest.

"You cover our breakfast and pack us a lunch, and we'll give you that horse for an even hundred."

"And don't forget the pie," Gator threw in.

Bryn chewed her lip, her gaze skimming over the diner patrons once more. Her eyes landed on Zane's, and he held them a moment, knowing already what she was going to say.

"Deal," she said. "Just give me a little time to drum up the cash. I'll make some calls while I put together your lunch."

Raleigh's lips curved as his eyes went to the clock above her head. He knew he had a live one—he just had to reel in the line. "You've got twenty minutes. Or we're leaving. *With* the horse."

Zane rifled through the bills in his wallet. He'd just gotten paid. In fact, one of his errands that morning was stopping at the bank. Even as he fought it, knowing how stupid the idea was, he knew his deposit was going to end up being a little slim.

He'd had the biscuits and gravy meal before and knew his bill normally totaled a little over ten dollars, so he usually left fifteen. He sighed as he took two bills from his wallet and slid them under the edge of his plate.

"Thanks for breakfast, Bryn," he told her as he slid off the stool. "I'll check back in later to see if you need a ride home."

"See ya, Zane," she said, then glanced at the bills on the counter, her eyes and her grin widening as she saw the twenty and the crisp hundred-dollar bill sticking out from under his plate.

He turned and walked out of the restaurant, knowing full well he was going to regret that move, but yet, somehow his steps seemed to be as light as his wallet.

CHAPTER 2

BRYN DREW THE BACK OF HER HAND ACROSS HER SWEATY forehead as she tried again to approach the anxious horse. It had let out an angry whinny at the hard screech of rusted metal when one of the men had released the latch and opened the back door of the trailer. Then it had bucked and pulled against the lead when Bryn had entered the small side door at the front.

She'd almost gagged on the stench of manure and decay, but she was determined to save this horse's life. Too bad the horse couldn't seem to get with the plan. She'd been bucking and fighting Bryn's efforts to get her out of the trailer for the last fifteen minutes. She'd barely missed getting kicked on her last try.

And the two jerks who'd sold her the horse stood by, duplicate smirks covering their smarmy-ass faces. She wouldn't mind if the horse kicked one or both of them in the head.

The inside of the trailer was rusted and foul, but Bryn tried to breathe through her mouth as she pulled an apple slice from a baggie in the front pocket of her uniform and held it out to the horse. She was standing just inside the door and jumped as Gator stepped into the doorway behind her.

"You need a little help?" he asked, his hands holding on

to either side of the door, blocking her escape. "I'm pretty good with getting the ladies to do what I want."

What she wanted was to kick this guy in his grimy crotch. Her fight-or-flight instinct was on full alert, and she swallowed back the fear rising in her throat. Sweat broke in the center of her back, and her chest tightened as she realized she was trapped between a pissed off horse and a creepy guy with a feral look in his eyes.

The horse didn't like him either, and Bryn dropped the apple slice and shrank back toward the door, and the slime-ball guy, as the mare stamped and whinnied her irritation.

"Why don't you take a step back?" a deep voice from outside the trailer commanded.

Bryn's shoulders sagged in relief as she recognized Zane's voice.

A sneer pulled at Gator's lips, but he backed out of the trailer and Bryn followed him, almost tripping on the edge of the trailer in her haste to escape the confined space.

Zane caught her, pulling her to him as he bent his head and spoke softly in her ear. "You all right, darlin'?"

She would be now that Zane was here. Although being pressed against his hard-muscled chest wasn't doing anything to slow her frantically beating heart. She nodded, her mouth too dry to speak. Her hands still felt shaky, and her fingers wrinkled the cotton of his T-shirt as she held the front of it in a death grip. But she wasn't quite ready to let it go.

He kept his arm firmly around her shoulders as he narrowed his eyes at the other man. "Everything okay here?"

Raleigh pulled Gator back another few steps and offered Zane an affable smile. "Yeah, Gator was just fooling around. Your girlfriend there seems to be having a little trouble getting her new horse out of the trailer."

Zane arched an eyebrow. "My girlfr—?"

Bryn squeezed her hands tighter against his chest, sending him a silent signal and hoping he'd play along.

He gently squeezed her shoulder. "Yeah, well, why don't you let me worry about my girlfriend? And I'll take care of the horse as well, and let you gentleman get on your way." He peered down at Bryn. "You okay if I take a turn at getting her out of there?"

"Yes, please," she said, letting out a shaky breath. She let go of his shirt and passed him the baggie of apple slices. "These might help."

"Good thinking." He dropped his chin and offered Bryn an encouraging smile. "You stay right here. I'll have her out in a minute." He let her go and stepped into the trailer.

Bryn instantly missed the heat of his arm but was impressed he didn't even flinch at the stench of the trailer. His ice-blue eyes were laser-focused on the horse's chocolate-brown ones, and he talked softly to her as he eased closer.

His tone was soothing, low and confident, as he held out a chunk of apple. "It's okay, sweetheart. I'm not here to hurt you. Nobody's gonna hurt you anymore. You're all right." The horse shook her head, sending a spray of slobber flying across the trailer, but the next stamp of her hooves didn't have the same weight behind it.

Rapt by the scene, and by Zane, Bryn couldn't believe the changes in the horse as she settled and calmed after giving another loud huff. She tentatively drew her head toward Zane's outstretched hand, rearing back slightly, then lowering her head again as her lips carefully nibbled the apple from his palm.

Zane held the gaze of the horse, not moving toward her or away, just sharing her space. Like the waves of a mountain lake gently lapping against the shore, the temperament of the horse and the charged atmosphere inside the trailer settled as the horse visibly calmed. She stamped her feet a few more times, then stood still.

She accepted a few more slices of apple before letting Zane gently brush his fingers across the side of her head. He continued to speak in hushed tones, to woo the horse, to soothe and pacify, as he slowly untied the lead rope and eased her backward.

Bryn rolled her shoulders, not realizing how tense she was, as she watched Zane with the horse. She was as transfixed as the horse, wooed by his gentle tone and calm demeanor. He was truly mesmerizing.

She knew he was gifted with horses, had heard the rumors, but had never seen him like this. She'd witnessed him talking an ornery goat off her kitchen table a few months ago, but this was different. This was an art form, like he was a composer of his own mix of mysterious music. Music that pulled her in and held her captive. Like the kind of music she felt in her chest that made it hard to breathe.

But Zane's composition changed and transformed the more time she spent around him. His refrain could be smooth and smoky, slow and hypnotic, like it was now as he wooed the horse. But she'd also felt the heavy rhythm of the blues rolling off him when he drew into himself and got that pensive look when he didn't realize someone was watching him. He could also be funny and charming like Southern rock, where his temperament could go from slow and easy to a sudden upbeat tempo she couldn't help but sing along with and get swept away in.

And then there were the moments when his leg brushed against hers or when he pulled her against him, like when she'd stumbled out of the trailer, and his low voice had caressed her ear and called her *darlin'*, and her heart had slammed into her throat like she'd been caught in the grasp of a rock ballad that caressed and seduced. It was a song that left her breathless and had her wanting to play it again and again.

There was something about this man—something that reached into her gut and drew her toward him. He was like gravity, and she seemed unable to resist his pull. He seemed lost and hurting, yet also strong and power-ful, a combination she found hard to resist.

He wore his sun-kissed light brown hair long, curling at the edges of his collar, and his bangs often hung down to cover the side of his face if he didn't smooth them back before putting on his cowboy hat. His hair reminded her of Chris Hemsworth's, somewhere between his surfer and superhero styles. Zane's jaw held just enough scruff to make her wonder how rough it would feel against her skin. The layer of whiskers wasn't enough to cover the scar that slashed from his eye and down his cheek—the two sides of his face were a stark illustration of his personality. One side was handsome and approachable, the other scarred and distant.

He reminded her of the stallions and skittish horses he broke: wild and wary until he earned their trust. And she wanted both to earn his trust and to shy away, to get close enough to feel his heat and stay far enough away to escape getting burned. And Zane Taylor was one hot fire. Tall and strong, his body was lean and hard, and he carried himself with the straight posture of a soldier. Not the typical loose, arrogant swagger of some of the other jerks she'd had the misfortune of dating.

The last one had been a thief, stealing not just her heart and her pride but also wiping out her bank account and taking her grandfather's truck *and* his prized rodeo buckle when he'd snuck out of town while she'd been at work. She got a bad taste in her mouth just thinking about it.

But she was done with that type. She was such a sucker for anything wounded and her natural instinct was to rescue and save. But she'd had enough of trying to save men who didn't want to be saved.

So why did her heart race like it was in the Daytona 500 and her palms start to sweat anytime she was within five feet of Zane Taylor? Why did her knees threaten to give way every time he walked into the diner or she saw his truck driving through town? On the surface, he may have seemed just her type—a bad boy who defied the norm. But there was something different about Zane. Something in his eyes, a shadow of pain. He wasn't really so much of a bad boy but more of a tortured lone wolf. All she wanted to do was rescue him. Could she?

No. She shook herself. *Don't be ridiculous.* She'd had her heart broken too many times. She wasn't going down that road again. Even if the road was a hot-as-hell cowboy who could charm a traumatized horse into trusting him.

But he just said he's fixing to leave town soon. He'd also told her she couldn't save them all. *Wanna bet?* He didn't know who he was messing with if he thought she wasn't going to at least try. So forget the wounded cowboy. She turned her focus to the horse—the one she could rescue.

The horse's back hoof slipped on the edge of the trailer, and she gave a frightened whinny, her eyes going wild with panic. But Zane remained calm, holding her lead tight with one hand as he gently stroked her neck with the other. "Easy, girl. Easy."

Her tail swished back and forth, whipping through the air, but she seemed to settle again once she was free of the trailer.

Bryn let out her breath and turned to Raleigh and Gator. "It looks like we're all set here." *So now you can leave, you disgusting jerks.* She'd already paid them, and they'd stowed the takeout cartons with their lunch in the cab. Now she just wanted them out of her sight, before they had a chance to change their minds or try to demand more money.

Raleigh nodded. "It appears so. It was a pleasure doing business with you." He closed the back of the trailer with a clang, then headed toward the front of the truck.

Gator opened the passenger door, then turned back and gave her body an additional cool once-over before offering her another of his repulsive grins. "Yeah, Bryn, it was a pleasure doing business with you. I'll be sure to look you up next time we're passing by this way. And maybe your boyfriend won't be around to mess up our fun."

She wrapped her arms around her middle, trying to stave off the shiver that ran through her at what felt like a barely disguised threat. But she was more worried about Zane. His expression had gone hard, his lips forming a tight line. The sleeves of his shirt stretched over his flexed biceps as his grip tightened on the lead rope, and he took a menacing step toward the truck.

Easy there. She held up a hand in warning. "He's not worth it," she told him, not wanting either him or the horse to get worked up.

Thankfully, Gator had already slammed the door, and Raleigh put the truck in gear and pulled out of the parking lot. They watched the truck speed down the highway, and the air seemed to feel cleaner now that they were gone.

"Assholes," Zane muttered not quite under his breath. He closed his eyes, took a deep inhale, then exhaled and opened them, rearranging his expression as he regarded Bryn. "You gonna come over and meet your new horse?"

His lips formed the slightest smile, and her stomach

dipped and swayed, producing the same wild panic that had been in the horse's eyes. Oh boy, was she in trouble with this man. She'd forgotten how intense he was, how exhilarating it was to be in his presence, to have him extend a rare smile, to be the one who evoked that emotion from him. It was addictive. And dangerous. And far from the nice, safe guy she knew she should be looking for.

Focus on the horse.

She approached cautiously, speaking softly and holding her hand out as she'd seen Zane do. "Hey there, sweet girl. You're safe now." She gently stroked the side of the horse's head as she continued to offer gentle assurance. The horse's tail swished a few times, but she held still, letting Bryn tenderly stroke her neck.

"You're doing great," Zane said, resting his hand on her shoulder. "She likes you already. Horses are good judges of character, and she recognizes you've got a good heart."

Bryn flushed at the praise—and at the sudden rush of heat that swept along her back from the spot Zane's hand was touching. Her mouth went dry, but she kept her gaze trained on the horse and prayed Zane couldn't feel her tremble. She did believe animals had an innate sense about people, had seen it many times with her dogs as they shied away from some, while openly licking the faces of others. She only hoped she could earn the trust of this horse, who had obviously seen enough of the bad in people to be wary.

"So what do we do now?" she asked. "Should we call Logan and ask him to bring over a trailer so we can get her back to my farm?"

Zane shook his head and moved his hand to gently rest it on the horse's neck. "No way. She's been through enough today. I'm not putting her through the distress of getting back into a trailer."

"Then how are we going to get her home?"

He tilted his head, eyeing the cloudless blue sky. "Seems to me like a good day for a walk."

"A walk? You know my farm is over two miles outside of town." Not that she hadn't ever walked home from town before, but she'd never done it with a three-legged dog, a traumatized horse, or a devilishly handsome cowboy in tow. And certainly never with all three at the same time.

Zane shrugged. "It's not that far. Probably won't take more than an hour. But you could call Logan to pick you up, and I'll meet you out there."

She cocked an eyebrow. "Not a chance. If you're walking, I'm walking."

"Don't you need to finish your shift?"

She shook her head. "Nah, we're dead today, and Vi is happy to pick up my tables. I already told Gil I was taking the rest of the day off to deal with the horse and my car. And he was good with it."

The corners of his lips tugged up. "Then I guess we're taking a morning stroll."

She held his gaze, her mouth curving into a grin. "I guess we are. I just need to grab my dog."

He glanced toward his truck, still parked under the tree. "Yeah, I should probably grab mine too."

She raised an eyebrow.

"Well, not *my* dog. I meant *the* dog."

"Uh-huh," she said, letting out a soft chuckle. "Why don't I grab them both?"

"Good idea. I'll stay here with the horse. No use getting her any more upset."

"Do you need anything else out of your truck?"

He looked down at the corroded and frayed rope knotted around the horse's head. Her skin was abraded in several spots where the rope had rubbed. "I've got a blue lead rope behind the seat of my pickup. Why don't you grab that when you get the dog?"

———————————

Ten minutes later, Bryn emerged from the diner. The two dogs pranced at her heels as she practically skipped toward Zane, bouncing on the balls of her feet. Her eyes were bright, and a huge smile broke across her face.

He chuckled softly. "What's with you? You look like you're walking across a trampoline."

"I *feel* like I'm on a trampoline, like I'm going to bounce into the air with excitement." She held the lead rope and her backpack, but dropped them to throw her arms around his neck and clutch his back. "I need something to hold on to so I don't float away."

He could feel her shoulders trembling as he pulled her against him. "You're shaking."

"I know. And I can't tell if it's because I'm so happy

and excited because I just bought a horse or if I'm terrified and panic-stricken because I just bought a horse." She pressed her cheek into his chest. "Can you just hang on to me for a second? Just until I feel steadier?"

He swallowed, wanting to say something witty or cute but unable to think of a thing, his brain too undone by the warmth of her body flush against him.

She tilted her head and let out a shuddering exhale. He could feel the warmth of it on his neck. "I can't seem to catch my breath." She looked up at him from under dark lashes, her eyes wide and frightened. "I think I might hyperventilate. I need something to ground me. Quick, do something to shock my brain out of this panic mode."

He didn't think, didn't analyze, he just did the first thing that came to mind. He leaned down and kissed her.

It was a quick kiss—a hard press of his lips against hers. But as he drew back, he couldn't help but steal another soft taste of her mouth, one more tender graze, but enough to leave him breathless for more.

She pulled away, her eyes round, her lips parted in a surprised "oh."

Was she mad? Had he overstepped? She'd said earlier she wanted to be friends. Did "friends" entail a shock-reducing lip-lock? Although it had been panic *inducing* for him—his heart was pounding like a scared rabbit facing a wolf.

He watched her face, waiting for a reaction. She just stared at him, wide-eyed, like maybe *she* was the scared rabbit. That seemed the more likely scenario, that he was the wolf. Sweat broke out on his back, and he raised one shoulder, trying for an offhand shrug. "You said to do something to shock you."

Her lips finally moved as the corners tugged up in the slightest grin. "I think I'm *still* in shock. You might have to do it again."

His lips curved into a smile, and he leaned in again just as his phone buzzed in his front shirt pocket. His grin turned into a scowl.

Only a few people had his number. It didn't matter. It could have been the pope and he still would have scowled at the interruption. He checked the caller ID, and his scowl deepened. "Hold on, I've got to take this."

"Go ahead."

He tapped the screen, then pressed the phone to his ear. "Hey, Dad."

"We're out of milk." Birch Taylor's voice was gruff and succinct.

"Is that your way of asking me to pick up another gallon, or are you just making a statement of fact?"

"Both. And we also need a loaf of bread. I tried to make a sandwich, but you must have left the bread out because it was all moldy."

Like I caused the mold spores to form. I'm pretty powerful like that. "Fine. I'll pick them up on my way home. If you think of anything else, just text me." He wouldn't. Birch hated technology and seemed to only use the new iPhone Zane had bought him for games of solitaire. "Did you take your medication?"

"Yeah. I took it," Birch grumbled.

"All right then. Get some rest. I'll see ya when I get home tonight."

"Yeah, see ya. Don't forget the milk. *Or* the bread."

"I won't forget, Dad."

"See that you don't."

Zane ended the call and pushed the phone back into his pocket.

"How's he doing?" Bryn asked, her eyes crinkled in concern, the kiss apparently already forgotten.

Thanks, Dad. Zane shrugged. "Good days and bad. The doctor said because he was a mechanic, his body was in pretty good shape, so that helps with the recovery." His dad had always been strong physically, just weak in spirit *and* when it came to booze. "It's a good thing he didn't have a liver attack. I don't think he would have come back so well from that."

She arched an eyebrow.

"I take him for his monthly checkups. Doc seems to think he's doing okay."

She studied his face. "How about you? Are you doing okay?"

"Me? I'm fine. I'm not the one who had a heart attack." Nope. His heart had been attacked a long time ago. Attacked and broken, and he'd since kept it locked up tight. Nothing could attack an organ he never used.

Not even an impulsive kiss with a beautiful girl, who had apparently already put the bold move behind them as she patted her backpack and changed the subject.

"I grabbed us a couple bottles of water," she told him, as if the kiss and her panic attack had never happened. "There's a hose around the side of the diner if we want to give the animals some too. And I brought more apple slices."

"Good thinking. She seemed to like the first ones." If that's how she wanted to play it, Zane could go along. He turned to the horse and carefully removed and discarded the rotted rope from her neck and replaced it with the soft blue one. Then they led the horse around the diner and cracked the water bottles while they waited for all the animals to get a drink.

Their motley crew now assembled and hydrated, Bryn shoved the water bottles back into her pack and raised it to lace her arm through the strap. Zane held out his hand to take it from her.

"You sure?" she asked, glancing down at the bright floral print.

He cocked an eyebrow. "You think I'm not secure enough in my manhood to carry a pink flowered backpack?" He slung it over his shoulder and lifted one side of his mouth in a grin. "Besides, I think the glitter on the purple pansies really brings out the blue in my eyes."

She laughed, appreciating, not for the first time, the gorgeous ice blue of his eyes. "It does indeed."

No amount of purple glitter could call into question

Zane Taylor's manhood. He exuded strength and masculinity, even with a flowery backpack riding on his shoulder. He seemed tough as hell, but she'd never seen him raise his fists or remember him ever getting in a fight at school. He didn't have to—one look at him told any adversary he was a man not to be messed with. His glare alone had just cut short the conversation of those two grimy men.

The size of his pecs and the straightness to his posture conveyed his strength, but he never came off as arrogant or cocky. He was dressed simply in jeans, square-toed boots, a faded blue T-shirt, and a straw cowboy hat, yet the fit of his clothes and the way the sleeves of his T-shirt stretched over his pecs showed off his muscled physique.

She liked that he was tall and strong, but she knew Zane was smart too. And funny. Plenty of guys she knew could joke around and tease, but she loved the way Zane could slay her with one of his well-timed wry jokes.

She hadn't been prepared for the way he'd slayed her with that kiss though. It was quick, over in a second, but for that one glorious second, it had heat coiling in her belly and robbed her of any coherent thought. And if the kiss hadn't stolen her senses, his impish grin after the fact surely had.

But *why* had he *kissed* her? When she'd told him to do something to shock her, she'd thought he would try to startle her, like one would do to someone with the hiccups. Most people don't try to *kiss* the hiccups away.

What would have happened if his phone hadn't rung?

Would he have kissed her again? Did she want him too? Did he want to? After the call from his dad, his charming manner had disappeared and his expression turned dark. She didn't know how to get back to that moment, so she'd changed the subject, figuring she'd think about it later. And Zane had certainly seemed okay with dropping the matter, so maybe the kiss hadn't meant anything to him. It was just a lark, a bit of fun.

Although Zane Taylor didn't seem the type to do spontaneous fun. But he had left her an impulsive hundred-dollar tip and helped her save this horse. Best to concentrate on that for now. She fell in step next to him as they set off down the road. The weather was gorgeous. A warm spring day in Colorado with lots of sunshine yet still cool enough.

Zane held the rope loosely in his hand, letting the horse set the pace as they walked next to her. They only spent a little time on the highway before they turned onto the quieter road that led to Bryn's farm. The dogs occasionally veered off into the grass or the ditch to explore a scent, but always kept them in sight.

Zane pushed his hat back and peered down at her. "So, now that you bought a horse, what are your plans for keeping it?"

"Don't you mean, now that *we* bought a horse?"

He let out a soft chuckle. "Hey, I'm just the investor. Think of me as more of a silent partner."

She liked thinking of him as a partner—and in more ways than just as co-horse-owners. She let out a breath. "I don't know what my plans are. Honestly, I still can't quite believe I just bought a horse. And for only a hundred dollars. Which I never thanked you for. So thank you. And I do plan to pay you back, you know. At least for my half."

"Don't worry about it. And that hundred bucks may have bought you more of a deal than you bargained for."

"More than a traumatized horse that I have no money to pay for the care and upkeep of?"

He nodded. "You might say you got yourself a two-for-the-price-of-one deal. This horse is pregnant."

CHAPTER 3

BRYN STOPPED IN HER TRACKS, EYES WIDE. SHE WAS stunned. "Pregnant? Are you sure?"

"Pretty dang sure." He ran a hand over the horse's rounded side. "She looks fairly malnourished, but there's no mistaking the movement of a foal inside her belly."

Bryn clapped a hand to her mouth. "I think I'm going to be sick. I already thought her previous owner was a monster, but this... Who sends a pregnant horse to slaughter?"

"Probably somebody who couldn't afford to keep even one horse, let alone two."

"Well, I can't afford to keep even one horse either, but I'll find a way."

His expression softened. "I believe you will. And I can help."

"You've already done so much."

He shrugged. "I haven't done that much. And I'm glad to help. I can pick up some grain and see to setting you up with some hay to get you by for a little bit. And I don't want you thinking you have to pay me back for the horse. That was your tip."

She laughed. "Neither Gil's biscuits and gravy nor my talent for pouring coffee would ever garner that kind of tip."

He lifted one shoulder in a shrug. "Your coffee-pouring skills might be better than you think."

She tilted her head and eyed him as they walked. "Your fibbing skills might not be as good as *you* think."

They laughed together as they approached the spot where Bryn's car sat on the shoulder of the road. Zane pulled the horse to a stop. "You want to give it a go? See if it starts up?"

"Sure. Good idea. It's been pretty temperamental lately, so it just might start." Bryn slid into the passenger seat, leaving the door open to let out the heat. As much as she wanted the car to start, she was enjoying this time spent walking with Zane. And the horse. And the dogs. She wasn't sure if she was more relieved or disappointed when she turned the key and nothing happened.

"Still dead," she told Zane as she got out and shut the door. "Stupid car."

"Don't worry. I'll come back and look at it later. It might just be a dead battery."

"Nothing is ever that easy."

Zane snuck a glance at Bryn as she walked beside him. A breeze picked up a loose strand of her hair and blew it across her cheek. She tucked it behind her ear as she raised her face to the sun. "What a perfect day."

He thought so too. But his thoughts had more to do with the company he was currently keeping than the temperature. Bryn was so easy to be around, whether they were talking or not. He wasn't used to being so comfortable in the presence of a woman, but Bryn had a way of making him feel at ease. Well, mostly at ease, if he didn't count the nerves that occasionally erupted in his gut when she touched his arm or her hand brushed against his.

It was just the backs of their hands, but a spark of energy shot through his body every time their knuckles bumped. What would she do if he casually took her hand? He reached out, ready to slide her palm into his, but the horse nudged his arm away with her head.

He frowned at the mare. *Thanks a lot. Jealous much?* He'd made a move and been cock-blocked by an envious equine. Sounded about right for his luck.

And Bryn hadn't even noticed. They were still close to a mile from her farm, but she seemed totally relaxed walking beside him, like it was an everyday occurrence for her to be taking her horse for a walk.

"You're being a pretty good sport about walking the horse home," he told her.

"It was the right call. There was no way we could subject this poor horse to the trauma of getting back in a trailer," she said. "Besides, I like walking."

"Me too. It's relaxing. Gives me time to think." He knew plenty of women who would balk at walking anywhere. Although Bryn wasn't like any other woman he knew. And he had picked her up this morning as she'd been walking to work. But that had been out of necessity.

"Yeah? What kind of deep things does a man like Zane Taylor think about?" she asked, offering him a playful smile.

"Oh gosh, *such* deep stuff. Just this morning I was walking across a pasture thinking about how much snow we might still get in this last week of spring, then I pondered some pretty philosophical ideas about what I was going to have for lunch today."

"Wow, that is deep," she said, teasing him as she put a finger to her chin. "I've pondered that lunch idea before as well. It can really be enlightening."

"You bet it can. The choices between a grilled cheese and a turkey sandwich can have all sorts of far-reaching implications. And when you throw in the options of available chips, it gets pretty mind-boggling."

She nodded sagely. "I can imagine. I've often thought Cheetos were pretty inspired."

"Mmmhmm. I'd have to agree. I do love Cheetos."

She chuckled. "Good to know. Especially since I'm planning to make you lunch for helping me out this morning."

Lunch? With Bryn? He didn't want to overstay his welcome, but he also didn't want to pass up the chance to spend more time with her. "You don't have to feed me."

"Yes, I do." She said the words with such finality he didn't bother arguing. "Besides, I owe you one, not just for helping me rescue this horse, but also for saving me from those guys."

"Seemed the least I could do, since, you know, it appears I *am* your boyfriend." His steps gained the slightest swagger.

It had surprised him how easily the words "my

girlfriend" had slipped from his lips. He hadn't said them in years—had planned to scrub them from his vocabulary after Sarah—yet the words had tumbled from his mouth as easily as leaves fell from a tree in autumn. And even more surprising, the words hadn't made his chest hurt, hadn't made his stomach pitch.

But if she knew the truth about him, she'd run away as far and fast as she could. Although *he* should be the one to run. He knew the truth—he wasn't good for her, wasn't good for anyone. He should call his old boss tonight and tell her he was coming back. Walk away now. Before someone got hurt.

"Oh yeah. Sorry about that." Bryn offered him a sheepish grin. "That Gator guy kept making revolting passes at me, and he was giving me the creeps, so I just picked out the toughest guy in the diner and said you were my boyfriend. You'd already left, but he'd seen you before and seemed to lay off a bit. It was either you or old Doc Hunter, and I thought you were just slightly more intimidating than the eighty-year-old guy with two bad hips."

"Just slightly, huh?"

She held up her thumb and forefinger to suggest an inch. "I hope you don't mind."

He shook his head. "Nah, I don't mind. You can use me as your badass fake boyfriend anytime." He offered her a grin. But the swagger disappeared from his steps. What had he been thinking? Of course she wasn't insinuating he was her *actual* boyfriend. Why would she? Who would want the son of the town drunk, and a scarred up ugly bastard to boot, as her boyfriend?

The horse nudged his shoulder, almost as if she'd read his mind. He ran his hand over her dusty, velvety neck. *At least the horse digs me.*

"I'll keep that in mind," Bryn said, teasing again.

Time to push away the bad memories and change the subject. "You know, those guys were more than just creeps. They were shady as the day is long and most likely con men."

"Wouldn't be the first time I've been taken in by one of those," she muttered, then shook her head as if to clear the thought and looked back to Zane. "What makes you think they're con men? For swindling me, and you, out of a hundred dollars? That doesn't seem to make them very good at their trade."

"It's not you they swindled." He patted the horse's neck. "You got the better end of that deal. But I'm sure they took whoever paid them to dispose of this horse, because they dang sure weren't taking it to a slaughterhouse."

"How do you know?"

"Because they outlawed slaughterhouses a decade ago. The last ones in Texas and Illinois closed down around 2007, when they banned the slaughter of horses."

"Then what were they going to do with her?"

He shrugged. "Who knows? My best guess would be that they took the money and were planning to take her out to the desert and put a bullet in her head."

Bryn gasped and put a hand over her mouth. "Oh my gosh. That's terrible. Why would someone pay them to do that?"

"They might not have known. Or they might not have cared. Keeping a horse is expensive, but so is disposing of one. Cremation can run seven or eight hundred dollars and trying to bury a thousand pound animal on your property has its own set of problems as well. It's tough all around to lose a horse. Maybe these people thought they were getting a deal or maybe they didn't care. Who knows?"

She shivered. "I don't know, and I don't care. All I care about right now is this beautiful girl and her new baby. And I'm thankful we were in the right place at the right time to be able to rescue them because this was not their day to die. Nope. Heaven can wait for these two."

He smiled down at Bryn, her expression so sincere, so full of love for a horse that she'd only just met. He understood it, had felt the immediate connection with an animal. "You've got a good heart, Bryn. And you're generous to a fault."

"Thank you. But I can tell you I don't feel very generous toward those two asshats who had this horse. There should be a special place in hell for people who would swindle folks out of their money for putting an animal down. And it's got to make it that much tougher for good people who are really trying to help in that tough situation."

"It does."

The sound of an engine had them turning to see a familiar silver truck heading up the road. It slowed when it drew even with them, and Zane's boss, Logan Rivers, leaned his head out the window. "Everything all right?"

Zane shrugged. "Yep. We're just out taking our horse for a walk."

Logan chuckled. "Seems like a reasonable way to spend the morning." His gaze traveled over the motley crew, then back to Zane. "I didn't realize the two of you *had* a horse."

"It's a recent acquisition."

"We just bought her off these two slimeballs at the diner who were taking her to be slaughtered," Bryn told him.

Logan's brow furrowed. "Why? She looks in pretty good shape to me."

"She is," Zane said. "A little malnourished, and needs some maintenance and a round of antibiotics, but otherwise she seems all right. We'll know more when we get her checked out. But I'm probably going to need to take the rest of the afternoon off. I can come back tonight to help with evening chores if you need me."

Logan shrugged. "You're good. Take the day. Looks like this need is more pressing."

"Thanks, Logan. I'll most likely call you later for a ride back to the diner. I left my truck there. And Bryn's car is broken down on the side of the road."

"I saw it when I drove into town. What's wrong with it?"

"Not sure. Figured I'd take a look at it, then get you to help me tow it back here if I need to work on it."

"I'm good with that. Call me when you're ready. Anything I can do to help now? Either of you want a lift to the farm?"

"We're good," Bryn said.

"You sure?" Zane asked her. "I can manage the rest of the way on my own."

She raised one eyebrow. Zane's lips curved into a grin as he turned back to Logan. "We're good. Thanks though. I'll call you later."

"Good save," she told Zane, then waved to Logan. "Thanks for the offer. We'll see you later."

Twenty minutes later, they ambled up the driveway of Bryn's farm. An old yellow two-story farmhouse with a wide front porch sat on one side of the drive, and a large barn with faded red paint sat on the other. Two nice-sized corrals flanked either side of the barn, and chickens roamed inside the fence surrounding a small chicken coop. A couple of outbuildings sat beyond the barn, but both looked like they hadn't been used in some time.

The farm was a little worse for wear, and Zane saw several things in need of repair, but he could see Bryn's touch in the cheery blue pillows on the porch swing and the array of colorful pots spilling over with flowers on the steps. She had a neat fenced-in garden next to her house, but her grass looked like it could use mowing. A couple dozen head of cattle filled the corral and the pasture beyond, and one let out a low moo, almost as if welcoming Bryn home.

"You got a place to keep this horse?"

"Oh sure. This farm is a little run-down, but I've got plenty of room. My grandpa used to have tons of animals. That barn has six stalls on either side. It could hold a dozen horses."

"That's good. You know, in case you decide to rescue any more damaged horses."

"Hmmm," she said, a wicked gleam lighting her eyes, then she let out a chuckle. "I'm just kidding. I think I'll have my hands full enough with just this one…two." She jogged ahead to pull open the big barn door.

Zane led the horse inside and down the middle of the alleyway of the barn. The air was cooler inside and smelled of cedar and the hay stacked up in the two far stalls. The rest of the area was well maintained—the empty stalls had been swept out and tools hung neatly from racks next to the door leading to the corral. The door stood open to a tack room that sat in one corner of the barn, and a couple of farm cats stretched out in the ray of sunshine coming in from a hole in the front of the barn.

He tied the lead rope to the post of one of the stalls. "You've got a good space in here. Except for that hole in the side of the wall."

"Yeah, that last big windstorm we got picked up this wagon I use in my garden and flung it into the barn there. It about scared me to death, the sound of it was deafening. The wagon was okay, bent one of the wheels a little, but it knocked that hole in the wall, and I just haven't gotten around to fixing it yet." She glanced up at the hole. It was a good twenty feet off the ground. "It's not so much fixing it that's the problem. It's where the hole is. To tell you the truth, I'm a little afraid of heights. Well, more than a little. I'm terrified of heights, so I haven't convinced myself to climb a ladder to fix it. I was eventually gonna get around to asking Logan to help me with it."

"I could help you. Wouldn't take much to patch it enough to keep the rain out." A couple of black rubber tubs sat in one of the stalls. Zane pulled them out, then filled a bucket with water from the spigot next to the tack room and poured it into one of the tubs. "You want to grab some of that hay?" he asked, curtailing any discussion about her letting him fix the hole. "We can give her a little something to eat while we look her over and get her brushed."

"Sure. Although I can't imagine she's still hungry. I swear we stopped ten times on the way here for her to eat some grass." Bryn laughed as she grabbed a portion of a hay bale that had already been split open and placed it in the other tub. The horse bent to sniff the straw, then pulled a portion loose to munch between her teeth. "Not that I'm judging. I've been known to put away half a pan of mac and cheese on a bad night." She offered Zane a sheepish grin. "Or a good night, depending on the quality of the mac and cheese and who I'm eating it with."

"Makes sense." He turned back to the horse. *Makes sense?* That didn't make sense at all. He floundered, having no idea how else to respond to what might possibly be a flirty invitation to eat pasta with her. He could have gone with something about how carbs look great on her hips… No, probably not. Maybe say he could be the mac to her cheese? His face flamed at the dorky responses.

What he really wanted to say was that he liked her, but he couldn't. He couldn't offer the stability of a comfort food like mac and cheese. He was more like buffalo wings with extra sriracha sauce—they might be good while you're eating them, but they only cause you pain later. Best to keep focused on the horse. "She's going to eat a heck of a lot more than that. We can give her some hay for now, then let her out into the pasture later. I'll stop in at the feed store when I head back to town and get her some oats."

"You don't have to—" she started to say, but he cut her off with a wave of his hand.

"You already told me your bank balance is hovering around six dollars, and one bag of good horse feed will run close to fourteen, so just let me get it. You're boarding the horse and providing the hay, the least I can do is buy some oats and pick her up some vitamins."

Bryn let out a sigh. "Okay. But I'd like to come along to see what you get. My grandpa used to have horses when I was growing up, so I know how to ride and probably just enough about them to be dangerous, but I don't know anything about their daily feed and care."

"I can help you with that." He gestured to the tack room. "You got some brushes in there? Maybe a curry comb? I'd like to clean her up a little, and we can check her for sores and injuries while we're brushing her. Plus it's a good way to bond with her."

Bryn disappeared into the tack room and came out with a handful of brushes and curry combs. She held them out to Zane. "Take your pick."

He took a curry comb, leaving a softer brush for Bryn. "I'm not sure if she's been groomed before, so we can take it slow and get her used to it. She's doing pretty well with us so far, but I don't want to spook her. I'll give her a little time to get accustomed to the brush before I try to check her feet. I can already tell her hooves are in terrible shape. Why don't you start, and I'll see if I can find a hoof pick and some nippers?"

Bryn nodded before turning back to the mare. "Help yourself. The horse tack is on the north wall. Grandpa always kept his tools organized, so you should be able to find what you need."

She was right. Her grandfather had kept an organized tack room, and Zane easily found a hoof pick, a rasp, and a nice pair of nippers. He walked out of the tack room, his concentration on the task of taking care of the horse's hooves. He looked up as he drew closer, then stopped, his heart jerking in his chest.

The ray of sunlight had moved and shone down perfectly on Bryn as she brushed the mare. She looked like an angel as the light gleamed across her blond hair.

But the thoughts Zane was having were anything but angelic. They were bordering on downright sinful as he watched her, mesmerized by her movements. Her body was voluptuous, with the kind of curves a man dreamed of skimming his hands over, but also graceful and elegant as she gently ran the brush across the horse's back. Something tightened in his chest as he watched her, and he let out a hard sigh. "Damn, but you are beautiful."

Bryn paused, her hand midstroke, her body tense, and she turned her head slightly toward him.

Criminy. Had he said that out loud? He held his breath as he waited for her reaction.

A long, painful second later, her shoulders relaxed, and she nodded at the horse. "Yes, she is beautiful. I can't believe someone would just throw her away."

He let out his breath. Did she *really* think he'd meant the horse? Should he remedy the situation by saying he was actually talking about her? Or would that just make the awkward moment worse?

Before he had a chance to say anything, Bryn turned and pointed the brush at him. "You know, that's not a bad name for this girl. Maybe not Beautiful, but what about Bella? Or just Beauty? Oh, I like that. It's like the character in the story."

He raised an eyebrow. "You mean the one who falls in love with a beast?"

"Yes, that one. I love that story." She smiled dreamily and clutched the brush to her chest. "It was complicated but still so simple. It got to the heart of every great love story and focused on how when you love someone, you see more than just what's on the outside."

"Yeah, but that's all it was—just a story. A fairy tale.

In real life, most people like that pretty exterior, and they don't really want to see the sullied mess that's on the inside."

She offered him a thoughtful look. "That seems pretty cynical. I think there are plenty of people who can handle a little mess and can look past the beast on the outside."

"Maybe," he said, lifting his shoulder but not breaking eye contact. "But sometimes there's a beast on the inside too."

The horse stamped her front foot and let out a whinny, and Bryn took a step back, breaking the connection. "I think Beauty disagrees with you."

"Wouldn't be the first time a horse had an opinion contrary to mine."

Bryn chuckled as she eased closer and resumed her gentle brushing. "No, I can bet not."

Zane set the tools on the ground and picked up the curry comb. He stepped in next to her and carefully drew the comb along the horse's neck, working his hand in slow circular motions as he loosened the dirt and inspected her coat for cuts and injuries. The horse leaned her neck toward him. "She seems to like being groomed, so my guess is someone must have taken care of her at some point."

"I agree, but it must have been a long time ago, because she doesn't seem to have been cared for recently." She pointed out a few places on the horse's skin where she'd found minor wounds.

They worked in easy unison, gently grooming the

horse, but Zane noticed every time her hand crept close to his or her fingers brushed his skin, his skin warmed as his blood pumped hot through his veins. It had been so long since a woman affected him this way. He kept telling himself Bryn wasn't important, but his body proved that lie to be false.

She *was* important. No matter how much he told himself she didn't matter, that she was just another pretty girl, he knew he was kidding himself. Bryn was so much more—she was funny and smart and didn't take the crap he continuously dished out. And they shared the same connection to animals—that soul-deep bond and the need to rescue and protect the ones who couldn't protect themselves.

But the heat on his skin had nothing to do with the way she loved animals and a hell of a lot more to do with the animal inside him—and the carnal things he imagined doing with and to her.

Hockey stats. The weather. Grandma's secret to a great piecrust. He tried to think of something to talk about to keep his mind off the thoughts he was having about her—about pulling her down into the hay and running his hands along her body. "So what did you mean earlier when I told you those guys were con men, and you said it wouldn't be the first time you'd been taken in by one of those?"

Her hand stilled on the horse's back. "I didn't really mean for you to hear that."

"Well, I did. So what happened?"

She shrugged. "I'm embarrassed to tell you. I was an idiot and did something stupid."

"There's nothing to be embarrassed about. I've done my share of stupid."

"Not like this. I thought I was helping someone, and they took advantage of me."

"You do have a tendency to take in strays."

"Yeah, well, this stray turned out to be a snake. And bringing a snake into your bed almost guarantees you'll get bit."

His chest constricted, and the muscles across his back tightened. He damn sure didn't want to think about someone else taking up space in Bryn's bed, especially someone who'd hurt her. He wanted to swear—hell, he wanted to kick the boards of the stall in—but he kept his tone even, knowing his temper wouldn't instill the trust she needed to tell him more. "You mean it was someone you were dating?"

"You could say that. We didn't really date as much as collided into each other. Then he said he needed a place to crash, just for a few days, and I let him stay. A few days turned into a few weeks, then a month. He helped me around the farm, and I thought he was helping me with the sale of a few cattle, but really he was just helping himself to the profits. And to my grandfather's truck, which he took off in after he cleaned out my bank account."

"Did you tell the police? Or file a report at the bank? Did they catch the guy?"

"No." She kept her gaze trained on the horse, her hand

moving in a steady circle. "Because I didn't tell the police. *Or* the bank."

"Why the hell not?"

"I told you: I was embarrassed and humiliated. And it was my own fault for trusting him. Plus, it was a friend of mine who worked at the bank who gave him my money, and she's a single mom, so if I filed a complaint, she could lose her job."

"Yeah, but you lost your money."

She shrugged again. "Believe me, that part wasn't a great loss. And neither was the truck. It probably broke down before he made it to Texas or Montana or whatever rodeo he was chasing next. It was losing the beef profits and my grandfather's prized champion rodeo buckle that really hurt. Although the buckle wasn't worth much either. Not to anyone but our family. I doubt he could even pawn the thing."

His hands tightened into fists. Who could do that to someone like Bryn? All she ever did was help others. "So he was a rodeo chaser?"

"Yep. Although when he stuck around here for that month last fall, I thought he might have settled. I thought it was because of me, but apparently he must have just seen the *sucker* sign plastered across my forehead." She let out a low sigh, and her chin dropped to her chest.

He hated that someone had made her feel less about herself and had taken that light from her eyes, even for a moment. She seemed so sad, so discouraged—his heart hurt just looking at her. He reached for her and pulled her into his arms. The smell of her hair surrounded him and his knees threatened to buckle at the intoxicating feeling of her body warm against his. He tipped his head and pressed his lips against her ear. "Trying to find the good in people doesn't make you a sucker. It just makes you kindhearted."

She held tightly to him as she let out a breath, a tremble barely evident in her voice. "Well, it sure makes me feel like a fool." She straightened, pushing away from him and forcing her shoulders back as she drew herself up to her full height and stared him straight in the eye. "Enough of that feeling sorry for myself nonsense—this kind heart is tired of getting stomped on. I'm done dating slick cowboys and trying to rescue men who don't want to be saved. I'm sticking to rescuing horses and three-legged dogs, and dating guys who are nice and safe, who have regular jobs and boring routines. I'll take slow and steady monotony over crazy collision heartbreak any day."

Before Zane could answer or find a way to get her back into his arms, the sound of an engine drew their attention. A white pickup pulled up to the barn door, and a tall man stepped out and waved. Looked like Mr. Nice and Safe had just arrived.

CHAPTER 4

Make that *Doctor* Nice and Safe.

The bed of the truck was affixed with a white vet box, and the man unfastened the side compartment to grab a box of supplies.

The passenger door opened, and a ten-year-old girl wearing a pink T-shirt, cut-off jean shorts, and a pair of cowboy boots with purple tops climbed from the cab. Her blond hair was long and pulled away from her face with some kind of braid that twisted across the side of her head.

A grin the size of Texas broke out on her face as she caught sight of Zane. "Hey, Zane," she called, loping toward him and throwing her arms around his middle. "I didn't know you'd be here."

Between the ragged scar and the scowl he usually wore, most kids were scared of him—or at least curious, like the ones in the diner that morning. He'd heard their not-so-quiet whispers about what happened to that man's face and seen the way they cowered behind their mothers at the grocery store. But not Mandy Tate. Zane wasn't sure that girl was afraid of anything, let alone a scarred up bastard like himself. He'd seen her pick up a snake, cuddle a pig, and dust herself off to get right back on a horse that had thrown her. She was a fighter, that one.

She'd only been a bitty thing the first time he met her, but she'd crawled right into his lap, oblivious to his imperfections. "Hey, kid," he said, ruffling her hair. "How'd you do on that spelling test last week?"

"Awesome," she told him. "I got a hundred percent— spelled every word right."

"Even *neutral*?"

"Even N-*E*-U-T-R-A-L, neutral."

"Nice work." He held up his hand for a high five, and she gave it a smack.

"Apparently, you need to help her with her spelling words every week," the tall man said, as he sauntered toward them. "Hey, Zane. Do you hire out as a tutor?"

"Brody," he answered, shaking the man's outstretched hand.

Brody Tate, wait, *Doctor* Brody Tate now, had been the golden boy in high school. He'd graduated with Zane, and they'd played hockey on the same team. But that's where the similarities ended. Brody came from a good family, a nice family who came to his games and had been at his graduation, cheering him on, instead of at the bar, tying one on. He was smart and earned a scholarship to Colorado State University, where he met Mary, a pretty little filly who was majoring in English.

While Zane had been sweating and fighting in the deserts of Afghanistan as he tried to shake the memories of his past, Brody had been building a future, getting married, thriving in vet school, and cuddling a new baby daughter. The happy couple eventually moved back to

Creedence, where Brody worked at his dad's practice, and Mary taught fourth grade. He'd seemed to have it all, until the day Mary found a lump in her breast. She'd been a fighter too, but in the end, Brody was left with a five-year-old daughter and an empty other side of the bed.

Bryn nudged his arm and offered him an amused side-eye. "I didn't know you helped grade-schoolers with their spelling words."

He shrugged, a grin hovering around his lips. "I'm a man of mystery."

Brody chuckled. "He's not that mysterious. Mandy and I were out at Rivers Gulch last week—Logan was having trouble with a horse, and Zane helped Mandy with her homework while I was working in the barn. Apparently, he's also quite good at fourth grade math."

"Just another one of my many talents."

Bryn raised an eyebrow, her lips curving into a coy smile. Zane held his breath, the anticipation of a flirty comeback already warming his chest. But then Mandy grabbed her hand and pulled her toward the mare.

"Show me your new horse," the girl said. "Did you really buy her from some slimeballs at the diner with your tip money?"

This time it was Zane's turn to cock an eyebrow.

"I called Brody from the diner and told him what I'd done," Bryn explained. "I asked him to come out and take a look at her if he was out this way."

How fortuitous that the good doctor just *happened* to be out this way. They'd only had the blessed horse for an hour.

But despite the twinge of jealousy he felt at the comfortable ease Bryn had with the vet and his daughter, Zane was still glad to see him. He liked Brody and respected his skill with animals. They needed to get the horse checked out and worm her anyway.

Brody approached the horse, offering her a couple of sugar cubes as he calmly introduced himself. "Hey, girl. You're a good horse, aren't you? I'm not gonna hurt you. I'm just going to check you over." He ran his hands over the horse, examining her back, her belly, her legs, peering at her infected eye and opening her mouth to check out her teeth. "I'd say you've got a pretty good horse here. Other than being a little malnourished and filthy, she seems in fair shape. She looks to be in her late teens, maybe early twenties, kind of on the late end to be in foal, so my guess is it probably wasn't planned. Not sure why someone would get rid of her, other than the fact that horses are expensive and maybe they couldn't afford to keep one horse, let alone two."

Bryn nodded. "That's what we were thinking."

"I can do a cursory exam, do some blood work to find out more, but how much do you want me to do? Blood work and tests can get expensive."

"I don't have much to spend. And by not much, I actually mean zero. Can you just do the basics to make sure she's healthy for now?"

"Sure. The blood work would tell us if she has worms, but my guess would be she does, so I can just give her a little dewormer and spare you that expense. I've got some in the truck, and I've got some antibiotics for her eye too—should clear that infection right up. That won't run you much, but if you're interested in our usual barter, I've got an overnight vet conference in Denver next week and could use a hand with Mandy. My folks are out of town; otherwise, she'd stay with them. I'd trade you the cost of the exam and the meds for an evening of babysitting. I'll even throw in some prenatal vitamins."

"I don't need a babysitter," Mandy scoffed.

"Of course you don't," Bryn agreed. "But how about planning a girls' sleepover for that night? We can eat junk food and paint our nails and stay up late watching chick flicks."

Mandy eyed her for a second, then nodded. "I guess I could agree to a sleepover. Could we get cookie dough ice cream?"

"Uh…yeah. Of course we can. I'm already mentally adding it to my shopping list."

"Okay, it's a deal then." The girl glanced at Zane. "Want to come to our sleepover next week? Sounds like we're doing manicures and eating ice cream."

The idea of a sleepover with Bryn had Zane's mind going to all sorts of places—most of them involving licking ice cream from Bryn's naked body. But he kept his expression in check as he glanced down at his fingernails. "I have noticed my cuticles could use a little work, but it sounds like this party is for girls only. Maybe next time."

"Sorry, Zane, no boys allowed." Bryn offered him another of those flirty smiles causing him to wonder if she hadn't had a passing thought about him sleeping over as well. But no, she'd just told him she wanted someone safe and boring. His life right now might check the "boring" box, but he wasn't the guy she was looking for if she wanted nice and safe.

"Speaking of cuticles," Brody said, drawing their attention back to the horse. "This mare's hooves need some work. They're too long and look pretty dry and cracked. You've done some farrier work, haven't you, Zane?"

"Yeah, and I can manage her hooves. Bryn's grandfather had a stocked tack room, so I've already got the tools I need." He gestured to the small pile he'd set on the ground earlier. "They'll look and feel a lot better once I trim 'em and clean 'em up."

"I agree."

Zane leaned a hip against the stall and watched Brody and Bryn further examine the horse. They were perfect together, with their blond hair and all-American good looks—they could have been the prom king and queen. And Brody was just the kind of guy Bryn needed—he had a good job, came from a nice, respectable family, worked hard. And had an adorable daughter. A ready-made family and everything Bryn said she wanted.

Now he just had to get out of their way and let it happen. "I'm going to call Logan, get a lift back into town so I can pick up my truck," he said, pushing off from the stall door.

"We can give you a ride," Brody offered. "I'm almost done here, and we're headed that direction anyway."

"I don't want to put you out." *So much for giving them time together.*

"It's no trouble."

"All right then. I'd be obliged if you could drop me at the diner. Then I can run into the feed store, pick up some supplies, and stop to check on Bryn's car on my way back out."

"I could come with you," Bryn offered. "Keep you company."

"Nah. It's all right. I've got the dog."

"Gee thanks, glad to know my company ranks lower than the dog."

Crud. "That's not what I meant." Heat flamed his skin, and he hoped his neck wasn't beet-red. This wasn't going as he'd intended. "You can come along if you want."

"I'm just teasing you." She nudged his arm. "But I do think I'll tag along. I want to see what you get at the feed store. And on the off chance all my car needs is a jump start, I can drive it home."

Brody spent another fifteen minutes with the horse. He rubbed worm paste along her gums and put a little goop in her eye, then showed Bryn how to use the eye drops. They talked through some general care, then all piled into the truck, with Zane, Brody, and the dog in the front, and Mandy and Bryn in the smaller back seat. Bryn had left Lucky in the house.

Even with the distraction of all the conversation and the dog resting her head on his leg, Zane was acutely aware of Bryn sitting behind him. Her arm was on the seat next to his neck, making his skin feel prickly and warm, and her perfume swirled in the air around him every time she leaned forward to ask Brody a question. He'd made a point the last few months not to run into her and to try to put her out of his mind, and now here he was, spending the whole day with her and imagining his hands on her skin as he inhaled her scent.

He could still smell the faint traces of her perfume in the cab when he opened the door of his truck after Brody dropped them off. Or maybe that was the scent of her hair as she climbed into the other side. Not that he preferred the normal smell of dirt, dog, and horse that usually permeated his cab, but this woman's scent was making him crazy.

They didn't talk much. She hummed along to the radio as they drove across town to the feed store. The collie followed them in, familiar with Zane's routine of picking up supplies for Logan. In a small town, especially a ranching community, dogs were welcome just about everywhere, and Sam, the proprietor of Creedence Country Feed & Supply, always had a box of dog treats behind the counter for his canine customers.

"Hey, Zane. Bryn," Sam called to them as they entered the store. "Coming in for some supplies for you-all's new horse? I've got some nice sweet feed that might help put a little weight on her."

News did travel fast in this town.

"Hey, Sam," Zane said. "How'd you hear about *Bryn's* new horse already?"

"Doc Hunter stopped in on his way home. Told me about it. He said he saw the tip money Zane left and didn't want to be shown up by a young buck in front of his favorite waitress, so he stopped in to add a hundred dollars to Bryn's farm account. He figured she'd eventually be by to get some grain."

"You're kidding me," Bryn said, her eyes going wide as she shook her head. "I seriously love that man. And I'm going to give him a big, fat, sloppy kiss the next time I see him."

Wait. Where was *his* big, fat, sloppy kiss? He'd done more than just lay down some money. Although Zane wasn't just interested in *one* sloppy kiss from her. He was ravenous for at least a hundred—a hundred slow and easy kisses followed by another hundred hard and fast ones.

Hell. He needed to get his mind off hard and fast tongue wrestling with Bryn before he gave himself a woodster in the feed and grain store—forget about Bryn's new horse acquisition; *that* would surely get the gossips' tongues wagging.

"So, about that sweet feed," Zane said. "We're going to need a couple of fifty-pound bags, a couple bags of grain, plus a salt block and a vitamin and mineral supplement. The horse is in foal."

"Got it," Sam said, guiding them toward the proper section of the store. He passed the dog a treat and gave her a pat on the head as he walked.

Twenty minutes later, they had the truck loaded with supplies and were back on the highway, headed toward the farm.

"I can't believe Doc Hunter stocked my farm account," Bryn said, rolling down the window and lifting her hair off her neck. "My luck has certainly turned today. I'd say if we pull up and my car magically starts, I think I need to run back to town to buy a lottery ticket."

"I probably wouldn't start counting your lottery winnings yet."

She cocked an eyebrow. "Well, not with that attitude."

He chuckled. "Fine, we'll hope for the best, but I wouldn't spend too much time thinking up your lucky numbers. It didn't start the last time we tried. But I'll take a look at it. I'm hoping it's just the battery and we can give it a jump start." Zane pulled off to the shoulder next to her inoperative vehicle. He motioned for the dog to stay as he got out and popped the hood. "Tell me what happened when you were driving."

She handed him the keys, hyperaware of his muscled back as she pressed her breasts against him to lean over his shoulder. His shirt was warm from the sun, and sweat broke out on her lower back from being this close to him. Every time he'd touched her today, she'd felt like a bottle rocket had shot through her spine. She hadn't seen him in months, had tried to convince herself he wasn't that good-looking, wasn't that charming, but one flash of his grin that morning had her melting like a Popsicle on a hot summer day. Her brain kept warning her to back off, keep away, but her traitorous body kept finding ways to touch him. "I was just on my way to work like normal, and the car suddenly died. Oh, and I think the check engine light came on."

The battery appeared old, the posts corroded with crusty greenish acid. "When's the last time you replaced the battery?"

She shrugged. "I'm not sure exactly. It's been four or five years though."

"Could be the battery, or could be your alternator if it just stopped running. There's a few tests I can run to figure out which is more likely." He slid into the driver's seat and spent a few minutes trying to start it, then went back to his truck and dug out the jumper cables.

It took another twenty minutes, but he got her car jump-started after diagnosing a faulty alternator. "Hopefully this will give you enough juice to get back to the farm. Why don't you drive my truck and I'll take the car, just in case it stalls again or the steering locks up?"

"I don't want you to get hurt if something happens. I can drive it," she assured him.

"I know you can, but I'd rather do it," he told her, then softened his tone as he placed his hand on her arm. "If that's okay."

She liked the way he tried to protect her without taking away her power. And she really liked the solid way his palm felt against her arm. Before she could argue more, a ringtone sounded from her pocket. She pulled out her cell phone and checked the screen. "Can you hold on a second? It's my brother."

"Sure. Take it."

She tapped the phone and pressed it to her ear, the familiar feeling of love and dread swirling in her chest whenever she saw his name on her screen. "Hey, Buck."

"Hey, Sis," his voice boomed in her ear. "What's up?"

"Not much," she said, keeping her answer intentionally vague. "Where are you?"

"Not sure. Some Podunk town in Utah. Another rodeo."

It was always another rodeo. Another purse. Another dream he never seemed to obtain. She strained to hear the sound of booze in his voice. Maybe this time would be different. "How are you?"

"I'm fine. Same old. Same old. Not like you. I heard you just bought a new horse."

How in the Sam Hill had he heard about the horse already?

"Rescued her more like. She's in pretty sorry condition."

"You must be in pretty *good* condition though if you had the money to buy her. You get a raise at the diner?"

"No. Nothing like that," she answered, sneaking a glance at Zane, who stared at the field across the highway as he rested his hip on the hood of her car. "A friend actually helped me to buy her."

"Oh yeah? I wish I had a friend like that. Things are pretty tight for me right now." *Annnd here it comes. Wait for it…* "I was thinking if you had come into some extra cash, you could float me a few dollars. You know, just until after the rodeo. The rough-stock events start in a couple of days, and I think I've got a pretty good shot with these bulls."

She hated to think about her little brother on the back of a thousand-pound bull, but he'd been bull riding for years and seemed addicted to the rush of the rodeo and the occasional win. He did all right, well enough to survive until the next town, the next rodeo, the next event. Well, with a little help from her.

"Listen, Bucky, I'm a little strapped for cash myself. In fact, I'm standing on the side of the highway right now trying to get my car back to the farm. It broke down on me this morning." She promised herself the last time she sent him money that it *would* be the last time. But she'd made that promise many times before. And she always gave in. *Stay strong. Say no.*

"Why don't you drive Gramps's truck?"

Ugh. His comment was like a sucker punch to the gut. A hard reminder of another man she'd let take advantage of her good nature. She hadn't had the guts to tell her brother yet that their grandfather's truck had been stolen. She'd been too ashamed. He'd asked about it last time he'd been home, and she'd given him the lame excuse that she'd let a friend borrow it. If she'd said she sold it, Buck would have his hand out for half of the profit.

"It's not really an option right now either," she told him. Which wasn't entirely a lie.

"Well, I don't want to bother you, but I could sure use a little help. I don't need much. But I understand if you can't do it. I don't want to put you out. And I've survived on ramen noodles before."

The guilt twisted in her chest. She might not have much, but she had food in her cupboard. And more than just a few packages of ramen noodles. Hadn't she just been glibly boasting about her luck a few minutes ago? Zane, Doc, and Brody had all helped her out today. How could she refuse to help her own brother? Surely she could figure out a way to send him something. Maybe she'd pick up an extra shift this weekend at the diner.

Her shoulders sagged as she let out a sigh. "Sure, Buck. I'll send you what I can. But it may be a couple days before I can earn some more tip money."

"You're the best, Sis. I'll text you the information for the Western Union here."

"Okay."

"Well, I'd better go. It sounds like you're busy and all. Good luck with your car. I'll text you that info. Love you, Sis."

"Love you too," she answered, but was pretty sure he'd already clicked off.

Zane narrowed his eyes. "Seems to me you've got enough of your own financial troubles without trying to find extra cash to send Buck. Although it's not my place to say."

"You're right," she told him, heat burning her neck. "It's not your place to say." If only her brother had waited five more minutes to call, she'd have been alone in the truck, and Zane wouldn't have had to hear her side of the conversation.

He held up his hands. "It's your money."

"He's my brother."

He nodded, not saying anything more.

He's my brother. She'd been using the same justification for years. The same rationale for why she let him take advantage of her, why she went hungry so she could send him money. She'd been taking care of him since they were kids, and he was the only immediate family she had left. What else could she do?

"Let's just focus on getting the car back before it dies again." She glanced at the pickup. "You sure you want me driving your truck? Most guys are pretty possessive about their pickups."

"I trust you," Zane said. "Plus, you'll have the dog riding shotgun." His lips curved into the slightest smile before he turned and slid into the driver's seat of her car.

That smile had her heart racing as she climbed into the cab of his truck and followed him back to her house. He might trust her, but right now she wasn't sure she trusted herself. She didn't seem to be making the brightest decisions today.

A few minutes ago, she'd thought luck was on her side, but luck was a fickle bitch and the realization sank in that Bryn didn't have a car that worked, had just promised to send her brother money she didn't have, and had just bought a horse and a half that she couldn't afford to feed. Not to mention the other gut-curdling fact that by purchasing the horse with Zane, she'd tied herself to a man who went against every principle she'd just sworn herself to follow.

Zane might be compassionate and warm with animals, but every other part of him, from his stiff posture to his hooded eyes, gave off the aloof vibe of a guy who kept his distance—a forbidding lone wolf. Sure, he could make her smile with his wry wit, but the things his grin did to her body, the way he had her skin heating and her chest tightening with nerves promised danger and risk.

She was done with emotionally distant guys she thought she could save. Talking to her brother and thinking about the things that asswipe Pete had stolen from her, not just her money but her pride, had her stomach churning and her heart hardening with resolve that she wouldn't be taken in again by a man who resonated that kind of danger. Not that she dreamed Zane would ever hurt her physically, but he had the capacity to wreck her heart. And her body. That one peck of a kiss had left her breathless and fired a shot of desire down her spine that reached all the way to her toes.

But then one phone call, and he'd completely shut down. She wouldn't risk her heart again no matter how tormented and wounded Zane seemed—no matter how much she wanted to save him.

She was done saving others. She wanted security and stability. Safety. And when it came to being around Zane Taylor, her heart was anything but safe.

CHAPTER 5

Birch Taylor was sitting in the kitchen that night when Zane walked through the door. His lips were pressed together, and a paper plate and an empty tumbler sat on the table in front of him. Zane couldn't tell what had been in the glass, but the air in the house held the sharpness of his father's temper. His chest tightened, and Zane fought to steady his breathing as he nodded to Birch. "Dad."

Birch didn't answer, but his eyes narrowed in a steely glare as he watched Zane put the milk in the fridge and set the loaf of bread on the counter. The collie stuck to his heels as he took a glass from the cupboard and filled it with water at the sink.

"You eat?" Zane asked his dad before taking a steadying sip of water. He was a grown man. Birch hadn't beaten him in years. So how did his father's glare still cause the hair on his neck to rise and every flight instinct to go on high alert? He wrapped his fingers around the edge of the counter, his knuckles going white as his grip tightened.

"No, Son. I did *not* eat," Birch stated through gritted teeth. "I'm hungry, and I would have like to have eaten. But as I told you earlier, there was no bread in the house. So I couldn't make a sandwich."

"Why didn't you open a can of soup?"

"Because I didn't feel like a friggin' can of soup. I felt like having a sandwich. And I didn't know you wouldn't be home until eight o'clock at night."

"You been sittin' at the table waiting for me since suppertime?" They usually ate around six. If Birch had been sitting there for two hours, he'd had plenty of time to work up a good head of steam.

Birch narrowed his eyes to small hard slits. "Yes, Son. I have."

"Sorry. I didn't know. I can put a sandwich together for you." He opened the refrigerator and took out a package of lunch meat and some Miracle Whip and set them on the counter.

Birch pushed back from his chair so fast, it fell over behind him. He grabbed the loaf of bread and shook it in Zane's face. "And just what the hell is this supposed to be? I asked you to get some bread."

"Take it easy, Dad. That is bread."

Birch slammed his fist onto the counter. "Don't tell me to take it easy. I've been waiting on you for two damn hours to bring home a loaf of bread so I could make a sandwich, and you can't even do that right. How hard it is to buy some bread? Only a dumbass would bring me this shit. Some hippie-dippie loaf of nuts and grain."

"It's whole wheat, Dad. It's not hippie-dippie. And they were out of white, this was all they had. Besides, the doctor said you need to eat healthier anyway."

"So, what? Now you're my doctor? Yeah right. I don't think so. You need brains for that, and you seem to be lacking in that department. Or are you trying to say that I'm the stupid one? You think I'm too dumb to know how to take care of my own health?"

Obviously. Since you're an alcoholic and you had a heart attack. Zane pressed his lips together, having learned a long time ago that keeping silent tended to end a lot better for him than mouthing off. He just needed to shut up and let his dad blow off the worst of the steam.

"Here's what I think of your healthy, piece-of-shit whole wheat bread." Birch crushed the loaf between his hands, then twisted the bag, tearing the plastic apart and flinging bread and crumbs across the kitchen.

A piece hit the floor in front of the collie, who stood steadfastly pressed to Zane's leg. The dog leaned her head down to sniff the bread.

"Get the hell away from that, you stupid mutt," Birch screamed and kicked the fallen chair toward the dog. It flew across the floor, but the collie yelped and jerked out of the way, narrowly missing getting clipped in the leg.

Zane didn't think. He only reacted as he shot forward and pressed his forearm into his father's chest and pushed him against the kitchen counter. He glared into his father's eyes as he spat out the words: "You can say whatever you want to me, call me every idiot name in the book, but don't you *ever* hurt that dog."

Birch glared back. "You think you're a tough guy now? So big and strong you can beat up an old man?"

His dad was far from an old man. Birch had the sinewy muscled arms of a man who had worked in a garage his whole life. Hauling tires and lifting car parts had made his body strong, and Zane knew all too well the strength of his father's hands.

"You think *you're* so big and strong you can beat up a defenseless animal?"

The collie stood fiercely by Zane's leg. A low growl emitted from her throat, then she let loose with three sharp barks at Birch.

"You better shut that damn dog up."

"Get back, girl," Zane told the dog, who obediently stepped behind his legs.

Birch shoved back against Zane's arm, raising his chin and pushing his shoulders back. "Don't test me, Son."

"Yeah, I know. You brought me into this world, you can take me out."

A wicked gleam lit Birch's eyes as he sneered at his son. "No, *I* didn't bring you into this world. Your mother did that, and you killed her in the process. It's almost a blessing she didn't live to see the despicable excuse of a man you turned out to be."

Zane huffed out a disgusted breath, the hateful words having less power over him than they'd once had. "Yeah, I've heard this all before, Dad. You need to come up with some new material if you really want to hurt me."

Birch shoved away from him and grabbed his jacket from a peg on the wall. "I don't need to take this bullshit from you. I'm walking down to the store. I'll buy my own damn bread."

"Fine. Next time, do that in the first place." He winced

as the walls shook from Birch slamming the front door. Zane knelt on the floor, and the dog whined as she leaned her head into his shoulder. "It's all right, girl." He ran his hand down her legs, examining her for any sign of injury. "He's an asshole, but I won't let him touch you. I may not be good for much, but I promise I can keep you safe. Nobody is going to hurt you while I'm around."

It was close to midnight when Zane heard the soft whisper of his bedroom door opening. He hadn't been quite asleep, but the dog had been lying next to him and snoring for the last half hour. She lifted her head at the sound, her hackles rising and a growl formed in her throat.

"Shhh," Zane whispered softly, stroking the dog's neck but otherwise not moving.

Birch didn't turn on the light, but Zane knew it was his dad and waited for the weight of his father's body to sit on the end of his bed. They'd been here before. Many times. But not since the heart attack. It wasn't the first time his dad had slung hurtful words in his direction since then, but it was the first big fight—the first time his dad's temper had torn loose—and Zane wondered if maybe his empty tumbler from earlier had held more than iced tea.

Zane held his breath and tried to push back the emotions of his ten-year-old self—the yearning for love, the bone-deep desire to hear the apology and the kind words that followed a beating. No wonder he was screwed up. His whole life love had been intertwined with pain—he suffered through one to get the other.

Birch laid a heavy hand on Zane's leg. In the dark room, Zane could still make out the shadow of his father, the slump of his shoulders, the hanging head. "I'm sorry for what I said earlier, Son. I didn't mean it."

Yeah, you did. Birch could apologize a million times, but the first time he'd said the words aloud—placing the blame of his mother's death on his birth—Zane knew his father believed them to be true. It was a heavy burden for a child to carry—one he'd been trying to lay down since he'd become a man.

Zane tensed his shoulders, waiting to hear what came next, his heart already thirsting for the meager words of affirmation Birch offered after a fight.

Birch softly patted his leg. "You're a good boy, Zane. A good man."

Zane didn't say anything. He never did. He just waited for his dad to push off his bed and carefully pull his bedroom door shut behind him.

He finally let out his breath as the dog cuddled in closer to his side. She pushed her nose into the crook of his neck and gave his ear a quick lick before laying her head on his shoulder. He pressed his forehead against hers as he ran his hand through her fur and over her back. She let out a doggie sigh, and his body finally relaxed. He closed his eyes and tried to sleep.

The next afternoon, Zane twisted a piece of wire around the corral fence he was mending and tried for the hundredth time that day not to think about Bryn.

She'd kept her word and not only fed him lunch the day before, but supper as well. He'd been eating meatloaf and mashed potatoes and flirting with a beautiful woman while his dad had been waiting for the bread. A tendril of guilt tried to work its way through his gut, but he pushed it back. It wasn't his fault his dad hadn't opened a can of soup. And he was allowed a life. Wasn't he?

It had felt like he was living a life yesterday as he'd spent the afternoon and most of the evening with Bryn, working on her car and fixing up the corral and a stall for Beauty. He hadn't wanted to leave, which was why he'd gotten home so late. But he knew it wasn't the kind of life he'd ever get. Bryn was sweet and kind, and he was damaged goods. The fight with his dad the night before had solidified his notion that he didn't want to bring that kind of darkness into Bryn's world. Which was why he shouldn't be spending the majority of his day today thinking of ways to get back there.

But he couldn't help it. He wanted to see her again. Be with her. Find ways to touch her, to hug her, to make her laugh again. Last night, he'd offered to drive her to and from work today, and she'd tentatively accepted the ride home but claimed she was fine walking into town.

He checked his watch. Still another few hours before he could pick her up.

He crossed the corral and stepped into the barn, where Logan stood with a couple of the James brothers from the neighboring ranch. Although they hadn't been friends per se—he hadn't let himself have many of those—he'd known Mason and Colt most of his life and had played hockey with both of them in high school. They were good men, and he respected the work they'd done with their ranch.

He tipped his head as he entered the barn. "Mason. Colt."

"Hey, Zane," Colt answered. "How's it going?"

Zane shrugged, not a huge fan of small talk. "It's going."

Mason stretched out a hand. "Heard you and Bryn Callahan rescued yourselves a run-down mare yesterday."

"Bryn did the rescuing. I was just along for the ride," Zane said as he shook Mason's hand.

"I heard the horse wasn't in the best shape."

"No, she wasn't. But she will be. A little malnourished, a nasty eye infection, and a little skittish. But that's to be expected. She'd been tied up in a filthy horse trailer for I don't know how long and the scumbags who had her obviously weren't taking care of her. I don't think they'd even given her water."

Mason winced. "Assholes."

"It's a good thing you and Bryn found her then," Colt said.

"Yeah. She's older, but still a good horse. And she's in

foal. I'm a little worried Bryn might be in over her head, financially speaking. One horse is expensive enough, but two can really tax you. I know her heart is in the right place, but heartstrings don't buy hay bales."

"I've known Bryn a long time," Logan said. "She has a way of landing on her feet."

"That's true enough. By the time she and I went back to town yesterday, Doc Hunter had already put a hundred dollars on her feed store account."

Logan grinned. "That doesn't surprise me. He's one of her regulars at the diner, and Doc's always had a bit of a crush on our girl Bryn."

It surprised Zane how much he liked the idea of being included in the consideration of Bryn being *our* girl.

"Yeah, well, I figured I couldn't let an eighty-year-old man show me up, so I'm planning to pick up another hundred dollars of feed and supplies and take it out to her today."

Logan pulled out his wallet and passed him a couple of fifties. "Add this to her account too. And I can pitch in some hay. We can fill up that small horse trailer with a bunch of bales, and you can take it over this afternoon."

"Sounds good." Up until his dad's heart attack, Zane had been away from Creedence for close to ten years, and he'd forgotten the generosity of the community. Well, toward one of their own who was someone like Bryn. Growing up the son of the town drunk had not afforded him the same kind of generosity. Or his dad's pride hadn't let them accept it.

Birch would rather split a can of baked beans for their Christmas meal than accept any kind of charity from those "busybody women at the church." Zane remembered that the women had still tried, at least when he was a boy. But Birch's mean-spirited comments finally drove them away. Just like they'd driven Zane away.

Except he always seemed to come back for another dish of pain. Birch might not lay hands on him anymore, but his father's words could bite and cut just the same.

Logan turned to Mason and Colt and held out his hand. "Pony up, boys, it's for a good cause."

Mason pulled out his wallet and held it open. "Looks like I've got sixty-three dollars to add to the pot." He passed Zane the contents of his wallet.

Colt opened his billfold and pulled out the two twenties inside. "I'm a little light, but I can throw some money on her account the next time I'm in the feed store. And we'll tell Rock to pitch in when we see him," Colt said, referring to the oldest James brother who played professional hockey for the NHL. "His wallet's always full, and he loves Bryn."

"Thanks," Zane said, shoving all the bills into his pocket. "Bryn's gonna love this. I don't think she'd accept it for herself, but she'll take it for the horse."

"While you all are feeling so charitable," Logan said, gesturing to the barn door, "why don't you help us load up that horse trailer with hay?"

Mason nodded. "Sure. We've got a little time before we need to be in town."

Zane walked beside Logan as they followed the other two men from the barn. "That's pretty cool the way you all just tossed in cash to help Bryn."

Logan shrugged. "She'd do the same for any of us if she could. That girl is as generous as the day is long."

"Maybe too generous," Zane muttered, a scowl forming on his lips.

"What's that supposed to mean?"

"Nothin', I guess." He hesitated, wavering between wanting to help Bryn and not betraying her confidence. "Say, what do you know about this last guy she was dating? The one back in the fall. She was telling me a little about him, and he sounds like a douche."

"He was. I don't know what she saw in him. I didn't spend a lot of time with the guy, but something about him gave me a bad feeling."

"I think that feeling was warranted. Any chance you remember the guy's name?"

Logan rubbed a hand across the back of his neck. "Yeah, it was Pete something. I remember that much because when he introduced himself he said he went by Pete, but his given name was Peter, like Peter Parker. And he had this stupid tattoo of a spiderweb covering the back of his hand, like he had some kind of connection to the superhero. But all I could think was how his name was Peter and that sounded right because he reminded me of a pecker."

Zane tried to keep his tone casual. "So you have any idea where I can find this Peter Pecker?"

Logan arched an eyebrow.

"I'd just like to have a discussion with him. He may have accidentally left with some things that didn't belong to him," he said, not wanting to reveal any more of Bryn's situation. She'd probably already be pissed just knowing he'd talked to Logan about the guy.

"I have no idea where to find him. Probably under a rock at some rodeo or another. If I remember right, he was a bull rider."

That was okay. Zane had enough to go on. He'd worked on a couple of different ranches and knew several guys who rode bulls in the summer. They weren't best pals, but he could put out a few feelers to see if any of them knew where to find a guy named Pete who had a spiderweb tattoo covering his hand.

Bryn snuck a glance at the clock. Her shift was over in a few minutes, but she hated to leave a table she'd started out helping. She leaned against the counter and surveyed the remaining customers. The single dad who took his teenage son to lunch every week was just finishing up, and the couple by the door who had spent their entire meal with their faces directed at their phones had already paid. They'd only said a few words to each other throughout their whole meal, but Bryn had seen the girl take a selfie with her fork raised, so she was probably still sitting at the table updating her social media to post a lie about their happy life—had a lovely lunch with the BF #bestlife—before they drove off together to ignore each other some more.

A chestnut-haired woman sat alone at her usual table by the window, her meal barely touched. She was pretty, but in a sad way, her green eyes often staring at something only she could see as she gazed through the pane of the window. She came in several times a week, and Bryn had struck up a tentative friendship with her. They were close to the same age, which was way too young for the other woman to already be a widow.

Bryn placed a scoop of chocolate chip ice cream into a small bowl and carried it across the diner. She set it on the table in front of the woman before dropping into the booth's seat across from her. "How you doing, Elle? Wasn't your burger okay?"

Elle Brooks picked up a spoon and forced a smile. "It was fine. I'm fine. Just not very hungry today, I guess." She dipped the spoon into the ice cream and took a bite.

Bryn had known she would. They'd done this routine before. Elle was too thin, and every time she came in, Bryn tried something new to get some nourishment into her. She'd brought over several things—soup, pie, apple slices, then distracted the other woman with questions in the hopes she'd absently put a few bites in her mouth. So far, ice cream was the only thing she'd finished.

"I heard you bought a horse," Elle said between bites. *How has everyone heard about this horse?*

"I did. I named her Beauty."

"Aww. I like it."

"You'll have to come out to the farm to see her. She's gorgeous."

"I'd like that," she said, just as she always did when Bryn invited her to come out to the farm. But she never came.

She always claimed she was busy. Elle had some kind of fancy job, something to do with marketing, and it required her to dress up and to travel frequently. She was always either just going or just getting back from some part of the country. Some folks in town envied her the gorgeous clothes and jet-set lifestyle, but Elle never seemed happy. Bryn could get an occasional smile out of her, but she'd never heard the other woman truly laugh.

Elle lived in a beautiful sprawling four-thousand-square-foot home on the east side of town. Alone. Her late husband, Ryan Brooks, of the wealthy Brooks Building family, had commissioned it to be custom built for his bride. He'd brought her back to his hometown, so proud to show off his new wife and to introduce the town he loved to the woman he adored.

They'd been in a car accident. She survived. But he died before he had time to get the town to fall in love with Elle, and now she rambled around that big house alone, not even a cat to keep her company. No wonder she came out to the diner to pick at her food. It had to be better than picking at her food alone.

Bryn's cell phone buzzed, and she pulled it out to check the screen. Her heart leapt as she saw it was a text from Zane. I'm running a few minutes late. Working on a surprise for you and Beauty. Be there in fifteen, the text read.

"Sorry, Elle. I need to answer this text," Bryn said. "Apparently my ride is going to be late."

"I can give you a ride home." Elle spoke softly, her gaze focused on the ice cream bowl in her hand.

"Oh you don't have to do that," Bryn answered, surprised at the other woman's offer. As hard as she'd been trying to befriend Elle, she'd never reciprocated. This felt like a tentative move in that direction.

"I'd like to," Elle said, raising her eyes and pushing her shoulders back. "It's no trouble, and it will give me a chance to meet Beauty."

Bryn smiled. "Okay then. I'll text Zane." She typed a return message, trying to ignore the disappointment fluttering in her stomach at not getting to see him. *This is for the best.* Hadn't she spent the better part of her day trying not to think about him? Now she could put him out of her mind and focus on her new friendship with Elle. Although his mention of a surprise for her and Beauty did have her intrigued. No worries. I've got another ride home.

Okay. See you soon.

See you soon? Did that mean he was coming over later? Or was he already at the farm? Her fingers hesitated over the screen as she debated her response. Her body had just responded with a resounding *yippee* as her heart jumped to her throat, but her mind told her to stay cool. Zane Taylor was not the kind of guy she could count on. And he'd already said he wasn't sticking around Creedence.

Oh brother. *I'm writing a text, not composing a sonnet.* She tapped the screen and typed See you soon, then turned her focus to Elle. "Give me a minute to grab my purse."

By the time Bryn had gathered her bag and called to Gil that she was leaving, Elle had finished the ice cream and was standing by the door. Bryn followed her to an expensive SUV and was glad she hadn't brought Lucky today as she slid into the buttery-soft leather seat. She pulled at the hem of her waitress uniform, suddenly conscious of Elle's dressier outfit. The other woman looked like she'd just stepped off the pages of an Ann Taylor catalog in a beige linen suit with a cropped jacket and matching ankle pants. She wore a light-pink shell with a soft floral-print silk scarf tied neatly at her neck. Her hair was pulled back and clipped smartly at the nape of her neck, and her shoes were a block-heeled sandal in the same shade of beige as her jacket and pants.

Bryn considered the shoes she had piled in her closet and wasn't sure she had a single pair that were the same shade as any of her clothes. And she'd tried to wear scarves before, imagining a smart, stylish look similar to Audrey Hepburn. But she couldn't figure out how to tie or fold or whatever the heck you did with scarves and always ended ripping them off in a fit of frustration and more than a few colorful swear words.

"How long have you lived on the farm?" Elle asked. "Did you grow up there?"

"Pretty much. It was my grandpa's farm, but he left it to me after he died a few years back. I've lived there most of my life though. My mom had a lot of problems, and my dad was never around, so my younger brother and I moved in with our grandparents when we were kids."

"That must have been tough."

"It was." Bryn blinked back the sudden memory of standing on the front porch of the farmhouse, Bucky's hand clasped tightly in her own as they watched their mom drive away. She'd wanted to run after her, beg her mother to take her too. But she had her little brother to think about, and she'd never let him down. "But it worked out okay. We missed our mom, but moving to Creedence was the best thing that could have happened to us. Our grandparents offered us a stable home, and they loved us. My grandma taught me how to cook and garden, and my grandpa taught me how to fish and ride a horse. We lost our grandma when we were in high school, and that's about the time my brother went off the rails, acting out and finding trouble around every corner." Bryn sighed. "But that's a story that would take more than the few minutes it takes to get home."

Elle smiled ruefully. "At least you had a brother. I was an only child, and my parents traveled a lot. Your grandparents sound lovely to me."

"They were." Bryn pointed to the leaning mailbox on the side of the road. "That's my driveway there."

Elle turned the SUV onto the dirt drive and pulled up to the farm. Bryn's pulse quickened at the sight of Zane's truck in front of the barn, but her brow furrowed at the small horse trailer attached to the back of it. Was he planning to take Beauty somewhere?

Zane must have heard the SUV, because he came out of the barn, a scowl on his face. The border collie followed him. His scowl remained as Bryn climbed from the car and approached him, but the collie loped toward her, anxious for a pet.

He nodded to Elle's vehicle. "Looks like you upgraded your mode of transportation. That's quite a step up from my old truck."

Elle got out and cautiously approached them.

"Zane, this is my friend Elle Brooks." Bryn absently scratched the dog's ears, her gaze on Zane's face as she introduced Elle, already anticipating his reaction. Most men either got nervous, shy, and tongue-tied or stupidly arrogant and boastful around the gorgeous woman. But Bryn had forgotten for a moment that Zane wasn't like *most* men. In fact he wasn't like any other man she'd known. And his reaction fell in neither camp.

His eyes narrowed as he studied her, then his features softened and his lips formed a tender smile. He reached out his hand and gently shook hers. "Nice to meet you, Elle." His voice was soft, none of his normal snark, and his whole body seemed to relax, his usual stiff shoulders losing their tenseness.

Bryn's eyes widened, and she fought to keep her mouth from going slack at the stark change in Zane's behavior. She swallowed, fighting the twinge of jealousy at his reaction. Then she realized he was acting with Elle exactly as he had with the skittish horse the day before, as if he recognized the anguish she was in.

She knew Zane was a skilled horse whisperer, but watching him with Elle revealed his apparent skills as a widow whisperer as well. And she wasn't sure how she felt about it. She admired it when he was doing it to a horse, but seeing him tenderly take Elle by the arm as he offered to show her the horse had a funny wisp of envy curling in Bryn's stomach.

"What's with the trailer?" Bryn asked, her question coming out harsher than she'd meant it to. "Are you planning to take Beauty somewhere?"

Zane shook his head. "Just the opposite. I'm *bringing* Beauty something." He motioned for her to follow them into the barn.

Bryn gasped and pressed a hand to her chest as she spotted a previously empty stall now filled to the top with fresh stacks of hay bales. "Oh my gosh. This is amazing. Where did you get all this hay?"

"Logan donated it for the horse. Colt and Mason James were at the ranch this morning, and we were talking about Beauty—seems like the whole town has heard about this dang horse—and I told him how Doc Hunter had loaded your feed store account with a hundred bucks. Apparently none of us wanted to be shown up by the old geezer because we took up a collection and added another three hundred and three dollars to your account. That should get you by for a few months anyhow."

She couldn't believe it. Last night she'd lain awake thinking about what she'd done and wondering how on earth she was going to pay for this horse—and she'd also spent a fair amount of time imagining how it would feel to have Zane lying in the bed next to her—but she mainly worried about the horse. And how she couldn't afford to feed it or take care of it.

And now that worry was lifted from her shoulders. At least for the next few months. Tears pricked her eyes. Before she could think too much about it, her body reacted, and she threw her arms around Zane and pressed her cheek into his shoulder. "Thank you."

His body tensed; then his hands—warm and firm— slid up her hips and around her waist. He hugged her back, just for a moment. One glorious, delicious moment. Then he dropped his hands and took a step back, clearing his throat and looking at everything but her. "You're welcome," he muttered, then turned back to Elle. He nodded to the horse, who was leaning her head out of the stall, as if she wanted to be in on the conversation. "This is Beauty," he told Elle, running his hand along the horse's neck.

Beauty responded by leaning into him and nuzzling against his chest.

"I spent some time working with her after I unloaded the hay. Just some simple stuff in the corral, putting her through the paces, but she responded pretty well. She's a good horse."

"She's beautiful," Elle said in a hushed voice as she

raised her hand to gently touch the horse's velvety nose. Beauty dipped her head and nudged Zane's arm. "She seems quite smitten with you."

He chuckled. "Not smitten. Hungry. She's a smart one—she knows I've got sugar cubes in my pocket." He pulled a small white cube from his shirt pocket and instructed Elle to hold out her hand. "Keep your palm flat."

Elle did as he said, holding her hand perfectly straight. Her eyes went round as he set the cube on her hand and the horse nibbled the sugar from it.

He held another cube out to Bryn. "You want to give her one?"

"Sure." She stepped in close, her shoulder touching Zane's chest as she held out her hand. He didn't move into her, but he didn't back away, and she tried to control the shiver that threatened to run through her as he tenderly placed the sugar cube in her hand. She didn't have a ton of experience with horses, but her grandpa had taught her about holding her palm flat when she was little so the horse didn't accidentally bite her. But still, she curved her hand and looked up at Zane, so close she could see the flecks of navy in his blue eyes. "Like this?"

He narrowed his eyes. For just a second, she believed the jig was up—that he'd figured out she was just trying to get him to hold her hand in his—but he didn't say anything. Instead, he put his hand under hers, cupping her palm as he pulled it flat. The horse leaned over and carefully took the sugar from her hand, but all Bryn could focus on was the heat of Zane's hand as he held hers.

She started as her cell phone rang in her pocket. Bryn swallowed as she pulled it out to check the screen. "Sorry, guys, I've got to take this. It's Brody."

Zane nodded. Did his eyes darken for just a moment? What was that about?

She took a step back as she tapped the phone and held it to her ear. "Hello?"

"Hey, Bryn. Brody here. I hate to do this to you, but I've got a situation, and I think you're the best person to handle it."

"Ohh-kay."

Zane must have caught the unease in her voice, because he watched her, reminding her of a protective wolf as his eyes searched her face with apprehension.

Tendrils of alarm and dismay bloomed in her chest as she listened to Brody's *situation*, but she knew there was only one answer she was going to give him. "Yes, of course I will. Zane's here now. I'll ask him to help, and we'll go right away."

Zane took a step closer as she hung up the phone, his brows drawing together. "What's going on? Where are we going?"

She shrugged, fear and excitement clogging her throat. "Apparently we're going to rescue another horse."

CHAPTER 6

BRYN HELD BACK THE NERVOUS GIGGLE THAT threatened to bubble out of her as she watched Zane's eyes widen.

"*Another* horse?" he asked.

She nodded, her head bobbing in quick, sharp shakes.

"Where in the hell did Brody find *another* horse that just happened to need rescuing?"

"He didn't *find* it. Someone called the vet clinic and told him their neighbor took off three weeks ago and left the horse behind. He said it's in a run-down corral out at the old Lewis farm."

"The old Lewis farm? That place has been falling down for years. How could anyone be living there?"

"Sounds like they aren't. Not anymore." She nodded to the horse trailer. "Think Logan will mind if we borrow the horse trailer for another hour?"

"Nah. He won't care. But are you sure about this? You really want to take on another horse?"

"No, but I think I'm going to anyway. Give me five minutes to drop my stuff in the house and put on a pair of jeans, and I'll be ready to go."

"I'd like to go too," Elle said, her voice so soft Bryn almost didn't hear her. "If that's okay."

Bryn stopped short. She'd almost forgotten the

other woman was standing there. "Yeah, of course. But are you sure you want to? I don't know what we'll find."

Elle pushed her shoulders back and held Bryn's gaze. "I'm sure," she said, her voice gaining strength. "I'd like to be a part of saving something."

Bryn swallowed, emotion prickling her throat. She couldn't imagine what Elle had been through.

Her gaze fell to Elle's outfit. The other woman would swim in Bryn's clothes, but she was sure Elle wouldn't want to mess up her expensive suit. "Do you want to borrow some jeans or something? You're thinner than I am, but maybe we could find you some sweats with a drawstring."

Elle glanced absently down at herself as if she couldn't even remember what she had on. "I'm not worried about my clothes. It's not like I'm going to be *riding* the horse." A tiny grin pulled at the corner of her mouth.

Had Elle made a *joke*?

Bryn laughed, her heart happy that the other woman was feeling comfortable enough to throw a little snark her way. "As far as you know. This is only my second horse rescue attempt. I really have no idea what to expect."

Zane arched an eyebrow. "My guess is you'll both be *under*whelmed. All we're doing is driving fifteen minutes and possibly coercing a hungry horse into a trailer."

"Good point," Bryn said. "I'll grab some apples while I'm in the house. Back in a jiff."

Twenty minutes later, they were rumbling down the

highway. Bryn was squished, not uncomfortably, in the middle of Elle and Zane, her body acutely aware of the heat of his thigh, hip, and shoulder as they pressed against hers. She was so close she could smell his subtle aftershave and the clean detergent scent of his T-shirt. It took everything she had not to bury her face in his neck and inhale him.

Down, girl. Focus on the horse, not the horse whisperer.

With the bench seat taken, Zane's dog had been relegated to the floorboards, where she rested her head on one of Elle's knees and gazed at her in adoration. For her part, Elle seemed oblivious to the black and white dog hair clinging to her pants as she rubbed the dog's ears.

Zane turned onto a small dirt road, and Bryn's teeth clacked together as they lumbered over the washboard ruts. "It's just up ahead," he said, pointing to a dilapidated house and crumbling barn. Rusted-out fencing enclosed a corral on one side of the barn. At the back of the corral, a battered lean-to leaned so far it almost touched the ground.

As they pulled into the driveway, a gaunt gray horse, its silver coat so light it was almost white, eyed them from inside the fence.

"Damn," Zane cursed, not quite under his breath. "Horse looks half-starved." He drew the trailer up to the fence and rolled down the windows before he cut the engine. He gripped Bryn's hand as he eyed her. "You sure you're up for this?"

She gripped back. She was more than up for it. Her heart was already breaking for the dejected horse. "I'm sure."

He glanced around the yard and the farmhouse. It was eerily quiet. "Why don't you all stay in the truck a minute? Let me take a look around the place and make sure there's no one here."

Bryn's mouth went dry, and the hair on her neck stood on end. She'd been so focused on getting to the horse she hadn't considered someone could still be here or that they could be walking into a dangerous situation.

Zane exited the truck and cautiously approached the house. He held his hands out to his sides, his body tense and poised to fight. His eyes narrowed, his gaze sharp as he made his way through the weed- and trash-covered yard. Random objects littered the patchy grass in front of the house—a corroded push mower, a half-buried tire, and a box of what looked like tarnished kitchen ware perched on the corner of a faded, moldy recliner. An old washing machine sat on the porch, rust crawling up its sides like a vine.

Bryn exchanged a look with Elle. "You okay?"

The other woman let out a shuddering sigh. "Yeah. I'm scared. But it's good. I'm glad to know I can still feel *something.*"

Bryn reached across her leg and took Elle's hand, giving it a tight squeeze before turning her attention back to Zane. The front door hung from its hinges, and Bryn held her breath, cringing at the sinister creak it made as he pushed his way through it and disappeared into the house.

They waited. One minute. Two. An eternity. What

was happening in there? Had Zane found something? Some*one*? Was he in there now, fighting off an assailant? Or worse, had he found someone who was beyond fighting? A body?

"What's taking him so long?" she whispered, coils of fear tightening her chest.

Elle clasped her hand. Whether she was offering support or taking it, Bryn wasn't sure. Maybe it was both.

The women jumped as a loud crash and an alarmed shout came from inside the house. "Zane," Bryn called, dropping Elle's hand and scrambling from the truck. She sprinted for the house, grabbing the closest kitchen utensil's handle from the box as she ran past the recliner.

The door screeched open again, and Zane stepped out onto the crumbling porch.

The breath whooshed from her lungs as relief flooded through her. "Oh my gosh, are you okay?" Bryn asked, closing the distance between them. "We heard a crash, and you yelled. Was someone in there? Did they attack you?" She wanted to throw her arms around him but couldn't because she still had the utensil clutched in her hands. Her fingers didn't seem to want to let go.

"No. There's no one in there. And I'm okay," he assured her as he reached out and firmly clasped her shoulder. The heat and strength of his palm on her arm worked to settle her chest. "I was checking out the upstairs, and the damn floor gave way. I almost fell through but managed to grab the doorframe as I scrambled back. I don't remember yelling." He rubbed his hand up and down her arm for a few strokes, then eased the utensil from her hands and examined it. "Is this what you were going to use to save me? I'm curious if you were planning to use this to attack someone or to make them spaghetti."

She glanced down and realized for the first time she'd grabbed a metal colander. She let out a relieved laugh. "I didn't have a plan. I just reacted. I thought you were hurt or that someone was attacking you, and I just ran."

"Most people run *away* when they sense danger, not *toward* the threat."

She shrugged, unable to tell him she wasn't running toward danger but running toward *him*. "I guess I'm not most people."

"True enough."

"I'm just glad you're okay." She threw her arms around his waist, trying to calm her racing heart by pressing her chest to his.

He slid his arms around her back and held her close for a few seconds, then tipped his head toward her ear, the deep tone of his voice sending heat down her spine. "I like that you were coming to save me, but let's focus on saving the horse for now."

She nodded and pulled away, then waved to Elle. "He's okay."

Elle stood by the truck, one hand holding the collar of the collie, the other holding up her cell phone. "I was ready to call 911."

"No need for that. I'm fine," he said again as they walked toward her.

"Not for you. For me. You almost gave me a heart attack." She let go of the dog, and it loped toward Zane, nudging his hand with her head.

Bryn chuckled. Two jokes in one day. Elle must be feeling more comfortable around them. "So what did you find in there? Any sign that the occupants are coming back?"

"No way. It looks like they were just squatting on the property." He wrinkled his nose as he petted the dog's ears. "The place is disgusting—full of trash and drug paraphernalia—and it stinks like an outhouse. There's an old mattress in the living room, but I didn't see any clothes or possessions—nothing to indicate anyone is still staying there or that they'd be coming back."

Bryn had glimpsed a bit of the filth and squalor through the windows when she'd been on the porch with Zane. The house had given off a scent of foulness and decay.

Elle wrapped her arms around her middle. "Who would leave and abandon their animal?"

Zane shook his head, his lips set in a tight line. "Assholes. That's who," he muttered, as he scanned the corral. "The watering trough looks empty. Do you want to look around and see if you can find a spigot and something to carry some water in?"

"Sure, I'll see what I can find." She headed toward the side of the house.

"Be careful," Bryn called. "This place is a tetanus shot waiting to happen."

"I will," she answered over her shoulder, already picking her way across the littered front yard. The collie trotted after her.

Bryn turned back to Zane, who was studying the horse, his face set in concentration. She watched his gaze go from the horse to the barn to the field and back to the patch of tall grass that grew in front of the rusted-out fencing the horse stood behind.

The horse stared back at Zane, as if measuring up the man. Now that she really looked at the gray, she noticed how shallow his breathing was and how skinny he seemed. He let out a whinny and gave a feeble attempt at stamping his back feet.

All Zane's focus was on the horse, and his brow furrowed as he took a few tentative steps forward. "Holy shit," he whispered, a wince of pain narrowing his eyes.

Zane moved cautiously toward the horse, trying not to spook him. He should have realized something was wrong when they pulled up and the horse didn't move, didn't trot up and down the fence as they went into the house. He chastised himself for wasting precious time checking out the structure and not paying enough attention to the animal.

The weeds in front of the fence were thick, hiding the horse's legs, but as Zane progressed forward, he spotted the coil of rusted barbed wire wrapped around the gray's front leg. The animal must have pulled back as it tried to get loose, because the wire had tightened and embedded itself into the skin.

"Damn it," he swore softly as he put out a warning hand to Bryn who took a step toward him. "Stay back. He's got his leg tangled up in a coil of barbed wire."

Her hands flew to her mouth as her gaze lowered to the horse's mangled leg. "Oh no. What can I do?"

"Just give me a minute to assess the situation," he said, his voice low as he eased closer. "It's all right, fella. I'm not gonna hurt ya. I'm here to help." The horse had his head down, his tail limp. He appeared weak, his breathing shallow. Flies buzzed around the scrapes and tears in his leg, but he didn't seem to have the energy to try to shoo them away.

Zane dipped his head, pulling his hat down so as not to look the horse in the eye. Stuck in the fencing, he was prey, and Zane didn't want to do anything to spook him and cause more damage to the already-ragged leg. "Behind the seat of my truck is a pair of blue-handled fence pliers," he told Bryn. "Can you grab 'em for me so I can cut this wire fencing? Move nice and slow. And you probably want to grab that lead rope for when I get him free."

She was closer to the truck, and he heard her careful footsteps, then the creak of the seat. He waited a beat, noting the patchy dirt around the horse's head. He must have eaten all the grass he could reach. It was hard to tell how many days the horse had been ensnared in the wire.

"Here," Bryn said, her voice breathy as she eased up behind him and passed him the wire cutters.

"Thanks," he told her, stuffing the pliers in his back pocket. "Stay back. I don't want to frighten him any more than he already is. It's gonna take a lot of trust for him to let me cut those barbs out of his skin." He approached the fence and deftly snipped the three rows of fence wire so he could get to the horse.

As he stepped closer, keeping his head and his voice low, the horse's body flinched and tensed, and his ears went back. His tail swished, and he stomped his back feet as Zane gingerly pressed his hand to the horse's shoulder. He kept his hand there, applying steady pressure while murmuring soft assurances.

The horse stiffened again, tossing his head and giving another tail swish, this one weaker than the first. Zane held steady, keeping his hand in place and a calm composure. Finally, the animal took a deep, hard breath, then his body settled.

Round one went to Zane. But this fight wasn't over. He still needed to gain this horse's full trust if it was going to let him cut it free.

He slowly moved his hand over the horse's body, assessing and analyzing what he was dealing with. This horse hadn't been treated well. His back haunches had strips of thickened skin that were smooth and hairless, evidence of a whip or riding crop being brutally used. His flanks showed scars from where spurs had struck and split the skin.

Just like Zane's own skin, the scars told the story of this horse's life. And the stories of both man and beast told a tale of abuse and violence. They'd both been mistreated, which gave them a bond only the abused understood.

He smoothed his hand over the horse's belly, across his shoulder, and down the foreleg as he bent to his knee.

"Be careful," Bryn whispered.

"I'm okay," he said quietly. "This horse has to decide if he's gonna kill me or not, and I think we've made it past that stage. Now I've just got to convince him to let me hurt him to save him."

"Why are his back legs bloody? He's got wounds back there that I can't imagine came from the fence."

Zane peered at his back legs and grimaced as he shook his head. "Those aren't from the fence. My guess is they're from coyotes. They would have seen this horse as prey and attacked him as a pack in the night. He may have kicked and fought the bastards off last night, but he's weaker now, and I'm not sure he'd survive another attack."

"Oh, Zane," Bryn said, the tremble evident in her voice. "We've got to save him. Can you cut him free? Should I call Brody? Should we wait for him?"

A hard lump settled in Zane's chest. Of course she would think Brody could handle this better than he could. Brody was a doctor.

But Zane was a horse guy. He didn't just work with them—he *got* them. He connected with the animals in an almost otherworldly way. Not that he believed in all that spiritual woo-woo shit, but he knew he had a connection with horses that was something special—unique and mystical. Brody could administer a lidocaine injection that would help numb the area, but at this point, Zane just needed to get the horse free.

"He's waited long enough. The skin is already swelling around the barbs. And he's fought the wire so much that it's tightened like a snare around his leg. If he gets spooked again, he could make the damage even worse."

He brushed a hand over the horse's neck, shooing away the flies buzzing around its eyes and nose. The horse smelled of sweat and fear, and dust had settled on its damp skin. Zane pulled the pliers from his pocket and gripped the horse's leg. "This is gonna hurt like hell, buddy. But you've got to let me hurt you to save you."

He cut away as much of the loose fencing as he could, then he tightened his grip on the horse's leg and went to work digging the barbs from his torn and bloodied skin. The horse huffed and pulled against him, but Zane held tight and worked as quickly as he could. Sweat dripped down his back as Zane used his strength to hold the horse's leg in place while drawing the rusted spikes from the torn and damaged tissue.

"You're doing great. Hold steady, boy. One more and we've got it," he told the horse, blinking back the tears that threatened his eyes. He knew the pain the horse was in must be tremendous, and Zane's crude surgical removal of the barbs had to be painful as hell. But he had to do it. It was the only way to get him loose. The horse had to withstand the torment so he could put the pain behind him and be free to heal and recover.

Zane ignored the quiet voice that softly whispered

he needed to put his own pain behind him. There wasn't time for that now. This time was for saving this horse.

He let out a shuddering breath as he pulled the last spiny piece free. "It's done. You're okay." He released the horse's foot and patted him hard as he leaned his head against its shoulder. "You were a fine soldier." Zane collected himself, taking a few more deep breaths. It was over. His mouth was dry, and his throat burned with dehydration.

He looked up and his eyes burned again at the sight of Bryn huddled by the fence, clutching the lead rope to her chest with one hand and covering her mouth with the other as tears streamed down her cheeks. "It's all right, darlin'," he told her, his voice husky and low. "He's gonna be okay now."

"What about you? Are *you* okay?" she asked. "That had to have been so hard."

He swallowed. Leave it to Bryn Callahan to watch him pull rusted barbed wire from a horse's leg and worry if *he* was okay. This woman was going to break him yet.

He cleared his throat, trying to dislodge the emotion burning there. "I'm fine. But let's get this horse back to your farm. He needs food and water and proper medical care. Pass me that rope, would ya?"

She nodded, wiping the tears from her face with the back of her hand as she eased closer and handed him the rope. He fashioned a loose bridle and slipped it over the horse's head, then coaxed him through the open section of fence and toward the trailer.

The horse pulled back, its eyes going wide as Zane

approached the door of the trailer. Zane kept his voice steady, his demeanor calm, and led him inside, tied him in, then gingerly closed and secured the door behind him.

He let out a breath as he leaned against the door. "That sucked."

———————

"Yeah," Bryn said, reaching out a hand to rest it on Zane's arm. "You did amazing." She'd stood frozen by the fence, watching with awe and fascination as Zane had earned the horse's trust then painstakingly extracted the barbs from the torn skin.

The sight of Zane's tensed muscles and gritted teeth told her how grueling the task was, but his occasional wince as he sucked in a tight breath told her it was also breaking his heart. She'd seen how smoothly he'd won the trust of Beauty, and she'd been impressed with that performance, but this was a different kind of trust.

Bryn saw the pain that narrowed the man's eyes as he'd brushed his hands over the horse's scarred and abused body. She'd heard rumors about the abuse Zane had suffered at his father's hands, and something about watching this wounded man free a wounded animal from the torturous snare of the barbed wire shattered her heart.

Now all she wanted was to take him in her arms and soothe the hurt she saw etched in his face. She slid her palm down his arm and took his hand, holding it tightly as she tried to pour her feelings into him.

"Zane," she whispered, then pressed her lips together to keep them from trembling. She didn't know what to say, how to put into words what she was feeling.

But she didn't have to. He stared at her a moment, then pulled her to him, wrapping her in his arms and holding her tightly against him. She clutched his back, squeezing her arms around him as if her embrace could heal his brokenness, could mend the shattered pieces of him.

They stood that way she wasn't sure how long, maybe a few seconds, maybe an hour, but she didn't want to move, didn't want to let go. She didn't know how long they would have stayed there if Elle hadn't screamed their names.

"Bryn! Zane! Help me," she cried.

They couldn't see her, but Zane sprinted toward her voice, Bryn right on his heels.

A decaying storm cellar jutted from the side of the house, its wooden doors rotted and missing a few slats. Elle was sprawled on her stomach, her arm thrust shoulder-deep through a hole in the boards. The collie paced back and forth along the doors, whining as she watched Elle.

Bryn's heartbeat exploded in her chest. "Elle, did you fall? Are you hurt?"

"No, but they are," she cried, her voice trembling as she strained to push her shoulder against the boards. "You've got to help me."

Zane sank to his knees next to Elle, his sharp gaze

trying to assess the situation. "Elle, stop. Take a breath. Tell us what's happening."

She pulled her arm free, ignoring the rip of her jacket as a seam caught on a splintered board, and pushed up to her knees. Her hands clawed at the boards, trying to pry them free. "I heard her crying, but the door to the cellar is locked."

He leaned forward and looked into the cellar then swore under his breath. "Holy hell."

Bryn knelt beside Zane, not sure who to help. She peered around his shoulder and into the cellar, and her breath caught in her throat. A ragged brown-and-white cattle dog lay in the dirt, her head lolling to the side, her tongue hanging from her mouth as she panted, a handful of puppies nursing from her distended stomach. She clapped a hand to her mouth. "Oh no."

"It's okay," Zane told them both. "We'll get 'em out of there." He stood and gently pulled Elle back from the door. Her eyes were glassy, and she couldn't seem to tear her gaze from the hole. Her hands were shaking, and the tremors seemed to move up her arms and into her shoulders.

Bryn stood and put an arm around her, holding on to her as much as holding her up. Zane searched the yard with a quick glance, then grabbed a length of pipe and used it as leverage to break open the slats. He pried back the door and cautiously descended the rickety steps into the cellar, brushing cobwebs away with his arm. "Can one of you shine a light down here so I can see what's going on?"

Bryn let go of Elle and jerked her phone from her pocket. She tapped the flashlight app on as she knelt and shined the bright beam into the hole. The walls and floor were dirt, and a row of wooden shelves lined one side. One lone can, its seal rusted and label missing, sat on the middle shelf. A musty scent, mixed with the smell of cool earth and a faint whiff of mouse droppings, filled her nose.

Elle dropped to her knees next to Bryn, oblivious to the soil grinding into the fabric of her expensive slacks. "Pass us the puppies, then you can bring up the mama." She reached both arms into the hole, her hands outstretched.

Zane talked softly to the mother dog, holding his hand out for her to sniff. She tried to raise her head, but was too weak and dropped it back into the dirt. He tenderly patted her head, then gently eased two of the puppies free and passed them to Elle. "We need to hurry. This dog is in bad shape."

Elle took the puppies, cuddled them to her cheek for a second, then set them carefully on the ground between her and Bryn. Their eyes were closed, and they made tiny mewling sounds at being separated from the warmth of their mother. The border collie nosed between them to sniff the puppies as Elle reached down for the next two. There were five in all, two black, two brown, and the runt was a light beige.

Zane carefully lifted the mother dog, then ascended from the cellar. Elle shrugged out of her jacket and wrapped the mother in it before taking her from Zane and nestling the dog to her chest.

"I'll grab that box from the front yard for the puppies," Bryn said, scrambling to her feet and racing toward the front of the house. She wrenched the box from the recliner, dumping the last few items into the chair, and ran back to Zane. He lifted the pups into the box, and Bryn hurried with it to the truck. Elle was right behind her, cradling the mother dog and cooing assurances to her. Zane found a bottle of water in the cab and poured some into his hand, holding it under the mother dog's snout as he tried to coax her to take a drink. She was still panting, but she weakly lapped a few sips into her mouth.

Zane passed Elle the water bottle. "That's good that she's drinking. See if you can get her to sip a little more on the way back."

They piled into the truck, Bryn in the middle with the box of puppies on her lap. "I'll call Brody and see if he can meet us at the farm. The puppies look in pretty good shape. It's the mama we've got to worry about. She's obviously been giving everything she has to these babies."

"She must have crawled down there to have the pups, then was too weak to crawl out," Zane said, his eyes glued to the road as he tried to avoid as many ruts as he could. "I think she'll be okay once we get some fluids and some food into her."

Bryn called the vet clinic and left a message with the receptionist, who told her the doctor was out on a call but assured her she'd have him get in touch soon. Elle had gotten the mama dog to drink a little more water, and she leaned her head close to the box of her babies.

A shiver ran through Bryn as she clutched the box of puppies. What kind of person would leave their animals behind? Who would abandon the ones that counted on their care? The sudden flashback to the image of her mom driving away after she'd dropped her and her brother off at her grandparents' farm returned and had pain tearing at her chest. She swallowed, her voice hoarse as she told Zane, "We can't let her die. Her puppies need her."

His hands clenched the wheel as he maneuvered the truck and the trailer onto the highway, but he broke one hand free and covered hers. "We won't. She's gonna be okay."

She twined her fingers through his, clasping his hand tightly as she took assurance from his fierce declaration.

Twelve minutes later, they pulled into the farm, and Bryn was relieved to see Brody's truck in the driveway. Zane stopped the truck, and Elle practically fell out of the cab trying to get the dog to the vet.

Brody had the long cabinet door on the back of the truck open, and Elle carefully laid the dog on the make-shift examining table. He had already started a cursory exam by the time Bryn reached him and set the box of puppies on the table by their mother.

"Thanks for coming," she told him. "You got here fast."

"I was already on a call out this way and thought I'd stop to check in on the new horse. I wasn't expecting this." He pressed a stethoscope to the dog's chest, then her stomach.

"Is she going to be okay?"

"I think so. She looks pretty malnourished. Her coat's dull, but her gums are still pinkish, and she doesn't seem to be in any abdominal pain. Those are both good signs. She probably looks worse than she is because the puppies are taking all her nutrients and energy. Let's see if she can eat." He pulled out a sample-size can of dog food and peeled back the lid. Scooping some onto his fingers, he held it to the dog's mouth. "This stuff is steak-flavored and smells good enough for a human to eat. Most dogs lap it up."

The mother dog lifted her head, her tongue darting out to lick the food from his fingers. "Good dog." He dumped the rest into a dish and the dog greedily gulped it down while he looked over the puppies. "Let's give that a few minutes to settle, then you can give her some more. The pups look in good shape. I'll give them all a dewormer, and I'll leave you some flea shampoo. I'd probably give them all a bath, especially since they're going to be around your other dog. And if you want to bring them into the house."

"Of course I'm bringing them into the house. I'm not going to leave them in the barn."

He shrugged. "Plenty of dogs survive outside. And this one looks like she's been living outside for a while now." He squinted at Elle, who had her hand on the dog's side and was staring down at it, but her eyes seemed a little glassy, as if she were really staring at something else entirely. He rested a hand lightly on her arm. "She's going to be okay," he told her, his voice gentle.

Elle blinked and moved her head to look at the man's hand on her arm.

He gave it a gentle squeeze, then pulled his hand back. "I don't think we've met. I'm Brody Tate."

Her gaze moved from her arm up to his eyes. "Sorry, I was just caught up in the dog and making sure she was okay. Thank you for taking care of her. I'm Elle Brooks, a friend of Bryn's."

Bryn's heart warmed at Elle introducing herself as her friend. She wasn't sure the other woman had many. The waitress had never seen her in the diner with a companion.

"I'm happy to do it," Brody said. "You good keeping an eye on her while I check out the horse?"

Bryn had almost forgotten about the horse in all the drama over the half-starved dog. So much had happened in the short time they'd been at the dilapidated farm. She filled Brody in on the injuries of the horse as they walked across the driveway and wasn't entirely surprised to see Zane had already unloaded the gray and taken him into the barn. He'd also filled a tub with water and given him some fresh hay. The stallion was working his way through a pile of sweet feed Zane must have poured into the trough, and Zane was brushing down his haunches as she and Brody approached.

"This is the horse they called about," Brody confirmed, running a hand over the horse's head and pulling his lips back to check his teeth. He worked his hands over the horse's body in a cursory exam.

"That's good," Zane said. "Otherwise, we just horse-napped someone else's property."

Bryn shook her head. "This horse may have been someone's property at one time, but they gave up that right when they abandoned it. You should have seen the squalor of that place."

"I've heard it was pretty bad." He patted the horse's neck. "But this guy looks okay. Except for the leg and the bite marks. Looks like some coyotes got to him."

"That's what Zane said."

"He's skinny, but he must have found *some* grass to eat because he doesn't look as bad as the last one you brought in. And the leg looks worse than it is. This horse got lucky. There doesn't appear to be any tendon damage. I'll wrap it and give him an injection of antibiotics and some pain meds, and I'll think he'll be fine."

Bryn let out a breath. "That's a relief."

"He's gonna need some attention over the next few weeks. Make sure he's up and moving. You want to maintain mobility so the scar tissue doesn't create a stricture. But he should come out of this just fine."

"Thanks so much for calling us about him. And for showing up like this. You're a real lifesaver."

"Yeah, thanks, Doc," Zane muttered. His lips formed a scowl, and his shoulders tensed as he turned away and busied himself with picking up the grooming tools and taking them back to the tack room. *What's that all about?*

What happened to the sweet guy who was just holding her hand in the truck?

Her brow furrowed, but she didn't know what to say. Instead, she turned to Brody. "I didn't know we'd end up with a box of puppies too."

Brody chuckled. "I didn't either. They were just a bonus, I guess. But thanks for taking the horse. For taking all of them. You have a good heart."

She jumped as Zane dropped the tools on the counter. She could hear him putting them back in their places, but it sounded like he was jamming the tools against the wall.

He came out a moment later and tipped his head, his hat now pulled low over his face. "It looks like you're all set with the horse. I'm gonna take off, get out of your way."

He was leaving? Why? "Wait. You don't have to go."

"I need to head back and help Logan with the evening chores. And Brody can take care of whatever you need."

A hard knot formed in her chest as she feared that what she might need was *him*.

"You keep this up, you're going to become a full-time rescue ranch."

She laughed but worried she might be the one who needed to be rescued...from him.

CHAPTER 7

ZANE EXHALED A DISGUSTED BREATH AS HE DROVE UP Bryn's driveway the next afternoon. He'd sworn he'd stay away today. Just like he'd sworn he'd stay away the day before, then ended up offering her a ride home from the diner. Apparently he needed to work on his swearing, because so far, none of them had stuck.

He'd made himself leave the night before—forced his feet to carry him to his truck. His heart might be damaged, but it knew that Brody was a better man for Bryn. He just needed to get out of the way and let that happen.

So how was his driving up to the house with a cab full of dog food and sweet feed helping that? It wasn't. But at least he had the animals as an excuse. It made perfect sense that he'd be stopping by to check on the horses and the dogs. It was completely logical that he'd picked up supplies for her—he'd been at the feed store anyway.

Beauty was in the corral, already looking healthier even after only a few days. She trotted toward him as he got out of the truck, and he crossed the yard to give her a sugar cube. The gray horse must have smelled the sugar cube because he plodded over for one too. The border collie had followed him from the truck and sniffed at the horses' feet.

A compact blue car that Zane didn't recognize sat in

the driveway. Not that he knew every car in town, but he knew quite a few. He'd been trained to be observant. The front screen door slammed, and Bryn and a tall, dark-haired woman stepped out onto the porch.

Bryn waved and flashed him a broad grin. An embarrassingly sappy feeling of warmth bloomed in his chest. *Damn.* Why did Bryn make him feel like a pubescent boy who got flustered and shy around pretty girls? He hadn't felt flustered and shy around a woman in years.

That's because you haven't cared about what one thought of you in years, his subconscious whispered. He was trying not to care about what this one thought either. But he appeared to be failing at his efforts.

"Hey, Zane," Bryn said, her steps light as she practically skipped down the steps. She leaned down to rub the collie's ears. "I wasn't expecting you."

He shrugged as he sauntered toward them. "I was in the neighborhood. Thought I'd check on the animals." *And bring you a wheelbarrow full of food.*

Her eyes dimmed for just a second, then she regained her bright expression as she gestured toward the other woman. "Do you know Tessa Kane? She dates Mason James."

He nodded and smiled at the dark-haired woman. "Sure. How you doin', Tess?" Now that Rockford, the oldest James brother, and Quinn, the youngest Rivers sister, were married, the Triple J Ranch and Rivers Gulch often joined forces for ranching activities or shared meals. Even though he tried to avoid the social gatherings,

Logan usually talked Zane into at least grabbing a plate of food. He'd met Tess at several of those occasions, and he liked her. She was funny and sarcastic and gave as good as she got with the rowdy James brothers.

"I'm good," Tess answered. "And even better now that you're here."

He narrowed his eyes, instantly suspicious of anyone claiming to *want* to be around him. Not that he was a total antisocial asshole, but most people didn't seek out conversation with folks who gave off the loner vibe as strongly as he did. Although Tess had never shied away from him. "Oh yeah? Why's that?"

"I've been wanting to talk to you. I'm doing a human interest story on Bryn and the horse the two of you rescued. That was quite an act of kindness." Tess was a reporter for a popular Colorado-living magazine.

"You don't need to talk to me. That was all Bryn. She's the kind one."

Tess raised an eyebrow but ignored his comment. Which surprised him a little, since she didn't often back off of giving him a hard time. In fact, she'd often plunked down next to him at family gatherings and struck up conversations with wildly personal questions like *How's your day going?*

"I was excited to come over and get the story of you-all rescuing one horse," she told him. "But I got a surprise. Bryn said you-all also saved *another* horse *and* a handful of starving puppies."

"We were a little surprised about that too." He snuck

a small grin at Bryn, as if sharing a private joke. Although the joke was on her; she was the one now stuck with two horses and six extra dogs.

"Well, now that you're here, I'd love to get some photos of you and Bryn with the horses. And the puppies. If my article is accompanied by a swoony picture of a hot cowboy holding a handful of puppies, the magazine will sell out every copy."

His smile fell. "You're going to have to look somewhere else then because nobody around here fits that description." He gestured to the truck. "Look, I'm just dropping off some dog food and some grain for the horses. I think it's great you're doing a story on Bryn, but you can leave me out of it. Take all the pictures you want, but I don't want to be in any of them."

Tess studied him for a moment, then shrugged. "Suit yourself." She turned to Bryn. "I already got some great shots of the puppies. But I'd love a few of you with the horses."

"Sure," Bryn said, leading her toward the barn.

"I'll just unload these supplies and be on my way then," Zane said, already heading for the truck. He put the two bags of dog food on the porch, then carried the grain into the barn.

The sound of Bryn's laughter carried through the space, and Zane snuck a glance toward the corral where she and Tess were taking pictures. Bryn was cracking up as she leaned against the side of the barn door and made cheesy faces while Tess chastised her to be serious.

He absently rubbed the scar on his cheek, trying to remember the last time he'd let himself be in a photo. Damned if he could remember. He avoided most cameras like the plague and would rather take a bite of horse shit than take out his phone and pose for a selfie. Just one more example of why he wasn't suited for Bryn. He'd seen her taking pictures of the horses, and she'd done a selfie with Brody's daughter and the new horse the day before. Bryn would fit right in with Brody and Mandy—a happy, fun-loving family. He could just imagine the three of them grinning into the camera on a family outing, then posting the pictures on social media. Hashtag happy freaking day.

Not him. He didn't want anything to do with that business. Hell, he didn't even have Facebook. What would be the point? To remind himself how few friends he had? No thanks. He didn't need to be reminded of that.

Bryn laughed again, this time the sound a painful reminder of what he'd never have. He slipped from the barn and headed for his truck.

Despite his best intentions to stay away from the woman, Zane couldn't make himself stay away from the injured horse. Brody had said it needed exercise and to work the leg. Which was why he had snuck out to the Callahan farm before the sun had come up the next morning and looped a soft bridle over the gray's head.

He attached a lead rope and gently held it as he slowly walked the horse around the corral. The gray turned out to be a good listener, and they had a congenial chat about the weather, the land, and women. The horse didn't have much in the way of advice, but he made a good sounding board and occasionally nodded his head as if in agreement with Zane's thoughts. The leg seemed to be healing well, and the horse was putting good weight on it. He felt good about the horse's recovery.

Inhaling a deep breath of mountain air, Zane gazed over the horizon as the sun made its appearance against a backdrop of pink-and-blue sky. The air was ripe with the scents of spring transitioning into summer—pine, honeysuckle, fresh grass, and horse. Zane felt good in the corral, with the horse—as though this was what he was born to do. Working horses was the only place he truly felt good about himself, like he was doing something valuable, something worthwhile.

"Let's go around one more time, then I'm sneaking out of here before Bryn wakes up," he told the horse. The horse swished his tail and plodded forward. He was pretty good at reading horses, but Zane wasn't sure if the gelding thought sneaking out was a good idea or not.

Bryn slipped out onto the porch, a warm cup of coffee in her hand. Lucky came out with her and hopped down the steps and into the grassy patch of lawn. She was usually up with the sun anyway, but this morning the sound of the horses had drawn her to the window, where she'd spied Zane walking the gray around the corral.

Something about the horse and the cowboy walking through the pale early morning light had her chest tightening as her breath caught in her throat. There was just something heartbreakingly beautiful about this tough-as-nails cowboy gently leading the wounded horse patiently around the corral.

She smiled now as she leaned against the porch railing and watched them. She could swear it looked as if Zane had just told the horse a joke and danged if it didn't appear the horse had laughed.

Crossing to the corral, she leaned over the gate. "Mornin', cowboy," she said as Zane and the horse walked toward her.

"Sorry," he said with a sheepish grin. Dang, but he had a gorgeous grin. "Didn't mean to wake you."

"You didn't," she said. "I was up anyway." She held out her cup. "Coffee?"

He peered into the caramel-colored liquid. "I would say yes, but that doesn't look like coffee to me. That looks like creamer with a splash of coffee."

She chuckled and shrugged. "Suit yourself. But you're missing out on some delicious coffee-flavored creamer." She pulled a sugar cube from her pocket and held it out on her flattened palm. The horse took a tentative sniff, then snuffled the cube, his velvety lips tickling her hand. She smiled as she stroked the side of his head. "How's he doing?"

Zane nodded. "Pretty good. I was going to rewrap the bandage before I headed in to work. I didn't mean to bother you. He needed to be exercised, and I figured I could help."

"Thanks. I appreciate it."

"He's real gentle. I'm sure he'll let you walk him around tomorrow."

Was he trying to say he didn't want to come back out here, or was he trying to get her to invite him to come out again? He was a hard guy to read. And *did* she want him to come out again? Or was it better, easier, *not* to be around him? Not to be tempted by his muscular arms and that tight-lipped grin that did funny things to her stomach?

"I'd better get going. Logan's expecting me," he said before she had a chance to reply.

"Sure," she told him. "Hey, before you go, I wanted to tell you I came up with a name for the new horse."

"Yeah?"

"Yeah. I was thinking since we did kind of a fairy-tale thing with Beauty, we could keep with that theme."

He raised an eyebrow. "I'm not sure *we* did any kind of thing when it came to naming that horse, but go ahead."

"Whatever," she said, teasing him. "Anyway, I think every girl needs a prince, and since this guy will be sharing Beauty's space, he should be hers. So I thought we should call him Prince."

Zane shrugged. "Fine with me. It's your call. And it's a good name." He pulled the horse forward as he led him toward the barn, then called over his shoulder, "Just remember, not every guy is a prince."

She sighed. This was a fact she was well acquainted with. Not every man *was* a prince, but a few were. It was just a matter of finding the right one.

———————————

Two days later, Zane pulled up in front of the diner and waved to Bryn through the glass. He'd texted her the night before to tell her the new part for her car had come in and offered to drive her home from work and install it.

She hadn't worked the day before, and it had taken copious amounts of willpower not to drop by her farm. There was a fine distinction between showing up unannounced and making a nuisance of oneself, and he didn't want to cross that line. At least today he had a reason for spending time with her. Not that installing an alternator was exactly spending time with her, but it was at least a valid excuse for being there.

The door of the truck opened, and Bryn clambered into the seat and flashed him a smile. "Hey, Zane, thanks for picking me up." The heady scent of her perfume filled the cab, and he wanted to lean over and bury his face in her neck. Even after a full shift, she still looked gorgeous. Her cheeks were flushed pink, and she had her hair pulled up, a few escaped wisps hanging loose against her skin. Her lips shimmered with some kind of pale-pink gloss, and he was struck with the idea that if he kissed her right now, she would taste like cotton candy.

His mouth watered just looking at her. Although that

also might have to do with the fact she smelled a little like cheeseburgers and chocolate malts.

"Hey yourself," he said. "How was work?"

"Another day, another dollar. And yes, I'm speaking of the lousy one-dollar tip my last cheapskate customer left me for his twenty-five-dollar bill."

Zane shook his head. "Bastard."

Bryn chuckled. "I did feel a little like a celebrity though. At least three people mentioned they'd seen Tess's article about the horses."

"The article's out already?"

"Yeah, I guess one of their features had to be pulled and they stuck the horse rescue story in its place. The actual magazine doesn't come out until tomorrow, but the digital one came out today. She did a good job. The article is focused more on the dire need of the animals than it is on me, and she set up some kind of online donation fund thing so readers could donate money to help pay for the care of the horses. I doubt anyone will—I mean, they don't know me from Adam, but the few people in town who do know me and saw the article…" She paused and pulled a handful of bills from her pocket. "They gave me extra tip money today to help the animals."

He shook his head. "This town. Seriously, that's great. I'm glad you don't have to do this on your own. Maybe you should make one of those little donation jars and set it on the counter by the register."

She laughed. "Elle is already on it. She came over last night to see the puppies and told me she's working on making several to put around town. She must have cleaned out the pet store because she brought over a new dog bed, food and water bowls, some chew toys, the most adorable puppy collars, and some old blankets. Half the stuff they won't even be able to use for weeks. Their bed right now is a clean cardboard box, some newspaper, and Elle's jacket, which the mother dog seems to love. Elle also gave me a hundred dollars that she said an anonymous donor had given her to help with the puppies. I think it was her, but she'd really committed to the anonymous-donor ruse and I didn't want to insult her."

"Good thinking."

"She was actually pretty great. Brody had helped me give all the dogs a flea bath before he left the other night, but Elle spent close to an hour just sitting with the mother dog and comforting her as the puppies slept."

"It was probably just as helpful for her as it was for the dog. I asked Logan about Elle, and he said she pretty much keeps to herself. He doesn't think she has a lot of friends, so it's lucky she has you."

"Are you kidding? I'm the lucky one. Adding two horses and six dogs to my house hasn't been easy. She gave me a much-needed break last night."

He lifted a shoulder but kept his eyes on the road. "I'm around if you need help. All you have to do is call."

"I feel like you're already doing so much for me. I can't believe you're going to fix my car."

"It's no big deal. I'm just replacing the alternator."

"It's a big deal to me. I'm not used to asking for or accepting help. I'm used to being the one offering the help."

He thought of the call she'd taken from her younger brother. He'd asked Logan about Buck as well. Because Buck was several years younger, Zane didn't remember him from high school. In truth, Zane didn't remember much from high school. And what he did remember, he tried to forget. But he knew what it was like to have someone looking to you for help. Except unlike him, Bryn could actually be counted on to come through.

He pulled the truck into the driveway and squinted at the house. "What the hell is that on your front porch? It looks like someone tied a big shaggy dog to your railing. Damned if that isn't the sorriest lookin' dog I've ever seen."

She raised a hand over her eyes to shield the sun then let out a tiny gasp. "That isn't a dog. It's a pony. Oh my gosh, Zane, it's a miniature horse." She opened the door of the truck before he'd even put it in park and ran toward the porch.

He motioned for the border collie to stay in the truck, then followed.

Bryn had dropped to her knees on the porch steps and was carefully stroking the little creature's back. There were tears in her eyes as she looked up at him. "Oh, Zane. This poor baby. Look at him."

The miniature horse was indeed in bad shape. His hooves were too long and starting to curl, and the outline of his ribs was visible through the dull coat of brown fur covering his belly. Zane pushed back a tangle of the matted yellow mane that hung in the animal's eyes and stroked a hand down his neck. His hair was rough and hadn't seen a brush in months, if not years. He had white socks on his legs and a matching white spot on his forehead, between his eyes.

Bile rose in his throat, and his hand clenched into a fist. How could anyone treat an animal like this? The hot Colorado sun beat down around the house—at least they'd had the decency to put the horse on the porch in the shade.

A fluttering caught his eye, and he looked up to see a note stuck to the front door with a piece of duct tape. He ripped it free and read it aloud.

"My wife bought this horse as a gift for my daughter. Now my wife and daughter are gone, and I can barely take care of myself, let alone this dumb horse that thinks he's a dog. I heard you were taking in horses, and knew he'd be better off with you. His name is Shamus. He likes macaroni and cheese and is partial to orange jelly beans." Zane closed his eyes as he pressed a fist to his forehead. "Who the hell feeds macaroni and cheese and jelly beans to a horse?"

"It doesn't look like anyone's been feeding him much of anything lately," Bryn said, running a hand over his thin belly.

"No, you're right. But we can remedy that." He rubbed the horse's forehead. "I'll go grab him some grain if you want to find him a bowl of water." He hastened to the barn and filled an empty coffee can with feed, then grabbed a hunk of hay from a loose bale and hurried back to the front porch.

Bryn was just coming out of the house with a dog dish filled with water. She set it on the porch in front of the horse, then took the grain from Zane and poured it into another empty dish. "The note did say he thought he was a dog."

The horse didn't seem to care what kind of dish the grain was in. He bent his head and greedily dug into the feed. Zane set the hay on the porch in front of him. "We'll give him a few minutes to eat, then we need to get him cleaned up. We could brush out the other horses, but I think this guy needs an actual bath. You got anything around here we could fill up with water?"

"There's a plastic baby pool on the side of the house that Lucky likes to play in during the summer. We could use that."

"Perfect. I'll spray it down with the hose and find some brushes to use."

"Give me a minute, and I'll help. I need to change my clothes and check on the puppies."

"You got any of that dog shampoo from Brody left?"

She nodded.

"Grab that too. And a pair of scissors."

Ten minutes later, Zane had the baby pool cleaned and filled with a few inches of water. He'd let the collie out, and she'd played in the spray of the hose, then retired to sun herself in the grass. He'd assembled a selection of brushes and combs and brought out the nippers and a pick. He figured the horse's hooves would be easier to clean and trim after they'd soaked in the water.

The rhythmic thump of country music suddenly sounded through the open front windows, and Zane looked up to see Bryn step out onto the porch, her arms filled with towels. She'd changed into a pair of cut-off jean shorts and Teva-style sports sandals. The outline of a hot-pink bikini top shone through her white tank top, the strings winding up and tied around her neck.

She juggled brushes, combs, and bottles of shampoo on top of the towels. Zane hurried up the stairs to take the stack from her. "I think you've got every contingency covered here," he said, teasing her.

She held up a finger. "One more thing." She disappeared into the house and reappeared a minute later lugging a full bucket of water. "I filled this with hot water to add to the baby pool so the cold water wouldn't be such a shock to the horse."

He smiled, not having the heart to remind her that a horse's coat was pretty thick and that they often stood outside in the rain and snow. He didn't think the horse would care too much about the temperature of the water, but it would make it easier on them.

Untying the lead rope from the porch, he led the miniature horse to the swimming pool. "Shamus, my friend, it appears you're about to have a day at the spa." He glanced at Bryn, who was pouring the warm water into the pool. "You're not planning to paint little pink toenails on his hooves, are you?"

She grinned. "I am now." Her grin faded, replaced with a heartbreaking frown as she peered down at the horse. "Gosh. He looks like a sad little Eeyore the way he's hanging his head and kind of limping along so slowly."

"I imagine he's limping along so slowly because his feet hurt. Those hooves are in bad shape, and I can't imagine they're easy to walk on."

"Poor baby." She brushed her hand across the horse's head. "We're gonna fix you up, little guy."

The horse stepped into the pool, and Zane eased the filthy halter off his head. It was too small and left indents in his hair where it had pressed into his coat. Zane had found another one in the tack room; it wasn't new, but it was better than the crusted and disgusting one that had been around Shamus's head. He looped the lead rope around his neck, confident the little guy wasn't going to run off, and slowly scooped water across his back. Bryn filled her hands with shampoo and gently massaged it throughout his coat. They worked together, kneading the soap over his coat, then spraying it clean. Shamus seemed to enjoy the attention, leaning into Zane's hands as he rubbed his shoulder.

The pool was small, but Bryn got right in with the horse and dropped to her knees in the water. Zane stayed on the outside of the pool, yet they were still right next to each other, their arms crossing and shoulders touching as they soaped and rinsed the animal. Zane tried to focus on the little horse and ignore the delicious display of Bryn's skin as she worked next to him. Her tank top was soon soaked, and the white fabric clung to the hot-pink bikini beneath it.

He knew the horse was the priority, knew Shamus needed his attention, but it was hard to ignore the needs of his body. Especially since he was yearning to stroke his fingers down her tanned arm and across the smooth skin of her neck.

"I grabbed some detangling conditioner," Bryn told him, leaning out of the pool to pluck the bottle from the ground. She poured a dollop into her hand and worked it through the horse's matted mane. "I thought it might help with his mane."

"It will," Zane replied, swallowing hard. Her shirt had ridden up an inch when she'd reached for the conditioner, and his mouth had gone dry as he caught a glimpse of her luscious skin. He picked up the scissors. "And so will these. I'm going to give him a trim, cut back the forelock over his eyes so he can see, and try to cut out some of the worst mats." He combed out the hair across the horse's forehead and cut it to right above his eyes. Bryn detangled as much of the hair through his mane as she could, then they cut the rest free, still saving a good three or four inches of mane. "That's got to feel better, doesn't it, boy?"

The horse shook his head, sending water flying, then nudged his nose into Zane's T-shirt, leaving a huge wet mark across his chest.

Bryn peered at his chest. "Your shirt is soaked, and it's hot out here. It's okay if you want to take it off."

Any moisture he'd gained in his mouth dried up faster

than water soaking into the sands of the Afghanistan desert. She'd already turned away, but not before he'd thought he caught a ghost of an impish grin. Was she flirting with him or just concerned for his well-being?

He cleared his throat, trying to get his mouth to work. "I'm good." He wasn't good. Not at all. His shirt was wet, and he *was* hot—his skin was scorching with the warmth of the sun and the heat of her comment, but he wasn't taking his shirt off. No way.

Beyond the men in his unit, not many had seen him without a shirt. Even with the few women he'd known intimately over the last few years, he made a point either to keep his shirt on or the lights off. The scar on his face itched, the skin stretched and tight, and he tensed his shoulders, feeling the same stretch and prickle across his back.

He'd made a sort of peace with his dad as an adult, but make no mistake, Birch Taylor was a mean drunk.

A warm pressure leaned into him, and he peered down to see the collie pressed against him, her head slanting into his chest. He rubbed her ears, tilting his head to accept the lightest press of her nose to his cheek as he murmured, "Good dog."

"It seems to me that anyone you let kiss on you like that deserves to be called by her name."

What would you like me to call you?

He sighed, wishing Bryn were the one kissing him instead of the wet snout smelling faintly of dog breath.

"I'm working on it," he muttered, stroking the horse's

back and avoiding Bryn's eye, afraid she'd see the desperate hunger shining there.

"That's a start," she said softly, resting her hand on top of his for just a moment. The moment was interrupted as the horse dipped his head quickly into the water then let out a small whinny as he sprayed water across them both. Bryn's eyes widened, then she let loose a peal of laughter. "I think he's getting a little spunk back."

"It's amazing what a good meal and a nice bath will do for you." He couldn't help but smile at the little horse who did seem to be in better spirits. "Let's get him out on the grass, and you can brush him while I work on his feet."

They led the horse out of the pool, and he bent his head and chomped on the grass as Bryn toweled him off and worked his coat with a brush and curry comb. Zane cleaned and cut back his cracked and curled hooves.

Bryn stood back and studied their work. Tears sprung to her eyes. "He looks like a different horse."

"He's got to feel better too," Zane replied, buckling the newer halter around its head and clipping the lead rope to it. "Let's take him out to the corral and see how he does with the other horses." He pulled on the lead, and the horse took a few tentative steps forward, as if testing his freshly cut hooves. Limping a little still, his stride grew stronger as he followed them across the driveway and through the barn.

Zane led him out into the corral, then unclipped the lead rope and tossed it back toward the barn. "Let's see what he does." Bryn stood next to him, and he had a sudden urge to put his arm around her waist, as if they were proud parents who were watching their child head into school for the first time.

"Aww. I feel like we're the overprotective mom and dad sending our little son off to school."

He grinned, liking the idea that their thoughts had been so in sync. "Our four-legged hairy son who is smaller than all the other kids in the class."

She chuckled. "He *is* so tiny. Look at him. His head barely comes up to the stomach of the other horses."

Beauty eyed the small creature from where she stood by the fence, but Prince plodded over and bent his neck to touch his head to the smaller horse. The bigger horse sniffed the smaller one, then turned his attention to Zane as he trotted over looking for a treat.

Zane held his empty palms out. "I got nothing. Now, be a good horse and go show that little guy around."

The horse gazed at him a moment, then trudged back across the corral. Shamus tried to follow, hesitantly walking forward as if trying out a new pair of shoes. He shook his head, seeming to revel in the release of the snug and filthy halter. Zane wondered how long he'd been tied up. He took another few steps, then slowly picked up confidence and trotted a few feet forward.

"Gah. Look how cute he is." Bryn clapped a hand to her chest. "His feet must feel a ton better."

"They aren't a hundred percent. It's gonna take a few weeks and some more care, but yeah, just cleaning them out and trimming them back has got to feel like a vast improvement."

She laughed as the little horse sprang up and down and pranced toward them. "He looks like he's hopping. He's gone from looking like Eeyore to bouncing like Tigger."

Caught up in her laughter, Zane leaned down and called the horse, then raced around the corral, encouraging Shamus to chase after him. The little horse trotted and pranced after him.

Bryn joined in the fun, running after Zane and cooing to the horse, her laughter filling the corral and Zane's heart.

"We did it," Bryn cried, launching herself into Zane's arms. "We really did it. We saved this little horse. And now we've saved *three* horses. I'm so happy I think my heart is going to burst." She wrapped her arms around his neck as she hugged him.

He hugged her back, his hands automatically going around her back and pulling her to him. Emotions swirled through him—a pang in his chest that might have been his heart exploding mixed with the heat of want and need.

She pulled her head back and looked up at him, her eyes bright with excitement. "Thank you," she whispered. "I couldn't have done this, *any* of this, without you."

He shook his head, his neck and ears going hot. "I didn't do anything," he muttered.

"You did everything."

He held her gaze, the butterflies in his gut crashing into his stomach walls in kamikaze dive bombs. Which was how he felt—like this thing with Bryn was a kamikaze mission, and the only thing to come from it would be hurt and pain and loss.

Still. He wanted this. Wanted her. His gaze dropped to her lips. They shimmered with some kind of gloss, looking soft and plump as they parted—as if in anticipation.

Don't do it.

But her lips. They parted. She wants me to kiss her.

Doesn't matter. You're not the guy for her. She's good and sweet. You're only going to hurt her.

I know.

Want and need tightened his chest, every nerve singing with desire as he fought an internal battle with his subconscious. Should he? Shouldn't he?

He knew his subconscious was right. He wasn't the guy for her. He wasn't even sticking around. Why start something he couldn't finish?

Because it would feel so damn good.

Bryn was an itch he couldn't scratch. A want he couldn't have.

Except he could have her. All he had to do was lean down and press his lips to hers.

He'd kissed her once, outside the diner, but that was a peck, a whisper of the way he wanted to kiss her now. He wasn't interested in a peck. He wanted to crush her mouth with his, to take his time and kiss her good and thorough.

But that would only open the door—a door he couldn't make himself walk through and one he wouldn't be able to shut. Once he'd really kissed her, tasted her, he would only want more.

Which was why he should walk away.

That's what I've been trying to tell you.

His gaze was still on her mouth. *Walk away.*

He raised one hand to touch her cheek, resting his fingers lightly on her face as he drew the side of his thumb along the edge of her bottom lip. She hitched in the softest breath and pulled the corner of her lip—the spot he'd just touched—under her top teeth.

Ah, to hell with it. He'd never been very good at following useful advice anyway.

He leaned in, brushed her lips with his, the softest graze, but it was enough—enough to stir the longing he'd thought he'd long buried, enough to start his heart thrashing into the walls of his chest, enough to know he wanted more. He wanted it all.

CHAPTER 8

ZANE PULLED HER TO HIM, DEEPENING THE KISS. HIS hand cupped Bryn's cheek, holding her face as he took her mouth in an onslaught of heat and desire. His other arm tightened around her, pulling her close as she melted into him. Her lips were yielding, pliant at first, then hungry as she matched the intensity of his need.

Her hands moved up his back, gripping his T-shirt as she pressed into him. His hand moved from her face to her neck, his fingers plunging into her hair as his palm held her head.

Her lips parted, and he lost himself in the sensual glide of her tongue as he inhaled her, stealing her breath in a rush of hunger and heat. Their tongues tangled in a decadent promise of more as she gave back equal parts of passion and demand.

She tasted like honeysuckle and summer and everything good he'd ever wanted. And he couldn't get enough. He wanted to press her against the barn wall and take his fill. Then he wanted to carry her into the house, toss her into bed, and strip her out of those tiny cut-off shorts before peeling off that hot-pink bikini top—with his teeth.

His body flushed hot, the heat coursing through his veins as he savored the taste of her mouth, the feel of her breasts pressed against his chest. Her back arched as her fingers dug into his shoulders. When she let out the softest sigh of bliss against his lips, he thought he would completely come undone.

The rest of the world fell away, and it was only him and Bryn locked in this incredible moment, her arms wrapped around him and her chest pressed to his. Nothing else mattered…except the sound of an engine as a truck pulled into the driveway and tooted the horn.

Damn it.

Zane pulled away, dropping his arms as he tried to reorient himself. His breath, ragged, caught in his chest as he recognized the pickup. Dr. Brody. *Of course.*

Of course the universe would pick this moment for Brody to drive up, to remind Zane that he wasn't the one for Bryn. That she needed someone different, someone better. That he would never be enough for someone like her.

It didn't matter that her eyes were wide as she stared at him, or that her chest was heaving as she tried to catch her breath, or that her lips were swollen from being thoroughly kissed.

She blinked, not saying anything, but kept her gaze trained on his, as if waiting for him to speak.

But he had nothing to say. No words of encouragement, no undying oath of love, no warning of how this would never work. He could only stare back at her and wish things were different. Wish *he* were different.

The truck doors slammed, and Brody's voice called through the barn. "Bryn?"

"We're out here," she answered.

Zane turned toward the barn, and his eye caught on two gray squares affixed to the walls above the corners of the door. "What the hell are those?" He pointed to the squares.

"Oh, I forgot to tell you. They're cameras."

"Cameras?" He ducked his head, automatically turning the scarred side of his face away. "How long have those been there?" How had he not noticed them before?

"Not long. We just put them up yesterday."

"What the hell do you need cameras for? Nobody even wanted these horses. Now you think someone's going to steal them?"

"No, they're not that kind of camera. They're like webcams. It was Tess's idea. She loaned me the cameras and helped me set them up. They're linked to a Facebook account and show a live view of the horses. It's a marketing strategy to help get donations for their food and care."

He lifted his hat and scrubbed a hand through his hair. "So you're telling me you've set up cameras and invited half the world onto your farm to watch you all day every day. You might as well have included an invitation calling all perverts and stalkers."

"It's not half the world. I honestly doubt we'll even get five people who care to tune in." She planted her hands on her hips, her voice rising in indignation. "And what kind of a weird pervert would get off on watching a couple of horses walk around the corral?"

He raised an eyebrow. "They won't be looking at

the horses. But they will tune in to watch the gorgeous woman who's taking care of them."

She blinked, and a slight pink colored her cheeks. "I think you're overreacting. Besides, we only have the cameras scheduled to turn on and do a livestream feed for a few hours each afternoon."

"Well, I have zero interest in being on any kind of camera, so just make damn sure they're not on when I'm around." He regretted the harshness of his tone as she took a step back, but the rest of their conversation was cut off as Mandy squealed from the doorway of the barn.

"Oh my gosh, isn't he the cutest?" the girl cried, running up to Bryn and Zane, the heels of her boots kicking up little clouds of dust as she ran. "When did you get a mini-horse?"

Bryn laughed and looked at her wrist where a watch might be. "About two or three hours ago."

"Can I pet him?"

"Sure. Just be careful. His name is Shamus, and he seems like a sweetheart, but we don't know much about him or how he reacts around kids."

Shamus was already trotting toward Mandy. "Where did he come from?"

"He was tied to my porch when we got home this afternoon with a note that his owner couldn't keep him anymore."

The girl mock pouted. "That is now my number one wish for life—that someone would leave a miniature horse tied to my doorstep. Well, right after an owl drops off my admissions letter to Hogwarts."

Bryn chuckled. "I'm still waiting for my letter too."

The girl ran her hands over the horse's neck, and he leaned in, obviously enjoying the affection. "Who would give this baby away?"

"He's not a baby," Zane said, his mouth twisting into a scowl. "By the looks of his teeth, he's a middle-aged man, and they tend to eat a lot and get grumpier as they age." At least that's what his dad had done.

Mandy frowned.

"But he seems to like you," Zane told her, softening his tone and forcing his lips into a smile as he tugged on the end of the girl's ponytail. "He used to belong to another girl, so maybe you remind him of her."

"Well, I think he's adorable." She hugged his neck as her dad stepped into the corral.

"Another one?" Brody asked Bryn. "It appears you really are starting a horse rescue ranch."

She tilted her head as she studied the horses, then turned back to the vet. "It appears I am."

"Now all you need is a name."

"Oh, we can work on one tonight," Mandy said. "Did you remember I'm spending the night?"

"Of course I remember. I already stocked the freezer with ice cream."

A broad grin spread across the girl's face. "I brought snacks too. I made Dad stop at the grocery store on the way here."

"Hope you like Sour Patch Kids, Reese's Peanut Butter Cups, and Cheetos," Brody said.

Bryn laughed. "Those are some of my favorites. Maybe not the sour things, but I could eat Cheetos all day long."

"How about all night long?" he asked. "Although I told her she still needs to go to bed at a decent hour and not keep you up too late."

"Da-a-d," Mandy admonished, rolling her eyes as she looked at Bryn.

"He just doesn't understand how slumber parties work," Bryn said, earning a grin as she winked at the girl.

"I don't think I want to know." Brody ruffled the hair of his daughter. "Just try to be on your best behavior. All right, kiddo?"

"We'll be fine," Bryn assured him. "Have fun at your conference. Don't worry about us."

He checked his watch. "I should probably head out. You want me to look at the new addition before I go?"

"Nah. You should get on the road before you hit too much traffic. But I'd appreciate you checking him out tomorrow when you pick Mandy up."

"Will do." He waved a hand at his daughter. "Let's get your stuff, squirt."

Zane watched the three of them head into the barn, a hard knot settling in his chest. They looked like they could already be a family. They were so easy with each other the way they joked and teased. And Bryn and Mandy could pass for mother and daughter with their blond ponytails and their familiar manner of bending their heads together to speak.

He wished he could leave, just get in his truck and keep driving. But he had the new part for Bryn's car, and he'd told her he would install it tonight. Besides, the quicker he got her car up and running again, the fewer excuses he'd have to come see her or offer her a ride.

———————————

Two hours later, Bryn and Mandy had finally settled into her house. Bryn held up the menu to the only pizza place in Creedence. "Should we order a pizza?"

"Yes, please. Can we get pepperoni?"

"Of course. That's my favorite." Her cell phone buzzed in her pocket, and Bryn was pleased to see Elle's number pop up on the display.

She and Mandy had spent the last few hours taking care of the animals, feeding and brushing the horses, putting scraps out for the few farm cats that roamed her barn, and cuddling Lucky, the mama dog, and the puppies. Zane had stomped off after their discussion about the cameras, and all she'd seen of him the last few hours was his muscled back and jean-clad butt as he leaned over the engine of her car. Which wasn't actually a bad part of him to see. The cowboy did have a great butt.

Thoughts of their earlier kiss had heat rising to her cheeks as she tapped the phone and put it to her ear. "Hey, Elle."

"Hi, Bryn. It's Elle. Well, shoot, I guess you knew that. I…um…I hope it's okay that I called."

"Of course it is. That's why I gave you my number. What's up?"

"Oh gosh. Nothing really. Nothing that important, I guess."

"Are you okay? Did something happen?" Bryn asked, detecting a note of something in the other woman's voice.

"Yeah, I guess. I mean I guess I'm okay, but something did happen." She let out a long sigh. "Apparently, I've been let go from my job."

"What? You got fired?"

"I believe the term they used was a 'career change opportunity.'"

"Oh no. I'm so sorry."

"I'm not. I mean, I know I *should* be upset, but really, I just feel relieved. Is that weird?"

"Not if you didn't like the job."

"I don't really know what I like anymore. But I liked hanging out with you. It was nice to feel like I had a woman friend again. So I was wondering if you might want to go out and grab a coffee or a pizza. Or a margarita or two? Or five?"

Bryn laughed. "I'll do you one better. It sounds like you could use some ice cream, girl time, and puppy therapy. And I happen to be having a sleepover tonight with five puppies and an adorable ten-year-old. Why don't you grab your most comfy pajamas and a toothbrush and come out here and join us?"

"Okay, you had me at puppies and ice cream, but why are you having a sleepover with a ten-year-old?"

"My friend had an overnight conference, so his daughter is spending the night with me. Our plans tonight involve a sappy chick flick and gorging on pizza, popcorn, ice cream, and puppy kisses. We were just getting ready to order the pizza. We'd love to have you join us."

"How can I refuse an offer like that? Give me twenty minutes to put some stuff together and I'll be out. Why don't I pick up the pizza on my way?"

"Perfect."

Thirty minutes later, Elle arrived with two pizza boxes in one hand and a large duffel bag in the other. "I wasn't sure one pizza was enough, so I had them make two."

"You can't have too much pizza," Bryn said, taking the boxes from her and placing them on the counter. She gave Elle a hug, then glanced down at the duffel bag at her feet. "I'm glad you're here. But you know it's just for the one night, right?"

Elle shrugged. "I've never been to a slumber party. I didn't know what to bring. So I threw in everything I could think of. And I wanted to contribute to the fun, so I brought some fancy face masks from the last time I spent a day at the spa and thought we could do facials."

"I've never had a facial," Mandy said, peering around Bryn's side.

"That's because you already have gorgeous skin," Elle told her, eliciting a beaming smile from the girl.

Bryn introduced the two, then pointed down the hall. "Your room is the first one on the left. The one with the blue comforter. Now go get in your cozies, and I'll pour you a drink. Although I'm afraid root beer is the strongest ale I've got."

"I haven't had a root beer in ages. That sounds perfect." She lugged the bag down the hall and emerged a few minutes later in a pink-and-purple flannel onesie and pink fuzzy slippers on her feet.

"Wow," Bryn said, covering her mouth as she tried not to laugh. "You do look cozy."

Elle grinned. "What? I get cold. And you did say to bring my comfiest pajamas."

"I love them," Mandy said. "I think you look beautiful."

"Thank you," Elle said. "I think you are my new best friend."

Bryn popped the lids on three bottles of root beer and passed them around. She held hers up. "A toast. To comfy pajamas, good pizza, and new best friends." They laughed, then clinked their bottles and drank.

The old farmhouse had a spacious kitchen decorated in light blue and sunny yellow with lemon accents. A small herb garden sat in the window above the sink, the long narrow pot spilling over with mint, basil, and dill. The hardwood floor was original and scuffed from years of bootheels and shoes, but still shone from the weekly scrubbing Bryn gave it. A long counter separated the kitchen from the dining area. On the other side of the round table and chairs, a cozy living room sat with a big overstuffed couch and a reclining rocking chair, both covered in fat pillows and soft throw blankets. The walls were painted a soft gray and matched the subtle gray hints in the blue and white pillows. Bryn's touch was everywhere, from the blue-and-white braided rag rugs on the floor to the white milk pitcher overflowing with fresh lilac stems on the side of the counter.

Mandy had helped earlier with setting out plates, silverware, and a stack of napkins, and Bryn passed them around, then lifted the lid on the top pizza box. She inhaled the scent of warm cheese and spicy pepperoni. "This smells amazing. Dig in, y'all."

They filled their plates with hot slices and settled on the sofa to watch an episode of the newest romantic comedy series on Netflix. Before the show was over, they had polished off the first pizza, a sizable bowl of popcorn, and six bottles of root beer. They had set up a spot on the sofa between Elle and Mandy for the mama dog to lie and have her puppies cuddled in with her, so they could love on the mama and give occasional pets to the tiny puppies. The mama dog rested her head on Elle's leg, keeping an eye on both her puppies and the woman who had originally rescued her.

Zane leaned over the engine of Bryn's car to reconnect the battery. The alternator had gone in smoothly, but now he needed to test it and make sure the battery didn't need a jump. The collie lay in the dirt by the front tire, her ears up and alert, ready in case he needed her to offer some advice or chase a ground squirrel or bunny away from the car.

The evening was warm, and he'd taken his flannel shirt off and had been working in just his undershirt. He'd just wiped a smear of grease on his jeans when a movement caught his eye. His shirt, which lay on the corner of the hood, seemed to be sliding slowly backward, almost as if being pulled by an unseen ghostly hand.

What the heck? Zane leaned over the side of the hood. *Hmmm.* Not a ghost. And not a hand either. Not unless Bryn's grandfather's spirit had come back in the form of an ornery billy goat who currently had the sleeve of Zane's shirt securely chomped in his mouth. The sneaky devil was slowly backing up and pulling the shirt toward him as if he thought he could sneak the thing away without Zane noticing.

"Drop it, you ornery cuss," he told the goat.

The collie's ears perked up higher, and she trotted around the front of the car, her haunches forward, ready to defend her master against the evil flannel-filching felon.

The goat froze. He knew he'd been caught. But he didn't drop the shirt. Instead, he lowered his head, and Zane knew he was going to make a break for it.

"Don't do it." Zane leapt forward and made a grab for the corner of the shirt. But the soft fabric slipped through his fingers as the goat skittered backward. The collie was quicker and snatched a corner of the shirt as it fell off the side of the car. She let out a low growl as she dug in her heels and pulled.

Zane sprinted around the hood, determined to help

the collie save his shirt. He grabbed a piece of the hem. "Otis, let go, you crazy coot," he commanded, then let out an exasperated chuckle.

The laugh must have confused the collie, because her head snapped from the goat to Zane as if trying to figure out if this was serious or a game. She must have decided it was a game, because she dropped her side of the shirt, let out a yip as she raced around the goat, then grabbed onto the sleeve of the shirt the goat had in his mouth.

"What? You crazy mutt. You're supposed to be on my side," he told the dog. She answered by shaking her head and pulling harder. He tightened his grip, mystified at how his night had just turned into a wacky tug-of-war with a goat, a dog, and one of his favorite shirts. And the worst part was that he was losing.

A loud rip sounded, and he stumbled back as the sleeve of his shirt tore away. The dog let go and raced to grab a new section of the fallen shirt, ready to continue the game, but the goat ran off with his prize.

Zane ran after it, the collie at his heels, determined not to let the buck get the best of him. But the goat was wily and quick-footed and snuck through the fence into the pasture. The dog followed and tried to herd the goat back toward her master, yipping and running circles around it. Zane changed tactics and ran to the barn to grab some feed. Maybe the goat would trade the sleeve for some food. Although by the way the dang thing was chewing on the flannel, the shirt might very well end up as food. He filled a coffee can with grain and tried to entice the goat to make a trade, but Otis wasn't having it. That shirt was apparently a treasured prize, and not even grain could coax it away.

"Oh, keep the shirt, you idiot," Zane hollered, waving a hand at the animal and shaking his head as the goat pranced away. He couldn't help but laugh as he whistled for the dog and headed back toward Bryn's car. Otis had won this round, but Zane had a feeling this wouldn't be the last argument he had with the greedy goat.

———————

Bryn eased Lucky off her lap and carried their discarded plates into the kitchen. *Romantic comedy—check. Gorged ourselves on bad food—check.* "Who's ready to do facials?"

Mandy thrust her hand into the air and opened her mouth to answer. But instead of words, a belch loud enough to rival a grown man's ripped from her lips. Her eyes widened, as if the ferocity of the belch surprised even her. She clapped her hand over her mouth and dissolved into hysterical giggles. "Excuse me."

Elle offered her a high five. "Good one." She tapped her chest. "It's the root beer. And drinking it out of the bottle." She opened her mouth and let out a tiny burp. Which only made Mandy giggle harder.

"That was weak," the ten-year-old said.

"I know. I'll work on it. Now that I no longer have a job, I'll have more time to work on my belching skills."

Bryn laid the packets of masks on the table and patted

the chair in front of her. Mandy slid into it, and Bryn drew the girl's long blond hair into a ponytail and away from her face. She pulled her own hair into a messy bun on top of her head, then tore open a packet and squeezed a glob of bright green goo onto her fingers.

"Eww! It's green," Mandy said, wrinkling her nose. "It looks like the gross kale smoothie my dad tried to make me drink once."

"Your dad drinks kale smoothies?" Bryn asked as she dabbed the goo lightly over Mandy's cheeks. The girl's skin already had all the glorious youthful glow the mask promised it would provide, but Bryn wanted Mandy to feel included, so she kept it to a thin layer.

"No, but he read an article about how to get your kids to eat more veggies and thought he'd try it. Like I said, it was only once." She sniffed. "This stuff doesn't seem so bad though. It smells kind of minty. And it's cold on my cheeks."

"It's nice," Bryn agreed, squeezing the rest of the packet onto her fingers. She watched the way Elle smeared it over her face, then globbed it liberally over her own cheeks and forehead. She *could* use a more youthful glow. "So, Elle, I know it just happened, and you're probably still reeling and maybe haven't had time to think about it, but besides improving your belching skills, do you have any idea what you want to do next?"

Elle shook her head. "No, not really. And I don't actually feel like I'm reeling that much from it. I know what reeling feels like, and this isn't it. Sure, I enjoyed the job.

But I didn't really like the travel and spending all that time alone in hotels and always eating by myself. Granted, I do the same thing here. As you may have noticed, I don't have a lot of friends, but it somehow feels lonelier in a hotel by yourself. They gave me a nice severance package and Ryan left me more money than I know what to do with, so I think for the first time in my adult life I'm just going to relax and take the summer off."

"Good idea," Mandy replied. "I'm taking the summer off too. And I don't have a whole lot of friends either. But I'll be your friend. And you could come to the swimming pool with me."

Elle covered Mandy's hand with her own, her eyes blinking back a sudden swell of tears. "Thank you, Mandy. I'd like that. Some time at the pool with a friend sounds wonderful." She smiled at Bryn, who had to swallow at the sweet show of emotion. "I also need to do some spring cleaning and get rid of some stuff in my house," Elle continued. "And I thought I could try to do some volunteer work and maybe meet some other people in the community. When Ryan first died, so many people reached out to me, but I wasn't ready, and I think I gave off the impression that I didn't want or need their support. And maybe I didn't. I just wanted to lie in bed and cover my head with the blankets and sleep every day. But my husband loved this town, and it's probably time I figured out why. And hopefully some of the people here will give me another chance."

Bryn squeezed her arm. "I'm sure they will. Creedence is a nice town filled with lots of good people."

"I'm sorry your husband died, Elle," Mandy said, her voice soft as she twisted a paper napkin that had been left on the table. She stared at her hands as she swallowed. "My mom died, and some days it makes my stomach hurt because I miss her so much." She peered up at Elle. "Does that ever happen to you?"

"It does," Elle whispered back, a lone tear escaping her eye as she took in a shuddering breath. She forced her lips into a smile. "But I'm sorry that happens to you."

Bryn blinked back tears, wishing she could offer some kind of remedy, anything to ease the pain of these two people she cared about. "Anyone want more pizza? Or ice cream? Or a puppy?"

Elle breathed out a laugh and pushed her shoulders back as she patted her stomach. "I'm stuffed, but I'm not done cuddling those puppies. I'm going in for another quick snugglefest while this mask dries."

"Me too," Mandy said. "I think that little black-and-white one likes me."

"I think she does too." The air lightened, and the tightness in Bryn's chest eased. She glanced over at Elle. "If you're serious about doing some volunteering, I've suddenly found myself with a whole lot of animals that I need to take care of, and I could definitely use the help."

Elle's eyes lit, and a grin spread across her face. "Yes. For sure. Whatever I can do." She held up a finger. "Oh, that reminds me. I stopped at a couple of places on my way here and collected the money from some of the donation cans I put out for you." She crossed the room to her bag and pulled out two jars full of coins and cash. "I haven't counted it yet, but I'm sure there's well over a hundred dollars in here."

"Wow. Already? I can't believe it."

"I can. People love you. And that article your friend Tess wrote was really great. Plus, didn't you say you started a social media campaign?"

"Campaign is a strong word. Tess made me a page specifically for the horse rescue, and she set up some livestream-video thing that runs for a couple of hours at different times in the day that shows viewers what the horses are up to. I don't get how it all works, but she does. I'm terrible at all that junk." She tilted her head and eyed Elle. "If you're really serious about this volunteering thing, besides helping with the animals I could really use some help with all this publicity stuff. With your background in marketing, maybe you could help with the social media aspect."

"What a great idea. That's the kind of thing I do at work all the time. Well, that I *used* to do at work all the time. But helping you sounds like a lot more fun. I'd love to work on your social media, and I can set up a website for you too. And I'll check out the Facebook page you've already got and see what I think."

"That sounds amazing."

Elle smiled, and Bryn loved the slight bit of pride that shone through her grin. Sometimes it helped to have a purpose. And anything Elle could do for her on the social media front was a huge blessing.

Bryn jumped as a knock sounded on the door behind her. She turned to see Zane at the screen door, and she waved him in. It wasn't until he stepped through and she saw his eyes widen that Bryn realized their faces were all covered in green goo.

Zane raised an eyebrow. "I've always wondered what happened at these sleepover parties, but I had no idea you smeared guacamole on your faces." He glanced toward the kitchen. "Did anybody bring chips?"

Mandy giggled. "It's not guacamole," she told him. "It's a beauty mask."

"Well, that seems ridiculous since you're all three already beautiful in my book."

Bryn was thankful the green goop covered her cheeks so Zane wouldn't see the pink color she was sure was heating them. Which was ridiculous. He hadn't exactly called her beautiful. It was more of an offhand compliment to both women and a ten-year-old girl. She was sure he was just being nice.

He seemed uncomfortable too as he raised his hand and rubbed the back of his neck.

"Oh my gosh. What happened to your shirt?" she asked, staring at his missing sleeve. "Did you hurt your arm?"

"Nah, just my pride. I took my shirt off to work on the car and next thing I know that dang goat Otis grabbed it. I ended up in a tug-of-war with him, the shirt, and the dog, and my sleeve was the loser. I tried to chase him down, but he got away. I even tried to barter with him, offered him some nice grain in exchange for giving me my shirt back, but your goat is sorely lacking in negotiating skills."

Bryn pressed her lips together to keep from laughing. "So you lost your shirt to my goat?"

"Essentially, yes." The corners of his lips tugged up in a sheepish grin. "He may have tried to apologize later by getting overly friendly with my leg when I was trying to finish up on the car, but I'm not sure if he was apologizing or flirting with me."

"With Otis, it could have been either." She ducked her head. "Sorry about that."

He shrugged. "It's okay. He and the dog kept me company while I worked. And regrettably, it's not the first time a farm animal has tried to get frisky with me."

Mandy wrinkled her nose. "What do you mean by frisky? Like a cow wanted to play a game with you?"

He chuckled. "Something like that. Anyway, I don't want to interrupt your girl time. I just wanted to let you know that despite being attacked by and losing half my shirt to your goat, I got the alternator in and your car is running fine," Zane told her.

"Oh, you're kidding. That's great. Thank you." Bryn stood but didn't know what to do. She couldn't exactly give him a hug with the green goo covering her face. And he'd already told her he wouldn't take any money as payment. But she wanted to offer him something. *Besides myself.* "Can we offer you some pizza? We have plenty."

He peered at the pizza boxes. "You could probably talk me into taking a slice or two to go. I don't want to interfere with all this fun happening in here. I just wanted you to know I finished the car and am heading out."

"You don't have to go," Mandy told him as Bryn moved into the kitchen to grab a plate. "Take off your hat, and we can give you a beauty mask too."

He shook his head and kept his smile in place, but Bryn caught the sadness that passed over his eyes. "There ain't enough guacamole in the world to make this mug beautiful, but I appreciate the thought."

"You're beautiful to me," Bryn said so quietly she wasn't sure he even heard the words. But the awkwardness of the phrase being out there had her swallowing and avoiding his eyes as she busied herself with putting two giant slices of pizza on a plate and covering them with foil. "Really, Zane, thank you so much. A couple slices of pizza doesn't seem like enough for fixing my car, and helping with the horses, and, well, just…everything." *Oh yeah… and for kissing me senseless and leaving me weak in the knees.*

"It was nothing."

It hadn't been *nothing* to her. It had been everything. Everything she'd imagined—hot, passionate, thought-robbing. And everything she didn't need. She wanted safe and nice, and nothing about that kiss was safe. It was fraught with heat and danger.

And it was senseless because Zane was leaving anyway—there was no point in starting anything with him. But hearing him say it was *nothing* accompanied by the slight shrug of the shoulders had her chest tightening and left an ugly rock-sized pit in her stomach.

He tipped his head to them. "I'll see you all later."

"Thanks again," Bryn said as she passed the plate to Zane. Their fingers brushed, and she thought she caught a quick catch of his breath. She wanted to hug him or offer to make him dinner or say something, anything, to tell him how much she appreciated all he'd done for her. But she couldn't—not with Elle and Mandy watching their exchange.

She already felt like a fool for standing there gawking at him, green gunk sliding off her cheeks. He looked uncomfortable, like he didn't know what to say either. He was probably anxious to get out of there, already regretting their earlier kiss. She raised a hand in a weak wave. "See ya around."

"Yeah, see ya around," he answered before slipping out the door.

An hour later, Mandy was tucked into bed. The girl had made a valiant effort to stay awake, but Bryn thought she might have been asleep before her head had even sunk into the pillow.

Their faces now washed and moisturized, Bryn and Elle sat on the sofa sipping wine from a bottle Elle had extracted from the cavernous duffel bag.

"Your duffel is like Mary Poppins's carpetbag," Bryn told her, eyeing the duffel. "What else are you going to bring out of there? A spoonful of sugar or a handsome chimney sweep?"

Elle shrugged and offered her a sheepish grin. "I think you've already got your hands full enough with a handsome cowboy who seems to be doing more than sweeping your chimney. He seems to be sweeping you right off your feet."

Bryn laughed. "Not hardly. My feet are still firmly planted on the ground." Even if her heart was trying to soar.

"Are you sure? Because from my vantage point, it seems pretty obvious you like him." She leaned forward to grab her laptop from the coffee table, then sank back into the corner of the sofa.

"It doesn't matter if I like him or not. He's going back to his old job in Montana, so he's not sticking around. And besides, he's so not my type."

Elle arched an eyebrow. "How can tall, dark, and delicious not be your type? Isn't that everyone's type?"

Heat flared to Bryn's cheeks. An impish grin stole across her face. "The man is delicious." She swallowed, flooded with the memories of their kiss, of the way his strong arms had circled her waist and drug her against his solid chest. *Shut it down, girl.* There was more to Zane Taylor than soft lips and hard muscles—but *oh*, his lips were so soft. She cleared her throat. "But being hot isn't always enough. He's also broody and wounded and—"

Elle covered her heart with her hands and let out an exaggerated love-struck sigh. "*Sooo* gorgeously broody."

Bryn cocked an eyebrow.

"And?" Elle asked, ignoring the glare and opening her computer to sign on.

"And I'm done trying to save men," Bryn told her. "And hurting myself in the process."

Elle had been clicking the keyboard as they talked. She let out a tiny gasp, then raised her eyes, offering Bryn a measured look and a smirk over the edge of the laptop. "So, are you *not* trying to save him by kissing him like your life depends on it?"

Bryn gasped. "What are you talking about? How do you know I kissed him? I mean…" She cut her eyes to the empty popcorn bowl on the coffee table. "I never said I kissed him."

Elle chuckled. "Apparently six hundred and twenty-four people know you kissed him. At least that's how many have reacted to the Facebook live video so far." She turned the laptop so Bryn could see the screen.

The display was open to the horse rescue Facebook page that Tess had set up. And frozen in the middle of the screen was a picture of Bryn and Zane, their arms wrapped around each other and their lips locked in a passionate kiss.

CHAPTER 9

"Oh no," Bryn said, her voice a hushed whisper.

"Oh yes," Elle said, studying the screen. "And you're getting more likes and several heart and smiley-face reactions as we speak."

Bryn's eyes widened as she raised her hand to cover her mouth. "Zane is going to be so mad. He hates having his picture taken, and he already told me he didn't want to be on the camera."

"Well, he's on it now. And he's a hit. Although his cowboy hat covers most of his face. Which is actually kind of great because the majority of the comments have to do with trying to figure out who the mystery cowboy is that you're sucking face with. This is so great."

"This is so *not* great. I told him we just set the cameras up for people to watch the horses, and that no one even knew about the video feed."

"Maybe they didn't then. But they do now."

"How did this even happen? I thought the feed ran for like an hour. How did it stop on that one spot?"

"This is just a few minutes of the feed. Looks like someone snipped just the kiss and reposted that tiny segment. It could have been your friend who was helping with the page, or it could have just been someone who saw the video and clipped that one part."

Bryn dropped her head into her hands. "This is awful."

"No, this is awesome," Elle said, her voice rising with giddiness. "We couldn't *pay* for this kind of marketing. An organic viral spread is the best kind of advertising you can get. You might not be excited about having hundreds of people seeing you make out with a hot cowboy, but this is the perfect thing to help with the horse rescue operation. People love a good romance. I'll bet the donations start pouring in." She clicked a few more times and let out a squeal. "Gah! Your GoFundMe campaign already has close to five hundred dollars in it."

"Five hundred dollars? Are you kidding?" Well, dang. Zane was going to be mad, but her horses were going to be fed. She could afford a lot of hay and grain with five hundred dollars.

"No, I'm not kidding." She turned the screen back toward Bryn. "I'm telling you, people love a good story. And your page is giving them one. You've got these poor abandoned horses, which would have been enough to tug at anyone's heartstrings, but now they have a budding hot romance to watch too."

"Our romance isn't budding. Or hot."

Elle lifted a brow.

"Okay. It is hot. Like crazy hot. I thought I would die this afternoon when he kissed me. But it was only the one kiss. And then Brody drove up, and Zane pulled away like I'd suddenly caught fire." She picked at the seam of her pajama pants. "That doesn't sound like a guy who's interested in any kind of romance, budding or otherwise."

"In my opinion, actions speak louder than words. And by the looks of his actions, and the way his hand is gripping your waist, he is plenty interested."

"Thanks for having her over," Brody said the next morning when he picked Mandy up. "I know she had a great time."

"We all did," Bryn said, squeezing the girl in a hug, then helping her load her stuff into her dad's truck. Mandy climbed in and pulled the door shut, giving Bryn a little wave through the window. She waved back, then walked with Brody around to his side of the truck. "I think all three of us needed a girls' night in." Bryn had texted him the night before to make sure he was okay with Elle spending the night at her house. He'd answered he was fine with it and that he trusted Bryn's judgment.

Which was kind of funny, since she wasn't sure she trusted her own judgment lately.

"Well…uh…I'm glad you had fun. And speaking of fun…" He studied a spot in the driveway where a weed was coming up through the dirt. "I was thinking if *you* wanted to have some fun. Or like, you know, if you think you might need a night out instead of in, I'd be glad to take you." He ground the weed with the toe of his boot. "Just something simple. Like going to dinner, maybe. Or whatever. If you want, I could take you to Taco Tuesday at the Creed. They put on a pretty good spread," he suggested, referring to the local restaurant and pub, the Creedence Tavern.

"Oh. You mean like a date?" *A date?* With Brody? Where was this coming from? Although, wasn't this what she'd been saying she wanted? A nice, safe guy who was steady and reliable? But it was Brody. She'd known him forever. He was more like a brother—albeit a really cute brother—than a dating prospect.

He shrugged, his cheeks brightening with the slightest shade of pink. "I guess. Or like a whatever."

"I usually help out with senior bingo night at the community center on Tuesdays." Why did she say that? This was her chance to go out on a date with a real live nice guy, and she'd just made it sound like she'd prefer senior bingo night to his company. "But maybe I can get out of it this week."

"Okay. Yeah, sure. No problem. Whatever you think. It was just an idea. You know, a way to say thanks for keeping Mandy for me."

Oh. So maybe he wasn't thinking it was a date-date. But he'd said the word *date.* "It was no trouble. I love Mandy. And besides, our sleepover was supposed to be a way for me to say thanks to you for helping with the vet visits."

He shrugged again. "I was glad to help. And not everyone is willing to hang out with a ten-year-old girl. Even if she is as charming as that one." He jerked a thumb toward the girl in the truck.

"We had a great time. I was happy to do it."

"All right then. I'll be back in a few days to check on the horses." He gave her an awkward hug. Which was weird since he'd hugged her many times. But not usually after he'd colossally failed at asking her out on a date.

"Okay. Sounds good," she told him. "And I'll let you know for sure about Tuesday."

"Sure. You've got my number. Call anytime."

Bryn had showered and dressed for her afternoon shift and was sitting on the floor watching the puppies when she heard a car drive up. Her house had become more popular in the last few weeks than it had been all year.

Four of the puppies were asleep, but one was rooting around and climbing over two of the others, trying to wiggle into a warm spot between his siblings. Bryn grinned at his little puppy tail furiously wagging as he squished himself into a comfy new spot. Their mother—which she, Elle, and Mandy had decided the night before to name Grace—licked their little multi-colored bodies. They had thrown around names for the puppies as well, but Bryn had been reluctant to name them all, since the idea was that she would eventually find homes for them and the new owners would want to name them.

Thinking about splitting up the puppies or giving them away had Bryn's heart aching, but the idea of a rescue wasn't to keep all the animals, but to house them until she could find better homes for them. If she kept them all, she wouldn't be able to help more. And the more thought she'd given to this horse (and puppy) rescue ranch idea, the more she liked it.

She had the room. And if Elle was right, and they could collect donations to help house and feed the animals, she didn't see how she could *not* do it.

A timid knock sounded on the door. Bryn opened it to find Rosalee Boswell, her sixth grade teacher, standing on her porch holding a birdcage with what looked like two miniature parrots inside.

"Mrs. Boswell, hi. Come in," Bryn said, stepping back to let her enter.

"I haven't been your teacher in many years, Bryn. I think you can call me Rosalee." The woman stepped into the house and set the birdcage on the kitchen table. Lucky scrambled over to check it out.

"Yes, ma'am. I mean yes, Rosalee." She gestured toward the kitchen. "How have you been? Can I get you some water or a cup of coffee? The pot should still be warm."

The woman stared down at her hands. "No, thank you, dear. I can't stay. I've come to ask you a tremendous favor though. I've heard that you've started an animal rescue here at your ranch."

"Well, I didn't exactly plan it, and it's more of a horse rescue, but yes, I guess."

Rosalee's eyes welled with tears, and her hands fluttered in her purse for a tissue. "I'm afraid I'm in need of a rescue."

"Oh no. What happened?" Her past teacher had

always lived in a neat yellow house a few blocks from the school. "I mean, of course. I've got a spare bedroom, if you need it."

The other woman chuckled. "Oh, you are a dear, Bryn. But I don't mean *I* need to be rescued. It's my birds. I'm moving back to Kansas to live with my son and his family, and I can't bring the birds with me. One of their kids is allergic. I've tried everyone I can think of. Well, everyone I would trust with my birdies. But I can't find them a home. I'm hoping you can keep them and hopefully find a suitable place for them."

"Wow." Bryn peered into the birdcage, relieved that her former teacher wasn't actually planning to move in. "I've never had a bird before."

"These are lovebirds. Their names are Ralph and Rosie. And they haven't been apart in over a decade."

"I'm sorry. This must be so hard for you." Bryn patted her shoulder.

"It is. But I'm at my wits' end. I can't take them with me, and I know you've got a good heart and will take care of them. I trust that you'll do your best to find a good home for them."

"I will. I promise." The birds were cuddled together on a perch in the cage. One tweeted and ruffled its feathers. "They're gorgeous."

"They are, aren't they? See how the one is a little rounder and has just a bit darker blue to his tail feathers? That's Ralph. Rosie is a little more delicate." She peered lovingly in at the birds. "They'll sit on your finger, and they love to listen to music. Did you know lovebirds mate for life? These two will feed each other. And they pine for each other if they get separated."

Bryn had a feeling Rosalee would be pining for her two sweet pets as well. "I'll take good care of them. Don't worry."

"Oh, I know you will. I've got all their toys and food and snacks in the car. I stocked up so you wouldn't have to buy anything for them for months. I also wrote out some instructions on how to care for them and things they like."

"Smart. I'll come out with you and help you carry it in." Bryn followed Rosalee to her car, wondering how the heck she was going to find a home for two ten-year-old lovebirds. She would have to ask Elle to come up with a cute post about them for her Facebook page.

Rosalee filled Bryn's arms with bird food, toys, a mini birdbath, and an industrial-size container of millet sprays. The idea of having the lovebirds was growing on her. They were so cute, and she loved the notion that they mated for life.

She hoisted the box of bird baggage into the house, wistfully wondering if her lovebird life mate was somewhere pining for her.

———————

That night, Bryn found herself pulling up in front of Zane's house. She hadn't planned to drive there. It was almost as if the car had driven itself. So it was really the car's fault. Yeah, and *the car* had also neatly packed a to-go carton with a piece of Zane's favorite pie. She tried to convince herself she was only there to tell him thank you for fixing the vehicle. She'd had a good shift at the diner that afternoon and had enough tip money to offer to pay for at least part of the alternator.

Everything in her was screaming to pull away, keep driving, go home, and eat the lemon meringue pie herself. No good would come from this. A nice guy had asked her out. All she had to do was say yes. So what the hell was she doing sitting in front of Zane Taylor's house, and why couldn't she stop thinking about that last kiss? She turned off the engine and got out before she lost her nerve. She'd never been to Zane's house before. But she'd always known where he lived—in a small rundown house on the outskirts of town, just a few blocks down from the Dairy Queen.

It was dusk, but Bryn could tell someone, she was sure it was Zane, had been recently working on the upkeep of the house. It looked better than it had in years. The lawn was still patchy but had been freshly mowed— she could still smell the fresh-cut grass. The front screen door had been replaced, and the siding wore a fresh coat of blue paint. She could hear the noise of the television and what sounded like a hockey game through the open windows.

Letting out her breath, she clutched the pie container as she walked up the porch steps and knocked on the front door. She heard the volume lower, then jumped as the door jerked open, and she came face-to-face with Zane. She didn't know what she'd expected—a look of surprise or maybe one of his rare smiles that he got when something really tickled him—but it wasn't the angry scowl on his face.

"What the hell are you doing here?"

"Um, well, I…" She took a step back, her breath catching in her throat. What the hell *was* she doing here? And had she really expected Zane to go all giddy with joy at her unannounced visit? "I just stopped by because I wanted to tell you how great my car was running and to say thanks again for fixing it."

"You could've called. Or just sent a text." He looked different. He had on gym shorts, an old faded T-shirt with the sleeves ripped off, and running shoes. She didn't think she'd ever seen him in anything but cowboy boots. And instead of his usual Stetson, he wore a blue-and-red Summit hockey cap turned backward.

"I know. But I wanted to stop by." *I wanted to see you.* "And I had a good day at the diner today and wanted to offer to help pay for the car parts."

"I don't want your money." He pulled the door shut behind him and took her arm to guide her away from the house and toward her vehicle. "Look, I was glad to fix your car. But I don't need you to stop by my house. My dad's not really up for visitors."

His dad, or him?

"Sorry. You're right. Of course. I should have called."

He took off his cap, scrubbed a hand through his hair, then jammed it back on and huffed out a breath. "No, I'm sorry. I'm just not used to having unexpected company."

She stared down at his feet. "I'm not used to seeing you in sneakers. I don't think I've ever seen you wear tennis shoes before." Wow. That was a random reply. But at least it might get them off the subject of her awkward, spontaneous arrival.

He shrugged. "I went for a run earlier."

Her eyes widened. "You run?"

He cocked an eyebrow at her obvious incredulity. "Yes. I run. And not just when someone's chasing me." He offered her the smallest hint of a wry grin, and for the first time since she'd driven up, the tightness in her chest eased. "I picked up the habit when I was in the military, and I guess it stuck. I like it. And it helps to relieve stress."

"Do you have something you're stressed about?"

He glanced back at the house and shrugged again. His eyes were sad as he turned back, but he didn't look at her. Instead, he seemed to look over her shoulder, at something in the distance. He cleared his throat. "You want to walk down to the Dairy Queen? Get some ice cream or something?"

She was definitely interested in the "or something." She thrust out the paper bag containing the takeout container. "Actually, I brought you some pie. It's lemon meringue."

Another smile tugged at the corners of his lips. "That's my favorite."

"I know."

She took a step closer, the pull of him like a magnet drawing her in. Something about him seemed different. In these clothes, this setting, he seemed younger, more vulnerable. And all she wanted to do was wrap her arms around his waist and hold him to her.

His shoulders relaxed, and he leaned in to her—just the slightest movement, but she felt it. Felt the nearness of him in the way her skin tingled and the sudden shortness of her breath. She wanted to reach out, to touch him, even if it was just to rest a hand on his arm or press her fingers to his chest. Or press her body against his and climb him like a tree.

Whoa. Okay, maybe that went a little too far. But seriously, she'd never seen him dressed like this, with so much skin and so freaking darn many muscles on display. His body was like an unexplored playground and she was suddenly ready for recess.

"Hey, boy," Birch's deep voice bellowed from inside the house. "You better get in here. The game's back on."

Like a rubber band snapping back into place, the tenseness returned to Zane's body, and he took a step away from her as the scowl settled back on his face. "I should probably go."

"Of course." The moment was lost, and now she didn't know what to say, how to act. A second ago, she was ready to offer him a hug or throw him down behind her car and jump him, but now she just felt self-conscious and uncomfortable, like she was pushing herself on someone who kept pushing her away. She stared at his shoes again, trying to think of something more to say. "The horses are looking good. If you want to come out and see them tomorrow. Brody said Beauty is putting on weight."

"Good. I'm glad the horse is doing well. I'll try to make it out, but I've got a lot of stuff going on." He avoided her eye as he stared at a spot on the sidewalk. A crop of dandelions sprouted through the crack, their cheerful yellow color in contrast to the stinging barbs on their leaves.

"Oh, yeah. No problem." She stared at the dandelions too, feeling as if Zane's words stung like the sharp points of the weed. Was she pushing herself on him, inserting herself into his life like this dandelion was pushing through the crack in the hard concrete? Did he imagine her as the same kind of nuisance one felt with a dandelion? They were a nice color, but no one wanted them in their yard, and seeing them only caused annoyance.

"So I heard Brody asked you out," Zane said, still staring at the sidewalk.

She glanced up. "How'd you hear that?"

He shrugged. "I don't know. He was out at Logan's this afternoon checking on one of the calves. He must have mentioned it."

Did she detect a trace of jealousy in his voice? Did she want there to be? "He didn't really ask me out. Not like on a date or anything. He just asked me to go to Taco Tuesday with him."

"Sounds like a date to me." He scrubbed a hand across the back of his neck. "Although if he were going to ask you out, it seems like he'd treat you to something better than tacos at the Creed. Their Mexican food leaves something to be desired."

"It's not about the food. It's about the company you're keeping."

He shrugged as if the company she kept was none of his concern. "So what'd you say?"

"I haven't said anything yet."

"Why not?"

"I don't know. Why? Do you think I *should* go out with him?" Gah. Why did she ask that? Was she hoping he'd jump in and tell her not to go? To go out with him instead?

"You're a grown woman. You can go out with whoever you want."

Apparently not. Because the guy she really wanted to go out with was standing in front of her acting like a grade-A ass. She pushed her shoulders back. This was why she wanted to date someone nice, someone without a giant chip resting on his shoulder. Zane always seemed mad at the world, where Brody seemed to stay positive in spite of what the world had thrown at him. Why was she even wasting her time here, sweating through her shirt with nerves, when she could be hanging out with a perfectly nice guy? She should have taken Brody a piece of pie.

She'd show Zane she didn't give two hoots about him. "Maybe I will then."

He finally looked up. Staring into her eyes, his face betrayed no emotion. "I think you should."

She swallowed, fighting not to take a step back. It felt as if he'd punched her in the stomach. Acid seemed to bubble and swirl in her gut as bile rose to her throat. What had she been expecting? For him to beg her not to go and profess his undying love? *Yeah right.*

"Fine," she said, narrowing her eyes as she held his stare. "I will."

"Fine. Do it."

"Fine." He wanted to call her bluff? She'd show him. She pulled out her phone and tapped Brody's number. He answered on the first ring. "Hey, Brody. This is Bryn. Is your offer still good for *taking me out* to Taco Tuesday?"

"Of course," he said.

"Then I'm in. It sounds like fun."

"Great. Pick you up at your place around six tomorrow night?"

"Six o'clock sounds perfect," she said, her gaze drilling into Zane's. "See you then." She jabbed the screen to disconnect the call and stuffed the phone back into her pocket.

"Sounds like you've got yourself a date," Zane said, his expression still a hard blank.

"Sounds like I do." She turned and yanked open her car door. "I'll see you around, Zane. Enjoy the pie." She slid into her car and started the engine, tearing away from his house before he saw the stupid tears welling in her eyes.

Zane slammed through the front door and swore as he caught his toe on the edge of the sofa.

"Watch your language," Birch scolded. "And sit down. You're missing the game. The other team just got a penalty, and we've still got a minute and a half on this power play."

Zane rolled his eyes at the hypocritical reprimand. His dad swore like a sailor. He tossed the bag onto the coffee table and slumped into the ratty recliner across from his dad. The collie had been waiting for him by the door and now sank down onto the floor by his feet. She rested her head on the top of his shoe.

"Was that little gal the one that waits tables down at the diner? Callahan's granddaughter?" Birch asked.

Zane grunted his concurrence.

"What'd she want?"

"I did some work on her car, and she just stopped by to tell me thanks."

"What kind of work?"

"Switched out the alternator."

"Did you clean the battery terminals and posts before you installed it?"

Zane sighed. "Course I did."

"Did you balance the fan and pulley?"

"Yes, Dad," he snapped. "I know how to install an alternator."

Birch held up his hands in surrender. "All right. Geez, calm down. I just asked a simple question." He pointed to the coffee table. "So what's in the bag?"

"She brought me a piece of pie to say thank you."

"I figured it was something like that. Can't imagine a pretty girl like her being interested in an ugly mutt like you."

An inky darkness settled into his gut. He couldn't imagine what Bryn would see in an ugly mutt like him either. He pushed the container toward his father—the thought of eating it now causing his stomach to roil—then sank farther into the chair and turned his focus to the game. "You can have it," he muttered. "I'm not hungry anyway."

———

The next night, Bryn leaned into the bathroom mirror as she stroked on a last dab of mascara and applied a smear of shimmery pink lip gloss. That was about the extent of her makeup expertise. She took a step back and studied her reflection. Not bad. She'd chosen a simple black skirt, some low wedge sandals, and a soft pink button-up blouse for her "date" with Brody tonight. She knew it wasn't *really* a date. No matter what Zane said. It was just Taco Tuesday at the Creed, just a casual dinner out.

She'd embarrassed herself in front of Zane the night before. He'd called her bluff, but she'd show him. She was determined to have fun tonight. And why wouldn't she? Brody was a terrific guy. They got along great, and he always made her laugh. Plus he was crazy cute. He was just the kind of guy she was looking for—nice, cute, sweet, funny. Did she already mention nice?

Stop it. Nice was a *good* thing. Just the kind of thing she wanted. Not dangerous or pulse-pounding, but there was still something to be said for steady and dependable.

She let out a sigh, then forced her lips into a smile. *Tonight will be fun.* She glanced at the clock—still close to an hour before Brody would pick her up. Time to throw in a load of laundry and take some sugar cubes out to the horses.

Turning from the sink, her heart jumped to her throat as she heard a noise coming from the kitchen. It sounded like bootheels on the hardwood floor.

Someone was in her house.

CHAPTER 10

BRYN TENSED, HER MUSCLES TIGHT AS SHE STRAINED to hear another movement. Glancing around the bathroom, she searched for a weapon, something she could use to protect herself. Her choices were limited unless the burglar was averse to having his hair conditioned or his nails painted. She patted her pocket for her cell phone to call the police. Shoot—she'd left it lying on the counter in the kitchen.

Poking her head out the door, she spied the ironing board set up in the spare bedroom and the iron sitting on top of it. It had been her grandmother's, so it was the old style and still had some heft to it. It wasn't the greatest weapon choice, but it was better than the colander she'd tried to save Zane with the other day.

She snuck across the hall, grabbed it, then crept slowly down the hallway, the iron held tightly in her hand. Who would break into her house? Although "breaking in" was a bit of a stretch, since she didn't often lock her doors. And even Otis, the goat, knew how to sneak his way in. But as pesky as that goat was, he didn't usually wear boots, and she was sure she'd heard bootheels walking across the floor.

But what could they possibly want? It wasn't like she had a lot of valuables—no new electronics or fancy jewelry. She did have a laptop, but she was frugal with her money and hardly ever purchased anything new. Hence why she was facing down an intruder with a twenty-year-old iron.

A sudden thought sent ice through her veins. Could it be one of the guys she bought the horse from? Raleigh? Or had Gator come back to make good on his promise of getting her to do what he wanted or to try to take the horse back? Or worse, to try to take her?

She'd shut all the dogs in her bedroom before getting in the shower, since the hair dryer tended to scare Lucky. Now she wondered if she shouldn't let them out. Not that a three-legged mutt and a half-starved mama dog with five puppies in tow would do much to protect her. But maybe their fierce barking might scare an intruder off before she had to face them down.

Deciding against riling them, best to let sleeping dogs lie and all that, she gripped the iron tighter as she cautiously leaned out of the hallway and peered around the corner.

In the kitchen, the refrigerator door was open and a man was leaning into it. All she could see were jean-clad legs and large male boots, and both were scuffed with red dirt. What kind of burglar robs the fridge?

Apparently a hungry one. But maybe this could work in her favor. Maybe she could get the jump on him while he was distracted with searching for the bologna. She crept closer, then froze as the fridge door slowly shut.

She tensed, ready to attack, the iron held high as the man came into view.

"Holy shit, Buck," she said, lowering the iron and pressing her free hand to her chest as she spied the familiar face of her brother, a slice of cold pizza hanging from his mouth. "You scared the hell out of me."

"Sorry, Sis. I didn't know you were home. I was looking for something to eat."

"Looks like you found something."

He tore a bite off the crust and talked while he chewed. "Good pizza."

She set the iron on the kitchen counter, then stepped forward to give him a hug. Holding him close, her emotions warred with thoughts of how glad she was to see him and know he was okay and wondering what he wanted this time. "What are you doing here?"

He pushed back his hat and leaned his hips casually against the counter. "Can't a guy come home just to visit his favorite sister?"

"I'm your *only* sister," she said, ignoring the trademark Bucky charm that he often used to get him out of scrapes or uncomfortable situations. "And you're evading the question."

"Geez, lighten up, Sis. I'm just passing through on my way to a rodeo in Fort Collins. Stopped in to say hi. I thought you'd be glad to see me."

Another warning bell went off in her head. Her little brother knew how to play her like a fiddle, employing a tactic he often used of trying to make her feel like she was the one who was wrong or being too sensitive. Unfortunately, his tactics too often worked.

"Of course I'm glad to see you," she assured him. And she was. She'd spent way too many nights praying over the well-being of her brother. He lived a crazy life of chasing rodeos and climbing onto pissed-off eighteen-hundred-pound bulls. But he looked good. A little skinny and in need of a haircut, but still, he looked good.

"I didn't think you were here," he told her as he jerked a thumb toward the driveway. "I mean, I saw your car outside, but not Gramps's truck. So I figured you were out."

Didn't stop you from coming in and helping yourself to my food though, did it?

Stop it. He's your brother, she argued with herself.

She'd been taking care of and feeding him for the better part of her life. Why would he expect anything different from her now? Just because he hadn't lived here in years didn't mean he wouldn't assume he could still help himself to the refrigerator.

He eyed her suspiciously. "You didn't sell the truck, did you? 'Cause I know you can sometimes get a pretty penny for an old classic like that one."

"No, I didn't sell it. I just loaned it to a friend." Okay, that was a bit of a stretch. More like *he* borrowed it from her. And without any intention of ever giving it back. But she wasn't ready to share that with her brother yet.

Buck grunted. "Must be some friend."

Yeah, Pete was *some friend* all right. The kind she could do without. But thinking about Pete was another good reminder of why going out with Brody tonight was a smart move. The likelihood Brody would take off with her car was slim.

Time to change the subject. "Did you see the new horses?"

"Yeah, they look pretty good." He chuckled. "That little one is cute, in like a funny old man kind of way."

She laughed. "He totally is. His name is Shamus. You should have seen him when he arrived. He was a mess."

"Have you decided what you're going to do with them? You planning to sell 'em?"

Why did everything come down to the almighty dollar with him?

"No, I'm not going to *sell* them. I *just* rescued them. And right now, all I'm working on is trying to keep them fed and alive."

"Yeah, I heard people all over town are donating money to your cause." His gaze raked over the donation jars sitting on the counter, and Bryn wished she had put them away earlier.

She grabbed the jars, shoved them into the pantry, and closed the door. "Don't even think about it. That money is to pay for the food and care of the animals. I don't just have the horses. I've got six dogs now, plus Otis is still around too."

"Otis, that ornery goat?" Buck patted his stomach and offered her a charming grin. "You know, I'm a hungry animal too."

"You can find your own food."

"Yeah, yeah. I'm just teasing you, Sis." He gave her arm

an affectionate nudge. "I'm doing fine. It's amazing how little food you actually need to live on. And I like boxed mac and cheese and peanut butter and jelly sandwiches. Although I might talk you out of that loaf of bread and the package of bologna I saw in the fridge."

Guilt settled in her stomach like a rock sinking to the bottom of a lake. "Of course you can have it. I'll put some stuff together for you to take. How long are you staying?"

And *where* was he staying? She wished she had the guts to tell him he couldn't stay at the house. It wasn't that she didn't love seeing him, but it seemed like every time he came home, he left with something of hers. He didn't outright steal it. The things he took belonged to their grandfather or had been part of the house or the farm. And he always had a reason for taking them and left with a promise to bring them back just as soon as he got the next job or won the next purse.

Except he never seemed to get that next job and the purses he won seemed to disappear as soon as they arrived in his hands. She didn't really need all those things anyway. But she did need her brother. So what else could she do?

"I'm not staying," he told her. "Just stopped in to say hi as I drove down the pass. I need to be in Fort Collins by tonight, so I can get registered in the morning."

She wasn't sure if she was disappointed or relieved. She would have liked to have some time to catch up with him, to hear what was new in his life. And spending time with her brother would be a great excuse to wiggle out of her date. "Listen, I'm supposed to be going to dinner with Brody Tate tonight, but I'm sure I could cancel. Or maybe you could come with us. We're just going to the Creed for tacos."

He shook his head. "As much as I love the Creed's tacos and their frozen margaritas, I don't have time to stay for dinner." He glanced up at the clock above the stove. "I need to be on the road in about thirty minutes."

"Dang." And double dang that her scheme to sabotage her date had failed.

"You do look nice though," Buck told her, giving her outfit the once-over. "But since when did you start going out with Brody Tate?"

"We're not *going out*. We're just going to get some tacos. And it's kind of a new thing."

"Nice. Bagged yourself a doctor. Maybe you can get out of this dump and we can finally sell the place."

"I said we're getting tacos, not getting married. And I'm not interested in ever selling this place. I love it. It's my home. It's the only place I've ever felt *has* been a home to me. To us." She was surprised at the well of emotion in her throat.

Buck must have caught it too. His expression softened. "Sorry, Sis. I didn't come here to argue. I just wanted to see you and get a Bryn hug." He opened his arms, and she stepped into them.

———

Sweat soaked the back of his T-shirt as Zane ran down the side of the road. He'd spent the day trying to get his mind off Bryn and her visit to his house the night before, but all his attempts had failed. He'd changed into shorts and sneakers when he'd got home from work and had hoped a hard run would do the trick.

Taking off from his house, he'd tried to clear his mind, focus on the run. So how the hell had he ended up at the end of Bryn's driveway? He'd turned his brain off, tried not to think, or maybe he'd been lost in thought. Either way, his feet had carried him here...to Bryn.

He paced the highway, debating if he should walk down to her house. It wouldn't hurt to check on the horses. And he could just say hi to Bryn. Offer her an apology. She didn't deserve the way he'd treated her the night before. She'd brought him a piece of pie, for Pete's sake. He should have thanked her, invited her in. Yeah right. Then maybe she and Birch could have a nice conversation about what a loser he was. *No thanks.*

He checked his watch. A little past five thirty. Plenty of time before Brody picked her up for their date. Damn. This was stupid. He shouldn't be walking down her driveway right before her date. Especially a date he practically forced her into going on.

No, he didn't force her. She made the choice—the smart decision to go to dinner with Brody. Who was a great guy and perfect for her, he reminded himself.

But if Brody was so perfect, whose beat-up Chevy truck was parked in front of her house? It had Colorado plates, but he didn't recognize the rig. A knot formed in his chest. What if it belonged to that asshole Pete? Could the guy be brazen enough to come back and try to take something more from Bryn?

Or maybe it was Brody picking her up early. Cheap bastard was probably trying to get to the Creed in time for happy hour to save money on their drinks. Except Brody wasn't a bastard—cheap or otherwise. And he didn't seem the type to drive a beat-up old truck. *No, that's my deal.*

Just walk away. It wasn't too late to turn around. No dogs had barked a greeting. No one even had to know he was here. Except his feet kept walking, across the driveway, and up the steps of the porch.

The house was lit from within, and a movement caught his eye. Bryn was in the kitchen talking to a tall guy. Zane couldn't see his face but his build didn't match Brody's. And he *could* see Bryn's face. She was smiling at the guy with real affection. The man opened his arms, and Bryn stepped into his embrace. And it *was* an embrace. She wasn't just hugging the guy, but was really holding on to him.

Zane didn't know who the man was, but he obviously meant something to Bryn, and suddenly he felt like an intruder. Like a voyeur who'd just infringed on a private moment. He turned away, his face hot with shame.

Taking the porch steps two at a time, he took off at a sprint the second his feet hit the dirt. Arms pumping, he tore back down the driveway and onto the highway.

His heels flung dust in their wake as he flew up the road. Oblivious to the burn in his lungs or the pain in his side, he pushed his body as he tried to outrun the desperate insecurities clawing at his back.

———————

An hour later, Zane stomped through the Creedence Country Mart, a black cloud following him through the aisles of the grocery store. He'd taken a shower when he got home, trying to wash off the dust and the image of Bryn in another man's embrace. And not the man she was currently out on a date with. The shower hadn't worked and neither had watching television with his dad.

He was restless and cagey and needed to get out of the house. He'd pulled into the grocery store thinking he might pick up a steak and try to drown his sorrows in a thick slab of red meat. He tossed a bag of chips into his cart and wheeled it into the next aisle.

The brightly colored packages of cookies on the display shelves caught his eye, and he stopped to stare at the choices, trying to focus on the flavors. Did he feel like chocolate chip or peanut butter? Had Brody already picked Bryn up? Were they already at the Creed? Was he feeding her tortilla chips and telling her corny veterinarian jokes?

What did he care? He'd practically pushed her into the date. Forced her hand so she was now at the Creed, laughing and sipping margaritas with the good doctor.

That was what he'd wanted. Right?

He picked up a bag of Oreos and threw them toward his cart. They hit the edge and fell over the side, hitting the floor and sliding into the hot-pink high heels of the woman walking into the aisle.

"Whoa," she said, staring from him to the cookies and back to him again. "What did those cookies do to you?"

He let out a sigh. "Sorry, Kimmie. I didn't mean to launch those at you." He knew the woman from high school. She'd been in a different grade than him, but in a small school, everybody pretty much knew everybody. Plus at one point she'd dated Logan.

"I just go by Kim now. Or Kimberly. And it's okay. I have kids, it's not the first time food's been tossed at me." She smiled as she bent to pick up the Oreos and flashed him a view of her cleavage. He averted his eyes. There was only one woman he was interested in looking at right now, and she was eating enchiladas with the animal doctor. Kim's snug jeans hugged her body, and her hips swayed as she walked toward him and handed him the bag of cookies. "What's got you so worked up that you're pitching Double Stufs across the grocery store?"

"I'm not worked up," he growled. "Just had a bad day."

She chuckled in that knowing way that women did when they knew you were lying but they still understood. Her eyes narrowed as she offered him a seductive stare. "I've heard a cold beer and a warm body is the best remedy for a bad day."

He shook his head. "I'm afraid I'm not very good company."

Kim shrugged and glanced around the grocery store aisle. "You're better than the company I'm currently in, which is no one." She ran a long pink-tipped fingernail down his arm. "Come on. One beer. No strings. I could use one too. Or maybe we could grab something to eat. Just a couple of old friends sharing a meal. Have you had supper?"

"Nah." He hadn't been hungry. But now he studied the woman in front of him. He'd known her a long time. She had a hellcat temper if she was crossed, but she could also be sweet. He'd heard she was recently divorced and looking for the next Mr. Kimberly. That wasn't him. But it didn't mean they couldn't grab a bite together. As old friends. "You feel like tacos?"

She grinned. "Taco Tuesday at the Creed? Hell yeah. I'm in. I'd trade my firstborn for a margarita right about now."

"Keep your kid. I'm buying." He glanced at the bag of cookies she still held. "Ditch the Oreos. Let's go."

She tossed the bag into the cart, leaving it in the middle of the aisle as she followed him from the store.

Turned out Kimberly wasn't interested in having dinner as "old friends." Not if the way she'd grazed his thigh with her hand for the third time now was any indication. Zane scooted back on the barstool and popped another chip into his mouth. He peered over Kim's shoulder as he chewed.

He'd spotted Bryn and Brody in a booth in the back corner of the restaurant when they'd come in, so he'd picked one of the high-top tables in the bar area for him and Kim. She'd ordered frozen margaritas and was halfway through a basket of chips by the time the tacos arrived.

Bryn's back was to him, so she hadn't seen him yet. It wasn't too late to ditch this stupid idea and hightail it out of the tavern, leave the tacos and head home to lick his wounds. The better man had won. Leave it at that.

Except Zane hadn't even thrown his hat in the ring. Brody had won because Zane had forfeited the game. He hadn't even tried.

He tried to focus on Kim, but she was telling another story about her ex, and his gaze drifted back to the corner of the restaurant. His pulse quickened as Bryn slid from the booth.

This was it. One more second, and she would see him. The restrooms were behind him, so she'd have to pass by them if that was her destination. She turned and started walking his way, but her steps faltered, and she paused as she caught sight of him. Her mouth opened, forming a perfect O—damn, he did love her mouth—and her eyes widened as she glanced from him to Kimberly, then back to him again. After what seemed like ten minutes but was probably only ten seconds, she finally blinked. Then her posture changed, her shoulders tensing and her eyes narrowing as she marched toward their table.

She offered Kim a curt nod, then leaned in toward

him, the high stool he sat on making his head even with hers. "What are you doing here?" she asked, her voice low as her teeth practically clenched together. "I thought you said the Creed's tacos left something to be desired."

Her perfume swirled in the air around him, making it hard for him to come up with a coherent thought. He scoured his brain for hockey stats as he glanced at Kimberly, then back to Bryn, keeping his eyes cool, his expression bland. "I seem to recall you saying it wasn't about the tacos but about the company you were keeping." As if on cue, Kim lifted her hand and rested it territorially on his.

Bryn couldn't keep a bland expression if she tried, but the surprise and hurt that crossed her face both pleased and pained Zane. He didn't mind Bryn being a little jealous, but he didn't want to hurt her. He pulled his hand away from Kim's.

She pushed her shoulders back to stand taller. "Well, don't let me keep you from your company then. By all means, enjoy your food."

As hard as he tried not to, he watched her walk away. He had to fight to keep his dumb ass in the chair when what he really wanted to do was go after her, lift her off her feet, and carry her out of there. Screw the tacos and all this nonsense of keeping other company. The only company he was interested in was hers.

He drew his eyes away and turned back to Kim. She offered him a cool stare, one eyebrow lifted. "I wish I would've known the reason you asked me here was to make another woman jealous. I would have ordered a more expensive entrée."

"That wasn't the reason I asked you—" He stopped short as she raised her eyebrow higher. "Okay, maybe it was part of the reason."

"A woman knows when she's being used as a diversion."

"Every day is a diversion from something," he muttered, avoiding her eyes.

She shrugged. "True enough. And it's not that I mind being a diversion, but if I would've known, I could've at least played my role better."

He let out a sigh. "Sorry, Kimmie. I'm an asshole."

"Maybe. Probably. But I'm still getting a free meal out of the deal and something to do on the night my ex has the kids. Plus, I'm earning tons of street cred around town for landing a date with one of Creedence's most notorious lone wolves. I'll bet my phone will be ringing with questions from envious women or with another dinner offer by noon tomorrow."

"I don't know anything about all that, but I am paying for the meal and the margaritas. And you should order yourself some dessert."

"Oh, I'm planning to. I love their fried ice cream." She took another sip of her drink. "I don't get it though. If you like Bryn, why didn't you just ask her out instead of me?"

He let out another sigh. "Even if I did like her, which I'm not saying I do, that doesn't mean I'm any good for her. Bryn is a nice person. She deserves better than someone like me."

Kimberly burst out with a hard laugh. "Holy crap, I hope we don't all end up with the someone we *deserve*. If that's the way it's going to be, then I need to stop looking now and just resign myself to a life as a single mom."

"You can joke, but Bryn doesn't need a 'notorious lone wolf.'" *What a stupid expression.* "She needs someone good. Someone who will treat her right and keep her safe." *And not the son of the town drunk.*

"Do you think you wouldn't treat her right?"

He narrowed his eyes. "Come on. You know the life I come from. How the hell am I supposed to know how to treat anyone right?"

"Because you sure as hell know how *not* to treat someone."

He shrugged again. "Whatever. All I know is she deserves someone better than me."

Kim took another sip of her drink, studying him over the rim of her salt-crusted glass. "I didn't realize you thought Bryn Callahan was stupid."

He reared back, his shoulders tensing as if ready to fight. "I never said she was stupid. She's one of the smartest women I know. She's juggling a farm and a thankless job as a waitress, and she still has time to rescue animals in need."

"Oh, so you *do* think she's intelligent?"

"Of course I do."

"Then why don't you trust her judgment when it comes to choosing the kind of man she wants to go out with?"

Her reasoning hit him like a punch to his gut. He had no response. Then he remembered the last guy Bryn had gone out with, the one who'd acted like he cared then stolen her blind. "Bryn may be smart, but she's lacking in common sense when it comes to choosing men. Brody's a much better choice for her. In fact, I even encouraged her to go out with him."

"Speaking from the perspective of most women, I'm sure she appreciated you making that choice for her."

Her sarcasm was not lost on him. He tossed back the rest of his frozen margarita, cringing at the brain freeze. "I didn't realize you were such an expert at relationships."

Kim shrugged. "I'm no expert. In fact, I have a history sort of like yours, but I try to learn from my mistakes."

"I do too." Which was why he was staying away from Bryn. Kimberly may have had a similar background growing up—it was no secret in town her mom had a drinking problem—but she didn't know his history. Didn't know the things he'd seen, the things he'd done. She didn't know about Sarah.

He peered down at his plate, the congealed orange grease next to the taco shell suddenly making his stomach turn. His appetite gone, he just wanted to leave. This had been a dumb idea, impulsive and reckless. Just like him. "I'm done. You okay getting that fried ice cream to go?"

Twenty minutes later, he dropped Kim off at her car where she'd left it in the grocery store parking lot. She'd given him one last half-hearted offer of having a drink at her house, which they both knew didn't have anything to do with an actual drink. But he declined, and she didn't seem to really care either way.

"Thanks for dinner." She held up the take-out container. "And the fried ice cream."

"You bet." He was tempted to say maybe they could do this again sometime—it seemed the right thing to do—but he knew he wasn't interested in doing this again. And most likely, neither was she. It was kind of an asshole thing to do to just wave and drive off. But then again, hadn't it been well established already that he was kind of an asshole?

He did wait for her to get in her car and pull out of the parking lot before he muttered, "See ya around."

Putting the truck in gear, he pulled out behind her and turned toward his house. He caught a glimpse of himself in the rearview mirror, the jagged scar a constant reminder of his self-worth. Or lack of self-worth. He was nothing. Nobody. Bryn was good and kind, and she deserved a good man. One she didn't have to be ashamed of. One who didn't wake up at one in the morning with night terrors, and one who didn't hurt the people he loved.

She deserved a guy who took care of animals and was sweet to his kid. She deserved Brody Tate.

Later that night, after Brody had dropped her off, Bryn poured a glass of wine, then sank into the corner of her sofa. She'd changed into her pajamas, a pair of sleep shorts and a little tank top, and pulled her hair into a messy bun. Not the ending some women would hope for after a date with a handsome veterinarian, but it worked for Bryn.

She'd had a nice time with Brody. It was obvious as he picked her up and they drove into town that they were both a little uncomfortable in the role of "date" instead of "friend." They'd never had trouble chatting before, but tonight their conversation was initially stilted as they reached for things to talk about. But after settling into the booth and ordering some food, they fell back into more of their normal rhythm.

It helped that they'd known each other a long time, so they could talk about people in town, some of his latest cases, Bryn's new horses, and, of course, Mandy. That was a topic Brody could talk about all night. His eyes lit up and a broad smile creased his face whenever he talked about her. She was his pride and joy. And the feelings were well deserved—Bryn thought the world of the ten-year-old girl.

Their date might have gone better if she hadn't spotted Zane when she'd got up to go to the bathroom. The nerve of that guy. Pushing her into this date, trashing the food at the Creed, then showing up there with a date of his own. That took a hefty-sized set of cojones.

Not that she wanted to think about his cojones. Or about him at all. So why had she just pulled up the horse rescue page on Facebook and opened the video of them kissing? Because she was an idiot, that's why.

Maybe she just wanted to prove to herself that it hadn't been that big a deal. That her chaste good-night kiss earlier from Brody was perfectly acceptable, and she'd only made the kiss with Zane seem more heated and passionate than it really was.

She caught her breath as she stared at the screen, swallowing at the rush of heat that tightened her chest as she watched Zane pull her close and take her mouth in a hard kiss.

Uh, yeah. That was a little different than the kiss with Brody. Especially since they both had turned at the same time and his lips had only hit one side of hers. And there had definitely not been any tongue. Bryn took a long swallow of wine to try to quench her suddenly dry throat.

She watched the kiss twice more, her skin heating more with each viewing. *Stop it.* She had to stop. This was only making her crazy—in both her mind *and* her body. She switched to the live feed, hoping that watching the tranquil horses grazing would calm her.

Beauty and Shamus were standing by the fence. That was odd. They didn't usually stand right next to each other. The gray was across the corral, but he turned his head and trotted to the other two. What the heck?

Bryn touched the screen to make the view larger and let out a gasp. A chill ran through her as she stared at the dark figure of a man standing at the fence.

CHAPTER 11

BRYN COULDN'T MAKE OUT HIS FEATURES IN THE DARK, but she could definitely tell it was a man. And a tall one.

Seriously? What the hell was going on? First her brother mysteriously appeared in her kitchen and scared the hell out of her, now another strange man was sneaking around her corral. Well, this time she wasn't scared—she was pissed off. This was her property, and she was done being afraid of who was showing up on it.

She pushed off the sofa and raced to the front closet. Searching the contents, she grabbed an old baseball bat of her brother's. A can of bear spray sat on the top shelf, and she grabbed that too. Yanking open the front door, she stepped onto the porch and screamed into the dark. "Whoever the hell is out here, I want you to know I've got a gun, and I'm not afraid to use it."

The light from the porch only illuminated a small circle. She held her breath as she peered into the inky blackness of the farmyard. One of the horses whinnied, and she could hear hoofbeats trot across the corral.

"Don't shoot," a voice called from the dark. "It's just me."

"Zane?"

She let out a shaky breath as Zane stepped into the circle of light. He eyed the baseball bat in her hands. "Is that thing loaded?"

She lowered the bat. "No, but this can of bear spray is. And it will deploy a twenty-five-foot hot cloud of pepper spray if I press the nozzle."

"I'd rather you not press the nozzle then." He shielded his eyes with his hand. "Can you hit the light? The moths are going crazy."

She narrowed her eyes, studying him as she set down the bat and the can of bear spray. He was dressed in running clothes again, shorts, sneakers, and another T-shirt with the sleeves ripped off. What did this guy have against sleeves? The front of the shirt was dark with sweat. She swatted at a moth, then reached inside the door and turned off the front porch light. "What are you doing out here?"

He shrugged. "Couldn't sleep. Sometimes when my brain won't shut down, it helps to go for a run."

"And you ran all the way out here?" She leaned a hip against the side of the porch railing as her eyes adjusted to the dark.

He furrowed his brow. "It's not that far. It's only a few miles out of town. We ran farther than that in basic." He moved his head and scanned the corral, as if the horses somehow held the answers he was looking for. "I didn't know I was headed here until my feet turned in to your driveway. They have a way of doing that."

"What? Taking you where you don't want to go?"

He shrugged, then turned his gaze to meet hers. "I don't know. Maybe they take me where I *do* want to go but I'm too stubborn to travel there on my own."

Oh.

She swallowed, suddenly unsure of what to say and trying to look at anything other than the array of skin and hard muscle on display. "So why couldn't you sleep?"

He raised his shoulders again. "Too pissed off, I guess."

Bryn jerked back. "At me? Because you're the one who pushed me to go out with Brody, then showed up at the Creed with a hot date on your arm."

He blinked. "I'm not mad at you."

"Then who are you pissed off at?"

"Myself mostly." He blew out a breath, then turned and sank down onto the top porch step next to her leg. "And circumstances, I guess," she heard him mutter.

She took a tentative step forward and eased down on the step next to him. "What circumstances?"

Zane rolled his shoulders as he rubbed his hand across the back of his neck. "The circumstances that keep a guy like me from going out with a girl like you."

"What the hell is that supposed to mean? If you wanted to go out with me, why didn't you just ask?" Her temper flared at his detached response.

"Come on, Bryn," he scoffed. "You know why."

Okay. This guy was really starting to piss her off. "No, I don't know why. Why don't you enlighten me?"

He shook his head, not speaking, his lips pressed together in a tight line.

She stared hard at him, as if daring him to say he was too good for her. "Come on, Zane. Tell me why a guy like you doesn't want to go out with someone like me. Am I not good enough? Not pretty enough? Don't have boobs as big as Kimmie Cox?"

His eyes widened as he reared back. "Not good enough? What the hell are you talking about? You're *too* good. You're the most beautiful woman I know. And I don't have first-hand knowledge, so to speak, but your boo…" He dropped his gaze to her pajama top, then raised his eyes back to hers. "Your *chest* seems pretty great to me."

Her nipples tightened under his stare, and she suddenly realized she wasn't wearing a bra. And with the thin cotton pajama top, he probably realized it too. She crossed her arms over her chest and offered him a scowl. "Then I don't understand."

He scrubbed a hand over his whiskered jaw. "I know you've met my dad."

"Yeah. So?"

"So that's the kind of man I came from."

"And?"

"Damn it, Bryn." His voice came out in a tortured growl. "Don't make me say it."

"You're going to have to say it because I'm in the dark here. I don't get what your dad has to do with you asking me out."

"He has everything to do with me asking you out. Everything to do with why I can't, I *won't* ask you out." He stared at her, his pain-filled eyes beseeching her to understand. "That's the man who raised me. The only time my old man was nice to me was after he'd knocked me across the floor or whipped me with a belt. The rest of the time he was drilling into me what a no-good loser I am."

She sucked in a breath. "That's not true. You're not a loser."

He pushed up from the steps. "It *is* true. I'm not like you, Bryn. You're good. And kind. You've got a heart as big as that barn. My heart's broken. And I don't mean like that sappy shit in romance movies. I mean it doesn't work. I tried it out once, and that ended in disaster." His jaw tightened as he spoke, and his hands curled into rigid fists. He pounded one against the front of his leg. "Don't you see? I'm no good. I've heard it all my life, and I know it's true. *I'm* broken."

Bryn raised a hand to her mouth, her heart breaking at his words. "No, you're wrong."

His eyes darted up and down the driveway as if looking for an escape. "I *am* wrong. *This* is wrong. I shouldn't be here. You should be with Brody. He's a good man. Or maybe with that other guy you were with this afternoon."

"Other guy? What other guy?"

"The one you were hugging in your kitchen."

Her mind searched for what he was talking about. *Oh for Pete's sake. Seriously?* Her eyes narrowed. "How do you know I was hugging some guy in my kitchen?"

"Because I stopped by earlier. To apologize. Or whatever. But you seemed like you were indisposed."

She threw her hands in the air. "Are you kidding me?

Why didn't you knock on the door? Or let me know you were here? Then you could have seen *my brother*. Because that's who I was hugging in the kitchen. It was Buck. But no, you didn't knock, you just made up your mind and assumed you were right."

He shook his head. "Never mind. It doesn't matter. I should go." He turned and strode up the driveway.

Bryn shoved off the steps and ran after him. She grabbed his arm, and he spun back around, anger flashing in his eyes. His body tensed, but she didn't back down. She planted a hand on her hip. "You can stare daggers at me all you want, Zane Taylor. You don't scare me."

He leaned over her, his broad shoulders menacing as his arms pressed out from his sides. His jaw tightened, and his eyes narrowed into intimidating slits. His voice was low, threatening. "You *should* be scared."

Bryn pressed her shoulders back, standing taller as she jutted out her chin. Her pulse raced, but she didn't back down. "The only thing I'm scared of..." She paused to swallow and try to control the tremble in her voice. She could stand as tall as she wanted, but saying the next words took more than a raised chin. It took guts and the courage to pull up the declarations and say them out loud. She started again. Her voice was quiet, but her resolve was strong, and she didn't waiver. "The only thing I'm scared of is you walking away."

He sighed and dragged a hand down his face. "Damn it, Bryn," he muttered as he shook his head and stared down at his boots. He raised his gaze, his eyes beseeching her to understand. His voice was thick, husky, as if the words hurt his throat to speak. "Don't you get it? I'm trying to head this thing off at the pass before you get hurt. And I guarantee you, being with me is going to hurt. And I couldn't live with myself if I did anything to damage you. I'm not the guy who deserves that sweet look you've got in your eye. I'm not the guy you want."

"How do you know what I want?"

"Because you told me. You said you were looking for someone nice and safe. And I'm *never* gonna be that guy. I'm not the prince in this story. I'm never gonna ride up on a white horse to save the day."

"Who asked you to be?"

"Me," he snarled, leaning toward her and pounding a fist against his chest. "I asked me to be. That's the kind of man you deserve and the kind of man I *want* to be for you. But that's not who I am. And I never will be."

Her throat hurt with each breath she took, and her palms ached where her nails dug into them. *The nerve of this guy.* "You know what, Zane? You are really starting to piss me off." She uncurled one fist and jabbed a finger into his chest. "Do you think I'm stupid?"

He reared his head back. "No."

She jabbed him again. "Do you think I can't make up my own damn mind?"

He covered her hand with his and pressed it hard against his chest. "I think you see the good in everyone, and you're trying to see something in me that just isn't there."

She held his gaze, her jaw tight, determined. "Yes, it is there. I see you for who you are."

"No, you don't. You think you do, but you don't know the things I've seen and done." He slid his hands up her neck and cupped her face in his palms as he pressed his forehead tightly to hers. "You're kind and sweet and so damn beautiful. Sometimes I look at you and have to turn away because the things I feel for you make my chest hurt so hard I think my bones might rip apart. I don't know what to do with that, Bryn. I wish I did. I wish with everything in me that I knew how to be the man for you I want to be so bad. But all I know how to do is hurt people. You're always trying to save everybody, and I see it in your eyes that you think you can save me, but I'm beyond redemption. I'm no good."

"You're good for me," she told him as she reached up and covered his hands with hers. Her voice broke as she whispered, "And did you ever think maybe I'm the one who needs saving? I don't need a knight on a white horse or a storybook prince. I just need you."

His jaw tightened, and he closed his eyes as he pressed his forehead harder against hers. Pulling in a ragged breath, he opened his eyes and dipped his head to slant his lips along hers.

Heat shot through her veins as his mouth ravaged hers. His lips were soft but demanding, and she pressed into him, trying to convey the depth of her feelings through the intensity of the kiss. Which was really freakin' hard since her knees were threatening to give way. She wrapped her arms around his neck and held on to keep from melting into the ground.

He held her face, his palms tender as he deepened the kiss. One hand slid around the back of her head, his fingers tangling in her hair.

They stood in the driveway, holding on to each other as they kissed. A flash of lightning lit the sky—a warning from the heavens perhaps—and small drops of rain started to fall as thunder rumbled in the distance.

"Come on," she said, tugging his hand as she pulled him toward the house.

He studied her for just a moment, his eyes narrowing as if he were trying to make a decision. Another flash of lightning struck, and he twisted his fingers with hers and ran with her to the house.

They jogged up the steps and burst into the house. Lucky looked up from the dog bed in the corner, but Bryn barely noticed. All her attention was on Zane and the feel of his hands and his lips as he lifted her onto the counter in the kitchen and continued what they'd started in the driveway.

His hands were big, strong, and exhilarating as they pulled her to him, then moved over her body, exploring her curves. She pushed his hat off and dug her hands into his thick hair as she wrapped her legs around his waist and lost herself in his kiss, in the feel of him against her.

She'd dreamed, fantasized, wished for this moment, and it lived up to every aspect of her dreams. Except they weren't naked. Yet.

Time lost all meaning as Zane reveled in the feel of Bryn against him. Her lips were soft and yielding, yet the press of her body against his was firm and insistent. He loved the way she squirmed into him and the soft sighs she made as he trailed his lips down her throat.

Her fingers clutched his back, and she let out another soft moan as his hand skimmed over her breast. He wanted to pick her up, carry her to the bedroom, and strip her out of those pajamas. He wanted, needed, her naked and under him. Then naked and over him. Then under him again.

Which was why he had to stop.

"Wait." He pulled back, scrubbing a hand through his hair as he let out a shuddering breath. "This can't be happening."

Bryn cocked an eyebrow and fixed him with a seductive stare. "Oh, it's happening all right."

A grin pulled at the corners of his lips. "No, I mean it can't be happening because I don't have any...you know...protection."

"You don't?"

Now it was his turn to raise an eyebrow. "No. I don't. I'm a man, not some teenage boy who carries them around in his wallet in hopes of getting lucky."

"Well, too bad you weren't channeling your inner teenager because you were just about to *get* lucky."

He offered her a devilish grin. "Yeah?"

She laughed and hopped down from the kitchen counter. "Yeah, and you still might if I can find a box in my brother's room. He leaves all kinds of stuff here for when he occasionally comes back," she explained as she started down the hallway.

"We don't need a whole box," Zane said, stopping her in her tracks.

She planted a hand on her hip as she turned back to him. "We don't?"

He chuckled. "Nah. Five or six will do."

Her eyes widened, then she playfully wiggled her hips. "*Just* five or six?"

He shrugged. "For now."

She laughed and raised her hands to the ceiling. "I've never prayed for condoms to appear before, but I'm praying now. Like manna from heaven, please let me find a box!"

Zane chuckled, then sent up a silent prayer that echoed hers as she continued down the hallway. In an odd way, he was thankful she didn't have any of her own because that meant she hadn't been planning the same kind of night with Brody. Apparently, she hadn't been planning any kind of night with anyone. But neither had he.

He'd never imagined—well, he had imagined plenty but he'd never *believed*—this night could actually happen.

"Bingo!" he heard Bryn holler from down the hallway.

Heat shot up his spine. He felt like he'd just won the round and couldn't hold back his grin as he headed toward her.

She met him outside her bedroom—at least he assumed it was her bedroom from the pink and white décor he could see through the door. Shaking a purple box at him, she grinned. "I found a brand-new package. I guess you're going to get lucky after all."

"I already have. Just getting to kiss you is lucky in my book." He pulled her into his arms and tucked a strand of hair behind her ear. "This is an entirely new form of luck to me. It's like the Powerball number in the lottery instead of just a two-dollar scratch ticket." He leaned in and kissed her neck, loving the sound of her laughter. Pressing another kiss below her ear, he whispered, "I've never won a prize this grand before, and I'm not about to waste a minute of my winnings."

"Then I guess I'm a winner too," she said, pressing her lips to his and kissing him thoroughly. To his chagrin, she pulled away, taking a step back. She narrowed her eyes in a seductive stare and pushed up her chest. "If you've just won the lottery, don't you think you'd better get to unwrapping your prize?"

CHAPTER 12

ZANE DROPPED HIS GAZE TO BRYN'S PAJAMA TOP. The little tank buttoned up the front and the top button was already undone, showing just enough skin to torment him. His groin tightened at the sight of the taut nubs of her nipples pushing through the thin fabric of her pajamas.

Damn, this woman was going to kill him. He loved that she was beautiful and sweet, but dang if he didn't love this new side of Bryn he was being introduced to, the side that was flirty and beguiling. He loved her tantalizing playfulness, although she was killing him with this teasing.

Time to turn the tables and do a little teasing of his own. He nudged her another step, pressing her back and shoulders against the wall, then slid his hand over the top of her shirt and cupped her breast in his palm. He grazed the tip of her nipple with his thumb and grinned at her sharp intake of breath. Lowering his head, he pressed his mouth to her shirt, sucking at the hardened nub through the light fabric while his free hand slipped under her shirt and caressed her skin. She arched into him, wanting more. He obliged by pulling down the material and exposing one breast over the loose neckline of her top.

Slowly, so slowly, he ran his lips down her throat and

over the top of her breast, his breath a whisper over her skin. Circling her nipple with his tongue, he reveled in the soft whimper he heard as he sucked the nub between his lips.

Her arms were down, one hand still clutching the purple box, the other hand pressed to the wall, as he flicked open another button of her shirt. His gaze was trained on the rise and swell of her breasts, but he felt her swallow as he undid another button. Then another. Then the last. He caught his breath as the fabric fell free, baring her smooth skin and both luscious breasts.

He paused, suddenly feeling shy, like the nerdy teenage boy who had gotten the rare and extraordinary opportunity to make out with the prettiest cheerleader on the squad. He wanted to touch her, to taste her. Hell, he wanted to devour her. But he also wanted to savor this moment and not rush through what was quickly shaping up to be the best night of his life.

Reaching out, he ran the back of his fingers from her neck down the center of her chest, his knuckles grazing the side of her full breast as he went. He circled her belly button, then flattened his hand and smoothed his palm over her stomach and around her waist. Slipping his hand under the elastic band of her shorts, he tugged them over her hips and let them fall to the floor. He couldn't help it. He wanted to see her. All of her.

She still stood against the wall, her shirt opened in the front, her breasts bare, and the only thing left covering her was the thin scrap of lacy fabric that barely passed for panties. Women could rave about the benefit of no panty lines, but men were the ones who truly appreciated the invention of thong panties. And he was offering his appreciation now.

"Damn, you are beautiful." He raked his eyes over her body, admiring her sensuous curves and smooth skin. He leaned down and took her mouth in a hard kiss. Her lips were compliant, returning the kiss with passionate fervor. His hands roamed her body, skimming over her lush curves and caressing her breasts, her waist, her hips. His breath came in ragged gasps as he leaned down and swept her up into his arms, carrying her into the bedroom and laying her on the bed.

The room was lit by a lamp on her bedside table, and her skin glowed in the soft light as she shimmied the rest of the way out of the pajama top. She looked up at him.

He'd toed off his sneakers when they'd come through the door, but he still wore his running shorts and T-shirt. Her hands gripped the hem of his shirt and tried to drag it up. But he pinned the fabric down with his arms, then reached to turn out the lamp.

She put a hand on his. "Don't. Leave it on."

He pulled back, a scowl shadowing his face. "I don't do this unless it's in the dark."

"Zane." She said his name softly and rested a hand gently on his chest. Could she feel the thundering of his heart? He swore it had to be pounding like a hammer against her hand. "I don't want this to be a one-time thing with you."

His scowl deepened. "Did I give you some kind of indication that's what I wanted?" he growled.

"No, I didn't mean that. I just meant that I feel like this could be the beginning of something good. And I don't want to start it in the dark. I want us to start in the light."

He shook his head. "I'm not pretty in the light." He scrubbed a hand over his face. "Hell, I'm not even pretty in the dark."

"Stop. You're beautiful to me."

He huffed. "You're beautiful. I'm a scarred-up beast."

"That's not how I see it. You are more than your scars. But I think our scars tell our stories. They don't have to be marks of shame, they can be symbols of survival, even victory." She reached up and gently ran her finger along the jagged mark on his face. "You lived through the battle and came out stronger."

She reached for his hand and drew it to her side, using the end of his finger to trace a thin white line of tissue. "This scar is from when I was playing in the barn, and my grandfather told me to stay away from the tractor, and I didn't listen and fell off the seat and cut my side." She moved his hand to another scar on her leg. "I got this when I wrecked my bike and broke my leg because I was trying to keep up with my brother and his friends who'd dared me to try to jump the ditch. I spent two weeks in the hospital. And my grandmother brought me books from the library. I must have read twenty books that week."

"My scars don't tell those kinds of stories. You don't know what I've been through and what I've done." He thought of the strip of skin that had been torn from his leg when he'd been stabbed by an Afghani soldier. The welts that crisscrossed over his back and shoulders— gifts from his father. The jagged gash across his thigh where he'd drawn a knife across it the night Sarah died, his hands sticky with blood as he tried to punish himself for her death.

"But they do. Every scar tells a story. And every one teaches us something." She touched the scars again. "Like this one taught me that I'm not always right. And this one taught me my brother and his friends could be jerks and not to let myself get peer-pressured into doing stupid stuff I'm not ready for."

He shook his head. "I appreciate what you're trying to do. But I don't have scars from riding my bike and playing in the barn. Mine are wounds of war and chaos and from getting beaten by a drunk. The only thing these scars have taught me is that war is hell and I'd rather have my dad hit me with his fists than whip me with a belt."

She winced. "I know it's not the same. And I can't begin to imagine the things you endured growing up with a man like Birch. But what I'm trying to say is that your scars don't define you. They are just a part of you. But not all of you. And I want all of you, Zane."

"I want you too," he said, his voice hoarse, his skin hot with shame. Didn't she know how humiliating this was? Couldn't she tell how much of himself he'd already bared to her? He didn't want her to see this part of him, to hear the pity in her voice or witness the horror in her eyes.

"Show me."

He shook his head again but didn't stop her this time as she reached for the hem of his shirt and slowly eased it over his head. "You don't have to tell me the story of every one, but I want to see them. And I want you to know that I see more than your scars. I see you."

She was going to break him.

"There isn't more. And they do define who I am. Every scar, every wound tells you exactly who I am. A nothing. A nobody. Not good for anything more than as a punching bag for my old man. Don't you see? I'm damaged goods. Already broken. These wounds go deeper than my skin. They screwed me up."

"They didn't. They might have made you the man you are today, but they didn't break you." Her eyes tightened in the smallest wince as she drew her fingers across the small puckered circle on his chest where Birch had put out his cigarette the night he'd caught Zane smoking. He'd tried to make it seem like some kind of life lesson from a father to a son. *Yeah, your Father of the Year award is in the mail, Dad.*

She leaned forward and pressed a soft kiss to the circular scar. "Show me," she whispered again. "I'm not scared."

"I am. I've been in the trenches in the desert. And locked in a closet. Those things made me a tough bastard. I'm not scared of much. But right now, I'm terrified."

"It's okay."

All he'd wanted was to touch her, to kiss her. He wasn't good at words or expressing his emotions, but he could *show* her what he was feeling. He wanted the focus of this time to be on her, not him. And damn sure *not* on his damaged body.

But she wasn't going to let up. He hadn't known Bryn long, but he knew the woman had a stubborn streak in her a mile long. He sighed. *Fine.* She wanted to see all of him, the true beast. It was her choice. If this was all he got, this brief time of making out with her in the driveway and the kitchen and the hall, then he'd have to be satisfied. He'd still gotten to touch her skin, to run his hands over her curves, to kiss that soft spot on her neck between her ear and her shoulder.

He turned around, anticipating the sharp intake of her breath, the cry of alarm and horror. But all he heard was a soft inhale, then felt her fingers lightly touch his back as she traced his history through his scars. A shiver ran through him.

He turned and saw tears on her cheeks, but her eyes didn't contain judgment or fear. He wiped a tear from her face with the back of his thumb. "Hey now, don't cry for me. I'm tough."

"I know. I'm not so much crying for the man you are now, but for the boy you were then. I'm sorry you had to go through this."

He shrugged. "I'm sorry you had to see it."

"I'm not," she said. "And it doesn't horrify me like you think it does. You have more to offer than you think." She pushed his hair away from his forehead and stared hard into his eyes. "You're like the stallions that run free in the mountains, wild but beautiful. You might not see it, but I do. You know, butterflies can't see how beautiful their wings are, but the rest of the world can."

He arched an eyebrow and offered her a wry grin. "Are you comparing me to a butterfly? Just as we're about to have reckless passionate sex?"

She giggled, her eyes full of mirth as she nodded.

He laughed with her. This was all new to him, talking and laughing in the middle of making out. Baring their hearts, then joking and teasing in between kissing and shedding their clothes. "How about we go back to that part where you compared me to a wild stallion?"

Her grin widened.

The scent of rain mingled with her perfume, and he glanced toward the open window as another flicker of lightning streaked across the sky. His eyes widened as he stared at the two pairs of eyes peering into the window. He let out a laugh as he gestured toward them. "It appears we have an audience."

Bryn twisted her neck and burst out laughing as she caught sight of the goat and the miniature horse watching them through the screen. The goat had a scrap of red flannel fabric hanging from its lip as it let out a loud bleat. "Otis must have taught Shamus how to escape the corral. And I think that's a piece of your shirt he's snacking on."

"Damn goat."

"They look like they want to come in."

"I consider myself a pretty open guy, but I'm gonna draw the line at that."

Bryn giggled again, then pushed up from the bed and crossed to the window. She shooed the animals away. "Go on now." She pulled the shade, then turned and walked back to the bed.

Zane had enjoyed the view of her walking away but appreciated the sight of her walking toward him even more. Her hips swayed, and she offered him a seductive smile. His gaze raked over her bare skin, and he grinned as her nipples tightened under his stare.

He took her hand and pulled her back into bed. Her lips curved into another slow smile as she nestled her head into the pillow, and he rose over her. Leaning down, he kissed the smile from her lips, losing himself in the sensual glide of her tongue against his. He buried his face in her hair, then grazed his lips along the soft line of her neck. He pressed his mouth against the hammering pulse point in her throat. Was she as nervous as he was? Or just excited?

His own heart pounded hard as he hauled her to his chest, slanting his mouth over hers again as he kissed her with a fury of lust and abandon. He wanted everything, all of her. Now. But he also wanted to take it slow, to savor every moment, every touch of her skin, every soft sigh that escaped her lips.

He tried to linger at her lips, but her body called for his attention. Her soft, lush curves molded perfectly against his body, but he pushed himself up, wanting to look at her as he ran his hands lightly down her sides and over the contours of her breasts and hips.

A wicked grin curved his lips as he watched her skin erupt in goose bumps at his touch. He dipped his head, giving his attention to one perfect breast, then the other. His tender caress over her sensitive nipples had her arching her back, demanding more. Her breasts filled his hands, and mouth, perfectly. She let out the softest whimper as his tongue rasped the tip of her nipple, and he almost came undone.

"Now, please," she whispered.

He positioned himself between her legs and brushed the backs of his fingers along the bare skin of her waist. Her thighs trembled, awaiting his command, but he was the one utterly at her mercy.

He grabbed the box of condoms, his hands shaking as he ripped open a package, tossed the wrapper to the floor, and covered himself. His body flushed hot, the sight of her naked and writhing beneath him setting fire to his already feverish senses.

Then he claimed her, finally and fully, reveling in the sweet sigh of surrender Bryn uttered as she clutched his back. Losing himself in the intoxicating blend of skin and scent, he surrendered to the slow rhythm of movement.

He cupped her chin, forcing her gaze, as he rocked into her, pushing them higher, and immersing himself in the sensations he'd only dreamed of feeling. Arching her back, she offered more of herself to him, and he took it all, drowning in the heat of desire.

His jaw tightened as he tried to cling to some form of control. But when she moaned his name, he lost it, his chest expanding as a growl ripped from his throat. Her cries matched his as they soared over the edge, then collapsed onto the bed together.

He pulled her to him, nestled her body under his arm, and pressed his lips to the silky strands of her hair. "I think maybe I could get used to this sex-with-the-lights on idea after all."

She tilted her head to grin up at him. "Yeah?"

"Yeah. But we might have to try it again, just to be sure."

———

The next morning, Bryn was still asleep as Zane slipped quietly from her bed. He looked around for his clothes and found his shorts on the floor, but his shirt was lodged securely under Bryn's leg. He contemplated pulling it free, the need to cover his back still strong, but he didn't want to wake her. And besides, who would see him? The dogs didn't care, and the puppies didn't even have their eyes open yet. He could just grab it as soon as she woke up.

He pulled on his shorts as he went in search of caffeine. In the kitchen, the lovebirds tweeted a greeting as he started the coffee maker, then filled his cup before the pot finished brewing. He took a sip of the dark brew as he propped open the front door to let the dogs out.

He felt a pang of guilt at leaving the collie at his house the night before. He'd text Birch in a bit to make sure his dad let her out and threw some food in her bowl. Lucky clamored around his legs, whining and shaking his hind end as he begged to be petted, while Grace, the mama dog, hurried to the grass to do her business and get back to her pups. It was amazing what a few good meals and a little rest could do for a dog; she already looked healthier. Her body was still thin, but she didn't have the gaunt, half-starved look she'd had when she'd been giving all her nutrients to her puppies.

A wry grin curved Zane's lips as he peered into the cardboard box and watched two of the puppies scramble blindly over the pile, one trying to bite the tail of its sleeping sibling. He scooped the two scramblers up and cuddled them gently to his chest as he eased onto the porch swing and watched the sun come over the horizon. The farm was peaceful in the early morning light, the only sounds the occasional mournful bawl of a cow and the far-off hum of a tractor already running. Most days for a farmer started as the sun came up.

The sound of an engine broke the morning's peace, and Zane raised his hand to block the sun as he watched a long white van maneuver up the driveway. It pulled to a stop in front of the porch.

Zane studied the van. It was big, one of those giant twelve-passenger conversion ones they used to haul kids to camp. Church camp, he assumed, since the words *United Methodist Church* and some town he'd never heard of in Kansas were displayed boldly on the side.

He set his coffee down before he stood and walked across the porch. The puppies were asleep, and he held them against his chest, wishing he had pulled his shirt free from under Bryn's leg. Nothing he could do about it now, except to stay facing forward, so as not to expose his back. He leaned his hip against the porch rail and eyed the middle-aged woman who climbed from the van.

She stretched her back as she looked around the farm, her jaw dropping as she caught sight of Zane on the porch. She swallowed as her hands fluttered to her mouth. "Oh my gosh. It's you." She turned back to holler into the van. "Get out here, Shirleen. It's him."

The other woman clambered from the vehicle as if the seat had just caught fire. She smoothed her hair as she rounded the front of the van. Both women were in their midforties and dressed similarly in walking shorts, sneakers and T-shirts. They had the rumpled look of having spent hours in the van.

"It is him," Shirleen confirmed, her voice a low whisper of awe as she looked from her friend back to Zane. She fanned her hand in front of her face. "Lord have mercy, look at that head of hair. *And* he's got puppies."

He's got puppies? Is that was this early morning visit was about? Were these ladies looking for a dog? Maybe they'd heard about the puppies Bryn had saved and were in the market for one. But how in the blue blazes did they know him?

"Can I help you with something?" he asked. "You ladies lost? Need directions?"

"Nope. We know we're in the right place. Plus we recognize you."

They recognized him? What was that supposed to mean?

Shirleen jumped in before he had a chance to ask. "We've been driving all night to get here. We're just about wore out, but we're sure glad to see you."

"Pardon our manners," the first woman said, taking a step toward him. "I'm Annie Lane, and this is my best friend, Shirleen Scott. We're from Kansas."

"I gathered as much," he said. "Nice to meet you. I'm Zane."

"Oh, we know. We know all about you and Bryn and the horse rescue farm you're starting. We follow you on Facebook."

That damn social media shit. He knew it was going to lead to trouble. He hadn't anticipated trouble arriving in the form of two middle-aged housewives from the Sunflower State though. He eyed the van, still unsure why they were here. He was pretty sure they didn't have a horse buckled in there.

He could hear Bryn in the kitchen, and he leaned toward the front door and hollered through the screen. "Hey, Bryn, there's a couple of gals from Kansas here to see you."

"Kansas?"

"Ayup. You better come on out. And could you bring me my shirt, darlin'?"

"Oh you don't need a shirt on our account," Shirleen said, her statement followed by a girlish giggle as her friend's cheeks turned pink.

Bryn pushed through the front door, a curious look on her face. He noted she'd put her pajamas back on and covered them with a short cotton robe. He preferred her the way he'd left her in the bed—wearing nothing but a satisfied smile.

She passed him his shirt, and they juggled the puppies, her fingers on the bare skin of his chest sending heat darting down his spine. Hopefully the ladies from Kansas didn't stay long. He was ready to get Bryn back into bed and peel those little pj's off again.

He pulled the T-shirt over his head and took one of the puppies back. "Bryn, this is Ms. Annie Lane and Ms. Shirleen Scott. They've driven all night to get here from Kansas. Ladies, this is Bryn Callahan. Although you seem to know that already."

Annie stepped forward. "It's so nice to meet you, Bryn. We follow your Facebook page and think it's just wonderful what you're doing for these poor animals." She glanced down at Bryn's robe and winced. "We're so sorry to just show up like this. I hope we didn't interrupt anything."

"That's not true," Shirleen said. "We hope we did. We've been rooting for you two to get together."

Oh, no. It was too early in the morning, and he hadn't had nearly enough coffee for these women. "So, besides entertaining you with our burgeoning love life, what can we help you ladies with?"

Annie wrung her hands, twisting her fingers together as she glanced back at the van. "I hate to do this. And I sure don't like imposing on you-all, but I don't have anywhere else to turn. My daughter, Georgia, she talked me into letting her get a potbellied pig for her sixteenth birthday. At first, the pig was adorable. We set her up a little pen with a dog door that goes from the basement to the yard, and she acts like she's our dog. But now Georgia's halfway through college and she's out of state, and I just can't take care of the pig anymore. Like I said, we've been following you on Facebook, and you seem like good people, and, well, we were just hoping y'all might take her in."

"Sure," Bryn said without hesitation. That girl's heart was bigger than the Rocky Mountains. "I don't know a lot about pigs, but I think potbellied pigs are adorable. I'm sure we could make room for her."

"Well," Annie said, glancing nervously toward her friend. "The thing is, when we got her, my daughter *thought* she was getting a potbellied pig. But whoever sold it to her either tricked her or didn't know what they were doing. By the time we figured out she wasn't a potbellied, we'd already fallen in love with her personality, and we couldn't give her up. But she kept getting bigger…" She gazed back at the vehicle. "That's why we had to borrow the church van."

Zane was starting to get a bad feeling. He took the other puppy from Bryn and stepped inside to set them back in the box with their mother, then came back to the porch and motioned to the van. "We'd better take a look at her."

"She's very sweet," Annie explained, leading them around the back of the vehicle. "Her name is Tiny. She was pretty little when we first got her. And Georgia spent so much time with her, so she loves to cuddle and get her ears scratched. Like I said, she acts like she's a dog. She comes when you call her, and she's really very cute. In her own way."

Methinks the lady doth protest too much. Zane had a feeling there was more going on than the sweet Annie was letting on. "I think it's time you just introduce us to Tiny."

"Yes, of course. This is just hard on me, ya know? She's my daughter's pet, and we're going to miss her, but I just can't take care of her anymore. I don't have the space or the means to keep her, and with the extra expenses of college, I frankly can't afford to feed her." She opened the back doors of the van.

Bryn took a step back and drew her hands up to cover her mouth. "Oh my." She blinked, her mouth opening, then closing again. "In the words of the famous spider, that is *some pig*."

CHAPTER 13

"I KNOW," ANNIE SAID, REACHING IN TO RUB THE animal's ears. The pig was light pink with a couple of black spots across her back. She was lying on a blue blanket, and a bucket of scraps was turned over next to her head. She leaned into the scratch, closing her eyes in swine bliss as she let out a muffled snort. A bright pink ribbon with a large red daisy attached to it was wrapped around her neck, like she'd gotten dressed up for the occasion. She looked clean and well cared for, despite the loose piece of wilted lettuce stuck to her snout.

Zane looked from Annie to the animal, then back to Annie again. "That's not a pig," he said. "That's a hog." The beast was easily two hundred pounds.

Annie covered the pig's ears and gave him an admonishing look. "We don't like to call her that." She turned to Bryn. "It's been a couple of hours since we last stopped. Would you mind if we let her out to use the facilities?"

"By all means."

Annie pulled out the ramp, and Tiny stood and daintily walked down it and across the driveway to the grass. She relieved herself, then wandered around the yard and finally plopped down in a shady spot under the elm tree. Lucky cautiously approached the pig and sniffed her snout. The tripod dog must have deemed the hog okay because he laid down in the grass a few feet away.

"Lucky seems to have given her his stamp of approval," Bryn said.

"They're so cute together," Shirleen said. "And those puppies you were holding are to die for."

"You want one?" Zane asked. "We could box up a couple and send them back to Kansas with you."

"We could not." Bryn nudged him in the arm. "They're nowhere near old enough to be away from their mother yet."

"I'm kidding." He wouldn't really separate the newborns from their mother. But eventually they would have to consider it.

"That's how I feel about Tiny," Annie said, her voice choked with emotion. "I know she was my daughter's pet, but with Georgia away at college, this pig keeps me company. And she's the only one who greets me when I come home from work every night." She wiped at her nose with the sleeve of her T-shirt. "I'm so sorry to do this to her. We really do love her. She's been part of our family for years. I just can't do it anymore. And you folks seem so nice. And you've got such a lovely farm. I felt like you were an answer to my prayers."

"You might not have prayed hard enough if we were the answer you came up with," Zane muttered.

Bryn nudged him again. "Shush."

"I've been praying about her for months, and last night the answer suddenly hit me. I knew this was the place for her. So I called up Shirleen, and we borrowed the church van and drove all night to get here. I just know this is the spot she's supposed to be."

Bryn glanced at Zane and offered a slight lift to her shoulders. "We do have that old pigsty to the side of the barn." She turned to Annie. "My gramps kept pigs for a time. It hasn't been used in years and might take a little fixing up, but I'd bet it would work for Tiny. Why don't you ladies come on inside? I'll fix us all some breakfast while Zane checks out the pigsty to see if we can use it."

Twenty minutes later, Zane walked through the door to the sound of female laughter and the scent of fried potatoes and bacon. He lifted an eyebrow at Bryn. "It seems like you've become fast friends with the ladies from Kansas, but I'm not sure serving bacon was the smartest move. All things considered."

She chuckled and made room for him to wash his hands in the sink. "Good point. But it's too late now. And I am having fun with these two. They're hilarious." She nodded to the skillet sizzling with bacon grease. "How many eggs do you want?"

"Two's good. I take 'em—"

"Over hard. I know. I've served you breakfast at the diner, and I always remember the preferences of my favorite customers. I know how you like your eggs." She lowered her voice so only he could hear. "And after last night, I know how you like a few other things too."

A sinful grin spread across his face. He dipped his head to her neck, the tendrils of her hair tickling his cheek as he spoke softly into her ear. "I've yet to learn enough things you like. I made a fair start, but I think I need another month in bed with you to really perfect my knowledge." He ran his hand down her side and grinned wider at the shiver that ran through her.

"You *do* realize we are in the room with you, right?" Shirleen said, teasing. "The way you two are heating up the kitchen, maybe you should tell us where the fire extinguisher is kept."

Zane chuckled as he tilted his head toward the pantry. "It's in there. Just in case."

"Stop it," Bryn scolded, swatting him with a towel, then smiling sheepishly at the two women seated at her kitchen table. "You-all are making my cheeks burn so hot, I may need to use the fire extinguisher on myself."

They'd probably spent enough time embarrassing Bryn. Zane glanced at the stove. "Anything I can do to help?"

"Sure," she said, shooting him a thankful smile. "I fried up some potatoes, if you want to put them in a bowl. Then get yourself some coffee and tell us how the pigsty looked."

He scooped the potatoes into a bowl and set it on the table, trying to ignore the goofy grins on the faces of the two women seated there. "Can I get you gals some more coffee?"

Shirleen giggled. "I just love the way you say 'gals.'"

"Is that a yes to the coffee?"

She giggled again as she shook her head. "No, I'm good."

He poured himself a cup and dropped into the seat at the end of the table, stretching his legs in front of him as he took a sip of the hot brew. "Your grandpa knew how to build stuff to last," he told Bryn. "That sty was in pretty good condition. I replaced a couple of boards and hitched up the gate. But otherwise, I think it'll work great for the pig. Or the giant pink dog, or whatever you're calling her."

"So does that mean you'll keep her?" Annie asked, her eyes welling with tears.

Zane peered at Bryn. "It's up to you." Although he already knew what she was going to say.

"Of course we'll keep her." Bryn nodded to the lovebirds. "I notice you've barely been able to take your eyes off the birdcage, Annie."

The other woman smiled wistfully. "I just love them. They're adorable. I used to have a parakeet when I was younger, and I could watch that little bird for hours. I could open her cage, and she would fly out and sit on my finger or my shoulder."

"That's what these will do too," Bryn said. "Their names are Ralph and Rosie. Rosalee, their owner, is a retired schoolteacher and she is moving to Kansas to live with her son, so she can't keep the birds anymore. I'm looking for a good home for them. Maybe we could make a trade—I keep Tiny and you take the lovebirds."

Annie's hand fluttered to her mouth. "Really? Oh, I would love that. I've been worried about the house being so lonely with Georgia and Tiny both gone. Having these two cuties would give me something to focus on and keep the house from feeling so empty."

"Plus they'll be a hell of a lot cheaper to feed," added Zane, earning a playful nudge from Bryn.

"You should take them, Annie," Shirleen encouraged. "This other woman, Rosalee, she's a Kansas woman too. Seems like it's meant to be."

Annie wrung her hands. "Oh gosh. I really did love having a bird when I was younger, and I've always thought someday I would get another one."

"Seems like your someday is today."

Annie gave a resolute nod. "Yes, it does. Okay. It's a deal. I'll take them."

Bryn smiled. "Perfect."

"I'm not sure who got the better end of that deal," Zane muttered.

After breakfast, they got Tiny situated in her new home. The pig roamed the fence line, sniffing its new surroundings, then took a carrot from the pile of produce Bryn had dumped into the trough and settled in a shady spot.

"Welcome to the family, Tiny," Bryn told the pig as she leaned over the fence and scratched her behind the ears. The pig blissfully closed her eyes and leaned into the scratch. She really was a cute thing.

"You sure she'll be all right outside like this?" Annie asked. She twisted the fabric of the small stuffed animal she held in her hands. "She does spend a lot of time outside in our backyard, but she usually sleeps in the basement."

"We'll keep an eye on her. Don't worry. She'll be fine," Zane assured her. He gently pried the stuffed animal from Annie's hands and placed it in the pen next to Tiny's snout. The pig rested her nose on the toy. "After they leave, I'll hose down the dirt in the pen and give her a good muddy spot to roll around in. She'll love it," he quietly told Bryn as they followed the ladies back to the van.

Zane loaded the lovebirds and all their gear into the back seat and buckled it in. "You ladies have a safe trip."

Both women hugged Bryn. As Annie tearfully thanked Bryn again, Shirleen opened her arms and wrapped Zane in a hug too.

"It was so nice to meet you," she said, closing her eyes as she rested her head on his chest. "Thanks for taking the pig and setting up the sty and feeding us breakfast and giving Annie the lovebirds."

Bryn pressed her lips together to keep from laughing. How many more things could this woman thank Zane for? The sun? The moon? Electricity? The invention of the cell phone? Chocolate? Netflix?

Zane patted Shirleen's shoulder in that awkward way that people who are uncomfortable with huggers do. But the woman didn't seem to get the hint and just held on to him.

"All right, Shirl," Annie finally said. "Let the handsome man go and get in the van."

Shirleen gave one more squeeze, then released Zane. "Really. Thanks for that hug too. It made my day."

"You're welcome, ma'am," Zane muttered, then

gestured toward the barn. "I'm going to go check on the horses." He ambled off and Bryn noted that all three of them watched his departure. The man did look good from that perspective. Actually, he looked good from any perspective.

Bryn hoped the women couldn't see the heat rising to her cheeks as she thought of the many perspectives of Zane she'd seen, and felt, the night before. She waved as they climbed into the van and turned around in the driveway.

Annie rolled down her window. "We'll keep in touch," she called before driving away.

Bryn checked her watch. They still had a few hours before Zane had to be at work and her shift started at the diner. Plenty of time for her to show Zane a few things she was thankful for too.

Later that afternoon, Bryn set a plate holding a pile of chips and two warm grilled cheese sandwiches on the table in front of Elle. After her shift, she'd come home and showered and dressed and had been watching the puppies when Elle stopped by. Bryn had been thrilled to see the young widow, who had dropped in to see if there was anything she could do to start her volunteer activities. Bryn had already eaten lunch but insisted on feeding Elle and loading her arms with squirming puppies as she filled her in on their early morning visitors.

"Seriously?" Elle asked, picking up a small chip and

popping it in her mouth. She shifted in her seat, careful not to displace the three sleeping puppies balanced in her lap. Lucky sat obediently by Bryn's chair, his eyes alert and watchful in case a loose chip or bread crumb happened to fall on the floor. "Two women drove all the way here from Kansas and dropped off a two-hundred-pound hog at your house? This morning?"

"Shhh," Bryn said, holding a finger to her lips. "She doesn't like to be called a hog. It's degrading."

"Oh, sorry." Elle pressed her lips together to keep from laughing. "I didn't realize she was such a sensitive soul."

"She's actually a very sweet pig. She even comes when you call her."

Elle struggled to hold it in, but the laugh burst from her. She covered her mouth with her hand and tried to control her laughter. "I'm sure she is a very fine swine." Curtailing another giggle, she stuffed a bite of sandwich between her lips and let out a groan. "Oh my gosh. This is so good. Speaking of being a pig, I'm planning to eat *both* of these sandwiches. I haven't had a grilled cheese in so long, I forgot how yummy they are."

"Thank you." Bryn was pleased to see the other woman eating. "I use two kinds of cheese, cheddar and provolone. And real butter on the bread."

"Sounds like I'll be as big as Tiny if I keep letting you feed me," Elle said around another bite of sandwich. She had already finished the first half and pushed the last of the second into her mouth.

"Good. You could stand to put on a few pounds. You're too thin."

Elle shrugged. "I didn't used to be. I used to love to eat. When we lived in the city, Ryan and I ate out all the time. We loved to try new restaurants and different kinds of entrees. Since he died, I just haven't cared about food."

"I'm sorry. I didn't mean to bring up Ryan."

"It's fine. In fact, it's good to talk about him. This was his town, he loved it here, but no one ever seems to want to talk to me about him. If they do talk to me, it's almost as if they do everything to avoid bringing up his name. Like they think maybe I've somehow forgotten he died and left me alone in his town, and if they say his name, I might suddenly remember."

"I'm sorry." Bryn didn't know what else to say. "That must be hard."

"It is hard. This whole freaking life is hard. But what am I going to do? I've tried barricading myself in that big house and all that accomplished was to alienate everyone in this town who might have eventually become a friend. Present company excluded. And I tried throwing myself into my work and staying so exhausted that I'd forget to eat and fall into bed at night. And that didn't work either because I don't actually sleep more than a few hours a night anyway. For the record, I don't recommend widowhood mixed with insomnia as a weight loss plan. All I achieved was to walk around like a zombie whose wardrobe didn't fit anymore. And now I don't even have that job to throw myself into, so instead I'm going to focus on you and what you're trying to accomplish out here. And maybe in trying to help someone else and save some animals, I might end up saving myself."

Bryn swallowed. That was the most she'd heard Elle say about her struggles after Ryan died. The other woman must have been feeling more comfortable with her. Plus, a good grilled cheese sandwich had a way of making everything better.

"Speaking of helping you," Elle continued, as if she hadn't just disclosed the struggles of her husband dying, "I've been going through the donations and the GoFundMe stats, and I think you need to create an LLC and set up a business bank account. I've already been working on your social media and researching the best place to set up a website for you."

"Okay," Bryn said, trying to switch to business mode.

"I thought I'd take some pictures of the animals this afternoon to use on the website. I've already taken about a million of the puppies, but I want some of the horses and, of course, of Tiny. And I was hoping you could get permission from your friend Tess to use a couple of the photos of you from the article she wrote. They were really good."

"I'm sure she wouldn't mind, but I don't think we need pictures of me," Bryn told her, imagining a shot of herself next to the giant hog…er…pig. "I'm not the important one—the animals are."

"Which is why you need to get your ducks in a row, so to speak. You've got these animals depending on you to house and feed them. And you've got people willing to help, so we need to make hay while the sun is shining. Which is why we need the bank account. But you've got to list the name of your business to get the LLC registered on the Colorado Secretary of State website. Have you given any thought to what you want to call this place?"

"Um, no. I've always just called it home." Bryn blew out a breath. "I had no idea rescuing a few horses would be so complicated. I don't even know what an LLC is, let alone how to register one."

"Well, that's why you have me. And don't worry, it's simple. I can teach you."

"I just don't know if we need to go to all that bother. I have a regular checking account—not that I keep enough in there to make much of a fuss about—but it seems like we could just use that and save ourselves all this hassle."

"It's not that much of a hassle. And you're going to need it. Regardless of how you manage your personal account, you don't want to mix the funds of your nonprofit with your consumer account. It'll make it hell on your taxes."

"Taxes?"

"Yes, my friend. Taxes. Welcome to the world of business."

Bryn dropped her head into her hands. "I just wanted to save a horse."

"And you did. You are. You're saving three of them. Plus a bunch of dogs and a delicate swine. But in order to keep saving them, and by that I mean *feeding* them, you need the account."

"But I don't have anything to put in it. So far the donations have just been made to the feed store."

"Which is awesome, but I've also collected over four hundred dollars so far from the tip jars, plus several hundred that's come in online."

"Six hundred dollars? You're kidding me!"

"Nope. People love animals. And they love what you're doing out here." She flashed Bryn an impish smile. "Plus they love the romance between you and the mystery man you were sucking face with on the video. Especially since it's so hard to tell who the man is. It's so mysterious, and that kiss was so hot. You and I know it's Zane, but the world of social media is still guessing. You know, online they're calling him the Kissing Cowboy."

"So I heard." Bryn told her how Annie and Shirleen had fawned over Zane when they'd first arrived. "He was on the porch with no shirt on, and I thought Shirleen was going to try to lick him and claim him as hers." The reason Zane was shirtless flooded Bryn's thoughts, and her body warmed with the memories of the night before and the feel of his skin against hers. She grabbed her glass and took a long swig of lemonade.

"That is awesome. And so cool to know that you, and the Kissing Cowboy, are getting more notoriety. All the more reason why we need to get your LLC in place."

Bryn shook her head. "Maybe. But I still have no idea what to name the farm. I'm terrible at stuff like this."

"Don't worry. We'll brainstorm something. We can work on that this afternoon." She popped her last chip into her mouth and leaned back in her chair. "Okay, enough about business. How was the date with the handsome veterinarian last night?"

"Uhhh. Well…"

Elle grimaced. "That bad, huh?"

"No, it wasn't bad at all. In fact, it was very nice."

"You say that like it's a bad thing."

"It's not a bad thing. It's a fine thing. He's a nice guy, and we had a perfectly nice time, and he gave me a perfectly nice good-night kiss."

"And?"

"And it was just kind of meh. We talked, we laughed, then he walked me to the door and gave me this funny little awkward quick peck—not quite like kissing my brother, just no real spark." *No spark, not even so much as a fizzle.* Bryn let out a sigh, then offered Elle a sheepish grin. "Not like the fireworks that happened later when Zane stopped by the ranch."

"Wait. Zane was here? The Kissing Cowboy? Last night? And there were fireworks?" Elle refilled her glass with lemonade. "You have my attention. Who cares about the nice date and the boring peck of a kiss. Tell me more about these fireworks. Are we talking like the little firecrackers you toss on the ground or the full-blown explode-in-the-sky ones?"

"The full-blown explosion ones. And *several* of them." Bryn's lips curved into an impish smile.

Elle let out a whoop and held up a hand for Bryn to high five. "You go girl. I'm glad for you. I can barely remember what fireworks feel like. The last time this body felt anything close to resembling an explosion was when I accidentally crossed the yellow line on the highway and drove down the rumble strip."

Bryn had been taking a sip of lemonade and almost spat it out as she choked on a laugh. "Oh my gosh. That is hilarious."

"No, it's not. It's sad." Elle gave an exaggerated wince. "But true."

Bryn raised an eyebrow. "Well, are you ready for an explosion? I mean one that's not induced by driving several yards down the rumble strip on the highway? Are you at the stage where you're thinking about looking?"

"No way. I am nowhere near that stage. I had my fireworks. Ryan was the love of my life, and I can't begin to imagine even lighting sparklers with anyone else." She stared down at the puppies asleep in her lap and tenderly brushed her fingers across the neck of the brown-and-white one.

Bryn reached out a hand and rested it gently on her friend's arm. There was nothing to say, nothing to do, nothing that would bring Ryan back.

Elle blinked at the well of tears shining in her eyes. "Wow. Enough of that sad business. Let's go back to talking about you and your wild night with Zane." She pulled her lips into a smile. "Tell me more. I know he is ridiculously hot, in that broody lone wolf sort of way, but how do you feel about the guy? Do you really like him?"

Bryn let out a shaky breath. "I do. So help me, I do. It

scares the heck out of me, but there's something about him that just pulls me in, and I'm powerless to fight it."

"You might have a right to be. Scared, I mean."

"Why?"

"I don't know. And maybe I shouldn't even say anything. I've been around Zane, and he seems like a decent guy—he helped save those horses and these little guys." She glanced down at the puppies again then back up at Bryn. "I've just heard some things, around town, you know. About him. About Zane."

An uneasy feeling crept along Bryn's spine. There was always gossip around town about anyone who was different or who didn't fit the small-town mold. "What kind of things?"

Elle gave a small shrug. "Just about how he used to date a local girl."

Bryn huffed out a breath. "I'm sure he dated a lot of local girls."

"No, actually, he didn't. They were talking about him at the hairdresser's today. I think the woman he was with at the Creed last night works there. Kim or Chrystal, maybe."

"Kim," Bryn confirmed, trying to keep her teeth from gnashing together. "Kimberly Cox. If it was at Carley's Cut and Curl. She works as a receptionist there."

"Yes, that's the place. Anyway, Zane used to date a girl name Sarah. Sarah Sears. Like the department store, I think. Does that sound right?"

"Yes. I mean, I didn't know her. She was older than me

and went to school a couple of towns over. But I knew her sister, Stephanie. She left town for a while, went out of state to nursing school. But now she's back and working as an RN at the hospital."

"Well, apparently this Sarah and Zane were pretty serious. She was the first girl he'd dated for more than a few weeks. But it didn't end well."

"Since when do serious relationships ever end well?"

"This was different. When I say ended, I mean Sarah died."

CHAPTER 14

Bryn swallowed. "She died? How?"

Elle picked at a stray thread of her placemat. "I guess of a drug overdose. They didn't say if it was accidental or on purpose."

Bryn covered her mouth with her hand. "Oh no."

"There was some speculation about how much Zane was involved in all of it, but no one really said for sure. I guess she was only eighteen when she died. They said Zane left town right after that. Apparently he got in some big fight with his dad, then took off and joined the military. These last few months are the first time he's been back in town for any length of time in years." This time it was Elle's turn to cover Bryn's hand. "I'm sorry. I know this is all just beauty shop gossip, but I thought you should know. It sounds like Zane's got some pretty rough history."

"We've all got history. And the only ones who would really know what happened are the people involved. I've got history too. But this is Zane's story to tell. I'm not going to judge him until he chooses to tell me his side of it, if he does." Elle's revelations might explain some of the comments he'd made the night before.

"You're right," Elle said. "I shouldn't have said anything. I'm a little embarrassed telling you anyway. I don't usually pass on gossip. Goodness knows enough of it has flown around this town about me."

"It's okay. I know you didn't have malicious intent, and you were only trying to protect me. That's what friends do."

Later that night, Zane pulled into Bryn's driveway and parked next to the barn. Bryn had texted him earlier to ask if he was hungry. He'd replied Always, but his response was a reaction to the kind of hunger that didn't have anything to do with food.

He hadn't been able to get his mind off Bryn and the time they had shared the night before. If she hadn't invited him to supper, he'd planned to show up with a pizza.

The collie jumped from the truck and trotted toward the porch, already comfortable enough with Bryn's place to race up the front porch steps. Although that dog seemed to make herself comfortable wherever she went. Including his bed. After he'd let her up that one time, she'd now taken to jumping up on it every night and curling against his leg. He'd allowed it, just because he was too lazy to make her move. *Yeah, sure.*

His dad had said she'd slept by the front door the night before, like she was waiting for him to come home. And then he'd bitched and moaned about having to let her out and toss her some kibble. Zane had brought the dog tonight. Not that he was planning to spend the night with Bryn again, but it didn't hurt to be prepared.

Zane grabbed the project he'd been working on the past few days and pulled it from the truck. He'd wrapped it in burlap, and the fabric was rough on his hands. Not that he'd needed to wrap it. He'd sanded the wood so many times it was smooth as glass.

A platoon of butterflies took off in his gut as he approached Bryn's front door. He'd made her a sign to proclaim her farm was now an official horse rescue ranch. But had he overstepped his bounds? Would she think the sign was stupid? Would she think *he* was stupid? Would things feel different tonight? Would she act different? He'd left her this morning with a goodbye kiss that had curled his toes and had him seriously contemplating calling in sick to work, an action he'd never done. Not that he hadn't ever had a cold or been sick, he just hadn't let it interfere with his job. Although the idea of spending all day with Bryn had enough appeal to consider it—and it wouldn't exactly be lying if he called in claiming he needed to spend the day in bed.

The sign was awkward in his arms as he shifted it to knock. But the door was flung open before he had a chance to raise a hand.

Bryn stood in the doorway, a grin bursting across her face. "Hi, Zane."

His lips curved into a smile. "Hey, Bryn." That was it—all he could think to say. The sight of her in a light blue tank top and cut-off jean shorts took his breath away. Her tanned legs looked a mile long and her feet were bare, her toes shiny with some kind of glittery pink polish that reminded him of cotton candy. Her hair was loose and curled softly around her shoulders, and the woman looked good enough to eat.

"You gonna come in, or are you just gonna stand on the porch and stare at me all night?" she said, teasing.

His smile curved wider. "From where I'm standing, the view is just about perfect."

Her grin turned shy, and she ducked her head. "You do surprise me, Zane Taylor."

He surprised himself. Where had that flirty comment come from? He was usually terrible with any kind of sappy lines. He'd never had to use them before. The kind of women he'd been with—when the need had arisen—hadn't needed to be wooed or pursued. They'd usually come to him—probably after all their other options had run dry—and all it usually took was purchasing a round of shots and a grunt of agreement to end up in someone's dark bedroom. There was no conversation, no expectation of a relationship, just a need to be filled.

His throat tightened, and his heart raced with panic in his chest. He took a step back, suddenly as skittish and spooked as a wild stallion penned in a corral for the first time. What was he thinking? He shouldn't be here, shouldn't be smiling at Bryn and saying flowery words, shouldn't be setting up the expectation that he was worth getting involved with.

Bryn reached out a hand and took his, twining her

fingers with his and holding him still. "Whoa there, cowboy. Don't go backing out on me now." She smiled again, but this smile was different—it wasn't flirty or excited; it was calm and full of steady reassurance. It was like she knew what he was thinking and she was telling him with her eyes and the firm pressure of her fingers interlaced with his that it was okay, that he was worth something.

Instead of pulling away, instead of backing off the porch and driving off in his truck, he let her lead him inside and push the door closed behind him.

"So, are we gonna talk about the elephant in the room?" she asked.

Aw hell. Was she really going to make him talk about his feelings of inadequacy? Make him admit that he knew he wasn't worthy of a girl like her? Well, he might have dropped a few sentimental lines, but he wasn't about to go pouring out his heart. Better to act dumb than to start rambling more gibberish about how darn pretty she was. "What do you mean?"

She chuckled and pointed to the package in his arms. "I mean this big ol' wrapped-up thing you're holding. What is this thing?"

He let out a breath. *Whew.* She meant the sign. Of course she meant the sign. Why would she want to talk about their feelings? They'd only been together for one night. *Damn, Zane, this girl is making you soft.* He set the sign on the kitchen counter. "I made you something. It was just an idea that came to me, and I thought you might like it."

"You made me something?" Her eyes were wide. "Wow. That's so cool."

"Don't go getting too excited. You don't even know what it is yet. And if you don't like it, it's totally fine. Don't feel pressured, like you have to use it or anything. It was probably a stupid idea."

"Oh my gosh, would you just shut up and show it to me?"

"Okay. Okay." He watched her face as he pulled back the burlap.

She clapped a hand over her heart as her eyes went wide and welled with tears. Reaching out her fingers, she traced the letters of the sign: HEAVEN CAN WAIT HORSE RESCUE RANCH, CREEDENCE, COLORADO. Her face beamed with joy as she looked up at him. "It's perfect," she whispered.

He swallowed, surprised at the burn in the back of his throat. He hadn't realized until this moment just how much he'd wanted her to love it. "Yeah?"

She nodded and stepped toward him, throwing her arms around his neck and pulling him into a tight hug. "I love it. It's absolutely a thousand times exactly perfect."

He held her close, burying his head in her neck. "You're a thousand times exactly perfect." He'd thought the words in his head and hadn't meant to say them out loud, but they hung in the air, a whisper of promise waiting to be taken.

Bryn pulled back and looked into his eyes, that same reassurance she'd shown him a few minutes before still shining there. She reached up and traced her finger lightly down the scar marring his cheek. "So are you, Zane. So are you."

His heart felt like it was being squeezed in a vise and the burn deepened in his throat. He didn't know what to say, how to put into words what her words meant to him. All he could do was show her. He pressed his lips to hers and kissed her with everything in him.

She met his passion and pressed herself into him as she kissed him back. She felt so damn good, fitting perfectly into the circle of his arms. He could stand here and kiss her all night. Except now she was pulling him back and down onto the sofa. Writhing under him, she wiggled her body, pressing against all the good spots—the spots that hummed and sizzled and sent heat surging through his veins. He actually felt a vibration between them. Wait. That was an actual vibration. It was the cell phone he'd jammed into his front pocket.

Bryn pulled back and grinned at him. "Is that your phone vibrating, or are you just happy to see me?"

He grinned back. "Oh darlin', I'm very happy to see you." The phone ceased its buzzing. Zane leaned down to kiss her again, but the pulsations started again.

"I think you either need to answer it, or shift your hips about three inches lower, and we'll hope they keep calling."

He chuckled, considering the idea, as he sat back and dug the phone from his pocket. It was Logan. He didn't call often. If he had something on the ranch that needed his attention, he usually texted. He tapped the phone and held it to his ear. "This is Zane. And this better be important."

"It is," Logan said, unfazed by his gruff greeting. The two men were used to each other after spending the last several months working together. "I just got a call from a buddy of mine who rides bulls, and he found your guy. He's in Fort Collins."

"You sure it's him?"

"I'm sure," Logan confirmed. "Besides the description and the stupid spiderweb tattoo on his hand, the guy introduced himself to my friend. And he confirmed he's driving the truck. He said it's parked at the fairgrounds right now. If you've got time, I'll pick you up, and we can head down there and initiate Operation Dick Parker."

Zane looked down at Bryn. Her cheeks were flushed and her hair was mussed from his fingers splaying in it. She looked good enough to eat. As much as he wanted to get back to sampling her, he knew she'd rather take the opportunity to get her stolen things back. At least he hoped she would. There was a strong possibility she'd be pissed and tell him to mind his own damn business. "You want to go for a ride?"

Her eyebrows raised, but she nodded, as if she could tell he wouldn't be asking if it weren't important. "Sure."

"I'm at Bryn's. She's coming with," he told Logan. He didn't have a problem confronting the guy on his own— he had a few choice words and actions for the guy—but it wouldn't hurt to have Logan along as backup.

"Good. Be there in fifteen," he said, then disconnected the call.

Zane pushed off the sofa, already missing the feel of Bryn next to him. "Logan is picking us up. He'll be here in fifteen minutes."

"Where are we going?"

"To take back what's yours."

"You found Pete?"

He nodded. "And the truck. You wanna go get it?"

She scrambled from the sofa and pushed her shoulders back. "Hell yes I do."

Zane narrowed his eyes. "You mad?"

"At him? Or you?"

"Yeah."

She shrugged. "Course I'm mad at him. I'm still pissed as hell that he took my money and my stuff and stole my grandpa's truck. As for you, and Logan apparently, I'm going to assume your hearts are in the right place."

He nodded again. "Yeah, and my foot's gonna be in the right place when I kick this guy's ass for stealing from you."

"Get in line."

Fourteen minutes later, Logan's truck pulled into the driveway. Zane and Bryn had each scarfed down a couple of the tacos she had made them for supper. Then Zane had fed the dogs while Bryn packed a small cooler with drinks and snacks for the road, and they'd grabbed jackets and were waiting on the porch for Logan. Zane had considered bringing the baseball bat Bryn had wielded a few days earlier, but he figured between him and Logan, they had enough muscle power to take on one slimy bull rider. And the assault charge would probably be less if he only used his fists.

They'd decided to leave all the dogs at home, and Bryn and Zane climbed into the pickup with Logan.

"Hey, Lo," Bryn said, scooting onto the bench seat next to him and digging for the seatbelt.

"Hey, Bryn." He took the buckle she handed him and clicked it into the clasp. "You mad?"

"She hasn't decided yet," Zane said by way of greeting. He pulled his door shut and clicked his belt into place. "She packed us drinks and snacks though, so she can't be too angry."

"Snacks are always a good sign." Logan laughed as he pulled the truck out onto the highway. "And we only did it because we love ya and hate that this asswipe took advantage of your kind heart."

Zane looked out the window, trying to keep his body from tensing at Logan's easy use of the words "we love ya."

There was only one person he'd ever said "I love you" to. And she had died the same day he'd uttered the words.

He pushed thoughts of Sarah from his mind. Bryn wasn't her. And he wasn't the same guy he'd been back then, he tried to convince himself. He was older, but he wasn't sure he was any better.

Zane felt a warm pressure against his palm and looked down to see Bryn twining her fingers with his. It was a small thing, but it meant everything.

Traffic through Denver was a bitch, so the trip to Fort Collins took over two hours, and Bryn's nerves were frazzled by the time they exited the highway and drove toward the city. It was nerve-rattling enough to imagine facing down Pete, but sitting next to Zane for the last two hours had her nerve endings spinning like a million tiny tops.

The guy was wound tighter than a drum, and she could tell by the way his shoulders tightened and hunched in that something had been bothering him. She knew him well enough by now to know he wouldn't want to talk in front of Logan. Although she wasn't sure he'd want to talk at all. She'd seen this silent, broody mood of his before, and the best way she'd figured to deal with it was to offer him reassurance that she was there and let him be for a bit.

She turned to Logan. "I saw Harper in town the other day. She had the goofiest grin on her face as she told me how great you-all were doing. She couldn't stop talking about how good you are with her boy."

Logan shrugged, but the grin spreading across his face displayed his pride. "Floyd's a great kid. I love hanging out with him."

"Me too. He's adorable. I told Harper she should bring him out to see the horses."

"He'd like that. And so would she."

"She seems happy. I'm glad. And don't forget, I'm the

one who set this whole happy-couple thing in motion by introducing the two of you."

He gave her a sideways grin. "How could I forget when you take every chance to remind me?"

She chuckled. "Well, remind Harper she owes me a peach cobbler."

"I'll tell her."

"She said Floyd did really well on the hockey team this year. Having you as his coach must have really helped."

Logan shrugged. "I don't know about that, but I have fun doing it." He reached over Bryn's head to nudge Zane on the shoulder. "How about you? You ever miss playing? We could use you on the alumni team."

Zane shook his head. "Nah. I wouldn't be much help. I haven't been on the ice in years."

"You'd be surprised. You used to be really good. I think once you put the skates on, it would all come back to you."

"I forgot that you two played hockey together in high school," Bryn told Zane. "I'm so used to seeing you on the back of a horse with your feet in the stirrups, it's hard to imagine you on the ice with them in a pair of skates."

"He was our best defenseman," Logan told her. "I never saw him throw a punch, but he just looked mean, and he was big, so kids got out of his way before he even had the chance to check them."

Apprehension tensed Bryn's shoulders. "Well, I hope you're not planning to throw any punches today. I didn't bring any money to bail you out if you get arrested." She nodded at the bag of snacks on the floor of the truck. "Not unless they take beef jerky and Oreos as payment."

She was trying to make a joke, but a scowl crossed Zane's face. His voice took on a hard edge. "I'm not planning to get arrested."

Bryn frowned as they turned into the parking lot of the fairgrounds. He hadn't said he wasn't planning to throw a punch though. "There's the truck," she cried, pointing to the old blue pickup. She'd know it anywhere. Besides the recognizable dent in the front fender she'd put there when she'd been learning to drive and had underestimated the distance she was to the barn, the back bumper still had the American flag sticker that read *Support Our Troops* affixed to it.

Logan parked next to it, and they got out and looked through the window. The cab of the truck was strewn with fast food trash and empty beer cans, but a new gear bag, saddle, and helmet sat on the seat. A sleeping bag was balled into one corner of the floor next to an old duffel overflowing with clothes.

"It looks like he's living in here," Zane said.

"He probably is," Bryn replied, trying the door handle. "Dang. It's locked."

"Hey, get the hell away from my truck," a voice yelled.

They turned to see Pete walking toward them. Bile rose in Bryn's throat, a combination of nerves and fury. She hadn't realized how mad she was until this very moment. She stomped forward, curling her hands into fists to keep them from shaking. "Actually, it's *my* truck."

Pete stopped in his tracks and took a few stumbling steps backward. The color drained from his face as he looked from Bryn to the two angry cowboys flanking her sides. His gaze darted from her to Zane to Logan, then behind him as if he was looking for a place to run. Then he took a breath as if composing himself and changed his expression, like a snake shedding its skin. His appearance went from alarmed to friendly, and he held out his arms. "Hey, Bryn. Good to see you, baby. You know I was just borrowing the truck. You know, like we talked about. I told you I was going to bring it back after rodeo season. Remember?"

Did he really think she was this stupid? She planted her hands on her hips and fixed him with her most steely stare. She'd been worried about what she'd say, but she shouldn't have. It was easy to know how to respond. "First of all, I'm not your *baby*. And second of all, we never talked about you *borrowing* the truck. *Or* my bank account. Or my grandfather's belt buckle."

"Did she say her bank account?" she heard Logan ask Zane behind her.

Zane grunted an affirmative response and took a step closer, so he was almost next to her but still letting her take the lead. She chanced a quick look to her right, where he stood like a six-foot-four grizzly bear protecting his mate. He didn't take his eyes off Pete, and she knew that menacing stare had to have the other man shaking in his boots.

"Now hold on there. This is all just a misunderstanding," he countered, moving his arm to cover his waist.

Bryn's heart leapt to her throat as she looked down and realized Pete was *wearing* the buckle. As if he'd won it himself. She pointed to his waist. "Take it off. Now."

"Bryn. Baby. Come on now."

"I believe the lady asked you *not* to call her baby," Zane said, his voice ominously deep and threatening. "And she told you to take the buckle off. Now."

Pete held his hands up in surrender. "Okay, fine. No problem. I was just wearing it as a lark anyway." He must have realized he wasn't going to charm her, and his tone turned from persuasive to condescending. "The thing isn't worth anything anyway. Nobody wants a buckle from a washed-up has-been like Cal Callahan."

"Well, I do. I want the buckle, and I'll be taking his truck back too." She held out her hand. "So hand over the keys while you're at it."

"I'll give you the stupid buckle, but you can't take the truck."

"I can. And I will."

"Listen, Bryn, I need that truck." His voice sank into a whine. "If you take it, where am I supposed to sleep?"

"Don't know. And I don't care. How about you creep back under the rock you crawled out from and sleep there?"

He narrowed his eyes as he passed her the buckle. "Now you're just being bitchy."

Zane took an aggressive step toward him, his arms pushing out from his sides in a fighter's stance. "You want to watch your mouth."

Pete shrank back. He dug the keys out of his pocket and tossed them on the ground in front of Bryn's feet.

She bent to pick them up, but Zane held his arm out in front of her. "Why don't you pick those up and hand them to the lady?"

"Why don't you kiss my ass?"

Zane didn't dignify Pete's question with a response. Instead, he just held still, his icy gaze trained on the other man.

Pete offered him a sneer, but when Zane's hands tightened into fists, he grudgingly bent forward and picked up the keys, then held them out to Bryn. "Whatever. That truck's a piece of shit too. Just let me get my stuff, and you can have it."

"Don't trouble yourself," Zane told him. "We'll get your stuff for you." He held his hand out to Bryn, who put the keys in his palm.

Pete followed them to the truck. Zane unlocked the door and passed the keys back to Bryn. He opened the door, and she reeled back at the mix of body odor, stale fast food, and feet.

Bryn put a hand on Zane's arm as he leaned into the truck. "That's awful."

He fixed her with a stare almost as hard as the one he'd given Pete. "I've shoveled out stalls filled with manure. I can handle the filth of this pig." He nodded to the other side of the truck. "Why don't you give Logan the keys, and he can open the other door and start airing the cab out?"

She passed the keys to Logan.

Zane started pulling stuff from the cab and tossing it to the ground. First the sleeping bag, then the duffel, and then the gear bag, helmet, and a pair of sneakers. Logan opened the other door and rolled down the window, then grabbed an empty plastic bag from the floor and started filling it with trash.

Pete shifted his weight from one foot to the other. "Look, it's my stuff. I can take care of it."

"You seem awful worried about what we're going to find in here, Peter," Zane said. "You hiding something from us?"

"No," he sneered. "It's just my stuff, and I don't want you pawing through it."

Logan popped the glove box. "Zane, he's got a pistol in here." He pointed to a handgun sitting amid a scatter of receipts, a stick of deodorant, and a black-and-gold box of condoms.

Bryn leaned in next to Zane, then turned back to Pete, a frown on her lips. "Magnums? Really, Pete?" She dropped her gaze to his crotch. "I don't think those are necessary."

She wasn't a mean person, but she felt mean. She wanted to make him pay. And she couldn't exactly beat the guy up, but she *could* embarrass him.

Zane offered him a smirk as he dug his hands under the seat. "Is the Glock what you're so worried we'd find? Or maybe it's this?" He pulled a dented metal box from under the seat. "Whatcha got in here, Pete? Coke? Weed? Another gun?"

"None of your business," Pete said, his eyes going a little wild as he pushed forward. "Just give it to me. It's mine."

He must have sensed a shift in Pete's behavior, because Logan slammed the door and came back around the truck to stand closer to Bryn.

Zane set the box on the seat and popped the latch.

CHAPTER 15

BRYN GASPED AS SHE SAW THE CONTENTS OF THE BOX. It did have a lighter, a pipe, and a Ziploc bag filled with weed in it, but it also had cash inside. There were two strapped bundles of twenty dollar bills totaling two thousand dollars each plus an assortment of loose bills in the bottom of the box.

Zane eyed Bryn. "I think we found the money from your bank account."

"But where's the other half?" she asked Pete before she could catch herself.

"Wait," Zane said, his eyes going wide. "This asshole stole eight thousand dollars from you?"

"Borrowed," Pete interjected.

"Shut it," Zane commanded as he held up his hand. "I didn't realize it was that much. I think we need to get the police involved."

"No, we don't," Pete said. "We don't need the cops. We can work this out ourselves."

Bryn leaned in toward Zane and lowered her voice. "I told you I don't want to involve the police. Or the bank. I know the teller who gave him the money. She's a single mom and a good person. And she can't afford to lose her job."

"She *should* lose her job. This isn't a little mistake."

Bryn sighed. "He didn't get all that from my account. Most of it was from the sale barn where we auctioned off the calves, but if we start an investigation, the teller could get caught in the crossfire. And really, how can I fault her for getting taken in by this guy's charm and bullshit story when I fell for it too?"

Zane pressed his lips together but nodded his agreement. "I'll do whatever you want."

"You can't take all my money," Pete whined. "What am I supposed to live on? How am I supposed to eat?"

Zane pushed past her and grabbed Pete by the front of the shirt. He hauled him up against his chest and spoke directly into his face. "I told you to shut it. With everything in me, I want to kick your ass ten times to Sunday, but for the sake of the lady, I am doing a damn fine job of holding my temper. So far. But if I hear one more word out of your filthy mouth, I will let loose a can of whoop ass on you the likes of which you have never seen or imagined."

Bryn swallowed. She'd never seen this side of Zane before. He hadn't actually done anything violent, hadn't thrown a punch, hadn't lost his temper, but he gave off the impression that if he did, it would be scary as hell.

"Whatever," Pete muttered, glaring at Zane, but not saying anything more. Zane let him go and stepped back toward Bryn. He took the two straps of cash and held them out to her.

She hesitated. "He's right. This does look like everything he has. I don't want to take all his money and leave him with nothing."

Zane gave her a double take. "Why not? That's what this asshole did to you. And besides, you're not taking *his* money. This is *your* money. This is the money he *stole* from you. Although it's apparently not all of it. Did he really take eight thousand dollars from you?"

She gave a slight nod as she hung her head.

He reached out and lifted her chin to look up at him. "Don't you dare hang your head. This isn't your fault. This is all on him. You were being kind and generous. You trusted this guy, and he took advantage of you."

She nodded. "You're right. It is my money." She still held the belt buckle in one hand, and she took the cash with the other.

Zane offered her an encouraging smile. "Damn right it is." He turned to Pete, who was still glaring at him. "Bryn is going to take her money back, and we're going to keep the Glock and that new saddle too. On deposit. I'm tempted to keep all that fancy new gear that I'm sure you bought with her money, but I'm going to let you use it to win back the cash you owe her. For now. But if you don't start making payments to her, I'll find you and collect it. We're returning the saddle for a refund, and you can get the gun back when you've paid her in full. Otherwise, she'll sell it and keep the profit."

"That's bullshit. You can't take my stuff too," Pete protested. Zane scowled, and Pete dropped his head. "Whatever, man. Just take it and go."

Logan had gone back around the truck and finished clearing out the floor of the cab. He took the gun and a small box of ammunition from the glove box. After he dropped the magazine and emptied the chamber, he set it on the seat and swept the rest of the contents into the plastic bag with the other trash. He replaced the gun and ammo in the glove box. "I think we got it all."

Zane nodded. "I've checked everything over here." He looked at Bryn, who was still holding her grandfather's belt buckle in one hand and the cash in the other. "You good, darlin'?"

She nodded back, still a little in shock at the evening's proceedings. She couldn't believe she was holding four thousand dollars of her lost cattle earnings. She'd already given the money up in her head—denied it, raged about it, bargained to get it back, mourned it, and had finally accepted it as truly gone. And now, thanks to Zane, she had some of it back. "I'm good."

Zane closed the lid of the metal box, leaving the drug paraphernalia and the stray bills inside, and tossed it on the pile of stuff he'd liberated from the truck. He tapped the top of the truck. "Let's go, then." He paused and gave Pete a quick glance. "Unless you got anything to say to him. Then I can wait."

What? No. She had nothing to say to Pete except *good riddance.* Why would she want to tell him anything?

She looked from Zane to Pete, then realized she did have a few things to say. She took a deep breath and passed the cash to Zane. "Hold this for me, would you? I *do* have a few things to say."

Zane grinned and gave her an encouraging nod. "Thatta girl."

She took the courage Zane offered and marched up to Pete and stared him straight in the eye. "What you did to me was wrong. You took advantage of me, you stole from me, and you made me feel like crap about myself." She held up the buckle. It barely fit in her palm, but she tightened her fingers around it, drawing bravery from the cool steel prize that her grandfather had worked so hard to earn. "This buckle is worth ten thousand of you."

She kept her features hard, her chin high as she glared at him, but she was shaking inside.

Instead of any flicker of remorse in his eyes, he glanced down at the buckle with disdain. He offered her a scornful laugh. "That thing wasn't worth the time I had to spend with you to get it. I tried to sell the thing and couldn't even get ten bucks for it. It's as worthless as you are."

She didn't think. She just reacted, raising her hand and smacking him across the face with the buckle still cupped in her hand. The metal made a solid *thwack* against his face, and his jaw whipped to the side.

He let out a surprised grunt of pain, his expression indicating he never saw that coming. His hand went to his cheek as his widened eyes narrowed into furious slits. "You bitch!" He lunged toward her, reaching for her throat, but was knocked backward as Zane shoved him in the chest.

Bryn hadn't even heard Zane come up behind her, but she should have known he'd have her back. Pete stumbled back a step, then fell on his ass. The ground was muddy around the water trough, where he fell, and she was sure enough horses and cows had trampled through there to leave a little fresh poo behind. Grungy mud streaked his jeans, but the muck wasn't half as nasty as the filth he had said to her.

Zane took a menacing step toward Pete, towering over him as he glared down. "Don't ever speak to her like that again. In fact, don't ever speak to her again at all. We all know you still owe her money, and you better pay her back. Just because she hasn't gone to the cops yet doesn't mean she won't. We found you once, we can find you again. And believe me, if you don't start sending her cash, we *will* find you. And the outcome of that meeting will be much different from this one."

Zane turned and walked back toward her, wiping his hands on his jeans. "You got anything else you want to add?"

She shook her head. "Nope. Now I am good."

"Great. Then let's get out of here."

Logan had grabbed their jackets and the cooler from his truck. He grimaced as he put them in the cab of her grandfather's pickup. "You might want to use these jackets to sit on."

"Good idea." Zane shook the other man's hand. "Thanks for finding him and for the ride down here."

"Glad to do it."

Bryn gave him a hug. "Really. Thank you. This means a lot. Sorry you had to drive all the way down here."

"It's no problem. I've got some stuff I need to do in

Denver anyway. And I'm going to spend the night at Tessa's grandma's house." He gestured to the saddle. "I just saw that in the window of Colorado Saddle last month. I'm sure that's where he got it. I need to stop there on my way up the pass if you want me to return it."

Zane passed him the saddle. "That'd be much appreciated."

He shrugged. "It's no trouble. I'm going there anyway. And it's the least I can do to help." He tossed the saddle in the cab of his truck, then took off.

Bryn took Logan's suggestion and spread her jacket on the seat before climbing into the truck. "I think our first stop should be the car wash so we can try to clean this thing out."

"We passed one on our way into town," Zane said, not bothering with the jacket as he climbed into the other side. "There's a Walmart across the street from it. I need to make a quick stop there first."

They pulled out of the fairgrounds and drove the ten minutes to the store. Bryn waited in the truck while Zane ran in.

He came out ten minutes later, his arms filled with shopping bags. He opened the truck door and set the bags on the seat. "I just grabbed a couple of things I figured we'd need to get this rig back in shape." He pulled out each purchase as he talked. "I got you some Febreze, some 409, and some Armor All, as well as paper towels and Clorox Disinfecting Wipes. I threw in one of those car air freshener things that smell like baking cookies or some such crap. I grabbed the vanilla one, since it kinda reminds me of you. And I got one of those seat cover things to put over the whole bench after we vacuum this cab out. It should fit. They only had orange or blue, and I know you're a Broncos fan, but I still figured you'd like the blue better. And I grabbed a new set of floor mats. No use trying to vacuum those. They aren't the originals anyway, so we'll just toss 'em and replace 'em with new ones."

"Good thinking." She shook her head over the array of stuff. "Wow. I can't believe you got all this stuff. This is great. The truck will be cleaner than it's been in years." She gestured to the large bag still on the floor of the truck. "So what's in the last bag?"

He shrugged and looked away. "That was kind of an impulse buy. I saw it as I was rushing down the aisle, and it made me think of you, so I grabbed it. With your new business and all, I just thought you'd like it." He passed the bag to her.

A flutter bounded around in her stomach. "You bought me a present?"

He lifted his shoulders again. "Yeah. I guess. I mean, it isn't much."

She peered into the bag and let out a gasp as she pulled out the soft fleece blanket. The cozy fabric was light cream and had a picture of two brown horses standing by a mountain lake on the front of it. "Oh, Zane. I love it!"

A grin tugged at the corners of his lips. "It was nothing."

"It *is* something. I really do love it. It's perfect. And one of the horses looks just like Beauty."

"Yeah, that's what I thought. I mean…kinda."

She leaned over the seat and wrapped him in a hug. "Thank you. It's wonderful. This means a lot." She pulled back and wrinkled her nose. "I really do want to give you a big fat kiss and totally make out with you right now, but this truck stinks and it's really crushing the mood. I just want to go to the car wash and clean every speck of that jerk wad out of it."

"Agreed." He climbed into the cab and slammed the door. "Let's do it. Then we'll christen it with a first-rate make-out session later."

"Promises, promises," she said, laughing as she pulled out of the parking lot and into the car wash on the other side of the street.

They spent close to an hour vacuuming, scrubbing, and cleaning the cab to within an inch of its old life. It touched Bryn the way Zane took care working on the ancient dash, as if he recognized the truck wasn't just a vehicle but a part of her grandfather's legacy.

It burned her to think how Pete had trashed it, and she took out her frustrations by scrubbing the grime from the windows until they squeaked. They'd sprayed the seats down with Febreze when they'd first started and the fabric had dried in the time they'd been working on the rest of the truck. Zane put in the new floor mats, then they stretched the fresh seat cover over the bench and folded the fleece throw over the back of the seat.

Bryn took in a breath of fresh, cleaner-scented air and patted the seat next to her. "I think we did it. Now we just need to drive through the car wash and clean the outside."

Zane climbed in, and she started the truck and pulled it up to the car wash. Sticking in a twenty, she chose the most zealous cycle, then rolled up the windows and eased into the car wash until the light blinked red for her to stop. The arm of the washer came out and started the first cycle of sudsy spray over the hood.

She turned to Zane. "Did you say something about christening this cab with a first-rate make-out session?"

He chuckled. "I don't think there's enough time on the wash cycle to get to first-rate, but we can give it a trial run." He pulled her onto his lap and slanted a kiss along her lips.

She pressed against his chest, wrapping her arms around his neck as she melted into the kiss. He smelled like Armor All mixed with a hint of his aftershave—not a bad scent. His hand twisted into her hair as he cupped her head with his palm.

Her breath caught as his other hand slid under her shirt and into the cup of her bra. His tongue explored her mouth as his thumb grazed her tightened nipple, the sensations sending surges of heat to her happy place, and she squirmed in his lap.

She couldn't get enough of him—enough of his taste, his smell, the feel of his hands as they explored her body. Her fingers gripped the fabric of his T-shirt, wrinkling it in her grasp as she pressed closer to him.

A car horn honked. Bryn pulled away to realize the car wash had finished and the car behind them was anxious to get in next. The mother in the front seat wore an annoyed expression and the two middle school girls in the back seat had their arms wrapped around their shoulders as they mimed kissy faces and giggled.

"Oh shoot." She giggled herself as she scrambled from Zane's lap back into the seat and put the truck in gear. "We got busted."

"It was worth it," Zane said, his lips spreading into a grin.

With the truck cleaned and the exterior washed, Bryn pulled out onto the highway and headed for home. She caught a glance of herself in the mirror and gasped at the chunk of hair sticking up and out the side of her head. But Zane was right. *It was worth it*, she thought as she smoothed her hair, and her face split into a naughty grin.

Two hours and all the snacks later, they finally made it back to Creedence. The trip had been fun. They hadn't talked the whole time, but they hadn't needed to. They were okay sometimes listening to the radio or looking out the window, just being together.

As they approached the far side of her property, Bryn had an idea. She pulled off the road and up to a gate leading into one of their pastures. "Can you grab the gate?"

Zane didn't seem to mind the detour. "We need to check on your cows?"

"No. I just want to show you something."

He shrugged and got out to open the gate, then waited for her to drive through and closed it behind them. He climbed back into the pickup, and she drove through the pasture and into a stand of trees. "We've got a stream that runs through our property, and there's a little lake up here. I haven't been up here in a while, but it's pretty neat. A hot spring feeds into it, so the water's not hot, but in some places it's surprisingly warm," she told him as she pulled through a break in the trees.

She loved hearing his quick intake of breath as he took in the scene of the small quiet lake nestled against the side of the mountain. "It's beautiful, isn't it?"

"It is," he agreed, getting out of the truck and walking to the water's edge. She followed and stood next to him as they gazed over the water. "You say the water is warm?"

"Yeah, I love to come up here and swim in the summer."

He peered up at the moon. "It does seem like a fine night for a swim. Too bad I didn't bring my suit."

She shrugged. "Me either. Guess we'll just have to improvise." She tried to hold back her grin as she grabbed the hem of her tank top and pulled it over her head. Zane was already kicking off his boots and shimmying out of his jeans.

They stripped down to nothing, and she waded into the water. Bryn had always loved swimming in the lake. Loved the way the sun warmed it from the top down, so she could feel various temperatures of water along different parts of her body, like the assorted colored layers of Jell-O in a mold. Now that she was in the lake with Zane, the water felt different, silkier, like a caress against her skin.

She dipped under the water, the only way to get used to it quickly, then came back up with a shiver as she smoothed her wet hair back. With a whoop, Zane came crashing in after her, diving in and popping up several yards away.

He swam back to her, his muscled arms slicing easily through the water, then slid one of those arms around her waist and drew her to him. "You were right. This place is beautiful, and the water is amazing."

"You're amazing."

"Yeah, you thought my diving skills were that great, huh?"

She nudged his shoulder, acutely aware of the proximity of her naked body next to his. "I meant what you did for me tonight—finding Pete and helping me get my stuff back."

He shrugged. "It was mostly Logan."

"Don't do that."

"Do what?"

"Brush off the great thing you did and act like it was nothing."

"It *was* nothing. Not the part about you getting your stuff back. That was great. But the role I played in you getting it back was nothing."

"Not to me."

Zane was looking over her shoulder, avoiding her eyes. He pointed behind her. "What's up with the side of that hill? It looks like there's a rope ladder leading out of the water then some steps are dug into the dirt leading up to the top of the hill."

She turned to see what he was looking at. "There are. We built all that there years ago. Made it easier to climb up to that ledge—we used to jump off it when we were kids."

"Let's do it," Zane said, already untangling himself from her and swimming toward the rope.

"No way. I said we did it when we were kids. That rope is probably rotted through."

"Seems sturdy," Zane said, pulling on the ladder. "How deep is the water here?"

"Plenty deep."

"Any trees or anything under it we might hit if we jump in?"

"No. We swam all over it, plus I've seen this lake when it was half-empty during a drought year, and there's nothing in it except some fish and probably a few turtles."

"Then let's do it. Let's jump off."

"No way."

"Why not? You said the water hasn't changed."

"It's not the water that's changed. It's me. I've grown up, and I don't do much jumping off the side of ledges anymore."

"Then maybe it's high time you did." He grabbed her hand and pulled her through the water to the ladder. "You want to go first? Then I can admire the view."

She nudged his arm again. "No thanks. You go ahead." Then *she'd* get to admire the view. And what a view. In the moonlight, the scars on Zane's back were barely visible. Instead, his body looked like it was sculpted from alabaster. His muscles rippled and flexed as he climbed the ladder, then turned to help her. Once out of the water, she followed him up the steps, tiny pebbles digging into her bare feet and dirt sticking to her skin. A shiver ran through her as the cool mountain air blew over her wet skin.

"You ready?" he asked, taking her hand and leading her to the edge of the grassy ledge. "Let's jump together."

"No, I'm not ready." She took a deep breath, searching his eyes for encouragement. He smiled and nodded. "But I'll do it anyway. Just give me a second to find my gumption."

"You've always had your gumption. Don't think about it, just do it. One. Two…"

"Three!" She whooped, and they jumped in together. Splashing and sputtering, she came up laughing and swam toward him.

"That was awesome," he hollered. He pulled her close and kissed her mouth, the lake water cool and wet between their lips. Their bodies were slick and warm as they pressed together, their legs tangling as they treaded water in unison.

"I can't believe I did that," she said, a thrill of exhilaration coursing through her.

"Why not? You said you used to do it all the time as kids."

"I know, but we were kids. We weren't as afraid of falling."

He brushed her hair back from her forehead, his gaze intense and deep as he stared into her eyes. "The fallin' is easy, darlin'. It's the jumpin' that takes the strength of will."

She swallowed, emotion suddenly thickening her throat, as if her body knew that he wasn't just talking about the ledge. She was already falling, and falling hard, for Zane Taylor, but was she really ready to jump headlong into this thing with him?

He dipped his head and kissed the side of her neck, the scruff of his whiskered chin scraping the delicate skin. She tipped her head back and sighed as she fell.

CHAPTER 16

BRYN HUDDLED IN THE WATER AS ZANE RAN UP TO the truck to grab the new blanket. They'd spent the last hour floating in the water, swimming, splashing, and kissing. It was the best swim of her life. She wasn't ready for it to end, but their fingers were getting prune-y, and it was time to get out. It hadn't seemed awkward when she was in the water with him, but now the idea of walking naked up to the truck while shivering in the cool night air made her feel embarrassed and shy.

Zane didn't seem bothered. She noticed a new confidence in him when he was around her. It wasn't that he hadn't been confident before—he had always carried himself with this straight-postured badass don't-mess-with-me/I-don't-need-anyone vibe. But he also wore his hat low and often held his head so the scar on his face was turned away from whoever he was talking to.

But he'd been different since that first night when she'd made him show her the scars on his back and she hadn't recoiled. He certainly walked with confidence as he strode back to her, the blanket held out in his arms, like he didn't even notice the rough ground underfoot. She tried not to wince as the rocks and pebbles dug into her feet as she waded out of the water and into the folds of the throw.

The fleece felt luxurious against her skin. She hadn't imagined using the blanket as a towel when Zane gave it to her, but it was perfect for the job. "You'd better get in here with me," she told him, opening one side of the blanket.

He slipped in next to her, the heat of his body warming her chilled one. Leaning in, he kissed her again, then kept kissing her as he walked her backward to the bed of the truck. He dropped the tailgate and lifted her to sit on the edge. Pulling out of the blanket, he turned back to get their stuff.

She swung her legs on the tailgate, her skin drying, a sly grin on her face as she enjoyed the view of his naked form walking back to the water's edge, where they had shed their clothing. He grabbed their things and tossed his boots and her shoes into the bed, but set their clothes on the tailgate next to her, then stepped back into the space between her legs.

"You ready to get dressed and head home?"

She leaned forward and placed a soft kiss on his neck. "Not particularly."

He chuckled, and she could feel the rumble in his throat. "Good. Because it seems like a perfect night to see the stars." He took the pile of clothes, folded them into a wrinkled square and set them behind her. He patted the makeshift pillow, then gently laid her back in the bed of the truck.

She looked up into the milky blackness. "It's a little cloudy. I'm not sure we'll see a ton of stars."

He peeled back the folds of the blanket and pressed a tender kiss on her bare stomach next to her belly button, then another one an inch lower. His tongue slid along her belly, his lips skimming over her skin, and she couldn't think straight as warmth coursed through her body. "Those aren't the stars I was talking about," he said, pressing another kiss even lower.

Oh.

He lowered to his knees and gently eased open her legs on the tailgate. Leaning in, he laid a trail of hot kisses along her inner thigh.

Oh. Oh. Ohhhhh.

He shifted again, then his mouth and his hands were on her, touching, caressing, stroking, licking. His lips lingered over her legs, her thighs, stopping to languish a slew of slow kisses in the soft spot inside her knee. His whiskers scraped her thighs, and she feared she would pass out from the anticipation of his mouth on her most sensitive spot.

His hands were warm on her cool skin and spirals of lust swirled through her body as she luxuriated in the bliss of Zane's attention. The heat and desire surging through her combined with his tender kisses had her body feeling as if it were melting into the warm metal of the truck. His sure touch had pleasure coursing through her, and her knees would have buckled if she hadn't already been lying down.

Her nerves sizzled as heat coiled in her belly and spread through her limbs, relaxing, then tensing, then easing again as the sensations climbed and built. Zane's touch was soft then firm, tender then strong, as he skillfully unraveled her.

A tiny shift here, a bit of pressure there, then solid strokes that made the muscles in her legs shake and the ache between her legs almost unbearable. His fingers tightened on her thighs as a tide of heat rose and crashed through her.

Her hands tensed, clutching the blanket, and her world exploded as she gazed into the night sky and did, indeed, see stars. A whole crazy sky full of incredible, mind-blowing stars.

Zane spent most of the next day thinking about those stars as he tried to focus on the work at hand. But his mind kept drifting to the time spent with Bryn tangled together in the back of the truck, and then the time spent in her bed when they got back to her house, and then the time spent that morning when they'd woken up wrapped in each other's arms and a mess of warm dogs curled around their legs.

It was all so domesticated, waking up together, feeding the animals, fooling around in the kitchen while they made breakfast. He didn't used to do sleepovers, didn't do breakfast. But everything seemed different with Bryn.

Maybe it was the way she'd faced his scars head-on the first night that made them seem less significant, or maybe it was the way when she looked at him, she seemed to really see *him*—her gaze didn't stray to the jagged tear across his cheek. And her eyes lit when he walked into the room as her lips curved into a smile that he hadn't ever seen her give anyone else. It always felt like it was just for him. He wanted to be better, to be more, to live up to the ideal of what she thought she saw in him.

She'd invited him for dinner again. This time they sat down at the table and talked as they made their way through the perfectly prepared chicken-fried steaks and mashed potatoes and gravy and buttery biscuits she'd baked.

Zane leaned back in his chair and patted his stomach when he'd finished. "Darlin', that was one amazing meal. You keep feeding me like this, I'm never going home." He hadn't meant it exactly like that, or at least he hadn't meant to say it like that. Although it was true: he preferred being at the old farmhouse a hundred times more than spending time at the house he shared with his dad. He didn't ever call it his home. *Home* was not a word that had a place in his vocabulary. It was just "the house," as in "I'm heading back to the house."

Bryn smiled coyly as she lowered her chin and looked up at him from under her lashes. "Do you *want* me to keep feeding you like this?"

The question came off as playful and flirty, but he knew there was meaning and intent behind it. His hand was lying next to hers on the table, and he grazed the side of her pinkie with his. A soft touch, but deliberate in its execution. "Yeah, I do." His voice came out lower and huskier than he'd intended. "But if I keep taking second helpings covered in your gravy, I'm going to be as fat as that new pig out there."

She chuckled, the enormity of the moment swept aside by his casual joke. "Speaking of that pig, she broke out of her pen today."

"Nice. Did she run off to another farm so now *they* have to feed her?"

She playfully nudged his arm. "No, she didn't run away. In fact, she made her way up to the house. When I got home from my shift at the diner, she was lying in a patch of sun on the front porch with a couple of the barn cats curled next to her. She got up when she saw me and came running like she was a dog that was glad I was home."

"She probably was. You can't feed her if you're not here."

"Stop it. I thought it was sweet. I let her into the house for a bit, and she followed me around as I cleaned up, then fell asleep next to the sofa with her head on one of the throw pillows."

"You let that pig into the house?"

"Of course. Annie said she was used to being a house pig. After a bit, I took her back to her pen, and she settled in like she'd had a nice visit and was plumb wore out. I'm considering leaving her gate unlatched so she can come and go as she pleases."

He shook his head. "Give it a shot. You've already got

a goat that roams this farm like it owns the place. Why not have a pig running around too? The worst that could happen is that it tries to run back home to Kansas. And I'm not sure that would be a bad thing. But I wouldn't recommend doing that with the horses or cows."

"Anyone ever tell you that you have a smart mouth?"

"Many times." He raised an eyebrow. "Anyone ever tell you that you have a gorgeous mouth?" He liked the way she ducked her head and her cheeks brightened with a touch of pink when he complimented her. "I'd like to spend a little time with that mouth, but I want to get your sign put up before it gets dark."

"This is really happening, isn't it?" Her voice held a dreamy quality and she let out a sigh.

His throat clicked as he swallowed. Yeah, this thing *was* really happening. It was barreling down on them like a train with no brakes. He'd never spent so much time just hanging out with a woman, living a life with her. Which seemed stupid because it had only been a few days, but maybe it seemed longer since he'd been thinking about it for so long. And apparently so had she—he couldn't remember ever having a woman talk about him with that dreamy look on her face.

She held her hands up and mimed the shape of a sign. "Heaven Can Wait Horse Rescue. Seriously, I can't believe I'm really doing this. Who would have thought I could turn this old farm into something so useful and instrumental in helping so many others?"

Dumbass. Of course she wasn't talking about their

relationship. Who even said they were *in* a relationship? He picked at a small scab on the side of his hand, scraping the dried skin away from the tender spot below. A small dab of blood bubbled from the wound, and he wiped the back of his hand on his thigh. "It's great," he muttered, though he did mean it. It *was* a great thing she was doing.

"Thank you," she said, seemingly oblivious to his uneasiness as she stood and picked up the platter from the chicken-fried steak. "I'll clean up these dishes if you want to go out now and work on the sign."

He shook his head. "Nah, there's not that big a rush. I can help."

She smiled. "Okay. I'll wash if you dry."

"Sounds good." He carried their plates into the kitchen and scraped them into the scrap bucket Bryn used for the cats.

"How about some music?"

"Sure."

A kitchen stereo was affixed under the cabinets, and she tapped the power button. The radio was tuned to an oldies station that played classic country music and the voice of Patsy Cline filled the kitchen. "I love this song," Bryn said, clearing the rest of the dishes as she softly sang along. The old farmhouse kitchen didn't have a dishwasher, so she filled the sink with warm sudsy water, then washed the glasses before dumping the plates and silverware in.

Zane leaned his hip against the counter, wiping the wet dishes with a tea towel before putting them in their place in the cabinet. He liked watching her, the quick, precise movements of a task she'd done a hundred times before. He liked the way she talked to the menagerie of dogs who padded around the kitchen, easily sidestepping them, unbothered by the fact they seemed to be constantly underfoot. Lucky liked to stay near her, usually dropping to lie by Bryn's feet wherever she was.

Grace mostly stayed on the dog bed in the corner, keeping a watchful eye on her pups. Much like the border collie kept a watchful eye on Zane. The collie didn't always have to be at his feet, but she could usually be found pretty close by.

Finished with the dishes, Bryn wrung out the rag and moved around the kitchen, wiping down the counters and stove. A new song came on, slow and bluesy. Zane watched, hypnotized by the swing of Bryn's shapely hips as she swayed to the music while she worked.

He stepped in behind her, sliding his arms around her middle and letting out a sigh as she leaned back into him. They swayed together, then he lowered his lips to her collar bone and placed a tender kiss there. "Wanna dance?" he asked softly against her neck.

She turned in his embrace and smoothly wound her arms around his neck as she laid her head on that spot between his shoulder and his chest. He slid his arms around her waist, one hand going flat against the small of her back and the other cupping her hip. They fit together, not like two pieces of a puzzle—he would never imagine that they came from the same kind of picture but were more like pieces of different puzzles that somehow seemed to still fit. She didn't clash and grate against him like other women in his life had.

No, Bryn seemed to fit flawlessly against him, her softness balancing out his rough parts.

"I didn't know you could dance," she said, her voice lazy and relaxed.

"I didn't know you could sing."

"I can't."

"I'm not much of a dancer either. But somehow when I'm doing it with you, you make it seem easy."

"Are you saying I'm easy?" she said, teasing.

"Gosh, I hope so." He chuckled as a new song came on, a faster song, and he reached for her hand and twirled her in a spin. He loved the way she laughed and followed his lead as he pulled her back against him, then swung her around again. Sarah had loved to dance, and she'd taught him the two-step and how to country swing that first summer they were together, spending hours in the cool rec room of her basement practicing to every country CD she owned.

He hadn't danced much since Sarah had died, but tonight, with Bryn, the moves came back to him and felt easy, natural, as he swung her around. He didn't know a lot of moves, just enough of the basics to get by, but Bryn didn't seem to care. She laughed as he spun her around and when she missed a step and collided into his shoulder.

A new song came on, another slow one. Without

his brain telling them to, his feet seemed to fall into the shuffle of the two-step, and he guided her around the kitchen. She fell into step with him, her hips swaying in time with the music, following his lead as he two-stepped her through the living room and down the hall toward her bedroom.

She smiled up at him, her tone playful as she asked, "What about putting up the sign?"

He grinned back. "What sign?"

An hour later, he was dressed and heading out the front door. He still had enough light to put up the sign, and he grabbed it from the front room. Taking his toolbox from his truck, he whistled for the collie, and she trotted happily along next to him as he sauntered to the end of the driveway.

A gathering of dark storm clouds moved across the mountains, and Zane could feel the hint of moisture in the air. Rain was coming, but he should have enough time to get the sign up. Knowing he wanted to get the sign put up that night, he'd dropped off a couple of cedar posts and a posthole digger at the end of the driveway on his way in earlier. He took his time, crossing the highway, then coming back and measuring and calculating the best placement for the sign to be the most visible. The dog ran up and down the road with him, then found a patch of dirt to lie in where she could supervise his work.

Deciding on the best spot, he picked up the posthole digger and sank it into the dirt. He felt good as he dug the holes and set the posts, then screwed the sign to the cedar supports—even caught himself humming the tune he and Bryn had been dancing to.

An ancient pickup approached and slowed as Zane pounded in the last post. The window was down, and old Doc Hunter leaned his head out. "Sign looks good. Bryn's really going for this horse rescue thing, huh?"

"She is," Zane answered, taking a step toward the truck. "She's taken in two more since that first one. Plus a handful of puppies and a sizable hog."

The old man shook his head as a wistful smile curved his lips. "Doesn't surprise me. She's a sweet girl. Always looking out for others. She'd give away her last dime if she thought it would help someone else."

Zane nodded. "I know."

Doc narrowed his eyes as he studied him. "She's got a big heart. I'd hate to see it get broken."

"Me too."

"I hope this rescue thing works out. That girl deserves to have some good stuff happen in her life. We all love her down at the diner—watch out for her where we can. We didn't say anything when she took up with that last fella, although I wish we would have. So I'm speakin' up now. We care about that girl, and we'd all sure like to see her end up with a good man who will put her first." Doc looked Zane squarely in the eye. "You get my meaning, son?"

Zane fought to keep his chin from dropping, to hold the gaze of the older man. "I hear you." *Loud and clear.*

"See that you do." Doc offered a sage nod, then pulled away and trundled down the highway, leaving Zane feeling like he'd just left the principal's office after a punishment had been handed down.

A hard ache tore through his chest. He knew that things with Bryn had been going too well. Dancing in the kitchen and laughing in the bedroom—that was the kind of stuff that happened in the movies. But not to him. His life wasn't a Disney film, he didn't get happily-ever-afters, and he sure as hell was no prince.

He searched the sky, watched the dark clouds rolling in over the mountains, and felt the storm settle inside him. A flash of lightning lit the sky, and something about the very air seemed to change, as if a warning had just been brandished.

That ominous feeling of something forbidding and dangerous in the air was all around him, and his chest burned with the knowledge of what he had to do. Doc Hunter was right. Bryn was a sweet girl who merited a good man—not a broken one with too much baggage and history to give her the life she deserved.

Maybe he should leave now, while things were still good. Leave on a high note, while Bryn was still fooled into thinking he was a semi-good guy, while she was still charmed by a few clumsy dance steps and a handmade sign. Before she found out the truth. About him. About Sarah.

Sarah's family had lived a couple of towns over, but still, the communities of the mountains were closely knit. People talked. And this town was too small for somebody not to talk to Bryn. To warn her away from him. To tell her what he did to Sarah.

Yeah, he should leave now. It was crazy he'd stayed this long. He would call his old boss tonight and tell her he'd come back to Montana, back to the desolate country of big skies and countless hours spent in solitude with only the cattle and horses for company. It wouldn't take him but twenty minutes to pack his crap and be on the road. Then he'd be gone, out of this town, and out of Bryn's life before something bad, something worse than this storm, happened.

The decision made, he gave the signpost one more whack with his hammer, then turned to head for his truck. He'd tell Bryn goodbye, tell her this wasn't working for him. Sure, she'd be surprised, especially after the last hour they'd spent together, and maybe a little hurt, but she'd get over it. Get over him. It was for the best.

Now he just had to get up the courage to tell her.

The front door of the house burst open, and Bryn came racing toward him. So much for having to find her to tell her. She was coming to him. And wearing a huge smile on her face.

"You won't believe the call I just got." She met him halfway down the driveway and threw her arms around his neck in a hug.

"From the way you're acting, I'd guess it was from the

state lottery office declaring your numbers were picked and you just won the jackpot."

She laughed as she released him but still bounced from one foot to the other. "Okay, it wasn't *that* great of a call, but I did win something. Or I don't know if I actually won, but I was nominated for something."

"Well, are you gonna tell me what it was? Or do I have to guess?"

"Oh gosh, now that I'm saying it out loud, it's sort of embarrassing." She covered her face with her hands.

"What could be embarrassing to win? Were you nominated for the Best Tail on the Edge of a Tailgate Award?"

Her mouth dropped open, then she giggled and shook her head. "No, of course not. And that's not even a real award."

He shrugged. "Maybe it should be. And you would definitely be the winner."

"Why are we even talking about this?"

He chuckled. "Just tell me who called."

"Right." She brushed her bangs from her forehead. "It was the Women's Club of Creedence, and they're having their annual volunteer banquet where they honor exceptional humanitarians around town. Or I guess in my case, it would be an exceptional animal-itarian, because they nominated me as the most innovative animal rescue volunteer."

"Nice. Although that title sounds a little like they made it up. But it also sounds pretty cool."

"Right? And who knows? Maybe they did make it up,

just for me. Which would be even more special. They said they were really impressed with the work I was doing out here with the three horses and all the dogs, and they somehow even heard about the pig and the lovebirds. I tried to tell them it wasn't a big deal and that anyone would have done the same."

Zane shook his head. "No, they wouldn't. It takes someone special to do what you're doing. To take in all these animals on just a hope and a prayer."

"Hope and prayers seem to be working so far." She blew out a breath. "I need to figure out something to wear, but I think I'm going to go."

"Of course you should go."

She looked down at her hands, then back up at him. "It's on Friday, so it's still a couple of nights away, but will you go with me? Like, as my date?"

He knew this was important—not just because she was being honored, but also because it meant the whole town would see they were together. But what about Doc's warning and the impending storm? What about his resolve to end things? He'd walked back here to tell her he was leaving.

But how could he do that now? She was on cloud nine. How could he destroy the memory of this moment when she was so happy? Because right now, they were the only ones who knew anything was happening with them— well, them and two middle-aged women from Kansas. And Logan. And a few thousand Facebook viewers had an idea. But as far as he knew, it hadn't leaked into town, and that was where it mattered. That was where gossip and innuendo could hurt Bryn. If he left now, only a handful of people would even notice he was gone, but once the whole town knew they were together and that he'd left her, Bryn would suffer even more.

Still, he couldn't bring himself to shatter this moment for her. He had time before the dinner. He would tell her tomorrow. He put his arm around her and pulled her close. "I wouldn't miss it."

She tipped her chin up and pressed a kiss to his lips—soft, light—then another, this one more demanding. His hands slid up her back and tangled in her hair as the first raindrops fell from the sky.

He barely noticed the rain even as it fell harder, hitting his arms and shoulders. The brim of his cowboy hat seemed to shield their faces, but he wouldn't have cared if it hadn't. All he could focus on was the taste of her lips and warm press of her body against his. Until a flash of lightning lit the sky followed by a quick clap of thunder. He pulled away, then rubbed her arms as a shiver ran through her. "We'd better get inside."

He spotted the collie on the other side of the highway and gave a whistle. "Come on, girl." The dog looked up and started to race toward him.

It must have been the noise of the rain that drowned out the sound of engine. Zane didn't hear it, didn't see it, until he caught the flash of silver from the corner of his eye. By then it was too late.

He raised his hands, sprinted toward the road, yelling, "No! Stay! STAY!"

Time seemed to slow down, the sounds magnified—the far-off roll of thunder, the roar of the car engine, the screech of tires, then the sickening thud followed by an agonizing whimper.

No. No. No. He raced toward the dog, rain pelting his face. He knew it. Knew he didn't deserve this kind of happiness. He'd been living someone else's life and that someone had just come back to claim it.

The car was gone by the time he got to the edge of the highway. The collie was lying on the side of the road. He skidded to a halt, frozen by the sight of the matted fur covered in blood, the bright red drops mixing with the rain pooled on the blacktop.

CHAPTER 17

No. Please, God. No.

The collie stirred and let out a whimper as she tried to lift her head.

Zane dropped to his knees, reaching a hand out to gently touch her shoulder. "It's okay, girl. It's okay." Grabbing the hem of his T-shirt, he jerked it over his head and wrapped the collie in it as he picked her up and gingerly drew her to his chest.

He'd thought Bryn was running behind him, but he didn't turn to look. His entire focus was on the small warm body clutched to his chest. This was what he got. What he deserved. But damn it, why did the dog have to suffer for his mistakes?

A car pulled up next to him. The door opened, and Bryn was there, touching his shoulder. "Get in," she ordered.

He didn't think. Didn't analyze the situation. Didn't say a word. He stumbled to his feet, his knees threatening to give way, as he got into the car. He cradled the dog on his lap as Bryn pushed the door shut, then ran back around to the other side. She slid into the driver's seat and had the car in gear before she'd even pulled the door shut. She fumbled for her phone as she raced down the highway, commanding it to "Call Brody."

Zane only heard one side of the conversation as Bryn told Brody that the collie had been hit by a car. She tapped the phone and tossed it onto the seat. "He's on his way. He's going to meet us at the vet clinic."

The windshield wipers slapped back and forth, their rhythmic thumping warring with the sound of his heart pounding in his chest. *Please, God, don't let this dog die.*

Bryn made it to the vet clinic in record time, but Brody's truck was already parked in the lot. His farm was only a mile or so down the road from the clinic. He held open the door and directed them to the first examining room as Zane carried the dog in.

"Just set her down here," Brody said, patting the exam table. "Let me take a look at her. Bryn said she was hit by a car?"

Zane eased the dog onto the table. "Yeah, and the bastard took off without even stopping."

"Let's just concentrate on fixing her up for now," Brody said, checking her gums then pulling the stethoscope from around his neck to listen to her heart and lungs. "What's her name?"

Shame burned through Zane's chest. He hadn't even given the damn dog a name. It would serve him right if she died. "She doesn't have one," he muttered.

Brody glanced up at him, then returned his focus to the dog, moving her joints and palpating her stomach. "It's okay, girl," he said soothingly to the dog. He pressed a pad of gauze to the gash in her side.

Zane had seen numerous gashes on horses and

cows—hell, he'd seen a horse's legs cut to ribbons after a fight with a barbed wire fence. But seeing the crimson blood seep through the white gauze had his chest tightening and bile rising to the back of his throat.

"Her gums are pale, her pulse is weak, and her abdomen feels full, so my initial concern would be that she's got some internal bleeding. I can do an X-ray, but the quickest way to check is to stick a needle in her." He reached behind him and pulled a syringe from the drawer. Sticking the needle into the dog's stomach, he pulled the plunger out and the vial filled with blood. "Damn. There shouldn't be blood. That means we have to do surgery. But if we can identify and stop the source of the bleeding, she should be okay."

"Do it," Zane said.

He heard a sharp intake of breath behind him and turned to see a small woman wearing pink scrubs with kittens on them enter the room. He caught the wince on her face and realized for the first time he wasn't wearing a shirt. She must have seen the scars. *Oh well, who gives a shit?* All he could focus on was the dog.

Brody nodded to the woman. "This is Val. She's the vet tech on duty. I called her and asked her to come in, just in case."

Val had composed her features and offered Zane a sympathetic smile. "Doc told me your dog was hit by a car. I'm so sorry."

"Val and I need about ten minutes to prep for surgery, then we'll take her in. You all can stay with her while we get things ready." Brody motioned the tech out of the room. "We've got some extra scrubs around here. I'll have Val bring you both something dry to wear."

Zane waved his concern away. "Just worry about the dog." He turned and caught sight of Bryn shivering as she stood silently in the corner of the examining room. Her wet hair dripped onto her shoulders, and her arms were crossed over her chest as if she were trying to hold herself together. *Shit.* He hadn't been thinking about how this was affecting Bryn. He wanted to hold out his arms, feel her against him as she stepped into them.

But he couldn't. He didn't deserve to be held, to be comforted. This was all his fault.

"She's gon-n-na be ok-kay," Bryn said, her teeth chattering as she hugged herself tighter.

Val appeared with a set of scrubs for each of them. She set them on the counter and quietly backed out of the room. "We're almost ready."

Zane picked up the smaller set of scrubs and handed them to Bryn. He took the blue shirt of the other set and pulled it over his head. She did the same. Neither bothered messing with the pants.

He looked down at the dog, guilt settling like a rock in his gut. He should never have promised he would keep her safe. People—and apparently dogs—who loved him always ended up getting hurt. He was always the bad factor in the equation. And now this dog was going to suffer. He shouldn't have fed the damn thing. He'd let her get too close. "I can't do this…can't stay here and wait for her to die. I've got to get out of here."

He took a step toward the door, but Bryn pressed her hands to his chest and glared up at him. "No way, you don't get to do that. You don't get to walk away. She is a good dog, a faithful companion. She loves you. Every time you've pushed her away, she's stayed and loved you harder."

"That's not my fault. I didn't ask for that." He shook his head, scrubbing a hand through his hair. *Where the hell did I lose my hat?* Didn't matter. His gut churned, and he eyed the sink, wondering if he was going to be sick. "I can't. I can't do this. I never wanted that damn dog in the first place. I never asked her to love me." He never asked *anyone* to love him. Because this was what happened when he let love into his life. In his world, love and pain equaled the same emotion.

Bryn grabbed his hand, held him in place. In truth, her hand holding his at that moment was about all that tethered him to the ground. If she let go, he was afraid he might drift away. "You didn't have to ask," she told him. "That's the thing about love. We don't ask for it, but sometimes we get it anyway."

Pull it together, man. Focus on the dog. He tried to shake it off, this feeling of helplessness, but a heavy dull pain filled his whole body. The constant burn in his throat had his voice sounding gruff and hoarse. "I can't. I don't know what to do to help her."

She squeezed his palm. "You can give her a name.

That's what you can do. She already knows you love her, but she needs a name."

His breath caught in his chest. This was why he didn't let himself love people or things—because it hurt too much to lose them. And he always lost them. His mom. Sarah. Now this frickin' dog. And he knew Bryn was next.

Stop it. He shook his head, only allowing himself to let in the grief of one loss at a time.

He reached out a hand and rested it gently on the side of the collie's face. The dog stirred, pushing her nose gently against his palm and letting out the softest whimper. "Don't die on me, you damn mutt." He swallowed at the emotion burning his throat and blinked back whatever the hell was making his vision blurry.

"Fine, I'll give the dog a name." He leaned down and brushed his hand tenderly along her neck. "You're a good dog. You're a fighter. And you're tough. You have to be to put up with a miserable cuss like me. I'm sorry I've been such an asshole. You didn't deserve that. You're a good girl. And I need you to hang on. I'm not good at this kind of stuff, but I'm not giving up hope." He blinked again, his chest tightening at the last word he'd spoken, and he knew that was it. "Hope? How about that for a name?" He peered up at Bryn and shrugged. "Is that a good one?"

"Yes, it's a good name." Bryn rested a warm hand on his shoulder. "It suits her."

He shook his head, swallowing again as he peered down at the dog. "It's sappy as hell, so I'm gonna need you to live just for the sheer spite of making me call you by it every day."

Brody stepped into the exam room. "We're ready for her." He'd changed into scrubs, and he carefully eased his arms under the dog's body to lift her. Hope let out a small whimper and turned her head, as if searching for Zane.

Zane took a step forward to help, then shrank back against the wall. There was nothing he could do. It was up to Brody now.

"Is there anything else we can do?" Bryn asked.

"She may need some blood. There's a good chance she'll need a transfusion, so we may need one of your dogs. Not sure the mama you just rescued is strong enough, but if you want to run home and grab Lucky, it couldn't hurt to have him here, just in case."

Bryn nodded. "I'll go get him now."

Damn. Now Bryn's dog would also get hurt because of him.

"You have time," Brody told her. "The surgery will probably take an hour or two."

"Okay. We'll be here." Bryn reached out a hand and gently scratched the dog's ears. "And she does have a name. Her name is Hope."

Brody glanced up at Zane and gave a slight nod. "We'll take good care of her." He carried the dog away then, the door of the exam room shutting softly behind him.

Zane balled his hands into fists. He wanted to punch something, to lash out, to tear something apart. He needed to run, to torture his body, to feel some other kind of pain than the anguish that was ripping through his heart.

And it wasn't just about the dog. He ached for the dog, but he ached for Bryn too. Because the dog getting hurt sealed the deal. He had to walk away. He was a wreck. He could barely stand the grief of seeing the dog get hurt; he wouldn't be able to live with himself if something happened to Bryn too.

He'd made a promise to the dog that he would protect her, and he'd failed. Just like he knew he would fail at all the promises he'd been silently making to Bryn the last few days with each heartfelt gaze and passion-filled kiss.

Panic rose in him like floodwater rising over the banks of the river and rushing down the street. He had to get out of there. He pushed away from the wall, knocking into a display of pamphlets addressing a dog's dental health as he tried to escape the room. The pamphlets scattered to the floor like confetti in a parade. He didn't care. "I thought I could do this, but I can't. I gotta go."

He charged through the lobby and pushed out the front door. Inhaling great gulps of air, he bent forward and braced his hands on his knees. The rain had stopped, but it was fully dark now, the sky an inky black that matched his mood.

He shivered as Bryn's hand touched his back. "Zane. It's okay. She's gonna be okay."

He stood. "No. She's not. Not if she stays with me. She's your dog now. I'm giving her to you."

"*Giving* her to me? What the heck are you talking about? You're not giving her to me."

"Yes. I am. I have to. If I want her to be okay, she can't stay with me. She has to go with you. And I can't stay here."

"You can't leave."

"I have to. If I stay—with her, with you—then someone else is going to get hurt."

She jerked her head back. "You're not making any sense. That's just stupid."

"You're right. It is stupid. Because *I'm* stupid. I know it. You know it. Hell, my dad's been telling me I'm a dumbass my entire life."

She shook her head as if the conversation baffled her. "What are you talking about?"

He scrubbed his hand through his hair. "I know it doesn't make sense. But it's the truth. People who love me always end up getting hurt. That's why I have to give the dog away. And why I have to break this off with you. It was selfish of me to let things get this far."

"Break things off with me?" Her mouth opened, then closed. "How did this turn into breaking things off with me?"

"Because I can't let you care about me. I'm not good for you. You need to get away from me. You need to be with someone else. Someone who can make you happy. Someone who won't hurt you."

She arched her eyebrows as she planted her hands on her hips. "So you're just going to make that choice for me? Because you know what's best for everyone else? Well, Zane Taylor, you really *are* a dumbass. Because I don't just *care* about you." She raised her hands and made air quotes around the word *care*. "I've fallen in love with you. And I'm not going anywhere."

Her words hit him like a splash of cold water to the chest. He couldn't breathe.

"Did you hear me?" she asked, raising her voice as she pressed a hand to his chest. "I love you."

He shrank back, as if the touch of her palm burned his skin. Raising his hand, he took hers and firmly pushed it away from him. "Don't."

Her mouth gaped as she let out an exasperated gasp. "*Don't?* What the hell does that mean? Don't what?"

"Don't love me."

He turned his back and walked away.

He made it about five steps before she yelled his name. *Keep walking. Don't turn around.* She called his name one more time; this time she didn't yell it. It came out as a whisper, and it nearly broke him. He turned back.

She launched herself at him. Ran toward him and threw herself into his arms. "I'm not letting you leave. Not until you tell me."

"Tell you what?"

"Tell me why you believe that the people you love end up getting hurt."

"Because they do."

She reached up and cupped his face, the tips of her fingers grazing the jagged skin of his scar. "Tell me."

The scar burned, the skin tightening against her touch. "I got that scar the night she died."

"Who died?"

"Sarah." His throat burned, and his voice came out hoarse just trying to say her name. "It was the first time I ever stood up to my dad. He was punching me, and I didn't care what happened to me, so I punched him back." He let out a harsh laugh at the memory. "Man, was he pissed. He busted a beer bottle on the side of my head, and the broken glass sliced my face open. But I didn't care. Sarah was dead, and I didn't care. I left that night—went into the military and volunteered to go to Afghanistan. Then I got shot, and they sent me home. So I did the only thing I knew how to do. Logan's dad, Hamilton, had taught me. I went to work on a ranch, spent my time herding cattle and breaking horses. My dad and I eventually made peace, and I came home when he had his heart attack last Thanksgiving. That's when I started working with Logan and spending time with you. This is the longest I've been in Creedence in years."

He'd been staring into the night behind her, but he stopped and looked down at her. "I stayed because I couldn't get enough of you. So help me, I tried. But you were the first woman who made me feel anything since Sarah. I tried to ignore you, and my old foreman was beggin' me to come back, but I couldn't leave. Then you bought that damn horse. And I still tried to push you toward Brody. He's the kind of man you deserve to be with."

Bryn stared at him, her expression unyielding. "Tell me about Sarah."

He swallowed and scrubbed a hand down his face. "Sarah was beautiful. She lived a few towns up the mountain from here, and we met at a party after one of my hockey games. It was our senior year, and I never went to stuff like that, but we'd won the game and I was feeling good. I somehow convinced myself I had a chance with this pretty blond, but I never really did. She was always too good for me. She was from a good family, had this nice sister. They all went to church together on Sunday mornings. Not like at our house, where the only thing Dad worshiped on Sundays was the football game and several cold beers." He took a deep breath, fighting the memories that he tried so hard to keep at bay. "Sarah was a cheerleader and so smart. She got offered a full-ride scholarship to one of those Ivy League schools on the East Coast."

"Did she go?" Bryn's question was asked softly, but it was the right question. The question of the hour.

"Nope. She did *not* go. She should have gone. But I begged her to stay. We'd been together for close to a year and were crazy in love. Her parents hated me. They knew I was no good for their daughter. She deserved someone way better than me. I knew it too. But I was selfish. I wanted her to stay. She gave up the scholarship for me."

"She must have really loved you."

He shrugged. "She said she did. But I could tell it really hurt her to give up that scholarship. She always felt things too much, like she could go from insanely happy to desperately sad in the space of an hour. And the next few weeks, she seemed to spiral. We got in a fight, and I told her she should see a shrink and get some meds. And apparently she did. She told me she went to a therapist and got some medication. And it seemed to help. She was happy again, back to her old self. I don't know what he gave her. Antidepressants or something. Whatever it was, taking half the bottle of it was enough to kill her."

Bryn took his hand, held it tightly in hers. "I'm so sorry."

He tried to clear the ache from his throat. "Me too. I was there the night she did it. We'd been watching a movie in her basement. Her parents were out, and I fell asleep on the couch. I found her when I woke up. I tried to save her. Stuck my finger down her throat to get her to puke 'em out. I tried mouth to mouth. Didn't know what I was doing, but I was trying everything. I called an ambulance. But it was too late. It was all too late."

He jerked his hand from Bryn's and used the back of it to swipe at his cheeks. "Have I ever told you how my mom died? She died giving birth to me. Complications, they said. Or that's all I ever heard. But according to my dad, she died because of me. That's why he's hated me my whole life. So don't you see? My mom was the start of it. She loved me, gave up everything for me, and she died. Sarah loved me, and in my selfishness, I asked her to give up everything for me too. And she did. Then she died." He jerked a thumb toward the vet clinic. "That damn dog decided she loved me, and now because of me, she might die too. That's why you have to take her. Because if she's yours, she at least has a chance to make it."

"Zane," she whispered and reached for his hand again.

But he pulled it away and pointed at the scar on his face. "The night my dad gave me this, I knew I deserved the pain. And every day I look in the mirror, I know I deserved this scar that marks my face and reminds me every day what I did to her. And what I won't do to you."

He took a step away from Bryn—a single step but it was one of the hardest he'd ever had to take. "I don't want you to love me, Bryn. Hell, I don't even want you to like me. I want you to be happy. And that's not going to happen with me." He took another step back. "I also want you to leave. Go get your dog and do what you can to save that damn mutt in there. Focus on that. Focus on being happy. And forget about me."

He turned his back to her and headed toward the road, pushing down the pain, the torment that was ripping his chest apart like the jaws of life tearing into a wrecked car. He forced one foot in front of the other.

This time she didn't stop him. She just let him walk away.

Bryn felt like she couldn't breathe, like all the air had been pulled from her lungs as she watched Zane walk away. She wanted to call his name again, run after him, demand that he listen to her, but she couldn't. Because he was right about one thing. She had to go home. She had to get her dog and bring him back and do what she could to save Hope's life.

Not for her. But for him—for Zane. To prove to him that his stupid theory wasn't true. She would take care of Hope, but she wasn't taking the dog. Hope was his—she belonged to him. And Bryn wasn't going to let her die.

She ran to her car and sped out of the parking lot. The hour was late enough that the roads were fairly empty, and it took her less than ten minutes to make the drive home. Brody had said she had time, but she wanted to be ready if Hope needed her—or her dog's—help.

She rushed up the porch steps and into the house. Grace and the puppies were curled in the dog bed in the corner of the living room, but Lucky came running to her. The dog had always been tuned in to her moods, and Lucky nuzzled his nose against her leg. She bent down and cuddled him to her, fighting to hold back the tears that burned her throat.

This was no time to cry. This was the time for action. Time to hold it together and take care of business. There would be time to cry later.

Letting go of the dog, she swiped at the few tears that had ignored her stern self-talk and headed down the hall to her bedroom. As long as she was home, she figured it was best to take a few minutes to change.

She shed her damp clothes and pulled on a clean pair of jeans, a T-shirt, and dry socks. She grabbed a hoodie and stuffed her feet into a pair of sneakers, the whole time trying to avoid looking at the bed, the rumpled sheets a stark reminder of the time she'd just spent there with Zane.

Ignoring the ache in her chest, she rushed through the house, collecting the dog and a blue blanket the collie liked to sleep on while she was there. In the car, her thoughts strayed back to Zane. He'd told her he wanted to call things off with them—but it was in the heat of the moment. He didn't mean it. Things would be different tomorrow. Once Hope was okay and Bryn had a chance to talk to him again. She wasn't giving up. She meant what she'd said.

She wasn't sure when it happened. If it was the moment he left her the hundred-dollar tip to buy the horse, or the first time he kissed her, or when he found Pete and got her truck back, or the moment after he'd jumped off that ledge with her and come up whooping and splashing and spouting beautiful words about falling. Or maybe it was all the moments combined. Whatever it was, it was real.

She was in love with him.

Lucky laid his head in her lap, and she scratched his ears. "Good dog." She pulled into the parking lot of the vet clinic, and the tripod dog followed her inside.

The door to the exam room was closed, but she could see light under the door and hear music playing. "Hello," she called into the empty room, praying that Zane had changed his mind and come back to the clinic. No one answered.

Her chest tightened as she searched the exam rooms and the bathroom. Lucky followed her back out to the parking lot, where she yelled his name. But he still didn't answer.

Zane was gone.

————————————

Zane crashed into his house, the door hitting the wall as it slammed open.

His dad was sitting at the table, a mostly empty bottle of Jack in front of him. He wore an old plaid bathrobe tied loosely over faded blue pajama pants and a stained and yellowed T-shirt. His eyes were bleary, and he regarded his son with disdain. "Whaz-a hell are you supposed to be? Is it Halloween or somethin'?" His words slurred together in an all too familiar sound.

Zane furrowed his brow, then remembered the scrub shirt the vet tech had given him to wear. He grabbed the edges of the shirt and pulled it over his head. "It's not mine."

His dad laughed—not a funny laugh, but a mean laugh layered with condescension. "Oh, I know izz not. Doctors wear scrubs. And you gotta go to college and earn a fancy degree to be a doctor. They don't take dumbasses like you who could barely pass algebra in high school."

"Whatever, Dad." A basket of clean laundry sat on the corner of the couch, and Zane grabbed a T-shirt off the top and pulled it over his head. Birch hadn't had any more schooling than Zane. "Hypocrite," he muttered not quite under his breath.

"What'd you say to me, boy?" His dad lurched from the chair, knocking it over. It crashed to the floor behind him, but he didn't turn around. His eyes were narrowed in fury. "You wanna get smart with me?"

"No, Dad. I just want to go to bed. I've had a shitty day."

"You had a shitty day? Poor baby. I've been sittin' in this house like a damn invalid for months. My chest hurts, my gut's all twisted, and I swear this house has been spinnin' all day." His voice rose with each assertion. "And I don't need your whiny smart mouth to come in here and give me sass," he bellowed.

He balled his hand into a fist and tried to raise his arm to take a swing at Zane, but his arm swung limply at his side. Birch looked down at the arm in disgust, like it had personally failed him, then turned back to his son just as his eyes rolled back and his body slumped forward.

Zane hurled forward and grabbed his father before he fell to the floor. He'd seen his dad pass out drunk many times. This was different. His dad's words echoed in his ears…chest hurt, gut twisted, house had been spinning. His dad was right—he *wasn't* a doctor, but he was pretty certain Birch had just had another heart attack. "Damn it, Dad."

CHAPTER 18

BRYN STUMBLED THROUGH THE NEXT DAY, GOING through the motions in a sleep-deprived haze. She'd spent most of the night at the vet clinic. Hope had come out of surgery around midnight, and Brody had said her prognosis was good. Lucky had been the hero of the night, offering his blood for the transfusion they eventually had to do.

Bryn had slept a little on the sofa in the waiting room, but Brody sent her home after the surgery. He told her he'd come back in around three to check on Hope, but there wasn't anything more for her to do that night, so she might as well get some sleep. She'd taken his advice, bringing Lucky home and falling asleep on the sofa with the dog curled in her arms. She couldn't face the bed yet.

She'd tried Zane's phone again as she drove to the vet clinic later that morning. She planned to check on Hope, then meet Elle at the bank. As much as she'd wanted to cancel, they'd already made the appointment to set up business accounts, and she knew she needed to get it done. It felt like something normal to do in an otherwise abnormal day.

Zane didn't answer. He hadn't answered all night. She'd considered going by his house on her way home the night before, just to tell him that Hope had come through the surgery okay, but had decided to text him instead. He hadn't answered that either.

Hope was doing okay. She wagged her tail a little when Bryn came into the room, but Brody said she was still pretty lethargic. They were going to keep her for another night, just for observation.

"Has Zane come in this morning?" she asked.

Brody shook his head, avoiding her eyes as he washed his hands. "No. He called and gave his credit card information to the receptionist to cover the bill, but he told her the dog was yours. I figured she must have misunderstood him."

So he was really going to play it that way, huh?

"Yes, I'm sure that's it. I'll take her home if he doesn't show up by tomorrow, but Hope is still Zane's dog."

Bryn left the vet clinic feeling as if twenty pounds had just been dumped on her shoulders. Her eyes were gritty and sore, and her body ached from the night spent on the old sofa. On autopilot, she drove to the bank and tried to concentrate on the information the banker was telling her. Elle met her there, and the banker helped them set up the accounts. Bryn had brought her laptop, and they worked through the process of transferring the donation money and the online GoFundMe account to the new bank accounts as well. Elle loved the business name. Bryn had told it to her the day before, and Elle had set up the LLC and obtained a tax ID number from the IRS using the new name.

What would she do without Elle? In the past few

weeks, the two women had really formed a bond. Bryn had called Elle about Hope getting hit by the car and going into surgery, but she hadn't told her anything about Zane. Her stomach churned with shame and embarrassment. Elle had cautioned her to be wary of Zane, warned her she would get hurt. Apparently her friend had been right.

Elle had brought the money she'd collected from the donation jars to deposit into the accounts, and Bryn realized she still had the first two jars crammed into her pantry. She'd meant to bring them, but her brain didn't seem to be running on all cylinders that morning.

"You want to grab some coffee?" Elle asked as they left the bank. "You look like you're about to fall asleep on your feet."

"I am." She covered her mouth as she stifled a yawn. "Thanks for the offer, but I think I'm going to go home and try to catch a few hours of sleep."

"Good idea. Anything I can do to help? You want me to come out and sit with the other dogs or feed your dainty pig?"

Bryn smiled. "No. I'm fine. I appreciate the offer though. You're a good friend."

A grin spread across Elle's face. "Why, thank you. That's the nicest thing anyone's said to me today."

Bryn let Elle pull her into a hug, then she dragged herself back to her car. She drove through the coffee shop on her way home and ordered a caramel latte with a triple shot of espresso for herself and a puppacino for Lucky, the hero dog. It was only a small cup filled with whipped cream, but Lucky licked it clean while Bryn sat on the front porch, nibbling half a sandwich and sipping her drink—and trying to convince herself she wasn't hanging out there waiting for Zane.

His truck had been gone when she'd come home the night before, but she figured he'd show up eventually. If not for her, then for the horses. He'd told her Beauty was within a few weeks of foaling and had moved the mare into the largest stall in the barn the day before. No matter how upset he was with her, or about the dog, she couldn't imagine he would neglect the horses for too long.

The latte didn't seem to be helping, she thought as another yawn overtook her. Maybe she'd lie down. Just for a little bit. She shuffled into the house and down the hallway, too tired for the sofa. She wanted her own bed, her own pillow.

Sinking into the bed, she closed her eyes and inhaled the scent of Zane still perceptible on her sheets. Lucky followed her in, jumped on the bed, and curled against Bryn's legs as she drifted off to sleep.

Bryn woke from the depths of a murky dream to the sound of someone in her kitchen.

Zane!

She threw back the covers and pushed off the bed, stumbling a little as her knees threatened to buckle.

Blinking her eyes, she shook her head, trying to get her body to match the alertness of her brain. Reaching out a hand, she steadied herself against the nightstand and took a second to catch her breath.

Lucky was gone from the bed, and she was surprised to see it was past five. No wonder she felt groggy—she'd slept for most of the afternoon. Lucky hopped into the room, gave her a doggie look that translated into something like *Help! Timmy fell in the well. Follow me*, then hopped back out again. Bryn straightened her shirt and smoothed her hair as she walked out of the bedroom. She ran the back of her hand over her chin, just to make sure she hadn't drooled.

She was excited to see Zane, but also apprehensive. It was about time he showed up, and her heart was racing in her chest, but she wasn't sure if it was pounding because she was excited or just pissed off.

Apparently it didn't matter, because it wasn't Zane in the kitchen anyway.

Although she did recognize the back of the guy currently digging through her pantry. Unfortunately, she didn't think he was searching for the peanut butter.

"Hey, Buck," she said, casually leaning her hip against the counter.

Her brother raised up and whacked his head on the shelf above him. He swore as he turned around, the two donation jars clutched in his hands. "Damn, Sis, you scared the hell out of me."

"Apparently not, because I think hell is still comin'

for the kind of guy who would steal money from helpless animals."

He furrowed his brow. "I wasn't stealing it."

She raised an eyebrow.

"I was just borrowing it. Come on. I heard you've got these jars all over town. No one's going to miss a couple of bucks."

"The horses will. And the dogs too. Because that's the money that's going to buy them food."

"What about me? I need to buy food too."

"Seriously?" She opened her mouth to say something more, probably something simpering and yielding before reaching for her purse and handing him the last of her money.

But this time she didn't. She snapped her lips shut and gritted her teeth so hard her jaw hurt. Why did she have to give him her money? What made her think she always had to take care of everyone else?

Warmth bloomed in her chest, a fiery fury that swirled and ached and burned her throat. All the craziness of the past few days, the dog getting hurt by a hit and run driver, Pete saying terrible things to her, and Zane... Well, Zane was a ball of fury all on his own. Who was he to tell her who she should be with? All the pieces eddied and churned, making her nauseous and feeling like if she didn't vomit out the sentiments building inside her, then she might actually puke on her freshly mopped kitchen floor.

She raised her hand, then slammed it down on the counter as she let out a cry of frustration through tightly gripped teeth. "Gahhhh. I'm so damn tired of being there for everyone else, of sticking my neck, not to mention my heart, out again and again and every damn time getting it stepped on. No, not even stepped on, but trampled, mashed, smashed, crushed, and massacred." She hit the counter again and again, smacking it with each new adjective describing the condition of her heart. "I'm tired of showing up every damn time for everyone who needs me, who needs anything, but never having anyone, not one single person, show up for me when I need them."

She'd thought Zane was going to be that person. But where the hell was he? He sure as heck wasn't here.

"Geez," her brother said, wrinkling his nose as if something in the kitchen smelled bad. "What's gotten into you? Why are you losing your shit?"

"Oh gosh, Bucky, I haven't even *begun* to lose my shit. This is only the top layer of the shit I'm about to lose. I have been keeping this bottled up in me for so long, pressing it down every time you asked for money, or some guy I'm dating asks to borrow my car, or some asshole who acts like he loves me steals my money *and* my truck. Well, I am sick and tired of stuffing the shit down. And guess what, Little Brother? You're the first one I'm going to start losing some of it on."

"Lucky me," he muttered.

"No, dear Brother, *not* lucky you. In fact, your luck in this house has just run out." She reached for the donation jars and snatched them out of his hands. "These are not yours. And you're not taking them. And furthermore,

I'm not giving you any of my money either. I work really freakin' hard for that tip money. I stand on my feet for hours on end and put up with bullshit customers who like to demand everything special, then stiff me on the tip. Granted, not all my customers are assholes, some are very nice, but nice doesn't always pay the bills. I have to clean up half-eaten food and spilled milk and mop floors and clean greasy pans. I work my ass off for every dime I make, then I hand it over to you out of some guilt-driven sense of responsibility. I give it to you because I'm your sister, and I should take care of you. Well, guess what, buddy? You are an adult. And it's time you start acting like one, starting with getting out of my house and going to find a job."

"I have a job."

"A real job. One that doesn't involve eight seconds of peril on the back of a thousand-pound bull." She let out a sigh as she set the donation jars on the counter and pushed them back against the wall, away from her brother's sticky fingers. "Actually I don't care what kind of job you get. Or *don't* get. Just quit calling me and asking me for money."

He huffed out an indignant breath. "Fine. I won't call."

"Grrr. That is not what I'm saying. I'm not telling you not to call. I just once, seriously, Brother, just one time would like to have you call me or stop by for a visit and not slip somewhere into our conversation a request for money."

"I don't," he sputtered.

"Yeah, you do. And until you realize it and stop freakin' doing it, I want you to go."

"Go? You're kicking me out of my own house?"

"*Your* house?" This time it was her turn to sputter. "When's the last time you paid the taxes or the homeowner's insurance? Or the electric bill? Or any freakin' bill?"

He shrugged. "Whatever."

"Look, Buck. This *is* your home. And it always will be. But this is *my* house. I don't expect you to pay the taxes or the insurance or the propane or the hundred other things I take care of around here. I just want you to quit taking away the money that does pay that stuff."

"Fine."

"I think you'd better go."

"I think so too." He scrubbed a hand through his hair as he ducked his head. "I'll call ya next week. Just to say hi." He leaned down and gave her a sort of awkward hug-type pat on the back. They'd never been big huggers, but her chewing him out must have hit a nerve for him to attempt one.

"I'd like that." She clasped her hands together in front of her, squeezing them tightly to keep from cracking open her purse and giving him the last twelve dollars of cash she had in her wallet. It could buy him a cheeseburger at least. *He can buy his own bloody cheeseburger. Remember? He's an adult.*

He gave her a little wave and slipped out the front door. She stood at the counter, still clasping her hands and willing her feet to stay in place so she didn't go running after him and beg him to take some of her money. She let out her breath, then collapsed onto the sofa as his truck barreled down the driveway and out onto the highway.

Lucky ran over and licked her face as if to say *Good girl*.

She sat there a few minutes, then her stomach growled. She heated up a bowl of leftover pasta and sat at the counter, staring at her phone while she absently shoved noodles into her mouth. Apparently staring at it didn't make it ring or ding or do anything at all. Neither did ignoring it while she rinsed her dish, then tried to watch a crime show on television.

So far, she'd tried eating, sleeping, and watching television, and none of them took her mind off the tall cowboy. Maybe she needed to go for a walk. She laced up her sneakers and let out a laugh as she pushed open the front door.

Tiny was sprawled out on the porch, four barn cats of various shades curled around her massive pink body, and all sound asleep. Otis had claimed a spot on the porch and rested his horned head next to Tiny's snout. Bryn's laugh and the squeak of the door must have woken them, because they all stirred and stretched, then the cats lounged back against Tiny's body. The pig raised her head, and Bryn swore it looked like she smiled at her.

Lucky had followed her out, and Bryn reached down to scoop up the friendliest cat and cuddle it to her chest.

"I'm heading to the barn to check on the horses, then I'm going for a walk, if anyone is interested in tagging along," she told the rest of the animal pile.

Apparently the idea was appealing to all except the cats, who didn't really find many things appealing, and if they did, they wouldn't dare stoop to mention it. But the pig, the goat, and the dog followed her down the stairs and across the yard. Laughing, she felt like the Pied Piper as she led the parade of pets into the barn.

Shamus and the gray horse stood at the entrance of the barn as if they were keeping a watchful eye on Beauty. The mama horse seemed to be doing okay, not that Bryn would know what to do if she wasn't. She'd assumed Zane would be here. And he always knew what to do, especially when it came to horses.

Pushing thoughts of Zane away, she gave some oats to the horses and passed out sugar cubes and puppy treats to the other animals. She held out a sugar cube in one hand and a dog treat in the other to Tiny. "I can't decide where you fit in the scope of farm animals, so you pick. Which do you want?"

The pig snuffled at the treats in her hand, then gobbled down both.

"That's kind of what I thought," Bryn said as she gave her a scratch behind the ears. Determined to finish her walk, she headed out of the barn. She'd get on the computer and google "how to know if your horse is about to give birth" when she got home.

Not sure she would enjoy the long walk, Bryn put

Tiny back in her pen. But Lucky and Otis decided they'd like to trail along. They crossed through the pasture, and Shamus kept them company for a bit, running along next to them and trying to get the dog and the goat to play. It was amazing to see the changes in the little horse. With proper care and plenty of grass and sweet feed, the horse had filled out and pranced around the corral as if showing off his new well-fed physique.

All the horses seemed to be doing well, and Bryn was proud of the changes she'd made to her farm to accommodate the rescued animals. She thought about the blowup she'd had with Buck. Apparently she was making a few changes to herself too.

But should Zane be one of those changes? She wanted someone she could count on, who would be there for her. Had he shown her he could be that man?

Not today he hadn't. Today, he hadn't even returned her messages.

It was almost dark by the time she made it back to the barn. She'd gone farther than she'd planned, her feet mechanically walking as her mind was lost in thought. Opening the barn door, she figured she'd check on Beauty one more time before she headed in and tried to drown her sorrows in some television and a glass of wine. Make that several glasses of wine.

Beauty was pacing her stall, and she let out a whinny as Bryn approached the gate. The horse seemed restless, and a fine sheen of sweat covered her coat.

Uh-oh. This wasn't good. Or maybe it *was* good. *Dang*

it. Why hadn't she come back sooner and spent the evening on Google, instead of wandering through the pastures staring at wildflowers and trying to convince herself she didn't want Zane and he could take a flying leap into the Arkansas River?

But it was too soon. Zane had said it could still be another few weeks before the foal arrived. Maybe she should call him…just to see if he thought the horse was okay.

No. Stay strong. The horse was just pacing and sweating. No biggie. Bryn had just been doing that herself out in the pasture.

Beauty swished her tail and swung her head back to try to bite her haunches. She tried to lie down, then got back up again and seemed to be sweating more than before. Okay, Bryn hadn't done any of that on her walk.

Bryn eased closer and noticed the mare's udder leaking milk. Yeah, she definitely hadn't done that either. But she remembered Zane telling her about it.

He'd said a little leakage was to be expected, but this wasn't a little. This was streaming down her leg. This definitely didn't seem good.

He'd told her to be on the lookout for behavior that was out of the ordinary for the horse. That the horse's owner, the one used to seeing it all the time, was usually the best judge of when the horse was in distress. Well, Bryn had been around Beauty enough to know this wasn't her normal behavior. And she didn't just seem anxious.

Bryn watched her for a few more minutes. The horse

paced harder, her shoulders now soaked with sweat. She went to her knees, then stood back up and let out a mournful moan.

No, this wasn't good. This horse was in trouble.

CHAPTER 19

BRYN PULLED OUT HER PHONE AND TRIED ZANE'S number. It went immediately to voicemail. So either his phone was off, or he was purposely not taking her calls.

She left him a message. "Hey, Zane, it's Bryn." Why did she tell him her name? It was on the caller ID. "I just wanted to tell you I think Beauty is going into labor. I remember you telling me she might leak milk when she's getting close, and milk is streaming down her leg. Plus she seems like she's in distress. She's pacing and trying to lie down, and she just made the saddest moaning sound that hurt my chest to hear. I know you're mad or upset or whatever with me, but don't take it out on Beauty. She really needs you right now." *I really need you right now.* "Call me back as soon as you can. Or better yet, just come out here. But hurry."

Oh yeah, that message didn't sound needy at all. Oh wait, yes, it did. Because she *was* needy. She *needed* help with this horse. She had no idea what to do.

Beauty sank onto the floor, lying down, then rolling to her back. She whinnied, then pushed herself back up again like she couldn't find a comfortable position. She lifted her back legs, one then the other, then the other again. The horse shook her head and kept making weird mouth movements like she was yawning.

Bryn tapped out a text message to Zane: "Help! I need you to call me! I think something's wrong with Beauty. She is really distressed. Call me!"

"It's going to be okay, Beauty," she assured the horse. And herself. Because really, how the heck was she supposed to know if it was going to be okay?

She called Zane again. "Pick up. Pick up. Pick up!" she yelled into the phone.

The trough that Bryn had filled earlier was still full of oats. The sweet feed mix was normally Beauty's favorite, and she usually gobbled it down the minute either she or Zane poured it into the trough.

She tried Zane's phone again. Straight to voicemail.

Beauty pawed the ground and curled her upper lip back.

"I know. I know. I'm pissed at him too. Why won't the bastard answer his phone?"

Beauty responded by lifting her tail and letting loose a stream of bodily fluids. She nipped at her belly again, then resumed her pacing.

Screw it. If Zane wanted to act like an idiot, she'd call someone she knew she could count on. She tapped the phone and almost cried with relief when Brody picked up on the first ring. "Oh thank God you're there."

"What's wrong? You okay?"

"Yes, I'm okay. But Beauty isn't. I think she's going into labor. She seems in real distress, and I don't know what to do."

"Okay, take a breath. Do you want me to come out there?"

Bryn slumped against the barn wall. "Would you?"

"Yeah, of course. I'm grabbing my boots. Talk to me while I'm putting them on. Tell me what's going on."

"She's really sweating, and she keeps pacing back and forth in her stall, like she's anxious and restless. She keeps trying to bite and kick at her belly. And she's making these awful moaning noises."

"That sounds normal. She's doing that stuff because she can feel her body getting ready to give birth. What else?"

"Um, she doesn't seem to be eating, and she keeps trying to lie down, then gets back up again."

"Good. Horses are pretty amazing animals. They know what to do. But they also like their privacy. As long as she has a quiet, clean place to foal, she'll be okay."

"Should I try to put some fresh hay in there? She keeps…um…going number one and number two at the same time."

Brody chuckled. "In the medical field, we call that urinating and defecating, but I get your meaning. Totally normal. You can try to spread some fresh hay in there, but I wouldn't stay long in her stall. Keep an eye on her, but don't hover."

"Got it. So watch her but act like I'm not watching her," Bryn said, imagining herself holding up a newspaper and discreetly peering over as if she were some kind of horse-breeding private detective. "She's also got some milk streaming down her leg," she told him.

"That could also be normal, but it could be something

to watch too. Depends on how much it is. What does Zane think? He's been working horses for years, and I'm sure he's seen countless foalings. Is he worried?"

"He doesn't appear to be because he's not out here. And he's not answering or returning my calls. It's just me. And the dogs. And the pig. And none of them are helping." She tried to keep her tone light and play off a joke to keep the bitterness from seeping into her voice. But she was mad, damn it. Zane *should* be here. Beauty was his horse too. They'd said they would do this together.

"Oh," he said, a thousand sentiments present in that one word. "Well, don't worry. I'm on call tonight, so Mandy is with her grandparents anyway. I'm locking up now, so I'll be there in ten."

Her shoulders sagged in relief. "Thank you, Brody. I can always count on you."

"I'll see you soon."

She hung up the phone and slumped against the wall in the barn. Brody was coming. Because Brody was a guy she could count on. She knew he wouldn't let her down. Unlike a certain jerk who wouldn't answer or call her back.

———————

Zane cringed as he walked into the house, his chest aching at the absence of the stupid dog running up to greet him. He'd had a shit day, and the dog could always seem to sense that. She wasn't overt about it but seemed to show up when he needed her, leaning against his leg or offering the back of his hand a quick lick. The house felt eerily quiet without the pattering of the dog's feet and the rumble of his dad's voice.

Birch was out of the woods at least. The heart attack had been minor, and he was already cussing out the doctor and flirting with the nurses. They were keeping him another day, just to monitor his vitals.

Zane let out a heavy sigh and practically fell into the recliner. All he wanted to do was slink off into a dark cave and lick his wounds.

He glanced into the corner where he'd hurled his phone against the wall. The phone still lay there, the screen black. It had died in his pocket sometime at the vet clinic the night before. Although he hadn't realized it until he'd pulled it out to call 911 and saw it had no juice. He'd flung it at the wall in frustration and for once was thankful his dad still had a landline.

He considered rescuing the phone and finding a charger to plug it in. He was sure it had some texts and probably a few missed calls on it, not that many people called him. In fact, no one really did except Logan and Bryn. And hers were the messages he was avoiding. Hers and the vet clinic's.

As much as he wanted to know how the collie—how *Hope* was doing, he knew it was better if he just cut ties completely. Like ripping off a Band-Aid, or in this case, like ripping a bandage from a raw, aching wound—it might be fast and thorough, but it hurt like hell.

He'd called from the hospital that morning to pay the vet bill, and the receptionist had told him the dog had come out of surgery and was doing okay. That was all he'd needed to hear. And that fact solidified his decision to sever ties with the mutt—and with Bryn. They would both be better off without him.

And so would his dad. Had the stress of having Zane around caused another heart attack? *But what if you hadn't been here?* a small voice tried to interject. Zane ignored the voice, disregarding the idea that his presence may have helped anyone or anything.

The only *things* he did seem to help were horses. He was good at that—his one talent. Horses didn't ask for much, which was perfect since he didn't have much to offer. Maybe that's why they were a good match.

As soon as he decided to rescue his phone, he would put in a call to Maggie, his former boss, and let her know he was coming back to work for her. It would be good to get back to the Montana horse ranch where all he had to focus on was getting horses fed and broke and bought and sold, and his days were measured in time spent in the corral rather than by what time Bryn was going to call or thinking about how soon he could see her next. Forget all that crap—he didn't need it, didn't want it.

All he wanted was a simple life, no drama, no emotional connections—get up in the morning, do the job, work so hard he fell exhausted into bed, then get up and do it again the next day. If no one expected anything of him, he never let anyone down. It was better than having all these people in his life. *Yeah, keep telling yourself that, buddy.*

A nauseating fist of guilt clawed at his gut. He was letting people, and animals, down right now. And he hated that feeling. He could call out to the ranch. Just to check on the horses.

Or he could charge his phone. He was pretty sure Bryn would text him an update if something was happening with Beauty. But she could also be texting him with questions about them, about their relationship—questions he didn't want to answer. A clean break meant he cut off communication. And the only way he was going to get through this break was not to talk to her at all.

That same tiny voice mumbled something about the only thing worse than his phone being filled with missed calls and messages would be to charge it and find that he had zero of either. He had told her they were through, that he was done with the dog and done with her. But he wasn't sure he was ready for the cold, hard truth that *she* was done with *him*. And no calls or messages would mean he hadn't mattered and that she realized he was right—she *was* better off without him.

Better not to know.

The house felt hot and humid, and the scent of mushrooms and old beef hung in the air from the dried up pan of Hamburger Helper stroganoff still sitting on the stove. He pulled off his boots and chucked them in the direction of his phone. They hit the wall with a *thud* that he'd thought would make him feel better, but didn't touch the misery sitting in him like the lumps of grease coagulating in the pan of forgotten hamburger mix.

He opened some windows, turned on the fan, and changed into shorts and a T-shirt. Leaning into the open door of the refrigerator, he tried to find something, anything, that sounded good to eat. He contemplated making a pan of scrambled eggs, but the effort didn't seem worth it. Giving up, he swung the door shut, grabbed a bag of corn chips off the counter, and slumped back in the recliner.

The chips were stale and a little like eating old cardboard—not that he tasted them anyway. He was just going through the motions of sticking something in his mouth. The clicking sound of the old box fan in the window grated on his nerves, and he wadded up the plastic bag from the chips and chucked it toward his boots. That corner of the room was accumulating quite a collection of angrily tossed items.

He pushed up from the chair, his body restless, his fists clenched in anger as he considered what in the house he could punch. But instead of destroying the house, he decided to punish his body instead. He shoved his feet into his sneakers, slammed out of the house, and tore off down the road.

The sky had gone dark, but his feet knew the way as they struck the pavement. His arms pumped at his sides as he sprinted, pushing his body harder and harder, until his muscles burned and his lungs ached.

Charging down the road, he kept pushing, driving his

body harder. He just wasn't sure if he was running toward
something or away from it.

———————————

Bryn checked her watch. It had only been seven minutes
since she'd hung up with Brody. She tried to be patient.
He'd said ten minutes, so he should be here soon.

The horse let out a low moan and went down to her
knees, then pushed back up again. Poor thing.

"You're doing great, Mama," she cooed to the horse
like she'd heard Zane do. Damn it. Zane should be here.
The horse always responded so well to him. Bryn knew
Beauty would be calmer with Zane near her.

Stop thinking about Zane. Instead of thinking about
the man, she tried to recall all the conversations they'd
had about this moment and sought to remember everything he'd told her about the birth of the foal and what to
expect. She knew just enough to be dangerous.

Beauty let out another moan, this one louder and
more distressful than the last. A white sac ballooned out
from under the horse's tail and two tiny hooves were visible through the milky material.

Oh my gosh, it is starting. Hurry, Brody!

The horse moved into the far corner of the stall and
laid down with her hindquarters pushed against the wall.

Oh no. That's not good. Bryn knew there had to be
enough room for the foal to come out, and there was
no space between the horse's tail and the wall. If Beauty

tried to push out the foal, either she or the baby could get injured. "You need to get up and move, girl," she pleaded.

The horse looked at her with an expression that was a cross between *you're crazy if you think I'm moving* and *please help, this hurts.*

Bryn had to do something. Hovering and frantically wringing her hands wasn't going to move the horse. That moment—the moment she chose to open the gate and step into the stall with an anguished half-ton horse who was making it clear she didn't want Bryn anywhere near her—was the moment she knew her life was truly changed.

She had taken on this horse without a clue in the world how to care for it or her baby. Then she'd taken on another one and another one still. In a matter of minutes, she was going to be the proud owner of *four* horses. Not to mention seven dogs, several cats, a cantankerous goat, and a curvaceous hog…er, pig. This was real. And it wasn't something she could just change her mind and back out of. Every one of these animals was now depending on her. She was doing this thing, starting a horse rescue, and she was doing it on her own. Truly on her own.

She'd just kicked her brother out. And by not showing up tonight, Zane had made it perfectly clear he didn't want to be part of her life. It was all up to her to feed and care for all these animals, and there were probably more to come.

When Zane had hung the sign and she'd registered

the business, it had felt real, but not like this. Not like stepping into a stall that smelled of fear and sweat and urine and trying to convince a distraught and hurting horse in labor that she needed to stand up and move to another part of the stall. This was the real deal, where the rubber met the road, and there was no going back.

It didn't matter that her hands were shaking and her heart was thrashing against her chest. She was scared, but so was Beauty. And they were in this together.

"It's okay, girl. I'm not gonna hurt you," she told the horse, taking another tentative step toward her. "I'm sorry, but you gotta get up."

Beauty swung her head, biting at her haunches, then moaning as her huge belly contracted. Bryn reached for her halter, slipping her fingers under the fabric. "Come on, Mama. You gotta move."

The horse pulled back, trying to free her head. Bryn held on. *I can do this. I have to do this.* She leaned back, putting her weight into it as she pulled on the halter. "Come on, girl."

The horse strained against her, letting out a hard bellow as another six inches of spindly legs appeared.

"Please, Beauty, you've got to get up." Sweat broke out on Bryn's neck and her arms trembled, but she fought the urge to panic as she pulled again, her need to help the horses, *her* horses, outweighing her fear. She *had* to move her. Before it was too late.

This time the horse rocked and moaned and pushed to her feet.

"Good girl, you did it!" Tears welled in Bryn's eyes, but she blinked them back as she led Beauty to the middle of the stall. The horse followed her a few yards, then went down to her knees again and rolled to her side. But it was enough to give her space to push the foal out.

Bryn patted the horse's neck and slipped out of the stall. She didn't want to upset the horse any more than she already had. "You're doing great, girl," she cooed, then gasped in amazement as another contraction hit, and the horse pushed the foal's head out. "Keep going, Mama. You're almost there."

The horse heaved and moaned, then pushed again. The foal's shoulders broke free, and the front hooves tore the sac. Another push, and the back legs were out.

The foal was here. "You did it, Mama. You did it," Bryn cried, pressing her hands to her chest.

The last push had drawn the sac back from the legs, but it was caught on the foal's head, the white casing covering its mouth and nose.

The foal wasn't moving.

It didn't shift its legs or try to lift its head. It just lay there.

Beauty raised her head in an attempt to get to the foal, but the effort was too much for her, and she dropped her head back into the straw.

Bryn held her breath, willing the baby to move, praying for its tiny chest to rise and fall, for it to wiggle its head free of the membrane. But it didn't budge.

Its small body lay deathly still.

CHAPTER 20

BRYN HAD TO DO SOMETHING.

Zane had told her when the foal came that it was important to try not to touch it and to stay out of the way of the baby's time to imprint on the mother. Bryn knew the first minutes were important, but she couldn't just stand there.

Not when the foal couldn't breathe. She had to do something. She opened the gate and raced to the foal. Falling to her knees, she lifted the foal's head.

The milky white membrane was thick and slick with fluid. She grabbed the edge and pulled it back, desperately trying to free the foal's mouth and nose. The tissue tore and pulled away, and Bryn pushed it off the foal's head and down its body.

The foal's head lay in the straw and Bryn lifted it again, clearing away fluid from its nose and rubbing the sides of its head. "Please, baby, please. Come on. Breathe."

Its head lolled to the side. *No!* Bryn rubbed harder, praying at the same time. "Please God, please God, please God."

The foal gave a sharp gasp followed by a snuffling sneeze. Bryn slumped forward, feeling giddy and drained at the same time. Her mouth was dry, and she let out a shaky laugh as she hugged her arms around her middle, pressing her hands to her sides to control their trembling.

Beauty raised her head and peered at her baby as the foal kicked its legs and flopped forward in the straw. Wanting to give the mother and baby bonding time, Bryn pushed to her feet and eased back.

Turning around, she gave a start and let out a little yelp at the figure of a man in a cowboy hat standing in the shadows of the stall.

"It's about time you got here," she spat at him, the relief at saving the foal replaced with anger at Zane.

But it wasn't Zane who stepped out of the shadows and held up his hands. "Sorry, I came as fast as I could."

Her shoulders slumped forward and her chin drooped to her chest. "Sorry, Brody. I thought you were Zane."

Brody held the door of the stall open then shut it after she'd walked through. "Looks like you didn't need either one of us." He tilted his head and studied her. "You okay?"

She pressed her lips together, fighting the emotions that struggled to break loose, as she carefully nodded her head.

He smiled and held his arms out. "Come here."

She took a shuddering breath and stepped into his open arms.

Zane heard their voices as he slipped quietly into the barn. He'd seen Brody's truck, so he knew the vet was here. He'd almost left when he'd seen his rig, but he figured the reason he was there had to do with Beauty, and Zane's concern for the horse and the foal drove him to sneak into the barn, just to see how they were doing.

He didn't expect to see Bryn stepping out of the stall and into Brody's arms. Her arms clutched his back and her shoulders shook like she was crying.

Damn. Had something happened to the horse? Or the foal? He took another step forward, trying to see into the stall without letting on that he was there and breaking up their intimate moment.

Bryn pulled away and swiped at the tears on her cheeks. "Sorry. I don't know why I'm crying. Everything's okay now. I guess I was just scared."

Brody put a hand on Bryn's arm. Heat rose up Zane's back, and he wanted to knock the guy's hand away. "It's okay," Brody told Bryn. "I'm sure you were scared. But you handled the crisis and saved the foal's life." He looked over her shoulder and into the stall. "Mama and baby look like they're doing just fine."

Relief flooded through Zane's body. *Thank God.* Both horses were doing okay. So he could leave now. Except his feet weren't moving, and his gaze was solidly stuck to the expression on Bryn's face as she gazed up at Brody.

"Thanks for coming all the way out here. I really appreciate you being here for me," she told him.

That mass of guilt that had been churning in his gut started tumbling again.

A hard ache ripped through his chest as he watched Brody lift his hand and cup Bryn's cheek.

"I'll always be here for you, Bryn."

She gazed up at the vet, a sweet smile on her face, as she covered his hand with hers and leaned her cheek into his palm.

Zane had to turn away. Had to *get* away. This was what he'd wanted. This was the way it was supposed to be. Bryn deserved a guy like Brody, and with Zane out of the picture, everything would fall into place. Just like it was supposed to.

He slipped back out the door, his feet itching to run as he sprinted toward the highway.

———————

Bryn held Brody's hand against her face. "Thank you. That means a lot to me. Especially after the day I've had today. And I'll always be here for you too." She squeezed his hand. "You are such an amazing guy. You are just the kind of man I've dreamed of finding and falling in love with."

"But?"

"But…" She lifted her shoulders in a helpless shrug. "I can't fall for you because I'm already in love with some-one else." Whether he wanted her or not, she was in love with Zane, and it was going to take a lot to get over that. And as much as she wished the cute doctor could be the remedy for her heartbreak, she knew he wasn't the cure.

"I wish I could be there for you in the way you want me to be."

He offered her a knowing smile. "You are, Bryn. You're my friend. And that's really all I need right now." He pulled his hand away and scrubbed it across the back of his neck. "I know I asked you out on a date, but that was more because my mom has been pressuring me to get back out in the dating world. I figured because we were already friends, you were a safe way to attempt my first date since Mary died."

Bryn smiled up at him. "And how did you think it went?"

"I think it was awkward and uncomfortable and also kind of nice. I really like you, Bryn. You're gorgeous and funny and smart, but I just don't think we have that connection. I know what real love is, and frankly, I'm not ready for that again."

She nodded her head. "I know. I feel the same way about you—you're gorgeous and funny and smart too. And I adore Mandy." She shrugged again. "But I'd still really like to be friends."

"Oh heck yes. I want that too. And Mandy would kill me if I wrecked anything between us and she didn't get to hang out with you anymore."

"So we're good?"

He smiled. "We're good." His lips tightened at the corners of his smile. "Although speaking purely as your friend, I am a little worried about you."

She was a little worried about her too. "I know," she whispered, already guessing what he was going to say.

"Zane's a tough guy. He's been through a lot and has a pretty rough history."

Why did everyone always bring up Zane's history? No wonder the guy wanted to stay away from Creedence. No one would let him forget his past.

"He just seems like a hard guy to hand your heart to," Brody continued. "You sure you trust him with it?"

"No," she answered. "But it's too late now. I already gave it to him. And you wouldn't want my heart anyway," she said, trying to control the tremble in her voice. "Because I'm pretty sure he already broke it." She swallowed back the lump in her throat and squeezed her eyes against the tears that were trying to sneak out.

Brody swore. "He's an idiot."

She tried to laugh, but it came out as more of a sigh. She forced her lips into a brave smile. "Enough about me. How's Hope doing? Is she feeling better today?" Bryn's stomach clenched at the frown that appeared on Brody's face.

"You know, I thought she was doing okay this morning, but when I left the clinic tonight, she still hadn't eaten. And she's been really lethargic—not her usual self. I'm glad she's staying another night, just so we can keep an eye on her."

"Should I go over there and see her?"

"Nah. You've got enough on your plate for tonight." He pointed to the stall where the foal was standing on wobbly legs next to Beauty and the mama horse was licking her baby's head. "You know, dogs are pretty devoted animals, and they can sense mood shifts and emotions in their owners. They can get depressed and despondent over the behavior of their alpha. So to be honest with you, I don't think you're the one she's waiting to see."

Brody was right, Bryn thought the next morning as she stared down at Hope's listless body. The dog did seem sad. Other than a small tail wag of greeting when Bryn first walked into the room, she'd barely lifted her head from the table. She looked pitiful in the harsh lights of the exam room. Her fur was still streaked with mud and blood, and a big patch of her fur had been shaved away from her abdomen and covered in bandages.

A vet tech walked into the room and smiled at Bryn. "Hey, girl, how are you doin'?"

"Hey, Maria, I'm doing okay. Better than Hope here." Bryn knew the other woman from school. Maria had been a few years behind her, but they'd had a few classes together and the other woman and her family often came into the diner to eat.

"Yeah. Health-wise, Doc says she should be okay. The surgery went fine, and most of the other cuts and abrasions are superficial."

"Then why does she seem so sad? She looks like she just lost her best friend." *I know the feeling.*

"She did," Maria said. "In a sense. Dogs are really in tune with their owners, and shake-ups in that relationship can affect them and can affect their recovery. We think she's just missing Zane."

"Has he been back in to see her yet?" Bryn brushed her hand over the dog's neck as she asked the question with what she hoped was nonchalance.

Maria shook her head. "No. But I wouldn't imagine he would. Not with his dad being in the hospital and all."

"Hospital?"

"Yeah, didn't you hear? Birch had another heart attack night before last. Friend of mine is a nurse over there, and she said he came in by ambulance. Zane stayed with him through the night and most of the day yesterday. Poor guy is probably wiped out. I guess it makes sense why he hasn't visited the dog yet."

Bryn was glad something made sense because nothing else seemed to be making sense to her right now. She gave the dog one last cuddle. "I've got to go. But one of us will be back to pick her up later."

"I'd call first. If she's still not eating, I'm not sure Doc's gonna let her go home."

Bryn walked out of the vet clinic and looked up and down the road, as if Zane might have left a trail of breadcrumbs when he'd left. She had no idea where to find him. She tried his phone again, no answer, then drove to his house, figuring it would be the most obvious place to check first. But no one answered her knock.

The curtains of the front window were open and she peered in, wondering if she might see him asleep on the sofa. But the living room was empty. She did spot his cell phone and a wadded up bag of chips on the floor in the corner though. So at least one mystery was solved.

She could try the hospital next. Or Logan's. But surely he didn't go to work. She pulled out her phone and dialed Logan's number.

He answered on the first ring. "Hey, Bryn."

"Hey, Logan. Is he there?" Neither of them had to clarify who she meant.

"Yeah. His rig is in the driveway, and I saw him carrying some steel posts out to the north pasture. He's been talking about fixing a section of fence by the pond there. But he's in a helluva mood, so if you've got a choice, you might steer clear of him for a bit today."

"Thanks for the advice, but it seems I don't have a choice. I'm heading your way now."

"Your decision. When you get here, just walk out that little trail to the north of the barn. You'll find him."

She was already in her car and headed toward the highway by the time she clicked off. She swallowed and tried to even out her breathing. Her heart was slamming against her chest, and she was equal parts mad and sad he hadn't called to tell her about his dad—hell, that he'd chosen not to call her at all.

Was she running a fool's errand, racing out to see him when his actions were making it quite clear he didn't want to see her? She didn't know why she was in such an awful hurry. She had no idea what she was going to say when she got there.

Fifteen minutes later, she parked next to his truck and

picked her way down the trail to the pond on the north side of Logan's barn. It was easy enough to find Zane—she just followed the path and the sound of hammering and his occasional swearing.

She came around the corner and saw him working on a bit of fence. He was shirtless and swinging a hammer, the muscles of his body flexed and tense. Heck, if she hadn't known what she was going to say before, she was speechless now.

The man looked like a Greek god, if a Greek god wore a tool belt and had been scarred by the torturous hands of his own father. Wait—that actually did sort of sound like a Greek tragedy. Oh gosh, she was getting way off track here. Suffice it to say, he looked hot as hell. Her legs turned to huckleberry jelly, and a fluttering started in her belly at the sight of him.

Zane looked up as she approached, his expression as hard as his muscles as he glared at her. "What the hell are you doing here?" His eyes cut to his shirt hanging on a fence post a few yards away. She could almost see the internal debate of if he should grab it and cover his back or not.

In the end, he stood his ground, pulling his shoulders back and standing even taller than he normally did. She assumed he took the stance as a way to intimidate her, but in fact it did the opposite. It softened her. The fact that he didn't cover himself—that he wore his scars in front of her, even as a shield—told her they'd crossed a major barrier in the huge wall of defense Zane had built around himself.

She swallowed, wishing she'd brought her bottle of water from the car. Her mouth was as dry as her great-aunt's Sunday pot roast. And there wasn't enough gravy in Colorado to moisten that roast. "I heard about your dad."

He shrugged. "So?"

Wow. This guy was tough. His expression didn't change a smidge. "So is he okay?"

"I thought you said you already heard about him."

"I heard he had a heart attack and that he was in the hospital. That's all." Well, that and that Zane had spent the better part of the last day and a half at the hospital.

"Then you know everything except I guess he's gonna live. And the doctors confirmed the fact he does indeed have a heart, which is a point that's been up for debate for years."

She was starting to wonder if the apple hadn't fallen far from the hard-hearted tree. *Stop it*. Zane was nothing like Birch. "Well, then that sounds like good news at least."

"Does it?" Zane dropped his gaze and picked up the next fence post. He rammed it into the ground and pounded the top of it with a hammer. *Bang! Bang! Bang!*

She jumped with each strike, the clang of the hammer on steel reverberating in her chest. And each smash felt like a shove to her body, thrusting her away from him.

"Is that all?" he asked, his gaze trained on his task as he wrapped wire around the studs of the steel fence post.

"I thought you'd want to know about Hope."

"I already heard she came out of surgery fine and she's going to be okay."

"You heard wrong. She's not eating, and they're keeping her another night."

His hands stilled for just a moment, then began their work again. "Not my problem. She's your dog now."

Who was this man? He wasn't acting like the Zane she knew. "Don't you want to know about Beauty? She had the foal, you know. No thanks to you."

"I know. I also know you didn't even need me. You took care of things yourself. You and Dr. Helpful."

"How do you know I did it myself? Did you talk to Brody?"

He picked up another post and shoved it into the ground. "I didn't have to. I was there. I came out to check on the horses and saw you together. It looked to me like he had everything handled—including you." *Bang! Bang! Bang!*

Shove. Shove. Shove.

"You were there? Why didn't you say anything?"

"I didn't want to ruin such a perfect moment." His sarcasm wasn't lost on her. She didn't need a GPS to find it.

"What are you talking about?"

He crashed the hammer onto the head of the post. "Don't bullshit me, Bryn. I saw the way he looked at you. And how you looked at him. That was all I needed to see. You didn't need my help. And you sure as hell didn't need me."

She reached out a hand to touch him, and her heart

shattered as he flinched. It was just the slightest of movements, but it was there. And it wasn't that he flinched at the idea that she was taking a swing at him. It was more like he flinched as if the touch of her fingers might burn him. "Zane," she whispered, her throat raw with emotion.

He pulled away, his eyes narrowing even more. She didn't think his glare could get harder, but if they passed out medals for the most terrifying glower, he'd take the prize, hands down. Except he didn't scare her. Not in that way, at least.

She knew he'd never hit her. But he could still hurt her—he *was* hurting her. With every clang of that damn hammer, he was chipping off another piece of her heart.

"Don't," he growled, leaning down to pick up the next few fence posts. "This is the way it's supposed to be. Brody's a good man. He'll treat you right. You don't need me."

A flash of anger tore through her pain, and she planted her hands on her hips and offered him her own glare. Enough was enough. She'd stood up to her brother; she could stick up to Zane. "I'm getting pretty damn sick and tired of everyone else thinking they know what's best for me. Since when do *you* get to decide what *I* need? And how *my* life is supposed to be?"

"You know what? You're right. I don't get to decide what you're going to do with your life. But I *do* get to decide that I'm not going to be in it. I already called my old boss and told her I was taking my job at the horse ranch back. I leave tomorrow. So there's no point in even talking about it anymore. You should just go." He hefted the fence posts over his shoulder and walked away.

She drew in a slow, unsteady breath and swallowed, her throat feeling like it had been sliced to raw ribbons. She fought the urge to completely lose it and scream at him. Instead, she swallowed and held it together, barely controlling her ire as she stated, "You know, I'm also getting pretty damned tired of you walking away from me."

He hurled the fence posts to the ground, but his voice stayed even, emotionless. "I'm getting pretty damned tired of you following me. I don't know any other way to put this. I don't want you anymore. The only thing I want is for you to leave."

Her breath caught in her throat. Then she couldn't seem to breathe at all. It was as if all the air had been sucked from the atmosphere and there was nothing for her to inhale. Her chest ached from the pressure of her failing lungs.

―――――――――

Please God. Why won't she leave?

The muscles in Zane's jaws throbbed from clenching his teeth so hard. She was killing him.

His head was pounding. His body felt numb, except for his chest and his throat—those both hurt like they'd been lacerated then set on fire. But he had to stay strong. Even though it was taking everything in him to keep pushing her away. But there was no other way.

"Zane. Please. I don't understand."

Just tell her. Tell her you love her, his heart screamed, while his brain scoffed, *No way. Let her go—she deserves better than a worthless cowhand like you.*

He couldn't back down now. Like a wild horse, he broke her again and again. He was tearing himself up as he did it, but *he* didn't matter. His feelings, his heart, didn't matter. He had to save her. Even if he had to break her—and himself—to do it.

He was so damned tired he just wanted to crumple to the ground and sleep. But he couldn't. He had work to do. *Concentrate on the work.* He wrenched a fence post from the ground and slammed it into the earth. His muscles ached and blood dripped from a fresh cut on his hand— when the hell had he done that?—but he couldn't stop. He had to stay focused—*so* insanely focused on the task at hand.

If he didn't keep his hands busy, he just might grab her and pull her to him and not ever let her go. And that wasn't what was best for her.

Even if she couldn't see it, he could. His hand was bleeding, and his heart was ripping apart, but he had to finish this, had to push her away. One. Last. Time.

It didn't matter that it hurt *him*. He'd been hurt before. Hell, he'd been whipped and punched and burned with a lit cigarette. And he would take that kind of pain over this any day.

Because he *could* take it. He would take any pain to save her. And pushing her away was the only way he knew how to do that—how to save her. Putting his needs and wants aside—and God knew, he wanted and needed her more than anything he'd ever wanted or needed in his life—but this time, he couldn't put his selfishness above what was best for her. And what was best for her wasn't him.

He gritted his teeth as he picked up the hammer. He couldn't look at her. Instead, he focused everything on the task at hand, on driving the next fence post into the ground. *Bang! Bang! Bang!* "You need to go, Bryn. We're through. I told you—I don't want you anymore."

He heard the soft hitch in her breath, could see the slump of her shoulders from the corner of his eye. *Go. Please, go. Don't make me hurt you again.* He twisted the length of wire around the post, cranking the wire tighter and tighter as he heard her finally walk away.

He tore the new post from the ground and hurled it into the pond, letting loose with a primal yell that was a cross between a swear and a shout. He shook his injured hand, spraying droplets of blood across the dust on the ground. *Damn it.* He was such a dick.

CHAPTER 21

BIRCH WAS ASLEEP WHEN ZANE WALKED INTO HIS hospital room late that afternoon. He'd told Logan he was done for the day and stopped at a gas station on the way into town to fill up and grab a couple of candy bars to eat for supper.

His dad stirred as he set the chocolate he'd bought for him on the tray next to the bed. Birch's eyes fluttered open and softened just the slightest as he looked at his son, then he let out a sigh and his normal *resting scowl face* returned. "What are you doing here?"

Zane slumped back in the hard plastic chair and stretched his legs out in front of him. "I honestly don't know." He sighed and gestured to the chocolate. "Figured you'd hate flowers, so I brought you a candy bar instead."

The tiniest of grins pulled at the corners of his mouth as Birch picked up the candy bar, then his features transformed into a glower. "What the hell kind of candy bar is this?"

"It's dark chocolate, Dad. Didn't you hear the doctor last night? He said you need to eat better. And he said dark chocolate's better for your heart than milk chocolate. That thing cost me twice as much as a Hershey's."

"Then I'll use twice the effort tossing it into the trash. You always were a sucker." Birch wrinkled his nose as he studied the package. "This says it's got seventy percent *caca* in it. See, it tells you right on the label it tastes like shit. Or at least seventy percent like shit."

"It's not 'caca,' it's 'cacao.' It's like a fancy word for cocoa beans."

"Then why don't they just say that? Why does every-body have to make things so complicated?"

Zane sighed. "I don't know, Dad."

"The only thing I want to eat beans in is chili and burritos," Birch muttered as he tore open the package and broke off a corner of the chocolate bar. He sniffed it, then gingerly put it into his mouth. He grimaced as he chewed. "I was right the first time. Tastes like caca."

"Then don't eat it," Zane told him. "I don't really give a caca."

Birch took another bite. "What are you all pissy about?"

"I'm not pissy. I've just got a lot on my mind. I called my old boss and told her I was planning to come back to Montana."

"Montana? Why?"

"For a job."

"You got a job here. And what about that Callahan girl I heard you been seeing? You just gonna leave her behind?"

"How did you hear I've been seeing someone?"

"I do have friends, you know."

Yeah, it was obvious. They might be friends when they were drinking in the bar, but where were they now? Had even one of them come to see Birch in the hospital?

Zane shrugged. "Well, your friends are wrong. I'm not *seeing* that Callahan girl. Not anymore."

Birch huffed. "I knew you'd screw that up."

"I'm sure you did, Dad," he muttered.

"I'm just saying it doesn't surprise me. A guy like you gets a chance with a nice girl like that, you're bound to screw it up. That's what you do, Son. You screw shit up."

"Yeah, I know." He did know. His dad had been telling him that his whole life. He'd screwed up both their lives just by being born. And even when he'd tried to get it together and have a life with Sarah, he'd screwed that up too. Which just solidified his choice to walk away from Bryn. He didn't want to screw her life up as well .

He clapped his hands on his knees and pushed up from the chair. "Well, this has been nice visiting with you, Dad. But I've gotta go." He didn't really have any place to be. He just had to get out of there. Away from his dad.

"You can't really go back to Montana, boy. Who's gonna take care of me?"

Zane pressed his lips together as he shook his head. "I don't know. Maybe all those friends you were just telling me you had."

"You're kind of an asshole."

"Like father, like son," he grumbled, then stopped at the door. "Let me know when they discharge you. I'll come back to bring you home."

"Thanks for the caca bar."

"No problem." Zane waved his hand, then headed down the hall of the hospital. His body felt beaten down, wrecked, and it seemed that the very air was full of molasses and pulled at his legs with each step he took.

He passed the chapel on his way out and something made him stop and turn and go inside. The room was quiet and cool, the walls a pattern of blues and greens as the late-afternoon sun shone through the big stained-glass window. Candles flickered on the altar, and the space felt intimate with only a few rows of pews.

Zane was almost surprised he hadn't burst into flames as he dragged his damaged soul across the threshold. He staggered forward and dropped into the last pew. Leaning forward, he rested his head on the back of the pew in front of him, the wood smooth and cool against his forehead.

It had been a long time since he'd been inside any kind of church. He'd always communed with God from the back of a horse on the open range or in the mountains as he stared across the vast scope of His creation. But he'd hit bottom, was at the end of his rope, and maybe the answer wasn't to let God come to him, but to show up at the door of His house.

He closed his eyes and prayed—prayed like he'd never prayed before. He prayed for wisdom, for guidance, for God to tell him what to do.

He heard a shuffling sound like someone had entered the chapel and walked up the aisle next to him. He raised his head, his eyes blurry with the grit of sleepless nights, and in the dim light of the room, he saw an angel.

Sarah was standing in the aisle, the glimmer of the candles flickering behind her. She looked older, her hair was darker and way shorter, and she was wearing purple scrubs with dancing puppies on them.

"Hi, Zane," Sarah said.

He let out a shuddering breath. It wasn't Sarah. It was her sister, Stephanie. He hadn't seen her in years. But he knew it was her. "Hey, Steph."

"How you doin', buddy?"

He shrugged.

"You look like hell."

"I feel like hell." He scrubbed a hand over his face. "Actually, I feel like I've been to hell and the devil sent me back."

She offered him a small attempt at a laugh and slid into the pew next to him. Up close, he saw her auburn hair was streaked with shades of purple and dark pink. She'd put on a little weight since he'd seen her last, but it looked good on her. She wore a gold band on her finger and a necklace with a couple of stick figures and little birthstones signifying she had a family. Good for her. He'd bet she was a great mom. She'd been the no-nonsense, snarky sister who called it like she saw it. But she was also funny and kind and always up for an adventure, like the time she'd talked them into a late-night ice cream run or the night she'd practiced shooting pucks in their driveway with him for two hours while he waited for Sarah to get home.

"How's your dad doing?"

He huffed. "Speaking of the devil."

She nudged his arm. "I'm a nurse now. I've been here for close to a year. I heard he'd been brought in, and I stopped to check on him during my rounds. He seems as ornery as ever."

"That's one way to put it." She would make a great nurse. He could imagine her bossing her patients around while still making them laugh. He pointed to the spot she'd been standing. "I thought you were her when I looked up, with the lights behind you and the way you've got your hair. I figured I must be going crazy because I thought you were an angel."

She chuckled. "I've never been accused of that." She gently rested her hand on his. "But I don't think you're crazy either. I think I see her sometimes too." They both knew who they were talking about. "Sometimes I'm driving down the road, and I think I see her at the DQ, standing out front, eating a chocolate-dipped cone like she used to. Or sometimes my phone rings and for just a second, I think it might be her. I've even seen her in places she's never been. I was at a conference in Atlanta last year and thought I saw her in the airport. Almost missed my plane because I followed this woman all the way down to her gate just to see her face."

He nodded. "I thought I saw her once in a market in Afghanistan."

"I'm glad you still see her sometimes and think about her."

"I do. A lot."

"I wasn't sure what you thought. You sort of dropped

off the face of the planet after it happened. I was really surprised you weren't at the funeral."

He lowered his head in shame. "I know. I'm sorry for that." His throat burned, and he couldn't look at her. "I'm sorry for everything. I couldn't go. Not knowing it was my fault."

"Oh, honey," she said, leaning her head against his shoulder.

He shrugged her off his shoulder. "Don't call me that. Don't even be nice to me. I don't deserve it."

"Why not? You lost her too."

"But it was *my* fault she died."

She jerked her head back. "*Your* fault? I don't understand. How could you possibly think Sarah's death was your fault? Did *you* make her take those pills?"

"No. But she wouldn't have done it if it weren't for me. I wanted her to stay. For once in my life, I acted selfish and asked for what I wanted. I begged her to give up her scholarship, and she did that for me. Then when she got so depressed, I'm the one who encouraged her to go see that therapist. And he's the one who gave her those pills. She wouldn't have gone there, wouldn't have had access to those drugs if it weren't for me. My putting my needs over hers drove her to do it. That's why it's my fault. She wouldn't have killed herself if it weren't for me."

"Oh, Zane." Her eyes softened, and she tenderly touched his arm. "Have you been carrying this around with you this whole time?"

He shrugged but couldn't speak through the pain in his throat.

"This wasn't your fault. None of it. My sister had a lot of problems. And she didn't go see a therapist because of you. She'd been seeing that same doctor for years."

"What? Why?" He blinked, and his brain felt dizzy as he tried to process what she'd just said. How could he not have known?

"Because she was messed up. She'd always suffered from depression. And she had a drug problem. Why do you think my parents moved us up here from Denver? To get away from the bad crowd of kids she was hanging out with at our old school. We thought she was doing better. She seemed to be so excited about college and her plans for the fall."

"But I screwed that up by asking her to stay. She gave up the scholarship and agreed to stay in Creedence for me."

Steph shook her head. "No, she didn't. I don't know what she told you, but she didn't give up the scholarship. She was planning to go to college. She'd enrolled in classes and had already accepted her dorm. She and her new roommate had connected on Facebook and had already picked the colors for their room. She and Mom had made plans to go shopping in Denver for the weekend after she died. They were going to get a comforter and all the stuff for her dorm room."

"Why would she lie?"

"Because that's what she did. She lied to all of us."

"I can't believe it." His shoulders slumped forward, the weight of what she'd said almost too heavy to bear.

"I'm so sorry. And I'm sorry you've been carrying this around with you. All of us have blamed ourselves at one point or another, but my mom and I have gone through a lot of counseling to help us deal with it. And neither one of us has ever blamed you. None of this was your fault. You made her happy—the happiest she'd been in years."

"But it wasn't enough. *I* wasn't enough."

She cocked her head to the side as her lips pulled together in a sneer. "That's bullshit. We're *all* enough. In my profession, I listen to a lot of life stories and some-one once told me, 'Don't believe everything you think.' Thoughts are just thoughts—don't give power to the wrong ones. Sarah loved you. She saw something in you that was worth loving."

He huffed. "She was the only one."

"I doubt that. I always thought you were a pretty great guy, especially when you let down your guard and were just yourself. My guess is that plenty of people have seen something in you, maybe even tried to love you, and I'll bet my firstborn child you've pushed them away."

"Keep your kid. You'd win that bet." *I'm pushing one away right now.* "But I push them away for their own sake. Being with me is how they get hurt, so I'm saving them that pain."

"Well, geez, aren't you just a mother-freakin' saint?"

"Not hardly. I do it for them."

She pulled her head back and gave him the famous

Stephanie Stink Eye. "I call bullshit on that as well. You're doing that for you. If you're pushing someone away, which I assume from the miserable look on your face that we're talking about a woman, you're not pushing her away to protect her. Women are tough, and we're also pretty smart. We know what we want, and we have a keen way of seeing the good in people. If you're trying to push a woman away, you're not doing it for her. You're doing it for you. Because *you're* afraid of getting hurt."

"I'm not afraid of pain. I've been hurt plenty. I can take it."

Her face softened. She knew about his history with his dad. "Heart pain isn't the same as body pain. And you can't let the hurts of the past keep you from having a future. You can't start the next chapter of your life if you keep rereading the last one."

He leaned back in the pew and offered her a wry grin. "You're just full of wisdom, aren't you? You sound like a greeting card."

She shrugged. "I might have read that last bit on a magnet in the break room. But falling back on sarcasm and charm doesn't change the truth of what I'm saying." She looked around the chapel. "And isn't wisdom what you came in here looking for?"

He let out a sigh. "Yeah, I guess it was. I just didn't think the Big Guy would send me wisdom in the form of a short, mouthy nurse with purple hair and dancing puppies on her shirt."

She laughed. "The Lord works in mysterious ways."

"That He does. And it seems like I've got some work to do." He stood and looked down at her. "I'm glad I ran into you."

"I am too." She stood and stepped into the aisle, then reached up and put her hand on his arm. "Just because you're strong doesn't mean you have to carry around everyone's baggage. If it isn't yours, let it go. Quit hauling around your dad's garbage and quit lugging around all of Sarah's sadness. Those aren't your burdens to bear. My grandma used to say you can't get to the next rung of your ladder without letting go of the old one and reaching for it." She gave him a hard hug. "Okay, I'll quit dispensing my awesome wisdom now."

He squeezed her back. "It was pretty awesome. And so are you. I'm sorry I didn't keep in touch."

She let him go and offered him a shrug. "Water under the bridge. We can't go back and change it, so why waste time worrying about it now?" She rolled her eyes and did a mock head-slap to her forehead. "I can't stop myself. I'm like a wisdom-farting fountain."

He laughed then. A real laugh. And it felt good.

She reached into her front pocket, then handed him a business card. "Here's my number. Don't be a stranger. And I'd like to meet her."

"Meet who?"

"The woman you're suddenly so anxious to go see."

He grinned. "I will go see her. But first, I have to go get my dog."

Bryn smoothed her dress as she approached her table. She'd considered flaking out on the awards dinner and curling up on her couch with a blanket, a bucket of rocky road ice cream, and a wineglass filled with merlot and misery. But some very nice folks had gone to the trouble of nominating her for this award and she didn't want to let them down. Plus she'd never received an award for anything before, so why let a little heartbreak and rejection stop her from accepting an honor that affirmed her best traits of being a good, animal-rescuing person?

In the end, she'd dug a fancy dress out of the closet and buckled on some strappy heels and convinced herself this was a grand idea as she drove into town. But now that she was here, all she felt was humiliation and embarrassment at the two place settings marked *Callahan* mocking her from her table.

She sucked in a breath. *Pull it together, girl.* She didn't need Zane.

In the last few days, she'd stood up for herself and accomplished things she didn't think she was capable of, but she'd done them. She was stronger than she'd first believed. And she could get through this night. She'd hold her head high and accept the award for most innovative animal rescue volunteer.

Then she could go home and have wine and ice cream. Maybe she'd have them together—a wine float. Hey, there was an idea. She should share it here and possibly nab another award for the most innovative idea to get through the breakup blues.

———————————

Zane's heart shattered as he looked through the bars of the kennel and saw his dog. A large bandage covered a shaved area of her abdomen, the fur around it still slightly matted with blood. A neat row of stitches secured the skin where she'd suffered the gash on her shoulder. Her body looked thinner, and she didn't turn her head when he entered the room the vet tech had pointed to.

"Hey, girl," he said, opening the kennel door. She was in the top kennel. It was one of the oversized ones for bigger dogs. She was curled up on a blue blanket, one he recognized from the farmhouse. Bryn must have brought it to the clinic for the dog. A food and water dish sat against the wall of the kennel, both full and seemingly untouched.

At the sound of Zane's voice, the border collie finally turned her head. She let out a soft whine and wagged her tail when she spotted him.

He gently rubbed her neck as she stretched her nose toward him. Whining again, she wiggled forward, trying to get closer to him. "Whoa there. It's okay, girl. I'm here." He blinked back tears as he carefully scratched her ears. "I'm here. But you gotta eat if you want to come home." He scooped some dog food into his hand and held it by her head.

She looked up at him, her eyes wary.

"It's okay. I promise. I'm really here."

He swore he saw the wariness transform into trust as she nosed his hand, then ate a few pieces of the dog food. "Good girl."

"That's the most she's eaten since you brought her in," a voice said from behind him.

He'd hoped he wouldn't have to see Brody. But the man did save his dog's life, and he owed him a debt of gratitude for that. He turned and eyed the veterinarian. Brody was wearing khaki pants and a white shirt with a blue tie under a navy blazer. Zane nodded to the dog. "Thanks for fixing her up. How's she doin'?"

Brody tilted his head toward Hope. "It seems like she's doing a lot better now that you're here. I wasn't sure she was going to come out of it."

"Why? I thought the surgery was a success."

"It was. But dogs are like people—they fight harder when they have something to live for. I think she sensed you weren't coming back, and it seemed like she was giving up. She hasn't eaten or drunk much water since the surgery. I was just stopping in to check on her and figured I'd have to put her on an IV tonight just to keep her hydrated."

The sound of splashing had Zane turning to see Hope lapping water from the dish. "She seems to be doing all right now."

"Yeah. She does. That's because you're here."

He shrugged. "I don't know about that. Maybe she just now got hungry and thirsty."

Brody huffed out a dry laugh. "I don't think so." He offered Zane a knowing look as the dog gazed up at her alpha, then dug into the bowl of dog chow.

Well, I'll be. Rather than admit the vet might be right, Zane nodded to his clothes. "Pretty fancy duds for this late at night. You on your way to a wedding or a funeral?"

Brody shook his head. "Neither. I was heading over to the Elks Lodge. The Women's Club is hosting a banquet tonight. You knew Bryn was getting an award, didn't you?"

That hadn't taken long. Bryn had already replaced him and invited Brody to attend in his place. Served him right for what he'd done to her.

"Yeah, I knew. And I'm glad you're going with her." He let out his breath and his pride with it. "You're a good guy. I told her she deserves someone like you, someone who will treat her right. I'm sure you two will be real happy together."

Brody chuckled. "You don't have a lot of experience with women, do you, Zane?"

He jerked his head back. "I've had my share of women," he assured the vet.

"I don't mean that kind of experience. I mean the experience of being in a relationship with one, being around one all the time and trying to understand them."

"Are you saying *you* understand women?"

He barked out a laugh. "Oh heck no. I can name three hundred bones in the body of a canine, but I haven't a clue about understanding women. But in my years of marriage, I did learn a few things. And one of those things is that you can't tell a woman how to think or what to feel. And you sure don't want to assume that you *know* what she's thinking or tell her *how* she should feel about something."

"What are you getting at?"

"You can't *tell* Bryn who she deserves to be with. And it's not me, by the way."

"Look, I saw you guys together last night. I stopped by the farm to check on the horse and saw the two of you getting all cozy. And if she didn't want you to be with her, why would she invite you to go to the awards dinner?"

"She didn't invite me. The clinic was nominated for an award."

Oh.

"And I don't know what you thought you saw last night. Yeah, we hugged, but you must not have heard our actual conversation or you would have heard us discussing how we're better off as friends. And how she isn't interested in me because she's in love with you."

Oh.

"Yeah, and from the look of your mopey face, I'd say you are in love with her too." Brody stared at him. "Did you hear me? The woman is in love with you."

"I heard you."

"Then why do you look gloomier than the dog? What's the problem?"

"The problem is that I went to considerable effort this afternoon to convince her I wanted nothing to do with her."

Brody shrugged. "I've also learned a little humility and a sizeable apology go a long way to mendin' fences you've torn down with a woman. And chocolate. That helps too."

"I don't know."

"What's not to know? Do you love this woman or not?"

Zane nodded. "Yeah, I do."

"Then what the hell are you doing standing here talking to me? Go over to the Elks Lodge and tell her."

Zane nodded and took a step toward the door. "Yeah, you're right. That's exactly what I'm going to do."

"Wait." Brody held up a hand and glanced down at Zane's shirt. It was a blue button-up, but he'd hit a bump in the truck that morning and spilled his coffee on it. Brown stains dripped down the center of his buttons. "You can't wear that."

"Shit, you're right." He glanced at the wall clock above the vet's head. "But there's nothing I can do about it. I don't have time to go home and change. The banquet started almost an hour ago."

Brody shrugged out of his jacket. "Here. Put this on."

Zane eyed the coat. "You sure? What about you? I thought you said you were getting an award too."

"I'm sure. I'd already decided not to go, so I sent one of the other vets in my place to accept the award."

Zane was already going to show up with his ass in his hand; the least he could do was not embarrass her any more by walking in wearing a coffee-stained shirt. He took the jacket and shoved his arms into the sleeves. It was a little snug, but it would work. "Thanks."

Brody pulled off the tie and held it out. "Better wear this too. It'll cover the stain."

"Smart." He took off his cowboy hat and pulled on the tie, then smoothed his hair back before replacing the hat. There was nothing he could do about the scar marring his face, but at least he'd be dressed in a coat and tie, a getup he hadn't worn in he didn't know how many years. Maybe the sight of him in a tie would be enough to distract her from his ugly mug.

Brody glanced at Hope. "I was going to do some paperwork anyway. I'll stay here with the dog until after the banquet."

"Thanks, man. I'll be back to get her right after. And I'll take her home tonight, if you think she's up to it." Zane reached out his hand. "You're a good man, Brody."

The vet shook his hand, giving it an extra hard squeeze. "So are you, Zane. Now go!"

CHAPTER 22

ZANE STEPPED INTO THE BANQUET HALL. THE ROOM was full of people. Dang. It must be a dead night in town because it seemed half of Creedence was in attendance.

Bryn was on the stage. She clutched the award to her chest as she profusely thanked everyone who had helped her with the horse rescue farm. She ended her acknowledgments with a shout out to old Doc Hunter and a special thanks to Elle, who sat in the front row and cheered the loudest.

Damn, he'd missed it.

Bryn had on a long blue dress that somehow sparkled as the lights hit it. The dress was gorgeous, but it paled in comparison to the woman in it. Her smile lit the whole room, and his chest hurt just looking at her.

She was so damn beautiful.

He sucked in his breath. This was it. Go time. This was the moment he laid it all on the line and prayed it was enough. God had already sent him a wisdom-spouting angel in the form of a spunky nurse. Zane just hoped He had one more miracle in Him, because that's what this would take.

Bryn waved away the applause as she walked to the edge of the stage, trying to focus on holding the award and making it down the steps without tripping on her dress.

Connie Dean, the president of the Women's Club, stepped back to the mic. "We're so excited about what you're doing out there, Bryn. Keep up the good work." She turned back to the audience. "Well, folks, I can't thank you enough for coming out tonight. That was our last award for the night, so—"

"Wait, I've got something I need to say," a deep voice spoke from the back of the hall.

Bryn shielded her eyes with her hand, trying to see where the voice—Zane's voice—had come from. At least it sounded like him. But maybe that was just her wishful thinking. She couldn't see anything beyond the glare of the spotlight, but she heard the hush of the crowd as a man walked between the tables and toward the front of the room.

Her breath caught in her throat. It *was* Zane. At least it looked like him. But she'd never seen him in a coat and tie—never even *imagined* him in a coat and tie. And she had imagined him a lot of different ways.

But never like this. Not dressed up and walking toward her with his lips set in a tight line, his expression full of determination, and his eyes full of purpose. He bounded up the steps, then stopped and looked down at her. "I've got some things to say, and I'd like you to stay to hear them."

She couldn't speak. Her mouth had gone dry, and her

chest had gone so taut she wasn't sure she could squeeze out a breath. She hoped he didn't feel the tremble in her hand as he picked it up and led her back to the center of the stage.

He leaned his mouth into the mic. "I've got—" The microphone squealed, and he jerked back. Clearing his throat, he tried again, this time with his mouth not so close.

Bryn was frozen, the steady pressure of his hand the only thing securing her in place. What was he doing here? What could he possibly have to say to her that he needed to say in front of half the town?

"Hi. Sorry to interrupt the banquet, but I've got some stuff I need to tell you and to tell her." He nodded to Bryn. "For those of you who don't know me, my name is Zane Taylor. I grew up in this town. Then I left the second I was old enough to get away. I've spent the last several years of my life running away from this town and the people and the memories in it. But it wasn't until I came back that I finally found something worth staying for."

He swallowed. "Which is why I'm standin' on this stage, making a fool of myself in front of you-all. Because I've already acted a fool, and this is the only way I know to fix it. I've spent my life trying to blend into the wood-work, which is why I needed to stand up in front of all of you and tell this woman how I feel. It's that important. I'm no public speaker. I hope you can't see how bad my hands are shaking. I'm a pretty tough guy. I can stare down a pissed-off stallion, but I've never done anything like this."

He pointed to his cheek. "This scar, the one you all know my dad gave me, reminded me every day that I am garbage even my own father didn't value. So, often, I hide my face. But then I met Bryn, and she looked at me." He swallowed, his mouth dry. "And she *loved* me despite my scars. She saw through the mangled tissue and shredded skin and saw someone worthy of love."

He let go of her hand and took off his hat. He set it on the podium, then brushed back his hair as he lifted his face to the audience. Other than the soft gasp that went up from the crowd, the rest of the room was deadly silent.

Bryn couldn't breathe. She was awed and humbled at the same time.

"I've spent the better part of the last several months doing my damnedest to screw up the best thing that's ever happened to me. I've always seen myself as broken and pushed others away." He turned to face Bryn. "Especially you. I keep trying to push you away from me and toward what I think is best for you. That stops tonight. Right now. As of this moment, I stop pushing and start trying to become what *is* best for you—someone worthy of the love you're offering."

She pulled the award to her chest, pressing against the tingling sensation surrounding her heart. Her stomach swooped and churned. He'd hurt her, broken her heart, and made her doubt him the last few days, but she could see the sincerity in his words and actions. She knew it took guts for him to come up here and bare his soul.

"You were honored here tonight for your efforts to

rescue animals that couldn't rescue themselves," he continued. "I feel like I should be included in that flock. For the first time, because of you, I feel like a man worth saving."

He looked at her—not just at her, but into her very soul. "I told you when we were out at the lake that the falling is easy, and it has been. Falling in love with you has been the easiest thing I've ever done. The fallin' was simple, but the jumpin' is what takes the strength of will."

He paused and picked up her hand again. "So, Bryn Callahan, and half the town of Creedence, this is me jumping. I've turned down the job in Montana. I'm staying right here, so you-all can get used to seeing me and my dog, Hope, around town. And with Bryn. If she'll have me.

"I can't promise I'll be perfect. Hell, I can pretty much promise that I *won't* be perfect. I'm battered and bruised, but I'm strong and I'm sticking. I'm not going anywhere. Bryn, I want you more than anything I've ever wanted in my life. I want to wake up in the morning next to you and fall asleep every night with you in my arms. I want to help you run that ranch full of misfit, unwanted animals and help you find homes for all of them. Because that's what you've done for this misfit man—you've given me a home."

Bryn shook her head and let out a shaky laugh. "You really are jumpin', aren't you?"

"With both feet," he told her with all the sincerity he could muster. "Or in this case, with just one knee." He took a deep breath and sank to one knee.

Bryn's knuckles went white as her fingers clutched the award tighter and tears sprang to her eyes. Her sharp inhale of breath was swallowed up in the gasp of surprise from the audience. The banquet had ended, but not one person had moved from their seat.

Zane reached into his pocket and pulled out a cheap, adjustable ring with a glittery blue butterfly affixed to it. He offered her an impish grin and held the ring up to her. "I got this for you last week as kind of an inside joke, because we'd been talking about butterfly wings. I've been carrying it around ever since, and now I want to use it to ask you to marry me. You don't have to say yes right now. Or even next week or next month. I'll buy you a diamond—hell, I'll buy you whatever you want. But for now, all I have to give you is this ring and a promise that I love you and I want to spend the rest of my life with you. I'm a patient man, and I can wait for as long as it takes to prove to you that I'm worth giving your heart to."

She let go of his hand and held her palm up. "Stop. Zane. Stop."

Another hush fell over the room.

She let out a shuddering breath. "You don't have to say anything more. And you don't have to prove you're worth giving my heart to."

He gave a hard nod as his eyes cut to the floor, and his lips pulled into a tight line.

She reached out, lifted his chin, and looked into his eyes. "You've already proven it a thousand times over. And I don't have to give you my heart now because my heart has belonged to you since the day you bought me that horse."

She watched him swallow against the emotion engulfing him. "Yeah?"

"Yeah." She nodded as she took in a breath, knowing she needed to make him see that she had changed as well. "I'm not perfect either. But over the last few weeks, I've discovered some things about myself too. From the time my mom abandoned my brother and me on our grandparents' doorstep, I swore to take care of him. And I've always felt that if I were taking care of everyone else, that it would somehow make me someone worth taking care of. But I've recently discovered that I don't need anyone to come in and take care of me. I'm actually a pretty strong woman, and I can do things I never dreamed I could. In saving all these animals, I've found that I can also save myself. In offering them a home, I've created my own home and I want to share it with you." She peered at the glittery butterfly and grinned. "I love this ring. It's perfect. I'm just waiting for you to actually ask me the question that goes with it."

He grinned, and her heart fluttered like the wings of a million butterflies. "Bryn Callahan, would you do me the honor of becoming my wife? Will you marry me?"

She smiled down at him, at the face she loved, the face *she* wanted to wake up to every day and fall asleep to every night. The face she wanted to see in their children. "Yes."

A cheer went up from the crowd as Zane pushed to

his feet and wrapped his arms around her. He twirled her in a hug and pressed his face to her neck.

Setting her down, he picked up her hand and slid the butterfly ring onto her finger. His face wore the goofiest grin. "Now that we've settled that, grab your purse, darlin', and let's go get our dog."

———————————

The next morning, Bryn woke to an empty bed. Well, not completely empty. A three-legged dog was curled by her feet. But no Zane.

The smell of coffee filled the air though, so she wrapped herself in her short fuzzy robe and stuffed her feet into slippers and went in search of her fiancé. He wasn't in the kitchen, but a note saying he was out working with the horses lay next to an empty cup. He'd drawn a heart at the bottom of the note. Dang, he *was* a changed man.

She filled her cup and took it out to the porch, smiling down at the blue blanket Hope lay curled on in a patch of sunshine. Tiny stood in the front yard, munching on a mouthful of grass. In the corral, Zane sat astride the gray horse, his feet tucked into the stirrups as he put the horse through its paces. Bryn's chest tightened and her heart sang at the sight of him.

A row of pansies lined the walkway from the porch, and she picked one and inhaled the sweet scent. Tiny crossed to her, and she gave the pig a scratch, then tucked the pansy behind the sow's ear.

The pig followed her as she crossed the driveway. Bryn climbed up to stand on the first rung and she leaned over the fence. "Good morning, cowboy," she called.

He rode toward her, a huge grin on his face. "Good mornin', darlin'." He peered down at Tiny. "Is that a flower behind that pig's ear?"

Bryn laughed. "Yep. She was feeling festive this morning. I told her we were gettin' married, and I think she wants to be considered for the flower girl."

He chuckled with her. "I'll keep that in mind."

She glanced down at the gray horse, the sun shining off its coat making him look even lighter than usual. "You know you told me once you'd never be the guy who rode up on a white horse to save the day, but you were wrong. This ranch seems to be the place to rescue things, and the horse might not be exactly white, but you've rescued me."

"Nah, you rescued yourself."

She grinned. "I like the way you think. Let's agree we rescued each other. That way I can still see you as a charming prince."

He shook his head. "You and your fairy tales. Just don't be disappointed when you realize I'm still more like the beast than any kind of prince."

She wiggled her shoulder and offered him a seductive smile. "Maybe I like a little beast in my charming prince."

He chuckled and held out his hand. "Wanna go for a ride?"

She grinned coyly. "Yes."

He laughed again. "I meant on the horse."

"Okay, we can do that first." She set her coffee on the fence post, then took his hand and let him pull her onto the horse in front of him. She snuggled against his chest. "I do love you."

"I do love you too."

"I'm sorry it was so hard for us to get here."

He took her chin and tilted her face toward his. His voice was deep and his eyes full of love and sincerity. "Honey, 'I'm sorry' are two words you *never* have to say to me."

She swallowed and smiled as she blinked back tears.

"Now like any good fairy-tale ending, we are going to dramatically ride off into the sunset." He pulled the reins and turned the horse toward the mountains.

"That's the sunrise."

She felt the rumble of laughter in his chest. "We've done everything else in this fairy tale backward. Why stop now?"

The End...

...and just the beginning...

ACKNOWLEDGMENTS

As always, my love and thanks goes out to my family! Todd, thanks for always believing in me and for being the real life role model of a romantic hero. You cherish me and make me laugh every day and the words it would take to truly thank you would fill a book on their own. I love you. *Always.*

I can't thank my editor, Deb Werksman, enough for believing in me and this book, for loving Zane and Bryn and for making this story so much better with your amazing editing skills. I appreciate everything you do to help make the town of Creedence and the motley crew of farmyard animals come to life. Thanks to my project editor, Susie Benton for all your encouragement and support, and a HUGE thanks to Dawn Adams for this amazing cover and every other awesome cover you've given me! I love being part of the Sourcebooks Sisterhood, and I offer buckets of thanks to the whole Sourcebooks Casablanca team for all of your efforts and hard work in making this book happen.

A big thank you to my parents—all of them. I appreciate everything you do and am so thankful for your support of this crazy writing career. Thanks to my mom, Lee Cumba, for so many lunches where we talk writing and plots. And thanks to my step-mom, Gracie Bryant, for your encouragement and support, and to my dad, Bill

Bryant, for spending hours giving me ranching and farming advice, plot ideas, and guiding me through some of the tough aspects of rescuing horses.

Special thanks goes out to Drs. Rebecca and Corbin Hodges, my sister and brother-in-law, who are always willing to listen and offer sound veterinarian council on my farmyard crew of animals. Special thanks to Corbin for spending an hour patiently helping me work through the hard scenes with Hope getting hit by the car and her subsequent stay in the clinic.

Ginormous thanks goes out to my plotting partner and dear friend, Kristin Miller. The time and energy you take to run through plot ideas with me is invaluable! Your friendship and writing support means the world to me—I couldn't do this writing thing without you!

I have to thank Anne Eliot and Ginger Scott, for the fabulously fun night of laughter and brilliance that we spent in Denver, drinking milk shakes and hammering out plot ideas for this book! You gals are the best!

Huge shout out thanks to my agent, Nicole Resciniti at The Seymour Agency, for your advice and your guidance. You are the best, and I'm so thankful you are part of my tribe.

Special acknowledgment goes out to the women who walk this writing journey with me every single day. The ones who make me laugh, who encourage and support, who offer great advice and sometimes just listen. Thank you Michelle Major, Lana Williams, Anne Eliot, Ginger Scott, Cindy Skaggs, and Beth Rhodes. XO

Big thanks goes out to my street team, Jennie's Page Turners, and for all of my readers: the people who have been with me from the start, my loyal readers, my dedicated fans, the ones who have read my stories, who have laughed and cried with me, who have fallen in love with my heroes and have clamored for more! Whether you have been with me since the first book or just discovered me with this book, know that I write these stories for you, and I can't thank you enough for reading them. Sending love, laughter, and big Colorado hugs to you all!

Keep reading for an excerpt from the first book in Jennie Marts's sweet and sexy Cowboys of Creedence series! These hockey-playing cowboys are hot enough to melt the ice, and your heart.

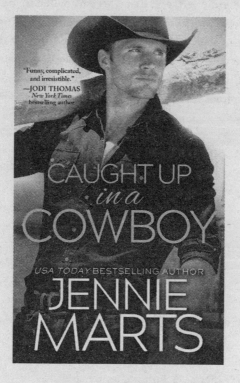

"Funny, complicated, and irresistible."
—JODI THOMAS
New York Times bestselling author

CAUGHT UP *in a* COWBOY

USA TODAY BESTSELLING AUTHOR
JENNIE MARTS

Available now from Sourcebooks Casablanca

CHAPTER 1

Bits of gravel flew behind the tires of the convertible, and Rockford James swore as he turned onto the dirt road leading to the Triple J Ranch. Normally, he enjoyed coming home for a visit, especially in the late spring when everything was turning green and the wildflowers were in bloom, but not this spring—not when he was coming home with both his pride and his body badly injured.

His spirits lifted and the corners of his mouth tugged up in a grin as he drew even with what appeared to be a pirate riding a child's bicycle along the shoulder of the road. A gorgeous female pirate—one with long blond hair and great legs.

Legs he recognized.

Legs that belonged to the only woman who had ever stolen his heart.

Nine years ago, Quinn Rivers had given him her heart as well. Too bad he'd broken it. Not exactly broken—more like smashed, crushed, and shattered it into a million tiny pieces. According to her anyway.

He slowed the car, calling out as he drew alongside her. Her outfit consisted of a flimsy little top that bared her shoulders under a snug corset vest and a short, frilly striped skirt. She wore some kind of sheer white knee socks, and one of them had fallen and pooled loosely around her ankle. "Ahoy there, matey. You lose your ship?"

Keeping her eyes focused on the road, she stuck out her hand and offered him a gesture unbecoming of a lady—pirate or otherwise. Then her feet stilled on the pedals as she must have registered his voice. "Ho-ly crap. You have got to be freaking kidding me."

Bracing her feet on the ground, she turned her head, brown eyes flashing with anger. "And here I thought my day couldn't get any worse. What the hell are you doing here, Rock?"

He stopped the car next to her, then draped his arm over the steering wheel, trying to appear cool. Even though his heart pounded against his chest from the fact that he was seeing her again. She had this way of getting under his skin; she was just so damn beautiful. Even wearing a pirate outfit. "Hey, now. Is that any way to speak to an old friend?"

"I don't know. I'll let you know when I run into one."

Ouch. He'd hoped she wasn't still that bitter about their breakup. They'd been kids, barely out of high school. But they'd been together since they were fourteen, his conscience reminded him, and they'd made plans to spend their future together.

But that was before he got the full-ride scholarship and the NHL started scouting him.

And he had tried.

Yeah, keep telling yourself that, buddy.

Okay, he probably hadn't tried hard enough. But he'd been young and dumb and swept up in the fever and glory of finally having his dreams of pursuing a professional hockey career coming true.

With that glory came attention and fame and lots of travel with the team where cute puck bunnies were ready and willing to show their favorite players a good time.

He hadn't cheated on Quinn, but he came home less often and didn't make the time for texts and calls. He'd gone to college first while she finished her senior year, and by the time he did come home the next summer, he'd felt like he'd outgrown their relationship, and her, and had suggested they take a mini break.

Which turned into an *actual* break, of both their relationship and Quinn's heart.

But it had been almost nine years since he'd left; they'd been kids, and that kind of stuff happened all the time. Since then, he hadn't made it home a lot and had run into her only a handful of times. In fact, he probably hadn't seen her in over a year.

But he'd thought of her. Often. And repeatedly wondered if he'd made the right choice by picking the fame and celebrity of his career and letting go of her.

Sometimes, those summer days spent with Quinn seemed like yesterday, but really, so much had happened—in both of their lives—that it felt like a lifetime ago.

Surely she'd softened a little toward him in all that time. "Let me offer you a lift." The dirt road they were on led to both of their families' neighboring ranches.

"No thanks. I'd rather pedal this bike until the moon comes up than take a ride from you."

Yep. Still mad, all right.

Nothing he could do if she wanted to keep the grudge fest going. Except he was tired of the grudge. Tired of them being enemies. She'd been the best friend he'd ever had. And right now, he felt like he could use a friend.

His pride had already been wounded; what was one more hit? At least he could say he tried.

Although he didn't want it to seem like he was trying too hard. He did still have a *little* pride left, damn it.

"Okay. Suit yourself. It's not *that* hot out here." He squinted up at the bright Colorado sun, then eased off the brake, letting the car coast forward.

"Wait." She shifted from one booted foot to the other, the plastic pirate sword bouncing against her curvy hip. "Fine. I'll take a ride. But only because I'm desperate."

"You? Desperate? I doubt it," he said with a chuckle. Putting the car in Park, he left the engine running and made his way around the back of the car. He reached for the bike, but she was already fitting it into the back seat of the convertible.

"I've got it." Her gaze traveled along the length of his body, coming to rest on his face, and her expression softened for the first time. "I heard about the fight and your injury."

He froze, heat rushing to his cheeks and anger building in his gut. Of course she'd heard about the fight. It had made the nightly news, for Pete's sake. He was sure the whole town of Creedence had heard about it.

Nothing flowed faster than a good piece of gossip in a small town. Especially when it's bad news—or news about the fall of the hometown hero. Or the guy who thought he was better than everyone else and bigger than his small-town roots, depending on who you talked to and which camp they fell into. Or what day of the week it was.

You could always count on a small town to be loyal.

Until you let them down.

"I'm fine," he said, probably a little too sternly, as he opened the car door, giving her room to pass him and slide into the passenger seat. He sucked in a breath as the scent of her perfume swept over him.

She smelled the same—a mix of vanilla, honeysuckle, and home.

He didn't let himself wonder if she felt the same. No, he'd blown his chances of that ever happening again a long time ago. Still, he couldn't help but drop his gaze to her long, tanned legs or notice the way her breasts spilled over the snug, corseted vest of the pirate costume.

"So, what's with the outfit?" he asked as he slid into the driver's seat and put the car in gear.

She blew out her breath in an exaggerated sigh. A loose tendril of hair clung to her damp forehead, and he was tempted to reach across the seat to brush it back.

"It's Max's birthday today," she said, as if that explained everything.

He didn't say anything—didn't know what to say.

The subject of Max always was a bit of an awkward

one between them. After he'd left, he'd heard the rumors of how Quinn had hooked up with a hick loser named Monty Hill who'd lived one town over. She'd met him at a party and it had been a rebound one-night stand, designed to make him pay for breaking things off with her, if the gossip was true.

But she'd been the one to pay. Her impulse retaliation had ended in an unplanned pregnancy with another jerk who couldn't be counted on to stick around for her. Hill had taken off, and Quinn had ended up staying at her family's ranch.

"He's eight now." Her voice held the steely tone of anger, but he heard the hint of pride that also crept in.

"I know," he mumbled, more to himself than to her. "So, you decided to dress up like a pirate for his birthday?"

She snorted. "No. Of course not. One of Max's favorite books is *Treasure Island*, and he wanted a pirate-themed party, so I *hired* a party company to send out a couple of actors to dress up like pirates. The outfits showed up this morning, but the actors didn't. Evidently, there was a mix-up in the office, and the couple had been double-booked and were already en route to Denver when I called."

"So you decided to fill in." He tried to hold back his grin.

She shrugged. "What else was I going to do?"

"That doesn't explain the bike."

"The bike is his main gift. I ordered it from the hardware store in town, but it was late and we weren't expecting it to come in today. They called about an hour ago and said it had shown up, but they didn't have anyone to deliver it. I was already in the pirate getup, so I ran into town to get it."

"And decided to ride it home?"

"Yes, smart-ass. I thought it would be fun to squeeze onto a tiny bike dressed in a cheap Halloween costume and enjoy the bright, sunny day by riding home." She blew out another exasperated breath. "My stupid car broke down on the main road."

"Why didn't you call Ham or Logan to come pick you up?" he asked, referring to her dad and her older brother.

"Because in my flustered state of panic about having to fill in as the pirate princess and the fear that the party would be ruined, I left my phone on the dresser when I ran out of the house. I was carrying the dang bike, but it got so heavy, then I tried pushing it, and that was killing my back, so I thought it would be easier and faster if I just tried to ride it the last mile back to the ranch."

"Makes sense to me." He slowed the car, turning into the long driveway of Rivers Gulch. White fences lined the drive, and several head of cattle grazed on the fresh green grass of the pastures along either side of the road.

The scent of recently mown hay skimmed the air, mixed with the familiar smells of plowed earth and cattle.

Seeing the sprawling ranch house and the long, white barn settled something inside of him, and he let out a slow breath, helping to ease the tension in his neck. He'd practically grown up here, running around this place with Quinn and her brother, Logan.

Their families' ranches were within spitting distance of each other; in fact, he could see the farmhouse of the Triple J across the pasture to his left. They were separated only by prime grazing land and the pond that he'd learned to swim in during the summer and skate on in the winter.

The two families had an ongoing feud—although he wasn't sure any of them really knew what they were fighting about anymore, and the kids had never cared much about it anyway.

The adults liked to bring it up, but they were the only kids around for miles, and they'd become fast friends—he and his brothers sneaking over to Rivers Gulch as often as they could.

This place felt just as much like home as his own did. He'd missed it. In the years since he'd left, he'd been back only a handful of times.

His life had become so busy, his hockey career taking up most of his time. And after what happened with Quinn, neither Ham nor Logan was ever too excited to see him. Her mom had died when she was in grade school, and both men had always been overprotective of her.

He snuck a glance at her as he drove past the barn. Her wavy hair was pulled back in a ponytail, but wisps of it had come loose and fell across her neck in little curls. She looked good—really good. A thick chunk of regret settled in his gut, and he knew letting her go had been the biggest mistake of his life.

It wasn't the first time he'd thought it. Images of Quinn haunted his dreams, and he often wondered what it would be like now if only he'd brought her with him instead of leaving her behind. If he had her to wave to in the stands at his games or to come home to at night instead of an empty house. But he'd screwed that up, and he felt the remorse every time he returned to Rivers Gulch.

He'd been young and arrogant—thought he had the world by the tail. Scouts had come sniffing around when he was in high school, inflating his head and his own self-importance. And once he started playing in the big leagues, everything about this small town—including Quinn—had just seemed…well…small. Too small for a big shot like him.

He was just a kid—and an idiot. But by the time he'd realized his mistake and come back for her, it was too late.

Hindsight was a mother.

And so was Quinn.

Easing the car in front of the house, he took in the festive balloons and streamers tied to the railings along the porch. So much of the house looked the same—the long porch that ran the length of the house, the wooden rocking chairs, and the swing hanging from the end.

They'd spent a lot of time on that swing, talking and laughing, his arm around her as his foot slowly pushed them back and forth.

She opened the car door, but he put a hand on her arm and offered her one of his most charming smiles.

"It's good to see you, Quinn. You look great. Even in a pirate outfit."

Her eyes widened, and she blinked at him, for once not having a sarcastic reply. He watched her throat shift as she swallowed, and he yearned to reach out to run his fingers along her slender neck.

"Well, thanks for the lift." She turned away and stepped out of the car.

Pushing open his door, he got out and reached for the bicycle, lifting it out of the back seat before she had a chance. He carried it around and set it on the ground in front of her. "I'd like to meet him. You know, Max. If that's okay."

"You would?" Her voice was soft, almost hopeful, but still held a note of suspicion. "Why?"

He ran a hand through his hair and let out a sigh. He'd been rehearsing what he was going to say as they drove up to the ranch, but now his mouth had gone dry. The collar of his cotton T-shirt clung to his neck, and he didn't know what to do with his hands.

Dang. He hadn't had sweaty palms since he was in high school. He wiped them on his jeans. He was known for his charm and usually had a way with women, but not this woman. This one had him tongue-tied and nervous as a teenager.

He shoved his hands in his pockets. "Listen, Quinn. I know I screwed up. I was young and stupid and a damn fool. And I'm sorrier than I could ever say. But I can't go back and fix it. All I can do is move forward. I miss this place. I miss having you in my life. I'd like to at least be your friend."

She opened her mouth, and he steeled himself for her to tell him to go jump in the lake. Or worse. But she didn't. She looked up at him, her eyes searching his face, as if trying to decide if he was serious. "Why now? After all these years?"

He shrugged, his gaze drifting as he stared off at the distant green pastures. He'd let this go on too long, let the hurt fester. It was time to make amends—to at least try. He looked back at her, trying to express his sincerity. "Why not? Isn't it about time?"

She swallowed again and gave a small nod of her head.

A tiny flicker of hope lit in his gut as he waited for her response. He could practically *see* her thinking—watch the emotions cross her face in the furrow of her brow and the way she chewed on her bottom lip. Oh man, he loved it when she did that; the way she sucked her bottom lip under her front teeth always did crazy things to his insides.

"Okay. We can *try* being friends." She gave him a sidelong glance, the hint of a smile tugging at the corner of her mouth. "On one condition."

Uh-oh. Conditions are never good. Although he would do just about anything to prove to her that he was serious about being in her life again.

"What's that?"

"I need someone to be the other pirate for the party. I already asked Logan if he would wear the other costume, and he refused. I was planning to ask Dad, but I have a feeling I'll get the same response."

He tried to imagine Hamilton Rivers in a pirate outfit and couldn't. Ham was old-school cowboy, tough as nails and loyal to the land. He wore his boots from sunup to sundown and had more grit than a sheet of sandpaper. The only soft spot he had was for his daughter. And Rock had broken her heart.

If there hadn't been enough animosity between the two families over their land before, Rock had sealed the feud by walking away from Quinn.

And now he had a chance to try to make it up to her. And to keep an eight-year-old kid from being disappointed. Even if it meant making a fool of himself.

He squinted one eye closed and tilted his head. If he was going to do it, might as well do it right.

Go big or go home.

"Aye, lass," he said in his best gruff pirate impression. "I'll be a pirate for ye, but don't cross me, or I'll make ye walk the plank."

Her eyes widened, and she laughed before she could stop herself. An actual laugh. Well, more like a small chuckle, but it was worth it. He'd talk in a pirate accent all afternoon if it meant he could hear her laugh again.

She took a step forward, reached out her hand as if to touch his arm, then let it drop to her side. "All right, Captain Jack, you don't have to go that far." She might not have touched him, but she offered him a grin—a true grin.

Yeah, he could be a pirate. He could be whatever she needed. Or he could dang well try.

The front door slammed open with a bang, and Quinn jumped. As if on cue, her brother stepped out on the front porch.

Anger sparked in Logan's eyes as he glared at Rock. "What the hell are you doing here?"

ABOUT THE AUTHOR

Jennie Marts is the *USA Today* bestselling author of award-winning books filled with love, laughter, and always a happily-ever-after. Readers call her books "laugh-out-loud" funny and the "perfect mix of romance, humor, and steam." Fic Central claimed one of her books was "the most fun I've had reading in years."

She is living her own happily-ever-after in the mountains of Colorado with her husband, two dogs, and a parakeet who loves to tweet to the oldies. She's addicted to Diet Coke, adores Cheetos, and believes you can't have too many books, shoes, or friends.

Her books include the contemporary western romances of the Cowboys of Creedence and the Hearts of Montana series, the cozy mysteries of the Page Turners series, the hunky hockey-playing men in the Bannister Brothers books, and the small-town romantic comedies in the Cotton Creek Romance series.

Jennie loves to hear from readers. Follow her on Facebook at Jennie Marts Books, or Twitter at @JennieMarts. Visit her at jenniemarts.com and sign up for her newsletter to keep up with the latest news and releases.

LUCKY CHANCE COWBOY

In Teri Anne Stanley's Big Chance Dog Rescue
series, everyone can find a forever home...

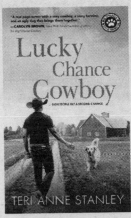

Emma Stern is barely scraping by while working and caring for
her elderly grandfather, but she's running out of options—and
hope. The last thing she has time for is Marcus Talbott and his
flirting, sexy as he might be. But every time Emma thinks she's
reached the end of her rope, Marcus is there to lend a hand.
Maybe there's more to the handsome playboy after all...

**"A real page-turner with a sexy cowboy, a sassy
heroine, and a dog that brings them together."**
—Carolyn Brown, *New York Times* bestselling author,
for *Big Chance Cowboy*